# Wild Heritage

Elisabeth McNeill was a long-established freelance journalist and broadcaster who wrote five non-fiction books and 26 novels. She lived with a miniature dachshund in the oldest inhabited village on the Scottish borders, where she spent most of her school days.

## Also by Elisabeth McNeill

*St James' Fair*
*Mistress of Green Tree Mill*
*Lark Returning*
*A Woman of Gallantry*
*Perseverance Place*

### A Bridge in Time

*A Bridge in Time*
*Wild Heritage*

### The Storm

*The Storm*
*Turn of the Tide*

# Elisabeth McNeill

## WILD HERITAGE

CANELO

First published in the United Kingdom in 1995 by Orion

This edition published in the United Kingdom in 2022 by

Canelo
Unit 9, 5th Floor
Cargo Works, 1–2 Hatfields
London, SE1 9PG
United Kingdom

A CIP catalogue record for this book is available from the British Library.

Print ISBN 978 1 80032 791 7
Ebook ISBN 978 1 78863 639 1

This book is a work of fiction. Names, characters, businesses, organizations, places and events
are either the product of the author's imagination or are used fictitiously. Any resemblance to
actual persons, living or dead, events or locales is entirely coincidental.

Look for more great books at www.canelo.co

Printed and bound in Great Britain by Clays Ltd, Elcograf S.p.A.

1

*'The seed of the cedar will become cedar; the seed of the bramble can only become bramble.'*

Saint-Exupéry

# Prologue

Ten years had passed since an army of navvies swarmed into the peaceful Border countryside to create an innovation which was to transform the lives of local people, though at first they were reluctant to accept its benefits.

When the navvies tramped away they left as their legacies a road to the outside world in the form of a network of railway lines, a beautiful railway bridge over the river Tweed, an unmarked grave-mound of their dead in the burying-ground of the abbey at Rosewell... and several fatherless children.

This is the story of three of these navvy bastards.

# Chapter One

*1866*

Nanny Rush lay dying.

She had grown so thin that her body made only a small mound beneath the white bedcover. Harsh raspings of painfully drawn breath from her half-open mouth almost drowned the sound of sobbing from a young girl kneeling by the side of the bed with her face sunk in her hands.

'Oh Nanny, dinna die, dinna die. What will we do without you?' this girl implored.

'Hush, hush,' said a small, stout woman standing by the side of the bed. Her voice was concerned and sympathetic, so the weeping girl turned towards her and was comforted by the touch of soft hands on her back and whispered words. 'You'll be all right, dinna greet, Marie.'

'Tch, tch, what a way to carry on,' said the dying woman's sister Martha who was standing on the other side of the bed, her hard grey eyes staring at the others. 'Take that greetin' bairn downstairs, Mrs Mather. She'll upset my sister,' she said.

With gentle hands Tibbie helped the girl to the door and whispered, 'Go and sit down in the parlour with David. Have a drink of milk and something to eat.'

The girl always seemed sickly. Although she was eleven years old, she looked about nine and there was a worrying transparency about her skin often seen in consumption sufferers. When she was told to eat, she refused with a shake of the head.

'I'd rather stay with Nanny. What if she wakes up and wants me?'

Tibbie soothed her. 'If she does, I'll call you, I promise.'

The girl closed the door behind her and the women heard her footsteps tiptoeing softly down the wooden stairs.

Then Martha raised her eyebrows and said, 'What right has she to be weeping and wailing as if she was real kin?'

3

'But she's as good as kin,' protested Tibbie.

Martha snorted, 'No she's not. She's greetin' because she's losing a soft berth. And she's from a bad background. What sort of name's Marie? It's a name for Papes.'

What she was saying was heard by the woman in bed, for Nanny's eyelids flickered, she gasped and reached out an emaciated hand as she groaned, 'Tak care o' my bairns when I'm gone.'

Tibbie hurried over to the bed and wiped the waxen face with the corner of her apron. 'Rest easy, Nanny. The bairns'll be all right,' she told the suffering woman.

Nanny's once bright blue eyes opened and stared into her friend's face. 'I'm dying, Tib,' she whispered, 'but I dinna want my bairns to go into the Foundling Home. I've left letters about them in a box on the downstairs mantelshelf.'

Wordlessly Tibbie patted her hand and soon Nanny was asleep again, her breathing harsh and shallow. The watching women glanced at each other for this signalled the approach of the end.

'She's nearly gone. I'm going to bring up the bairns so they can say goodbye to her,' said Tibbie, rising to her feet.

Martha frowned. 'You're being silly. They're just foundlings after all.'

Tibbie glared and replied fiercely. 'That doesnae stop them loving her.' Then she opened the door and called down the stairs, 'David, Marie, come up now.'

Two frightened-looking young people with poker-straight pale blond hair and vulnerable white faces came hurrying upstairs. Like his sister, the boy seemed younger than his real age for though he was often taken for eleven or twelve, he was actually fourteen. When they entered the room he was holding his weeping sister's hand.

'Say goodbye to her,' said Tibbie and obediently they bent over the dying woman, pressing their lips to her cheek. David was able to control his tears but Marie broke down sobbing. 'I dinna want you to go, Nanny, dinna leave us. You're all we've got,' she implored.

Martha pulled her roughly back from the bed. 'Get a grip on yourself, girl,' she said harshly.

In a swift movement the boy jumped between them and the ferocity of his stare was frightening. 'Get your hands off *my* sister,' he hissed.

Startled, Martha dropped her hand from the girl's shoulder but to cover up her confusion she said loudly to Tibbie, 'Did you hear that?

Did you hear the way that laddie spoke to me and him only a guest in this house?'

Scandalised at the prospect of a row breaking out beside a death-bed, Tibbie said urgently to the boy, 'Take Marie downstairs, David.' Without speaking he put an arm round his sister's shoulders and led her away.

Then the flustered Martha hissed, 'I ask you, did you ever hear the like? That laddie's a bad lot. Mark my words, he'll come to no good like all his folk before him.'

Tibbie's plump face was flushed. She was angry but fought to hide it for Nanny's sake. 'The bairns are upset,' she said grimly.

'Huh, he's no' shedding any tears. He's only bothered for himself,' replied Martha.

Tibbie turned back to the sick woman whose face was bedewed with sweat. 'I'm going down to get some warm water so's I can wipe her poor brow,' she said, lifting a china basin from the washstand. Having to talk to Martha was annoying her.

Downstairs David and Marie were standing in the tiny lobby by the front door and she could tell from the way they straightened up when they saw her that they were bracing themselves for bad news. She shook her head to tell them that Nanny was still alive.

'Is it certain that she'll go? She's been ill before and got better... maybe this time too...?' David's voice quivered as he spoke.

Tibbie shook her head. 'No, lad, I'm sorry, not this time. All we can do is try to make it as easy as possible for her.'

Grief for her dying friend swept over her like a wave as she spoke, for she had been holding her sorrow back so as not to upset the children. Now she could hold out no longer and sank down on the stairs with tears flowing down her cheeks. The young people stared at her. When they saw Mrs Mather weeping they knew that Nanny would soon be dead.

'I'm sorry,' sobbed Tibbie. 'She's my oldest friend. There'll never be anybody else like her. When she goes, a lot of me will go with her.'

Marie squeezed onto the step beside the weeping woman and put a hand on her shoulder.

'It's not fair,' she sobbed. 'Why does Nanny have to die when...?' Her voice trailed off as she looked upstairs and Tibbie knew she was wondering why God was taking Nanny when Martha, the oldest sister, was so obviously thriving. The girl had been too well trained in Christian consideration, however, to speak her thoughts.

David was more forthright. 'We don't like Martha,' he said.

'I don't care for her myself,' replied Tibbie, though she usually thought it unseemly to criticise adults before children.

'Will she want to take us away with her when Nanny...?' His voice trailed off for even he, trying so hard to be grown up, could not say the word 'dies'.

Tibbie shook her head. 'I don't know what she wants. Nanny left a letter about you. We'll have to see what it says.'

The children nodded. It was unthinkable for any of them to open Nanny's letter before she died. They would wait.

Then the door above their heads opened and Martha's footsteps were heard on the stairs. The boards creaked beneath her tread as she came slowly down towards them. When she reached the lobby she gave a nod, almost of satisfaction, and said, 'Well that's that, she's gone.'

Tibbie felt a surge of anger that made her cheeks flush. Not for the first time she wondered how sweet-natured Nanny could have a sister like Martha. 'You should have called us,' she snapped.

Martha raised her eyebrows. 'Should I? I'm her sister. I'm the only blood kin here. Anyway she went very quietly. Now we'll have to start arranging things.'

She stepped dry-eyed into the parlour, ignoring Marie and David who were clinging together weeping.

'Where's this box of letters she was talking about?' she asked advancing on the mantelpiece. Mutely David pointed to a battered red tin box that stood among bits and pieces of brightly coloured pottery.

Martha lifted it down and rummaged among the contents. 'There's two letters here,' she said in surprise, turning them over in her hands before she handed one to David. 'One's for me and the other's for you...' It was obvious that she thought it unsuitable that her sister should leave a letter for him.

To Tibbie's disappointment, Martha slipped her letter into her pocket. She wasn't going to read it in front of them. David wiped his eyes and turned his letter around in his hands as Tibbie asked, 'Do you want to read it now or keep it till later?' There was curiosity shining in Martha's eyes.

'I'll read it later,' he said and the letter went into the pocket of his jacket.

The ever-practical Tibbie made tea and poured it out. Although the children drank it rather than hurt her feelings, she could see they were both utterly exhausted, for it was almost midnight and they had been up, watching over Nanny since dawn.

'Away you go to bed and Martha and I'll do what's necessary,' she gently told them and they didn't argue.

'That pair'll have to go on the parish,' Martha told Tibbie the moment the parlour door closed behind them.

'Your sister wouldn't want that. What does she say in her letter?' was the bleak reply.

Martha brought the letter out of her pocket and opened it with her back turned to Tibbie. It did not take long to read and when she had scanned its few lines, she swiftly folded it up and put it away again.

'What does she say about the bairns?' asked Tibbie.

'Nothing.' Martha sounded shifty and an expression of incredulity crossed Tibbie's face. 'But…' she protested.

'But nothing. They've had all they're getting off my sister. They should have been on the parish years ago. They've been living off her charity too long, taking money she could ill afford.'

'She never thought about it like that. She loved them as if they were her own bairns. You heard what she said up there,' protested Tibbie. She wished she could get her hands on Nanny's letter and read what it really said.

Martha was intransigent. 'That was only because she never had any bairns of her own. She was a soft touch for that mother of theirs. And you know what she was, don't you?'

'Their mother was a poor soul,' snapped Tibbie.

Martha sneered. 'She was a whore and God knows who their father was, or even if they were fathered by the same man… They're navvy's bastards and blood will out, you mark my words. They'll come to no good, neither the two of them. It's as well my poor sister died before she saw them revert to type.'

Tibbie's face was scarlet in the firelight. She wanted to hit the self-righteous woman before her.

'You shouldnae talk like that about folk you never even saw. Not all the navvies were bad. My own lassie Hannah married a navvy and a better man never walked this earth.'

For once Martha was disconcerted. She had forgotten that Tibbie's girl Hannah had made a precipitate marriage to a navvy called Tim

7

Maquire who came to Rosewell to oversee the gangs of men building the new railway. It had been a scandal at the time but folk changed their tune about it when Hannah and her baby died in a cholera epidemic up at the navvy camp.

'There's exceptions to every rule,' she said in a mollifying voice. 'All I'm saying is that those two upstairs'll have to go on the parish. They've no money and no home and my man Willie wouldn't have them in our house.'

'That'll be a relief to them,' snapped Tibbie. She liked Martha's husband Willie even less than she liked his wife. He was a miller, gluttonous and mean-minded with a reputation for crooked dealing and giving short weight in his flourmill outside Kelso. Willie had done well in business by nefarious methods and Martha liked coming back to her native town of Rosewell to show off her fine clothes and smartly painted dogcart, but people who knew her only laughed and whispered to each other about how many sacks of oatmeal Willie had adulterated to pay for his cart and pony and Martha's feathered bonnets.

Stung by Tibbie's tone she glared and snapped, 'Dinna lose your dander because I forgot your Hannah ran off with a navvy. I'm just telling you I'm going to make arrangements with the parish for those two upstairs because I want them out of this house tomorrow.'

Tibbie was pulling her shawl over her shoulders preparing to go home. She whirled round to say angrily, 'Don't worry about making arrangements as you call them. I'll take them in. Nanny knew you wouldn't treat them right. She had you sized up. Tomorrow morning I'll take them away. They'll not bother you any longer than they have to.'

Martha bristled but all she said was, 'That's good.' She had got what she wanted.

—

Before nine o'clock next morning, Tibbie returned to Nanny's house in Rosewell and found Marie sitting with David in the parlour while Martha bustled about, very busy and preoccupied.

As soon as she saw Tibbie she announced, 'Go up and look at her. She's a perfect picture. I've dressed her in her best nightgown and made the bed with her wedding sheets. Go up and see her.'

Reluctantly Tibbie did as she was told, for she did not like looking at people when they were dead, preferring to carry a picture of them alive and happy in her memory. In the low-ceilinged bedroom she found everything as Martha had described. Nanny lay in state with her hands folded on her breast and ruffles of lace around her white face.

At the sight of her, grief hit Tibbie like a sharp blow in the chest and drove the breath out of her lungs.

'Oh my dear,' she sobbed, dropping onto a chair by the bed. She remembered her friend as she had been when they were both young – Nanny aged seventeen dancing in a flounced dress; Nanny aged thirty, in a stiffly starched white cap, weeping in sympathy when Tibbie's husband died; Nanny bravely accepting the fact that she would never be able to carry a child full term. But she was so sweet-natured that she did not envy her friend's daughter Hannah... And now both she and Hannah were dead. The pain of old grief mingled with the new stabbed Tibbie's heart.

Patting her friend's ice-cold hand for the last time, she sobbed, 'I'll miss you sore. I'm sorry you've gone.'

Then, wiping her eyes, she rose to go back downstairs where the children were waiting. By their feet lay two small baskets and they were dressed for outdoors.

'You must be in a hurry to get back home,' said Martha without even offering her guest the usual cup of tea or mug of ale that was pressed on callers in the poorest household at such a time.

Tibbie nodded grimly. 'I've things to do right enough. I see the bairns are ready. Is that all they're taking just now?' she asked, pointing at the baskets.

'That's all they've got,' snapped Martha.

'But what about their books and Marie's paintbox?' said Tibbie in surprise. Nanny, who taught a dame school in her parlour for many years before she took ill, had encouraged their love of learning. She had especially encouraged Marie's gift for drawing by giving her sketch books and boxes of paints.

Martha glared. 'The books and the school things are part of my sister's estate and she's left it all to me.'

A glimmer of suspicion showed in Tibbie's eyes. 'Is that what the letter said?' she asked.

'What business is it of yours?' Martha wanted to know.

'None, none. It's just that Nanny and I used to talk about things when she first got ill... She told me things,' said Tibbie.

The other woman began bristling like an angry cat. 'I can't help what she told you. All I know is what was in the letter and she never left a will. If she'd not wanted me to have her things she should have made a will. Not that she'd much to leave. She wasted a lot of money when she was alive.'

As she said this her eyes went to David whose cheeks flushed scarlet at the words.

Tibbie sighed. 'Poor Nanny trusted folk. That was her trouble. She probably thought she didn't have to leave a will. She'd have done the right thing and she expected other folk to act the same way.'

Her meaning was not lost on Martha, who turned away and stared out of the window as Tibbie said to the children, 'Come on then, let's get back to Camptounfoot. You're coming to stay with me now.'

She was rewarded by seeing Marie's peaked face light up and even grim David looked relieved for, more than his sister, he had been aware of the shadow of the workhouse hanging over them.

Suddenly Martha's conscience seemed to strike her and she turned back from the window to say, 'If you're going to find it hard feeding them, I could give you some money for their upkeep.'

Tibbie glared at her. 'I have more than enough money to feed two children. My son-in-law Tim Maquire, the ex-navvy you know, is very generous to me. He sends me more money than I need. It'll be good to have something to spend it on. Come on now David, come on Marie, let's be off.'

Martha thought of something else to say before they left. 'We're burying Nanny tomorrow.'

Tibbie paused. 'What time?'

'Eleven o'clock in the abbey burial ground.'

'We'll be there,' said Tibbie.

It was one and a half miles from the little town of Rosewell to Tibbie's home in the village of Camptounfoot and the easiest way was by a narrow path that snaked beneath tall beech trees along the face of a small hill overlooking the river. Tradition had it that the monks who built Rosewell Abbey made the path which still went by the name of the Prior's Walk.

The sorrowing trio went in single file over its stony surface, all of them sunk in private thoughts. Tibbie, who led the party, was a stout little body with pink cheeks and sparkling brown eyes that made her look like the sort of cheeky little robin that haunts cottage gardens and, from time to time, makes so bold as to hop into the house itself. Her still smooth-skinned face had a girlish quality, belied by the wisps of grey curls that escaped beneath the frilled edges of the demure cap she wore to signify her widowed state. She was completely unaware that the sight of her could still make old men's hearts beat a little faster, because she had been the prettiest girl in the district and there were many disappointed suitors when she walked up the aisle with Alex Mather, a skilled stonemason who was ten years her senior.

He died when their daughter Hannah was still a child and she had feasted emotionally on his memory since then. There was never another man like Alex as far as she was concerned. Not even when Craigie Scott, a rich farmer and the most important man in Camptounfoot, came courting her would she contemplate leaving her widowed state.

Oblivious to carnal passion, but full of love for her daughter and her friends, she sailed serenely through life. Even the devastating blow of Hannah's death had not soured her essentially optimistic and loving nature.

From time to time she looked back over her shoulder at her two companions. The sight of their woebegone faces saddened her and made her forget her own misgivings at saddling herself with two young people at a time of life when she was beginning to appreciate living alone.

'It's not much farther,' she said consolingly to Marie, and the girl nodded but did not speak. There were dark purple circles beneath her eyes and her skin was waxen-white. Tibbie remembered with disquiet how ghastly the girl's mother used to look and that her father had died of galloping consumption.

'Are you all right, lass?' she asked and Marie nodded as she said politely, 'Yes, thank you, Mrs Mather.'

Nanny had brought her up well and she was trying to hide from the kind woman who had rescued them from the workhouse that she was in a state of emotional turmoil. Everything had happened so fast. She could not get used to the idea that dear Nanny was really dead and that within hours she and her brother had been thrown out of the only home she could ever remember. Tears pricked her eyes, but she did not shed them for she felt it was important to put on a brave front.

It was not as if Mrs Mather was a stranger. Marie knew her well because she had been Nanny's closest friend, the one who came every Wednesday night to play cards and to gossip. On Sunday afternoons Nanny had always walked with the children to Camptounfoot to visit Tibbie, so her cottage was familiar as well, but Marie had never, as far as she could remember, spent a night in any house other than Nanny's and she was terrified of change, totally thrown off balance by the upheaval.

Her life had been very sheltered. She had not even gone to a proper school, for she learned her lessons at the dame school in Nanny's parlour. There were never more than four or five pupils at a time and they had all been biddable, polite children like Marie herself. David had gone to Rosewell school but Marie had always stayed at home and the outside world seemed like a dangerous jungle to the timorous girl.

Will I have to go to school in Camptounfoot? she was wondering as she walked along. What will it be like? If David went to school with her, she would feel safe but something told her that her brother had other plans. Though it was only a short time since Nanny's death, he had changed. Overnight he seemed to have grown up. She felt she did not know him any longer and that frightened her too.

To reassure herself she glanced back at him bringing up the rear of their little party. Poor David, he looked so sad, with his hands thrust into his pockets and his head sunk on his chest. His sister longed to comfort him but something held her back, for there was a look of suppressed rage in his expression that warned her he might thrust away her advances. He could be very impatient sometimes, treating her as if she was stupid and unable to comprehend his thoughts.

He'd been particularly close to Nanny and they used to enjoy sitting together in the parlour after Marie went to bed, talking about books and things they'd read in the newspaper. Oh poor David, thought his sister. Her awareness of his sorrow made her own grief even more acute.

What she did not realise was that, as well as being sad, David was angry. Resentment raged like fire inside him, first of all at God because he had taken Nanny away and then at Martha who had cruelly rejected him and his sister, throwing them out of their home like unwanted rubbish. He suspected he had been cheated but had no way of proving it, for Nanny had left no will and what she had written in her letter to Martha would, he knew, never be revealed. Her letter to him, which he read by candlelight before going to sleep, dealt with matters other than inheritance.

David was used to being scorned. He had grown up in the knowledge that he was a foundling, perhaps even a bastard, left behind by the navvy gang. The jeers of his fellow pupils at Rosewell school had thickened his skin and stiffened his resolve to beat them in every way possible, so he became a better scholar than any of them; a faster runner; a swifter skater on the frozen pond in winter. He was afire with urgent ambition to prove himself.

As she walked the familiar path to Camptounfoot, Tibbie was thinking how much she had grown to enjoy her privacy in the silent cottage that she shared with her cat and the parrot that Tim Maquire had brought back from the Crimea. Taking in Marie and David would disrupt this tranquil existence and what worried her even more was not knowing if having another girl in the house, sleeping in Hannah's old bed, might bring back sad memories. But she had a duty to Nanny and it must be fulfilled.

At last they reached her snug little cottage that stood by the side of the road with its front door opening straight onto the cobbles. She pushed a big iron key into the lock and ushered them inside... 'Welcome to your new home,' she said.

The kitchen was dim and shadowy but cosy and comforting because before she went out, Tibbie had banked up the fire in the grate and now it was glowing red. A black japanned kettle was steaming gently on the brass hob. Drawn up on each side of the fireplace were two wooden chairs with multicoloured cushions on the seats. Bonaparte the parrot watched beadily from his big brass cage.

'What a grand bird,' David exclaimed in admiration, his face lighting up as he turned to Tibbie to ask, 'Does it talk?'

She giggled. 'Yes, he does. And he swears. But a lot of it is in a funny foreign lingo... French, Tim says. He bought him in Sebastopol when he was there building the railway.'

'Can you make it say something?' the boy asked, bending close to the cage.

Tibbie shook her head. 'He only speaks when it suits him. Sometimes he says nothing for days and other times he prattles on for hours.' She was pleased that David was interested in the parrot because for the first time that day he had shed his grim look.

But he looked solemn again very quickly as he asked, 'Is the man who gave you the parrot the same one that was the navvy ganger on the railway line here?'

Tibbie nodded. 'Yes, he is. He married my daughter Hannah but she died... He's a big contractor now. He builds bridges and tunnels all over the world.'

'I hope I'll meet him one day,' said David.

'I'm sure you will. He always comes to see me when he's in this country. Are you interested in being a bridge-builder too?' she asked.

He shook his head. 'No, but I'd like to ask him about our parents.'

Tibbie went still. 'Of course, Tim knew your mother and your father.'

'Nanny's letter said our father was a carpenter with Mr Maquire's navvy gang,' said David, drawing it out of his pocket. His sister was watching with an intense concentration which told Tibbie that he'd said nothing to her about its contents.

'So he was,' she agreed.

'Did you know our father?' asked David.

Tibbie shook her head. 'No, but I met your mother once.'

Both of the young people stared at her and Marie gasped, 'Oh Mrs Mather, tell us about our mother please. I never liked to ask Nanny too much in case she thought... in case she thought I didn't love her enough... it was difficult.'

Tibbie gave her a sympathetic glance but turned to David and asked, 'What did Nanny say in her letter about your parents?'

He opened the sheet of paper. 'She's written down how our mother paid her to look after us when she went back to the camp after our father died. When she died too, Nanny kept us because we hadn't any other relations. She never knew much about who we were or where we came from except that our father's name was Benjamin and our mother was called Mariotta, so she registered us at the local census as David and Marie Benjamin, though she doesn't know if that was our father's first name or his surname... She thinks he was Irish. Mariotta was Irish too.'

'A lot of the navvies were Irish. Tim's Irish,' said Tibbie softly. Her heart was full of sympathy for the solemn-faced boy, for she wondered how much more he knew of his ancestry. She doubted if he could have spent much time at Rosewell school without some lad taunting him about it. Perhaps he was testing her to discover how much she would tell him and how honest she would be.

Marie interrupted them. 'Do you remember what our mother looked like?' she asked wistfully.

Tibbie turned eagerly, perhaps too eagerly, and said, 'Indeed I do. She was a bonny lassie with yellow hair like yours and great big blue eyes. You're going to look very like her.'

In fact, she had a flashback memory of Mariotta, waif-like and skeleton-thin with her bonny eyes blackened and lip split from a beating. Poor lassie, what a tragic life she had and a short one too, for she'd been dead before she was twenty-four. Tibbie also remembered the smell of gin coming from the girl on the day of their only meeting but it had been impossible to blame the poor soul for drinking because it dulled her pain.

Mariotta's children were intently watching her now, however, and she strove to hide these thoughts.

'She was a very pretty lassie,' she said again and hurriedly tried to remember other things to add. 'I think she told my Hannah that she'd no family except for your father. Her own father had been a navvy working in London and he was killed there. She spoke with a nice Irish accent but she didn't know where she'd come from or if she had any family in Ireland... It was the same with your father. He'd been born to a travelling family. And yes, there's something else I remember about her. She was very clever with her hands. She could paint flowers beautifully. Tim bought their house after Benjy died and the bedframe and the doorjamb were all painted round with wild flowers by your mother. They looked so real you could almost have picked them.'

This piece of information was seized on as if it were treasure. David's voice was excited as he cried, 'And Marie's a good painter. She can draw and paint flowers too. Is the house still in the field where the navvy camp was?'

Tibbie shook her head. 'No, it isn't. It burned down after Hannah and her wee baby died there of the cholera.' She didn't say that Tim, in his grief, set fire to it. That terrible time was best forgotten.

'Did our father die of cholera too? It killed lots of people in the camp, I've heard,' asked David.

Tibbie shook her head. 'No. Both of your parents were dead before it started. Your father died of consumption. Tim said he always had a bad cough.'

When the boy did not ask what had caused the death of his mother, she knew that he'd heard the stories, but obviously his sister had not for she asked, 'Was it consumption that killed our mother?'

Tibbie looked at David and saw entreaty in his eyes. He did not want his sister to know about their mother's terrible fate. It had been possible to keep it from Marie because of the semi-reclusive life she'd led with Nanny.

Tibbie shook her head and said, 'Not consumption. She had an accident. Her body was found up there on the hill.'

She pointed through her kitchen window to the flank of one of the three tall hills that brooded over the village like guardian giants. Marie looked shocked but seemed satisfied by that explanation.

David then said to his sister, 'Nanny took us to her funeral.'

Tibbie's face was full of pity as she looked at him. 'I was there too and so was my Hannah. She and your mother were friends.'

David smiled at her. 'And I'm very grateful that you're still our friend, Mrs Mather,' he said. It was the first sign of trust that he'd shown her.

—

Nanny Rush was buried next day in the shadow of the ancient Abbey of Rosewell. Her grave was dug in the dark soil in the middle of the velvety sward beside a broken red sandstone pillar which once supported the roof of a cloister where long-dead monks had walked. A crowd of mourners attended the interment because the dead woman was a well-respected member of the community and many of the townspeople had either been pupils at her little school or sent their children to her for education. They turned out to pay their respects, the men in stiff black suits and women with black linings sewn into their bonnets.

Martha, resplendent in midnight-coloured crêpe with maribou feathers around the edge of her cape, was chief mourner and when the ceremony was over she stood with a bowed head accepting commiserations. Tibbie, with David and Marie walking beside her, was one of the last to approach her and their exchange was stiff. It was obvious that Martha wanted to get away but Tibbie would not let her go without one last plea…

'Can't you see your way to letting the bairns have their books and paints?' She could not imagine what use Martha would have for children's treasures and it seemed unfair that they should be turned out of their home with only enough clothes to fill one small straw basket each.

Martha stiffened. 'I've told you already that my sister left me everything she possessed.'

'I find it hard to believe she didn't leave something to the children, because she loved them.' Tibbie's temper was up now. 'I'm beginning to wonder why you won't let me see that letter...' she went on.

'You've some impudence, Tibbie Mather! Are you calling me a liar?'

'Maybe I am. That's up to you. Where's the letter?' asked Tibbie.

'It's in the fire.'

Tibbie laughed. 'Isn't that handy!'

Red patches mottled Martha's cheeks and neck as she turned to look for her husband, who was standing a little way off with her sons and some friends.

'Willie, Willie,' she called. 'Are you going to stand there and hear your wife called a liar and a thief?'

He waddled over and glared at Tibbie, who stood her ground and glared back. 'What's this?' he asked.

'She's saying I've done the navvy's bastards out of an inheritance from my own sister. Did you ever hear the like? They were lucky to be kept for nothing all those years.'

Willie glared at Tibbie. 'You'd better watch your tongue, missus, or we'll have the law on you,' he threatened.

She shrugged. 'All I'm saying is I find it strange that Nanny didn't leave them anything, because she never liked Martha and she loved the bairns, so it's funny that she left nothing to them... That's all I'm saying.'

'Why should she leave anything to them? They're not blood kin. Family ought to inherit and she knew it! Anyway she didn't have much to leave. I don't know what you're making such a fuss about. You're meant to be so well-looked-after by that son-in-law of yours,' cried Martha viciously.

'And so I am,' snapped Tibbie. 'I'm not worried for myself. It's those two children being done out of their rights by somebody who doesn't need it, that's what's worrying me. It'll not do you any good, Martha, mark my words.'

Martha grabbed her husband's arm. 'Did you hear that, Willie, she's putting a curse on me!'

Willie gobbled like a turkey cock and it was obvious that he wished he was miles away from Rosewell at that moment. 'You watch your tongue, missus…' he said again.

'I know, or you'll put the law on me,' snapped Tibbie as she turned away and put an arm on each of the children's shoulders.

'Come on, let's go home,' she said.

This time the walk to Camptounfoot went quickly because they talked about Martha as they went.

'It makes me mad to think she's cheated you two,' raged Tibbie but David seemed philosophical.

'She's done it because we're not blood kin, but I'll be rich one day and able to look down my nose at people like her and her fat husband. I'm going to start tomorrow. I'm going over to Maddiston to see about a job in the big mill,' he said.

Tibbie stopped in mid-stride. 'Oh you cannae do that, laddie! Nanny wanted you to be a minister or a lawyer because you're so clever. If you go into the mills it'd be a terrible waste.'

'You can make good money in the mills,' said David grimly.

'You make more in the church or the law,' Tibbie reminded him.

'But that'll take too long. I want to make money fast so's I can get my own house and take Marie to live with me. I want us to be independent. We've been living on other folk's charity long enough!' His tone was vehement.

Tibbie looked at him with sorrow. 'Nanny never thought of it as charity… and neither do I.'

He shook his head. 'Maybe you don't but other folk do. They say we're foundlings taken in to save us going to the Poors' House. When I'm rich all the people who look down on us now will admire us. I'm going to get rich for Marie as well as for myself.'

He waved a hand at his sister who was listening wide-eyed.

'I'm sorry you won't go to college like Nanny planned,' Tibbie told him. 'If it's money you're worried about, don't, because I've more than I can spend. It would be a pleasure to educate you with it.'

He shook his head. 'We're not your kin any more than we were Nanny's. You can't spend money on us. I'm going to find work. I know the foreman of Henderson's weaving mill in Maddiston. He'll get me a place there and as soon as I can I'll take my sister to live with me. And when I'm working I'll pay you for looking after her.'

'Oh dear, that won't be necessary,' said Tibbie, but she knew she was wasting her breath. Nothing would ever change this boy's grim determination or deflect him from his purpose.

'Marie must still go on learning, though. I want her to be a lady,' he said.

'Camptounfoot has a good school,' Tibbie told him. 'The old master, Mr Anderson, died last year and we've a new one now, young Mr Arnott. Folk talk well of him.'

David nodded and said solemnly, 'That's good. Marie's only been taught by Nanny so she might be a bit behind. Nanny wasn't able to teach much after she got sick.'

It was obvious that he saw himself as his sister's provider and protector, the one who took all decisions concerning her. Already he was mapping out their future together and was setting himself to achieve his dream. Heaven help us all if things don't work out the way he wants, thought Tibbie with disquiet.

When they reached the corner by the Camptounfoot general store its door flew open and a child dashed out almost beneath their feet. Bob, the shopkeeper, emerged too, face red and yelling, 'That wee besom! Stop her. She's been stealing again!'

Tibbie did not seem surprised. 'Is it Kitty?' she asked.

Bob glared. 'Who else? It's aye Kitty. This time she's off with a chunk of cheese as big as a doorstop. The little thief that she is.'

'Tell her granny on her,' advised Tibbie.

'That'll no' get my cheese back, she'll have it all eaten by now. I don't think they feed her but that's no excuse for stealing,' said Bob righteously.

'Sometimes it can be,' Tibbie told him.

## Chapter Two

Kitty Scott was more like a wild animal than a child. Where other children had homes and families, no matter how poor, Kitty was a solitary; where they shivered in cold weather and sweated in the heat, she took the seasons in her stride and without any change in the rags she wore. Her feet were always bare, her wild hair matted, and her eyes and ears were not turned towards the games and chatter of other children but were alert for changes in the mood of the weather or for little signs that told her a strange bird or animal would soon cross her line of vision. She knew places in the village where none of the other children had ever been or which were forbidden to them, like the walled orchard behind Townhead farmhouse.

It was her favourite playing place because it was as impossible to keep her out as it would have been to ban the blackbirds. She made her way in through a low arched gap in the twelve-foot-high wall that had been cut long ago to allow the passage of a stream. She took good care, however, that no one ever saw her bending double and wriggling like an eel through the aperture, for she knew the two women who lived in the farmhouse had a neurotic fear of being spied on, and would have barred the stream hole against her.

Like an animal, from the time she was weaned she learned to forage for herself and at noon when the other children in Camptounfoot school went home to eat their main meal of the day, Kitty stole food wherever she could find it, before going to her favourite hiding-place in a thick hawthorn hedge that ran alongside the railway line at the back of the village. There, in a hole dug in the sandy soil, she secreted apples, crusts of bread, cold potatoes or raw turnips pulled from the farm's field. She kept all her finds till they became mouldy or smelt too bad to eat because she never knew when the day would come that she would find nothing for her dinner and she was always ravenously hungry.

What she liked best, because there was an element of danger in it, was to slip into Bob's shop while he was occupied with a customer and steal something, anything, from the counter. If he saw her he yelled, 'Get oot o' here, you wee besom!' but she usually managed to get away with a trophy of some kind. Perhaps it would be a handful of brown sugar from the big open bag that stood near the shop door, or a bit of raw bacon whipped off the counter under his nose. If she couldn't stomach what she'd taken – raw rice or dry barley was inedible without a fire and a cooking pot – she scattered it around her hiding-place for the birds to eat, sharing her spoils with them. In return the birds and animals showed her where the brambles were first ripe and which of the hazel trees had nuts, because she watched where they went and followed them.

On the day she stole the cheese, she sat in the shadow of the hedge and happily wiped her nose on her forearm as she stared out over her native village. She was nine years old but tall for her age with strong bones and broad shoulders, which was surprising because since birth neither her mother nor her grandmother had bothered to see that she was properly looked after, but Kitty had a strong instinct for self-preservation and quickly learned to be a good thief. The only place where she heard homilies about how children were expected to behave was in the schoolroom and she listened to these pieces of advice as if to a fairy story. Real life, she knew, was different.

Her career of crime in Camptounfoot, however, was badly handicapped by the fact that she was so conspicuous. It was difficult not to be noticed when you had bright red hair that flamed like a fire and a cheeky freckled face that caught the eye in any crowd. Kitty was also noticeable because she was dirty. No, not just dirty – very, very dirty. Her long thin legs were brown from lack of washing; her hair so tangled that it looked like wire wool and her clothes ragged and faded till it was impossible to guess what colour they had been originally. Once seen she was not easily forgotten and very easy to describe.

Her lack of fine clothes and her passing acquaintance with soap did not bother her, however, and on the day she bit into the hard yellow cheese she was happy. It would provide three meals at least.

Chewing, she relived the taking of it, how she'd slipped her hand up onto the counter from a crouching position on the floor while Bob was talking to Mrs Rutherford. Then she'd run out and almost bumped into Tibbie Mather... She'd had two young folk with her... Who were they?

Kitty's greatest interest was in knowing everything that happened to the families of the village. She turned in her hiding-place and stared out across the field. The place where she sat was a snug little den at the base of intertwined hawthorns and small beech trees with immensely thick trunks. The branches had grown into and through each other, forming an impenetrable tangle that shielded her from prying eyes, but she could see Tibbie's cottage, the last in a line of higgledy-piggledy houses overlooking the field that lay between them and the hawthorn hedge.

It was the prettiest cottage of all, she thought, because the garden had two low-branched apple trees and was full of flowers all summer long. It was closed in behind a stone wall with a gate in the middle, but the wall was low enough for sharp-eyed Kitty to have a clear view of the windows. She spent a lot of time staring into them because Tibbie was one of the few adults in the village who bothered to pass a kind word with her when they met in the street and, from time to time, even handed her a farthing or something to eat.

In the distance she heard the ringing of the school bell. Mr Arnott was summoning his charges back to their lessons but Kitty gave a shrug and decided to take the afternoon off. She'd had enough schooling for one day. Perhaps she'd slip into the orchard and play imaginary games among the ancient apple trees which had not been pruned or cut back for half a century and whose branches interlinked like friendly arms. Some of them were dying back and had become covered with pale grey lichen that made them look as if they were eternally gripped in ice.

If she did not do that, then she'd slip like a fox through the village alleys and see what was going on… Her curiosity about the lives of the villagers was as voracious as her appetite. She liked the idea that she was a pair of hidden eyes, watching everything.

A flurry of unusual activity at Tibbie's back door caught her attention. The two strangers she'd seen in the street came out with plates in their hands and sat down to eat in the sunshine. She regarded them with disfavour. They were both yellow-haired and very prim-looking with neat, tidy clothing and white faces. The sort of people who drew back from navvy bastards.

Tibbie came out next with a breadboard on which rested a loaf and a bright yellow square of butter. Kitty's mouth watered and suddenly the meal of cheese lay on her stomach like lead. She watched enviously as they ate.

When the meal was finished the boy went into the cottage and re-emerged carrying the brass cage containing Tibbie's parrot. Many times Kitty had peered at that wonderful bird through the cottage window when its owner was out but she had never been inside to speak to it. With all her heart she envied the strangers who were standing by the cage watching the parrot which sat with its head cocked and its feathers fluffing out in the warmth of the sun.

Tibbie peeled an apple and cut it in chunks, giving a piece to each of her guests who proffered them to the parrot. Something furious exploded in Kitty's head. These strangers were taking over Tibbie, worming their way into her affections so effectively that they were even allowed to feed the precious parrot! Fury filled her. She groped around on the earth and found a large lump of coal that had fallen out of the tender of a passing train. Like an avenging fury she stood up, took aim and threw it like a cannonball into Tibbie's garden.

Marie and David were enchanted with Bonaparte, who was eyeing them speculatively and making little muttering sounds under his breath as he accepted the bits of apple they held out to him.

'He'll say something in a minute,' Tibbie told them a few seconds before a lump of coal came whizzing through the air, missed David's head by inches and clattered against the bars of the cage. The bird gave an outraged screech and spread his brightly coloured wings wide.

'Devil, devil, devil…' he squawked in a marked French accent, fixing a furious eye on David, whom he thought was the perpetrator of this outrage.

Tibbie, however, was not under the same misapprehension. She ran to the garden gate and shouted across the field towards the hedge. 'Are you there, Kitty Scott? What do you think you're playing at? You could have killed somebody.'

There was strange silence and stillness in the hedge which told her that it harboured a hidden listener, a surprised listener too because Kitty had thought no one knew about her secret place. Even the field birds stopped chirping as if they were curious to hear what was going on.

Tibbie shouted again. 'Come out this minute. If you don't, I'll go and get your granny.'

There was a distant rustling, the long branches on top of the hedge began swaying and a bedraggled figure emerged.

'Aw dinna tell my granny, Mrs Mather... I didnae mean to hurt anybody,' it shouted.

Tibbie was furious. She gestured with her hand and called, 'Come here at once.'

Kitty came trailing reluctantly over meadow grass spangled with yellow buttercups, bright pink clover and big white daisies with brilliant orange hearts.

Tibbie stood with arms crossed watching her approach. 'Why did you do that? You know it's dangerous to throw rocks about, don't you?' she asked.

The red head hung down. 'Aye. But it wasnae a rock, it was a bit of coal.'

'It doesn't matter what it was. Why did you do it?'

'I dinna ken.'

'You must know. Think... Were you trying to hit my parrot?'

Kitty did not look up, only scraped in the dirt with a bare foot till words came from her. 'No, I didnae want to hurt the bird. I just felt angry. It sort of came over me when I saw you all there... You'll no' tell my granny, will you? I'll no' do it again, I promise.'

As she listened Tibbie's face softened. Now she felt pity instead of rage for the stone-thrower. There was something about Kitty that always touched her heart.

'You'll have to learn to keep a hold on yourself,' she said in a more gentle tone and lifted a half-peeled apple which she handed to the child on the other side of the gate. 'There, take that. You look hungry. Shouldn't you be at school? Hurry up or you'll get the strap for being late.'

Without another word Kitty took the apple and ran like a deer across the field, over the railway line, up into a wood on the side of the hill. Tibbie's face was sad as she watched her go.

'Poor wee soul, there's not much hope for that one, I'm afraid,' she said half to herself and half to her companions.

'Who is she?' asked David.

'Her name's Kitty Scott. Her mother and grandmother are bond-agers on the farm at the end of the village. Her mother's called Wee Lily and she's a bit simple because she was dropped on her head as an infant. Big Lily, the grandmother, is cruel to Kitty. I don't think she'd care if the bairn lived or died.'

Marie sighed. 'But hasn't she got wonderful hair? I've never seen hair that colour before. It's like a fire.'

Tibbie frowned. 'It would look better with a wash and a comb. When you go to school in the village, stay away from Kitty. She's not very clean and might give you lice. You've bonny hair and we don't want to have to cut it all off.'

The subject of their discussion did not go back to school but hid in the orchard until evening came. When dusk was about to gather she crawled out along the burn bed and headed down the slope towards the River Tweed, which twisted in a huge silver loop along the valley floor beneath the cliff on which the village perched.

On a steep gravelly bank where rabbits frolicked in the setting sun, she found black-clad Jo, the village undertaker, looking like a tall heron as he stood in the water fishing for trout.

She sat down behind him and watched without speaking, though she knew he was aware of her presence. Most of the village children were terrified of Jo because he was associated with death in their minds, and their mothers used the threat of getting Jo to them if they did not go to bed. When they were older they avoided him, for Jo was a strange bachelor, given to wandering the village at night, peering into folks' windows. Sometimes, gripped by a kind of religious mania, he preached sermons full of words like 'salvation', 'fornication', 'adultery', 'damnation' or 'redemption' outside the houses of people with secrets they would rather not have talked about.

Kitty rarely went to church but she liked to hear Jo shouting in the early hours of the morning when the world was dark and silent. The solemn sound of his utterances pleased her ear, though she did not know what the words meant.

He and she were friends because they shared a love of gossip. Kitty told him everything she found out by her assiduous watching and he supplied her with stories about the villagers' past peccadilloes, most of which would be condemned as unsuitable for a child's ears by Mr Arnott if he heard them. Jo's memory of the antecedents of the folk of Camptounfoot went back through at least four generations, which made many of them afraid of him but Kitty was not. In fact, she was afraid of very little because her lack of parental guidance meant that she had never been warned about dos and don'ts, rules of behaviour and etiquette, pitfalls to watch out for or things to avoid. She learned by her mistakes.

Now she asked in a friendly way, 'Caught anything yet?'

'No,' he said, reeling in the line. 'They're not biting tonight.'

'Dinna stop. You'll catch something soon and then I'll make a fire and we can cook it,' she said.

Jo knew she was always hungry so he offered, 'I'll gie you a penny and you can go up to Bob's for a bag of sweeties if you like.'

She pulled a face. 'He'll no' let me in. I stole some cheese from him at dinner time.'

Unlike most adults, Jo viewed this as perfectly acceptable behaviour and shrugged. 'Oh well, you'll just hae to do without the sweeties in that case,' he said.

Silence fell over them again for a little while till Kitty threw a stone into the river and said, apparently idly, 'Tibbie Mather's got two strangers staying with her.'

Jo did not let her down. 'I ken who they are. They're the two who lived with Nanny Rush in Rosewell. Their father was a navvy on the railway line and their mother was found up there on the hill with her heid bashed in. She was murdered...'

Kitty stared at him wide-eyed. 'They're awful proper-looking to be a navvy's bairns.' All her life she'd had the insult 'navvy's bastard' thrown at her and knew it meant the lowest of the low.

'Aw well they've been lucky, no' like you,' said Jo sympathetically.

Seeing that he was well disposed to talk, which he was not always, she seized her chance to ask more questions. 'Who murdered their mother?' she asked.

Jo looked sharply at her over his shoulder. 'They never really found out but folk thought it was the same man as fathered you.'

She stared at him with wide brown eyes that told she was genuinely shocked, and Kitty was hard to shock. Jo was sorry that he'd sprung it on her like that.

'They never really found out. It was just what folk thought at the time,' he backtracked.

'How could they think that?' she asked.

Jo always talked to her as if she were grown up, so he said, 'She was his woman. She lived with him in the navvy camp. He used to knock her about and one day she disappeared. Then they found her up on the hill.'

Kitty shook her head in disbelief. 'And the two with Tibbie look that respectable!'

'Nanny Rush did a good job wi' them,' said Jo.

'When did it happen? When was she found?' asked Kitty who was still recovering from the shock.

'Before you were born.'

Kitty had always known that she was the child of rape. Her grandmother flung it in her face, taunting her that she was unwanted because she'd been conceived in violence and borne with reluctance. She'd been told it so often that she accepted it as a fact of life and even had a lingering sympathy for the man who fathered her because he was awarded the same scorn by Big Lily, her grandmother, as was Kitty herself.

'What was my father like? Did you know him?' she now asked Jo, who was pulling in his line and preparing to go home.

'I boxed him,' he told her shortly and she was familiar enough with his parlance to know he meant he'd put her father in his coffin. It was the first time she'd heard that and her heart thudded because she sometimes secretly hoped that one day her father would come back to make amends for raping Wee Lily and take his child away with him. If he was dead, however, that dream would never come true.

'What was he like?' she asked again. That at least she wanted to know.

'Reed-headed, reed as you, and big, well over six feet. He had a chest on him like a barrel. I needed an extra-large box for him,' said Jo. He sounded impressed.

Kitty felt no sorrow over the death of this colossus, only curiosity.

'If he was so big and strong, what did he die of?' was her next question.

Jo glared at her with a strange shifty look in his eye and went secretive. 'You're asking too many questions. I dinna remember.'

She stood up and stamped a foot in anger. 'You do, you remember everything. I ken fine you never forget anything that's happened in this village.'

But she had run up against village secrecy. Not for nothing was Camptounfoot built like a honeycomb, with each house walled off from its neighbour, linked by alleys lined with walls so high it was impossible to see over them. Camptounfoot folk made a fetish of keeping their secrets and Jo, who knew most of them, could not be forced into talking when it did not suit him or when the story reflected on his community.

'I dinna remember what he died of. Ask your granny about him,' was all he would say.

Townhead farm, where Kitty lived with her mother and grandmother, was the last cluster of buildings in the village. The tall, bleak farmhouse stood at the eastern end of the main street and looked as if it had once been a guardhouse or a watchtower, for its wall marked the edge of the carriageway and the only windows on that side were set high up like watching eyes staring suspiciously out across the surrounding countryside. The entrance to the house was at the rear, facing the orchard, and its only gate, a wooden door set in the wall, was guarded by a vicious old sheepdog which snarled at every stranger.

For centuries Townhead farm had been owned by the Scott family, but the current head of it, Craigie Scott, was an absentee, languishing in an Edinburgh prison and unlikely ever to be released. For over ten years he had been shut up for murder and only escaped hanging because he managed to persuade the judge that he was insane. The villagers never talked about Craigie's crime for it was one of their closely guarded secrets. Kitty knew he'd killed someone but had never been told the identity of his victim and she accepted that, just as she accepted the vagaries of the weather, and rarely gave it a thought.

Craigie's two sisters, Helen and Joan, still lived in the farmhouse looking out into the enchanted paradise of an orchard. They never picked the fruit that was so abundantly produced by the trees that grew there and apples lay on the grass till they rotted because neither would they give anything away. Their greed was only exceeded by their terror of the outside world, which had grown worse since their brother was taken away to Edinburgh.

Across the street from the farmhouse were two cowsheds, a grain store, some sheds and a bothy, as well as a dairy which supplied the villagers with milk, cream and butter.

The Misses Scott, in spite of the turn in their fortunes, still had pretensions to grandeur, and kept apart from the rest of the villagers, thinking themselves superior to ordinary folk. They did no work apart from pocketing the money paid by the customers at their dairy and all the actual labour was done by two bondagers, Big Lily and her daughter Wee Lily, with the inadequate assistance of a lumbering simpleton called Jake, who received no thanks and the minimum of wages for their loyalty.

When Kitty returned to the farm after her evening on the riverbank with Jo, she found her grandmother alone in the dairy. Big Lily was a massive woman with broad shoulders and huge pendulous breasts, her face was brown and weather-beaten beneath the saucer-shaped black straw hat she always wore except when she was asleep in bed at night. Her spatulate hands were gnarled and marked on the back by ridges of raised veins like the hands of a working man.

'Where've you been?' she asked without looking up from some task she was performing with a bone-handled knife in a tangle of rope.

'Fishing with Jo.'

'Humph, you'd better watch out for him. He's funny about lassies.'

It was the first time Big Lily had ever warned Kitty against anything or anyone and she was surprised. 'Jo's all right,' she protested.

'No man's all right. The likes of you wouldn't be here if they were,' grunted Big Lily, slicing the rope in two with the sharp blade of her knife.

Jo's advice to 'Ask your granny,' came into the child's head and encouraged by the fact that Big Lily was at least speaking to her, a rare occurrence in itself, she ventured, 'Jo was telling me about my father.'

Big Lily stopped cutting and stood perfectly still. Then she turned slightly and stared at the child beside her. Her eyes were red-rimmed and deeply pouched like the eyes of a tired dog.

'Was he noo? I'm surprised he hasn't better things to talk about than that bastard. What did he say?'

'He said he was tall and had red hair like mine.'

'Huh, don't I know it. He left that mark behind at least,' said Big Lily sourly, beginning her cutting again, but there was a lack of intensity about it that told Kitty her grandmother was abstracted and listening to her.

'What was my father's name?' she asked.

Big Lily threw the knife down on a wooden shelf and snapped, 'He didn't introduce himsel' to your mither when he raped her. We could have done without you. You werenae wanted. Tibbie Mather tried to get rid of you with medicine but it didn't work… you hung on like the thrawn little besom that you are. You were asking his name. He was called Bullhead and that tells you what he looked like – like a red polled stirk!'

Kitty fled and for a few minutes stood in the cobbled yard with her legs shaking beneath her, knotting her fists impotently. She hated her

29

grandmother. Big Lily was cruel, always ready to administer beatings or verbal torments but never a kind word or an embrace.

There was a faint light glimmering through the unglazed window of the bothy behind the cowshed which was the bondagers' home and she ran towards it, knowing that while Big Lily was occupied in the dairy, her mother would be alone and less afraid of showing her child some affection. When Big Lily was present, she always acted as if it was shameful to be kind to her daughter.

The splintered wooden door was ajar and she pushed it open to reveal a dark, cavernous room with a fire of logs burning in a hearth at the far end. Smoke had blackened the rough stones above it for there was no chimney, only a hole in the ragged thatch. The walls were unplastered and unpainted; the floor trodden-down earth that turned to mud in wet weather; the furniture was two rough wooden chairs, a table, an iron bedstead that the bondagers shared and a pile of rags in the corner which was Kitty's bed.

Wee Lily, as tall as her mother but much thinner and surprisingly graceful, was standing by the fire with a wooden spoon in her hand and when she saw Kitty she cried out, 'Aw, bairn, are you hungry? Come on in and I'll gie you some broth. Hurry up and eat it before she gets back.'

She ladled out a plateful of steaming soup and laid it on the table, pointing at it with her spoon. 'Hurry up,' she said anxiously, fearful of her mother's return. The child did as she was told, gulping the soup down, although it was very hot, while her mother watched.

'Was it good?' she asked innocently when the plate was empty.

'Aye, very good, Mam,' said Kitty.

Wee Lily gave her a quick hug. 'You'll no' tell my ma, will you?' she asked. She always talked to her child as if they were the same age although, in fact, Kitty was more intelligent and worldly-wise than her mother. From as far back as she could remember she had always felt Wee Lily's senior and not the other way around.

She pressed her face in at her mother's waist, loving the soapy smell of the apron, for in spite of their neglect of Kitty, both of the bondagers were excessively clean and particular about their appearance. It was a miracle how they managed to turn themselves out so well because they were cripplingly poor and lived in primitive conditions, but they made their own soap, washed and bleached their clothes, blackened their boots till they gleamed and repainted their black hats every time the gloss wore off. It was as if they were saying to the world, 'We may only be farm workers but we're clean and decent.'

Kitty would have liked to stay in her mother's close embrace for ever but a sound outside the door made Wee Lily pull away. When she did so the child looked up at her and said, 'Jo was telling me about my father...'

Wee Lily froze, spoon upraised over the pot on the fire. Her voice was panic-stricken when she said, 'I dinna remember onything aboot it. It was terrible. Dinna ask me about it, bairn, just dinna ask.'

Kitty turned away and sat down in the wooden chair nearest the fire. 'All right, I won't, but it isn't my fault that I was born,' she said defiantly.

Wee Lily spread out her arms and cried, 'I know that. I dinna think it was your fault but my mither says I wouldn't have carried you if I hadnae... if I hadnae enjoyed it. That isnae true. I hated it. I thought he was going to kill me.'

Kitty sank her head in her hands; she didn't want to hear any more, not now, not ever. She wished she'd never opened this can of worms. 'All right, Ma, all right. I don't want to know,' she said.

But Wee Lily could not stop. She walked towards her daughter saying urgently, 'It wasnae my fault Craigie shot him. It's no' my fault Craigie's in the jile but my ma thinks it is.'

Kitty looked at her in horror. Her mouth felt dry and her ears were pounding. 'Craigie shot who?' she asked.

'That Bullheid. It wasnae my fault they took Craigie awa'.'

A sour taste of vomit filled Kitty's mouth. She wanted to be outside, away from those awful words... Craigie Scott shot her father... her father had killed a woman and raped her mother... Too much awful knowledge was being forced on her at an age when she should have been hearing fairy tales.

'I'm going to be sick,' she gasped and rushed for the door, and did not stop running till she was safe in the heart of the orchard. No one came looking for her and she stayed there with hunting owls and little animals going about their business around her till morning.

## Chapter Three

Next morning an unusually subdued Kitty turned up late at school and found the pupils all chattering together while Mr Arnott, the schoolmaster, talked to Tibbie Mather who was holding the girl with the yellow hair by the hand.

The school was just one big, wooden-walled room with a large potbellied stove standing in the middle and benches arrayed round it. Mr Arnott sat at a high desk by the door surveying his charges with what he hoped was a stern eye. In fact he was rather unsure of himself, having only graduated from college in Glasgow a year before and this was his first post. He had been chosen to succeed old Mr Anderson who had been the much-respected dominie at Camptounfoot for over forty years until his death.

When Kitty slipped in, Tibbie was introducing herself because Arnott did not yet know all the inhabitants of the village as Mr Anderson had done, having taught most of them.

'I'm Mrs Mather from up the street and this is Marie Benjamin who's come to live with me. I'd like to enrol her in the school please,' she said in her most polite voice.

Arnott saw to his relief that the child was clean and neatly dressed, as was her escort, so he held out his hand saying, 'I'm delighted to have another pupil. How old is she and where's she been at school before?'

'She's eleven but she's not had a lot of schooling because she was in the Rosewell dame school and the mistress there wasn't doing much teaching for a long time. She was ill,' explained Tibbie.

'I'm not very good at counting,' whispered the girl and Tibbie encouraged her with, 'But you're a good reader, Marie, and you do the loveliest drawings.'

Arnott came down from his perch, put a hand on top of Marie's head and looked around the class for an empty seat. The only one he could see was at the side of Kitty Scott, who moved along a little as if to make room for the newcomer. Tibbie saw this movement too and flashed the schoolmaster a warning look which he immediately understood, so he pointed a finger at a rough-looking little boy and said, 'Willie, come and sit in the front beside Kitty. Marie can have your place.'

When he saw Tibbie to the door, she said softly to him, 'Thank you for not putting her beside Kitty. I've nothing against the bairn but she's not very clean and she's as wild as heather. She chucked a stone at my parrot yesterday.'

He looked scandalised. 'But that was very dangerous.'

Tibbie felt she'd betrayed Kitty and wished she hadn't said it, so she hurried to add, 'It was a mistake I think and it didn't do any harm. She missed and the parrot's fine.'

'More by good luck than good judgement, I'll be bound,' said the disapproving Mr Arnott.

Back in the classroom he clapped his hands to call the chattering pupils to order and said, 'We'll do arithmetic now.' Taking up a piece of chalk he scrawled some figures with a flourish on the blackboard. His eye fell on the newcomer and he asked, 'Can you add those numbers together, Marie?'

She blushed and stumbled... 'Thirteen and fourteen is – twenty-six, is it?'

He shook his head. 'No. Can anybody tell me what thirteen and fourteen is?' A forest of hands shot up, all eager to show their superiority over the stranger. He looked around. One hand was not up. Kitty Scott was sitting staring into space as usual so it was her he chose to answer. 'What's thirteen and fourteen, Kitty?'

'Twenty-seven,' she said shortly.

'Why didn't you put your hand up if you know the answer?' he snapped, disappointed at being foiled in his plan to make a fool of her.

'There was plenty others wi' their hands up,' she told him insolently.

Soon it was mid-morning and time for a break. Bella Ferguson, the spoilt and petulant daughter of Bob who kept the shop, was the most important girl in the school and the others, with the exception of Kitty, followed her lead, so when she walked towards the newcomer with a smile on her face, they did the same. Because Marie was well dressed and politely spoken, Bella took her arm and said, 'Sit with me when we go back in and we'll be friends.'

Marie, who had never had the company of more than two girls at any one time, because female pupils were rarer than boys in the dame school, was overwhelmed by this apparent friendliness. Only Kitty Scott stayed away from her, staring in a hostile way from the farthest corner of the schoolyard, but when the bell rang to summon them back to lessons, Marie found herself in front of Kitty in the queue and turned to say in a friendly way, 'I wish I could count like you.'

Kitty was won over a little and her brown eyes flashed through her tangled fringe. 'It's easy. The answer just comes. I like figures. They're all different colours you see,' she said.

Bella, at Marie's side, pulled on her arm and whispered, 'You shouldn't be speaking to her. She's just a tink.'

At midday, when she served dinner, Tibbie was pleased to see how well Marie seemed to have settled in at school, for she'd been worried that the shy girl would not be able to cope without the protection of her brother, who, that same morning, had walked three miles to Maddiston in search of work and had not yet returned. Marie, however, was bright and happy, eager to go back for the afternoon session and at one o'clock she disappeared out of the door with a happy wave.

When she got back to school things were different, though. Hostility, as palpable as a wave of cold water, met her as soon as she stepped through the school gate. Bella was standing in the middle of her friends and, at the sight of Marie, pointedly turned away. Miserable and confused, Marie trailed into school alone when Mr Arnott rang his handbell. Just before the door closed, the red-haired rebel came squeezing in behind her.

During the afternoon reading lesson Marie had her moment of glory because she was asked to read a poem from a book which Mr Arnott handed to her. There were some hard words like 'dungeon' and 'meteor' but she managed without faltering and even infused some meaning into the lines. When she was finished the teacher held up his hand and said, 'Well done, very well done. That was Byron's poem about the Prisoner of Chillon. Did you understand it, class?'

The last question was answered by murmuring sounds of assent and once more Marie was told, 'You read very well.' A glow of pleasure still filled her when the children tumbled out into the yard, shouting and scrapping among themselves. Bella, her plump pink face set hard, was waiting for Marie.

'You speak awfy fancy for a navvy's bairn,' was her first accusing remark.

'Why shouldn't I?'

'I'd have thought you'd speak Irish like some of the other tinks who come through here in the summer.'

Marie blushed bright red, for she was unused to hostility, and wished David was with her. In a hurry to escape she tried to push her way through the little crowd but Bella held her back. There was worse to come. 'And that's not an Irish name you've got – Benjamin. What sort of name is that?' she demanded.

'It was my father's name. He was called Benjy,' said Marie innocently.

Bella sniggered. 'That's what my dad said. It was his first name – like mine's Bella and my father's called Bob. If I called myself by my father's first name I'd be Bella Bob!' The other girls giggled at this sally but Bella's blue eyes were hard and unamused. 'I didnae ken you were a navvy's bairn like that one over there,' she said, pointing across to where Kitty stood watching what was going on. 'Now we've got two of you.'

Marie was angry now. 'What's wrong with having a navvy for a father? Mine died of consumption in the camp.'

'Oh, aye, so he did – and what happened to your mother? Do you ken anything about her? I'll tell you. She was a whore, a bad woman, that's what she was.' The terrible word was hissed out like a curse in a sibilant whisper in case Mr Arnott should hear it being bandied about.

Tears sprang to Marie's eyes. 'That's not true, that's not true!' she cried, but Bella stepped nearer and whispered, 'It is true. When I went home at dinner time I told my mother and father that you'd come to the school and they told me that your mother gave you and your brother to Nanny Rush before she went off to live with another man when your father died. They said she wasnae properly married to your father either… and you know what that makes you! There was a lot of that kind of woman in the camp when the navvies were here. It was a scandal. So you needn't act so grand. We know what you are! You're a navvy's bastard like Carroty Kate.'

The words were hardly out of her mouth when what seemed like a human cannonball came bursting through the crowd of onlookers. Head down, Kitty charged at Bella's middle, making her double up with a gasp. Then Kitty's balled fist hit her full on the nose and a fountain of blood spurted out and splashed scarlet drops onto her immaculate white pinafore. Her friends set up a chorus of screaming that could have been heard in Rosewell and had the effect of bringing Mr Arnott rushing to the classroom door. When he saw what was happening, he waded in through hysterical girls and grabbed Kitty by the tail of her ragged dress, pulling her away from the screaming Bella.

'What in heaven's name is going on here? It's you is it, Scott? And you, Bella! This isn't like you,' he shouted.

Through hands spread over her face his favourite wailed, 'She hit me, she hit me, she's broken my nose. Oh look at all the blood! My dad'll get the polis to her.'

Arnott shook the struggling Kitty hard. 'Why did you do this?' he asked.

'She shouldnae call folk bastards,' shouted Kitty angrily.

'As far as I'm led to believe you are a bastard – and you certainly behave like one,' was his rejoinder. Kitty looked at him with scorn. 'Not me, *her*! She called her a bastard.' She was pointing at the new girl who'd read Byron so well. He looked from Kitty to Marie and then to Bella who was wiping her face with her pinafore and sobbing copiously.

'Is this true?' he asked Marie who nodded and said softly, 'Yes, she did.'

He did not want to enter into an argument about the rights and wrongs of this so he turned back to Kitty and shook her again. 'Even if she did, there's no need for you to fight other people's battles. You've hurt Bella badly.'

Kitty struggled out of his hold. 'Och no I haven't. She's just got a bloody nose. It'll do her good.' Then she dashed like a hare for the school gate and disappeared.

She knew she wouldn't get away with it, of course. Though she hid in the orchard till it was dark, she had to go home eventually and when she did, Big Lily was waiting for her, sitting in her chair by the fire with a stick across her knees and her face red and glowing with sweat and emotion.

'I've had Bob from the shop here,' she announced as soon as Kitty stepped inside the bothy.

Wee Lily was hovering in the background, wringing her hands and moaning, 'Aw, Ma, dinna be too hard on her, aw, Ma, she's only a bairn.'

Big Lily didn't look at her daughter but said out of the side of her mouth, 'If you dinna want to watch, get away out. You're far ower soft on her, always have been. That's half the trouble.' Wee Lily shrank back into the corner and said nothing more.

Big Lily glared at Kitty again and pronounced solemnly, 'Like I said, Bob's been here. He says you've split his lassie's nose and ruined her peeny. The bloodstains'll never come out apparently. He wants me to pay for it or he'll go to the polis. And he said the schoolmaster told him that you'd been chucking stanes at Tibbie Mather's parrot. Have you gone out of your mind altogether?'

As she spoke she stood up, rearing like a giantess above the child. A strong smell of sweat came off her and there were stains like half-moons on her blouse under her arms. She was obviously highly charged with fury and excitement. Kitty stood her ground and said nothing. There wasn't any point.

'Why did you do it?' asked Big Lily, flexing the stick between her hands so that it arched.

Why? wondered Kitty. All she could remember was the red rage that swept over her when she heard Bella jeering about navvy bastards. That and the fact that the blonde-haired newcomer needed a protector against the hard-eyed girls who had turned against her. She could not explain all that to her grandmother, however, so all she said was, 'I dinna ken.'

'You dinna ken much, do you? But you'll ken about this,' yelled Big Lily and whacked at the child's bare legs with the stick. Even though she expected it, the pain stung so badly that Kitty leapt in the air and gave an anguished yell. Her mother in the corner groaned, 'Aw, Ma, dinna hurt her...'

These reactions seemed to fuel Big Lily's rage and she stepped closer to the cowering child, slashing at her with the stick. Her eyes bulged and she grunted as if she were possessed. 'You're like that man that fathered you – a deil on legs. I'll learn you, I'll learn you...' As she spoke, Big Lily was continuing to beat Kitty who had backed into a corner, attempting to shield herself from the furious blows with arms crossed over her head, but there was to be no respite. Big Lily was out of control, glorying in cruelty, shouting as her arm flailed up and down, 'I should hae put you out on the hill when you were born... You wouldnae be any loss.'

A particularly vicious blow caught the child across the back and she gave a terrified whimpering cry. 'Oh dinna, dinna, I'm sorry...'

'Sorry! I'll make sure you're sorry. You'll no be able to walk when I'm finished wi' ye.' The stick crashed across Kitty's shoulders and she sank to her knees on the floor. There was blood in her mouth and it tasted sweet as she swallowed it. She closed her eyes and wondered if she was going to die.

When she saw the child fall down Wee Lily ran forward and tried to pick her up but Big Lily hit her too and yelled, 'Get oot o' there or I'll let you have it as well.'

'Ma, Ma, you'll kill her. She's only a bairn,' pleaded the child's mother but to no avail. Big Lily was bending over Kitty and still belabouring her. Wee Lily ran for the door and disappeared out into the darkness. Through mists of faintness Kitty thought that her last hope of salvation had deserted her.

Wee Lily knew what to do, however. She ran over the courtyard, down the lane, and across the road to Tibbie Mather's cottage. Though it was late and there was no light in the window, she hammered frantically on the knocker, crying out, 'Tibbie, Tibbie, come and save my bairn.'

Tibbie, who had been in bed, answered the door in her nightgown and gasped in amazement when she saw the frantic bondager weeping in the street.

Wee Lily reached out and pulled her into the open, gabbling, 'Oh, Tibbie, my Ma's killing Kitty because she bloodied Bella's nose and threw stones at your parrot. Come and stop her. She'll listen to you.'

It was common knowledge in the village that Big Lily was brutal to her daughter's unwanted child and Tibbie did not linger but grabbed a shawl to pull over her nightdress and ran to the bothy in the wake of Wee Lily, who was sobbing frantically as she went, 'Dinna let her kill my bairn.'

When they got there, Kitty was sprawled on the floor, fighting no longer, arms spread like a broken doll, Big Lily bent over her with the stick in her hands. If the child had moved, she would have started beating her again.

Tibbie strode up purposefully and ordered, 'Give me the stick. You should be ashamed, a woman your size hitting a bairn.'

Big Lily grunted, 'She's no' a bairn. She's that navvy's seed. We should have got rid of her at the time.'

Tibbie knelt down beside the half-naked child. White skin shone pathetically through the slashed cotton of her dress and her eyes were shut. There was blood on her face, matted in her hair and red weals from the stick marked her legs and arms.

'Kitty, Kitty, can you hear me?' she whispered, cradling the redhead in her arms. She wished with all her heart that she had not told the schoolmaster about Kitty throwing the coal at Bonaparte.

There was no response from the slumped body and Wee Lily gave an anguished groan. 'She's deed. I know she's deed. Oh, Ma, you've killed my bairn!'

Big Lily, apparently uncaring, strode over to the fireplace and sat down heavily in her chair without speaking. Tibbie stroked Kitty's face and held a hand to her lips before she looked up at Wee Lily and reassured her by saying, 'She's not dead. She's still breathing. Have you any whisky or brandy in the house?'

'No, but we've got ale,' said Wee Lily.

'That's no good. She needs more than that. Go to my house and you'll find a bottle of brandy in the cupboard by the kitchen fireplace. Bring it here.' Tibbie spoke with firm authority and Wee Lily did as she was told without as much as a glance at her mother, who was still staring fixedly into the fire.

When the brandy bottle was pressed to the child's white lips, she managed to swallow a little. Then she sighed, her eyelids fluttered and she moved her shoulders. When consciousness returned, Tibbie asked, 'Can you move your arms and legs? Is anything broken?'

First one arm moved, then the other. After that, with a wincing expression, Kitty moved each leg. 'Everything hurts,' she whispered.

'That's only the cuts. They'll heal. As long as nothing's broken,' said Tibbie with relief in her voice.

Then she looked over the child's head and addressed Big Lily. 'You're lucky. She's going to be all right. But don't ever do it again or by God I'll fetch the polisman to you myself. No decent person would beat a dog the way you've beaten this bairn.'

The woman in the chair was unrepentant. 'A hiding'll do her good. It'll knock some of the cheek out of her. She'll no' be throwing stones at your parrot again anyway,' she said.

Tibbie looked angry. 'I didnae want you to hear about that. She's just a child. Folk do daft things when they're bairns. You must have been daft yourself once.'

Big Lily's eyes were bleak. 'I was working in the field when I was her age,' she said.

Tibbie knew this to be true, for Lily had been born and brought up in the bothy and was sent out to the fields with her mother when she was old enough to toddle. A realisation of the barren cruelty of the other woman's existence silenced any more protests. Tibbie knew that Big Lily herself was a bondager's bastard, fathered by the farmer who employed her mother and gave the child his surname but nothing else.

That farmer was also the father of Craigie Scott, who, in his turn, had fathered his own child on Big Lily.

No wonder Wee Lily's simple, thought Tibbie as she bent down to lift up the third generation of that unfortunate family and put her to bed.

As the child lay in her arms she looked down at the white, heart-shaped face beneath the tumbling hair. Poor little soul, she thought, fathered by a brute, mothered by a simpleton, grandchild of a bitter woman and Craigie Scott who was shut up in prison for shooting the man who'd raped her mother. She hoped that no one would ever tell Kitty the secrets of her family, for they were very dark indeed.

'Where does she sleep?' she asked, looking around the cavern-like room.

'On the floor,' was Big Lily's indifferent reply as she indicated a dark pile against the wall near the door.

Tibbie looked shocked. 'Doesn't she even have a blanket?' she asked, for Kitty's bed was only a collection of tattered rags on dried bracken.

'No,' was the hard reply.

'Then I'll get her one,' said Tibbie, laying the child down on the rags before she went out of the door. When she came back she was carrying a white woollen blanket taken from the well-filled linen chest beneath her own bed.

'There, Kitty, cuddle into that,' she said, tucking up the child. Then she walked across to Big Lily, who sat by the fire smoking a clay pipe as if nothing had happened.

'Listen to me, Lily,' said Tibbie sternly. 'You've got to treat that bairn better. It's not her fault she was born.'

'I don't know why you're so bothered about her,' was Big Lily's sullen reply, but there was a shamefaced note in her voice that told Tibbie the murderous rage had left her.

'It was me helped to deliver the poor wee soul if you remember,' Tibbie snapped.

'It would've been better if you'd let her die. She's nothing but trouble and expense,' grunted Big Lily.

'Some expense. You don't waste any money on her. She's a disgrace to you. You should be ashamed of putting her out in rags,' was Tibbie's angry rejoinder.

This stung Big Lily who glared back. 'I'm too old to start wi' bairns again and her mother's no' able, so why should I bother? It's that yin's fault Craigie's where he is and all the work of the farm falls on me. His sisters don't do anything.'

She carried a heavy load. The only help given to her and Wee Lily was from lumbering Jake who slept in the outhouse and was paid a pittance. Jake's mother had come to the farm some twenty years before as a potato picker but died of consumption leaving her three-year-old son behind. He never left and had grown into a big, doltish man who could neither read nor write and found it hard to follow the simplest instructions.

The Scott sisters ruled their workers by fear, always threatening to send them away, a threat which terrified them, for they had never lived anywhere but on Townhead and the thought of facing the outside world was too frightening to contemplate.

'I don't know why you stay here. You could easily find yourself another place. You and Wee Lily are good workers,' said Tibbie, but Big Lily stared at her in astonishment.

'Leave here? I'd never do that. I was born in this bothy and I want to die here. This is my place as much as it's the sisters'.'

Tibbie softened slightly. 'I know it's hard for you but try to be kinder to that poor bairn.'

'Aye it's hard for me and having that navvy's brat to raise hasn't made it easier. My lassie didnae even have the sense to miscarry it!' Big Lily's face was a mask of misery as she spoke.

Tibbie sat down on the chair facing her and asked softly, 'But weren't you forced too, Lily?' She'd always thought that Craigie must have forced himself on his bondager.

She was in for a surprise, however, because Big Lily looked up and glared with eyes that glittered like steel with unshed tears.

'Me, forced? I was never forced. I loved Craigie. I love him still and I promised I'd stay here when he was taken awa'.'

This was hard to comprehend for Craigie was not a man to inspire love in any woman as far as Tibbie could see, but Big Lily obviously thought differently. She was staring into the fire and saying, 'I was glad to have his bairn. They say a woman willnae carry a child when she's raped unless she wanted the man to take her. I carried Craigie's bairn and Wee Lily carried that navvy's.'

Tibbie was shocked. 'Lily, Lily, you mind as well as me what state Wee Lily was in when we found her after that man had his way with her. Don't you remember how hurt she was, how she cried? It was just bad luck that my medicine didn't work and she carried the child.'

'I think she wanted it,' said Big Lily bleakly and Tibbie realised that this was the major grudge in the older woman's mind against her daughter's misbegotten child. Big Lily was jealous, jealous of the love between Wee Lily and Kitty. The emotions that ran among the three of them in that dark hovel were deep and complicated.

Suddenly she felt very tired and stood up, pulling her shawl over her shoulders. 'It's long after midnight. I'm going back to bed. Don't you dare touch that bairn again because I meant it when I said I'd report you to the polisman if you do,' she warned.

As she was going out she bent down and looked at the sleeping child. 'You'll be sore tomorrow, Kitty,' she said softly.

'In that case she'll no' do it again,' came Big Lily's unrepentant voice, but Tibbie knew she'd frightened her and that Big Lily would think twice before she administered another brutal beating to her granddaughter, for she was mortally afraid of falling foul of the law. A police case might give Craigie's sisters an excuse to get rid of her.

When Tibbie reached her own cottage she found Marie and David up and waiting for her in the kitchen because they had been wakened by the frantic comings and goings. 'What's wrong?' asked Marie anxiously when Tibbie came in.

'Big Lily beat Kitty and nearly killed her. I just got there in time to stop it,' she sighed.

'What did she beat her for?' asked the girl.

'I think she was only looking for an excuse, but she said it was because Kitty made Bella's nose bleed.'

Marie gasped. 'Then it's all my fault. Kitty hit Bella because of me. I'm so sorry.'

Tibbie consoled her. 'It's not your fault. What did Bella do to you?'

'She said I was a navvy bastard and Kitty just ran into her and hit her on the nose. She was flaming mad,' Marie said.

Tibbie sighed. 'The poor wee soul must be sick of folk talking about navvy bastards. Don't worry, Kitty's going to be all right and your mother and father were decent people. Hold your head up and ignore Bella. She's just a nasty wee gossip.'

It was still dark when Kitty was wakened next morning by the sounds of her mother and grandmother rising and dressing. She lay as still as a mouse and watched them through half-closed eyelids. Her grandmother was stooping over the ashes of the fire, breathing life into them by blowing gustily on the dull embers. Dust and ash flew everywhere but soon flames began to lick around the broken twigs she had placed on top of the pile.

Wee Lily was pulling on her clothes. Like her mother she was a big, handsome woman and from a distance looked imposing. It was only when you were close to her that you noticed the bland simplicity of her stare, the childishness of her smile. She sat on a wooden box and pulled on her boots, laboriously lacing them up and then giving the toes an extra polish with a bit of cloth. Kitty was filled with an immense love for her mother, and longed to rise from bed, throw her arms around the broad shoulders and kiss her cheek.

But the least movement hurt her as she silently tested out her body, luxuriating in the pain, flexing her muscles in turn but taking care to draw no attention to herself. Each movement made pain flood through her like a tide, building up to a climax and then gradually fading away as she lay still again. It throbbed inside her, taking its beat from the thudding of her heart. She must have given a sob or a sigh because she saw Wee Lily turn and stare in her direction, so she closed her eyes and pretended to be asleep.

Then Big Lily's voice rang out in the silent room. 'Dinna sit there staring. There's fifteen heifers to be fed before daylight and I've the sheep to check before we do the milking. Hurry up.'

'But what about the bairn?' Wee Lily asked.

'Leave her be. She's asleep. She can get herself up when she wakens.'

'But what if she's hurt? What if you did some damage to her last night?'

'She's not hurt bad. That kind don't get hurt.'

'Aw, Ma, you're ower hard on her. She's only a bairn.'

'Her kind's born to hang. You mark my words. The quicker you cut her off the better,' said Big Lily as she pushed her protesting daughter out of the bothy.

When their footsteps died away, Kitty crawled out from under her blanket – where had it come from, she wondered? – and, wrapping it around her shoulders, staggered over to the fire which was still burning cheerfully. Her bones ached, the welts on her arms and legs throbbed and when she put a hand up to her head, she felt throbbing lumps on her skull.

Usually she loved to be left alone in their little house but today she was too sore and too unhappy to really savour the experience. On the stone slab of the hearth, she sank down and let her tears flow, but not for long. Kitty despised tears. Angrily she wiped them away, furious at her own weakness.

When the door opened behind her, she thought it was her grand-mother, so she sat upright and blurted out, 'I'm no' greetin', I'm no' greetin'.'

'Then you should be. I'd be crying if I was you,' said a soft voice and Kitty turned her head to see the new girl from the school groping her way in through the semi-darkness.

'What do you want?' she asked.

'Tibbie told me what happened to you and I'm very sorry because I was the cause of it all. She sent me over with this dress because she said yours got torn last night. This one used to belong to her daughter Hannah.'

A dress of dark blue flannel was tentatively held out towards the huddled figure by the fireside. Kitty touched it. 'It's bonny,' she said in a changed voice. Though she never owned anything nice, she loved pretty things and the material of the dress was soft in her fingers. 'Is it really for me?' she asked.

Marie nodded. 'Yes, Tibbie said you were to keep it. There's a peeny that goes with it too…'

She held out a stiffly starched white pinafore with ruffles around the armholes, but Kitty shook her head. 'I couldnae wear that. It'd get dirty too quick.'

The other girl nodded in agreement because the idea of hoyden Kitty in a frilled pinafore was incongruous.

'When you're dressed, Tibbie said I was to take you back to her cottage so's she can have a look at you. She'll wash your hair,' Marie said next.

Kitty put a questing hand up to her head and found that the hair was matted with dried blood. It could obviously do with a wash. She rose painfully to her feet and started to pull the new dress over her head, refusing Marie's offers of help. It smelled of dried lavender and fitted her well.

'Isn't it braw?' she whispered.

Marie nodded in agreement. 'You look very grown up. How old are you?'

'Nine I think,' said Kitty.

Marie was surprised because they were the same height. 'You're as tall as me and I'm eleven!' Then she became brisk and hurried Kitty up with, 'Come on, let's go. Tibbie's waiting.'

When she saw the transformation in the bondager's child, Tibbie was glad that she had kept Hannah's clothes. She took Kitty's chin in a careful hand and examined her bruises. 'Are you all right, lass?' she asked gently.

'I'm fine. I hurt a bit that's all,' was the stoical reply.

'Good. Have something to eat and I'll wash your hair for you. It's got blood in it,' said Tibbie sympathetically.

Kitty nodded. 'I know. Thank you, Mrs Mather.'

She sat in a chair next to the parrot and watched the wonderful bird slowly and reflectively eat the seeds which had been scattered on the floor of its cage. A sigh escaped her. For years she had longed to be in Tibbie's cottage, watching the parrot.

'It can speak,' said Tibbie, who could see how fascinated Kitty was with the bird.

'What sort of things does it say?' she asked, big brown eyes wide open.

Tibbie laughed. 'He says my name, sometimes he talks about the weather, and says "Nice day" and things like that but sometimes he speaks in French… I don't know what he's saying then.'

Marie added, 'And sometimes he swears, doesn't he, Tibbie? He says, "God damn" and "blast me boots".'

Tibbie nodded. 'Tim must have taught the poor bird that. He was aye saying "blast me boots".'

She was bustling about, bringing out a tin basin and a towel, and fiddling with the kettle that boiled gently on the hearth. 'Come and sit down here,' she said, indicating a place on the rug where another towel was spread. Kitty drew back slightly. She had little experience of having her hair washed, though once or twice attempts had been made to comb it and that had always been very painful.

Tibbie began pouring steaming water into the bowl. 'Don't worry. I'll not hurt you,' she said.

Not wanting to show cowardice Kitty walked forward and knelt on the towel with her head bent forward so that she looked and felt like someone at the scaffold. Very gently Tibbie poured a jug of warm water over the bent head and massaged the white nape of the child's neck. As she worked she wondered how Big Lily could find it in her heart to be so brutal to her own flesh and blood.

Kitty sat submissive, luxuriating in the feel of Tibbie's capable hands gently rubbing her head, kneading and smoothing, smoothing and kneading. A sense of pure bliss filled the child and she wished that this ritual would never end, but when she was satisfied that the rinsing water was at last running clean, Tibbie told Marie to fetch another jugful of water from the well and mix it with the rest of the hot water from the kettle.

This last libation was poured over Kitty's head, drops coursed down her cheeks like tears and ran into her ears. Tibbie wrapped her head in a soft, warm towel and told her, 'That's it. You're clean as a whistle now. I'll brush it soon.'

As she untangled the child's hair, it seemed to spring into life and fill with colour glowing, gleaming and glittering like the leaping flames in a high fire on a winter's night when there is snow and frost outside. Marie watched with open-mouthed admiration as the thick tendrils uncurled and shone glossily. The artist in her gloried in the beauty of the autumn shades of deep red, amber, orange and burning brown.

'What wonderful hair, what a beautiful colour, it looks as if it's on fire,' she sighed.

Tibbie, gently brushing, replied, 'Aye, it's bonny hair right enough. My Hannah had red hair but it was more corn-coloured than this.'

Kitty, whose head was bent so that she could not look up, was genuinely surprised at their enthusiasm because her hair had always been a cause of shame to her.

'They call me Carroty Kate at school,' she offered.

'That's because they're jealous. Your hair's the most beautiful colour I've ever seen,' Marie told her.

Kitty, surprised, put up a hand and felt the new softness of her hair; took a curl in her hand and held it up so that she could see it. To her disappointment it still looked the same colour as the carrots that her mother and grandmother grew in the field behind Craigie's farmhouse.

'Take care of it,' Tibbie was saying. 'When you need it washed, come over here and I'll do it for you. It's a pleasure to work with hair like yours.'

For the first time in her life, Kitty felt she had something of which she could be proud. Her red-headed father had left her one good legacy after all.

The two girls were sitting side by side in the sun when David arrived back, dusty and tired after the walk from Maddiston. He was full of the news that he had been offered a place in the mill counting-house and was to start the following Monday. His face fell, however, when he saw a girl with his sister in the garden and he turned to Tibbie to whisper, 'Who's that?' Kitty's refurbished state had confused him.

She said, 'It's Wee Lily's bairn from over the road.'

His eyebrows shot up. 'The bondager's bairn? The one who stole from the shop? I thought you said Marie was to stay away from her? Why did you let her in here?'

Tibbie was surprised at his reaction. 'It's all right. I've washed her hair so she's no lice now. She's no' a bad lassie and they're getting on well together,' she told him.

He frowned. 'But she's the one that was fathered by the navvy called Bullhead, isn't she? My sister should find a better friend than that.'

Tibbie shot him a sharp glance and was about to make a sharp retort but bit it back. 'Let them be. Marie's enjoying looking after Kitty and the poor wee lass could do with a bit of that. It's good for both of them,' she told him.

'I'll speak to her about it,' said David sullenly and climbed the narrow stairs to the attic where she heard him throw himself heavily on the bed. He stayed there till Kitty went away.

That night, when they went to bed, and after David had broken his good news to Tibbie and his sister, Marie heard his voice coming through the curtain that divided their attic in half. 'Don't get involved with that Kitty Scott,' he warned her.

'Why not? She's a nice girl. She said she'd take me for a walk and show me where the rabbits play and where you can see lots of bonny birds,' she protested.

'She's from a bad family. We've got to aim for better friends than that. When I'm up in business, we'll have to know the right people,' he said heavily.

She turned on her side in bed and sighed. 'Oh don't be silly. It's a long time before we've got to worry about things like that.'

His voice rose angrily. 'Listen to what I tell you. You're judged by your friends. We're going to find it hard enough to make our way without being seen with the wrong people.'

She was used to deferring to him in everything and his vehemence frightened her. 'All right,' she said in a mollifying voice. 'Don't worry.'

When she woke next morning, however, for once she decided that she was not going to do what her brother told her. At school she took Kitty's arm, ignoring the jeers of Bella and her friends and after lessons were over, they walked along the riverbank while her new friend pointed out wonderful things – trailing waterweed with tiny white flowers like stars dotting its surface; still pools where fat brown trout lurked and allowed their bellies to be tickled by Kitty's poaching fingers; beds of yellow flag irises where little black moorhens paddled to and fro in the shallows; secret places in the riverbank where ducks made their nests; warrens of rabbit holes like little towns and badger holes with platforms of earth beaten down in front of them; swooping swifts, kingfishers and herons. Marie felt like Kitty's pupil because she realised the other girl was able to show her a wonderful new world, a world that had been hidden from her before. When she was living with Nanny, she had rarely ventured outside the streets and gardens of Rosewell.

They parted at sunset and Marie said, 'I hope we'll be friends from now on but my brother's funny about me going out with other people. He's working in Maddiston now and he'll only be coming home on Sundays though, so don't come for me then.'

Kitty understood what she was being told and nodded. 'I'll no' come on Sundays,' she promised.

That was how their alliance began; that was how Marie began leading a double life, hiding her friendship with Kitty from her brother. And it was a real friendship despite the difference in their ages, for while Marie was shy, withdrawn and romantic, Kitty was ebullient, realistic and worldly-wise. They complemented each other very well.

## Chapter Four

Languid would be the best word to describe the attitude of the tall, fair-haired man who was surveying passers-by from the first-floor window of an elegant house overlooking the trees of London's Berkeley Square. Long, heavy-lidded, hooded eyes made his face look impassive as he watched the labours of the crossing sweeper, a purple-faced man in a threadbare jacket and a red neckerchief. It did not take long before the unremitting stare made the workman look up and grimace in discomfort, wondering why the toff in the green velvet dressing-gown was staring so hard at him.

Pleased with the success of this aimless way of passing the time, Sydney turned back to the breakfast-room behind him where Norris, his valet, was pouring golden China tea from a famille rose teapot. His mind leaped back a decade to the time when his morning libation had been Major Bob's strong black tea from a rusty tin pot. Major Bob! – the strangely impressive ruin of a woman who had taken to drink and kept herself in brandy by taking care of ten men in a navvy bivouac.

He remembered the taste of her brew… black as tar and flavoured by peat from the brackish water of a stream that ran through the navvy camp where they were all living. His face darkened. Major Bob had died there, a horrible death from cholera but she'd endured her agonies with dignity and without complaint. What would she think if she saw the navvy she'd known as Gentleman Sydney wasting his time watching passers-by from a window, wondering how he was going to pass the rest of the day?

He drank his tea and then walked across the hall to his dressing-room where his clothes were laid out. A pair of brightly polished boots stood side by side on the carpet. Again his memory took a leap back to the dusty clothes he'd worn as a railway navvy. He still owned his old boots, all walked-down and split at the seams. He'd never allow them to be thrown out, in spite of his wife Bethya's horror of them,

49

because they were part of his memories, part of the time when he'd run away from his family and background and tried to be someone else.

Sydney was bored and only too well aware of his own shortcomings not to recognise that when he was in such a frame of mind, he had an unfortunate tendency to get into trouble.

'What's the programme for today?' he asked Norris, who had been with the household for several years and was totally devoted to the beautiful Lady Bethya. As a result he harboured a barely hidden animosity towards his employer, who not only had the luck to be married to her, but did not seem to appreciate his good fortune.

'Her ladyship is holding a luncheon party,' said Norris solemnly.

'Who's coming? The usual bores… the Parliamentary crowd?' Sydney asked.

'As far as I was told there are only two guests… your lordship's friend, Sir Timothy Maquire and his wife, Lady Emma Jane.'

'Goddamn, of course, I'd forgotten Black Ace was coming today. That's something to look forward to. I haven't seen him in three years!' Sydney's boredom flew away, changing the expression on his face, making him seem younger and happier.

'Can I inform her ladyship that you will be attending the luncheon?' asked Norris. On more occasions than not, he had the task of telling Bethya that Sydney would not be present at her entertainments, but now his employer regarded him with astonishment. 'Of couse I'm going, I wouldn't miss the Maquires, would I?'

'Of course not, sir,' said Norris, wondering how he was expected to guess whom his unpredictable employer found suitable and whom not.

It was a fine day so Sydney decided to drive away boredom by taking a stroll in the sunshine, but before he went out he looked in on his wife.

Bethya was in their huge bed with her pair of pet pug dogs sprawled on the cover and the pages of a letter strewn over her lap. She looked up at him through a pair of gold-rimmed spectacles perched on her pretty nose. He loved to see her wearing her spectacles because they made her look like a small and surprised mole peeping out of a hole. She was vain about them; never wore them in public and always snatched them off hurriedly when he caught her unawares.

'How's your mama and sisters?' he enquired, leaning negligently against the doorjamb.

She frowned. 'How do you always know when I receive a letter from them?'

'It's easy. There's one almost every day. Your family are wonderful letter writers.'

She looked sad. 'I miss them. I wish they would come here but they absolutely refuse to travel.'

He walked across the thick carpet and sat on the bed, displacing one of the pugs that growled slightly at him.

'What do you call that animal? You haven't named it after Norris, have you?' he asked.

She laughed. 'Of course not. It's called Oberon. Why do you think I've called it Norris?'

'Because it's almost as jealous of me as he is. It's very hard being married to you. All males – even pug dogs – loathe me because of it. They're all in love with you.'

She tossed her head and laughed sweetly, her melancholy gone. In a strange way his unfailing ability to lighten her mood annoyed him. He wished she was more difficult to manipulate, that her moods ran deeper and she was more inscrutable, but at least she was still very, very lovely.

Leaning on one hand he looked at her with pleasure. Bethya had luxuriant dark hair that was glossy as a raven's wing and her skin was satiny-looking and creamy-white like the petals of a magnolia. It was her eyes that enchanted him most, however, for they were aquamarine, slightly slanting, set wide apart above prominent cheekbones, and the eyelashes were incredibly thick and so dark that it looked as if she had drawn lines of kohl around her eyes in the manner of an Indian temple dancing girl.

He often wondered what story lay behind her mixed parentage… Had one of her male forebears gone to India as a soldier and met a dancing girl? Her parents had told her some romantic tale about an Indian princess and an English officer who snatched her off her husband's funeral pyre, a pleasant yarn that Sydney pretended to believe when Bethya told it to him, but he had noticed that, now their own children were growing up, she talked less of her mixed ancestry. As far as the children were concerned, their mother was a pure-bred Englishwoman. It was only when she was excited that a shrill, bazaar woman's note appeared in her voice, making Sydney raise his eyebrows and smile. When he did that she was always very angry.

'Norris tells me that Tim and Emma Jane Maquire are coming today. I'd almost forgotten,' he told her.

She frowned. 'I'm surprised you forgot that. They're your old friends.'

He stood up. 'Don't worry, I'll be in attendance. I'm looking forward to it. But you don't mind them, do you? I thought you'd be pleased they're coming, especially now that Tim's been given a knighthood.'

He always teased Bethya about being a snob and said she preferred titles to sainthood. Today she did not rise to the bait but returned to her letter with an abstracted air.

'I like them well enough… but she's such an unusual little woman, interested in building bridges and digging tunnels… so odd…' she said.

When she saw that he was on the verge of leaving, she added, 'Don't sulk. I will talk to you but first I want to finish this letter from Miriam… She always writes such screamingly funny letters.'

His hand was on the door. 'I don't know why you don't sail out to see them all in Bombay if they won't come here,' he told her.

'I can't go just now.' Her voice was so unusually solemn that he stopped and stared at her.

'Why not?'

'Because I'm expecting another baby,' she said quietly.

He groaned. 'Oh God, not another one.' They already had two sons and three daughters and as far as Sydney was concerned, that was enough. The succession to his title and property was assured and the nursery was full.

She frowned over the glasses which were in place again. 'For a man as sophisticated as you, it never ceases to amaze me why you don't associate one of your favourite activities with the size of our nursery.'

He laughed. At least pregnancy had not made her incapable of being biting when she chose.

He went to Hyde Park, which was looking exceptionally fine because the trees were in full leaf and the beds full of brilliantly coloured flowers. Fashionably dressed people were strolling along the paths, women in fluttering dresses and beribboned hats on the arms of more soberly dressed men. Little platoons of black-caped nannies ushered their charges along, some of the children trying to escape from supervision by running very fast behind gleaming metal hoops.

At Rotten Row the riders were out, parading themselves and their horses beneath the tall trees that lined the bridleway. Sydney scorned such an exhibitionist activity for himself – he was a serious hunting man – but he enjoyed watching the horses and admiring the skill of some of the riders, especially the women, many of whom were high-class tarts who used Rotten Row as a place to display their charms to their clientele. Bethya was a fine horsewoman but he would never have allowed her to ride in Rotten Row among the courtesans.

He strolled along, swinging his cane, with his hat rakishly tilted over the droop-lidded eyes, eyes whose sarcastic gleam had won him enemies. He was burning with a strange unease that made him want to throw up his comfortable and luxurious life and take off into the unknown. But he could not leave. He'd gone once before, and could not repeat the trick. Perhaps, he thought, when I have a chat with Maquire, this feeling of unsettledness will go. His old friend, whom he'd met when he was on the run the first time, always had a good effect on him.

It was near noon when he turned to go back home. Then he saw the girl.

She was mounted on a showy chestnut horse that he could tell looked more reliable than it actually was. Her tight-fitting habit was dark green and a thick braid of cream-coloured hair fell down her back like the hair of a schoolgirl who had not yet been 'brought out'. It was incredibly exciting to see this childlike braid of hair on a woman who was unashamedly advertising herself as sexually available.

For that was what she was. There was no mistaking her for a lady in spite of the expensiveness of her clothing. No lady cast her eye over the watching men with such open speculation.

She managed her horse well, making it prance and rear, curvet and bend into the bit like the horses on old Roman carvings. Because of its antics, other, more timid, riders gave her a wide berth, so she rode alone as if she were in a circle of light. That was obviously the way she wanted it.

Sydney leaned his arms on the top rail of the fence dividing the pedestrians from the riders and watched her. She shot him a stare from beneath her hat rim and raised her chin. He turned to ask an acquaintance who was also looking at the girl, 'Who's that?'

'Don't you know her? That's Lucy Beresford. At least that's what she calls herself now. She started off plain Minnie Clough, but she's gone up in the world since Allandale took her over from his uncle, old Maclean.'

Sydney laughed. 'She's Dickie's doxy, is she? She rides a horse very well.' The Duke of Allandale was an old friend of his, met first at school and later in the Scottish Borders, where Allandale had his lands, during the time when Sydney was in the navvy gang building a railway there.

The man by his side knew all about Lucy. 'So she should ride well. Her father was head groom in a racing stable. She knows what she's about.'

'In more ways than one I'll be bound,' rejoined Sydney, still laughing. It amused him that the Duke of Allandale, who masqueraded as a woman-shy bachelor under the thumb of a domineering mother, should be associating with such a girl.

'They say she costs him a pretty penny,' Sydney's informant was hissing in his ear.

He turned and grinned as he said, 'My dear chap, it's wrong to count the cost of some things in life. There can't be many like her in town. Allandale's quite right to run that filly for as long as he can.'

-

'Wha-hay!' With a huge yell that rattled the Dresden vases on the drawing-room mantelpiece, Tim Maquire advanced on Sydney. His arms were spread wide and, the two men were soon clasped in an affectionate embrace, clapping each other on the back and laughing aloud in their pleasure at meeting again.

The women looked on this exuberance with slightly embarrassed smiles and both wondered silently at the strangeness of men. Tim and Sydney seemed like little boys, so pleased were they to be in each other's company.

'By God I'm glad to see you, Black Ace. You're looking well,' cried Sydney, stepping back from his friend.

Tim, dandified as ever in a pale pearl-grey suit of foreign cut and a purple silk cravat, ran a hand down his black beard and said, 'I am well. France suits me. I like the food and the wine – and so does Emma Jane.'

He put out a hand to his little wife, the girl he'd fallen in love with and married when she was finishing the bridge-building contract of her dead father at Camptounfoot. She was dressed in a gown of cherry-and-grey-striped taffeta and a perky little hat which gave her a cosmopolitan air as well.

Her voice was sweet as she said, 'We're so pleased to see you again, Sydney. Tim hardly slept last night thinking about this meeting… and we're pleased to see you too, Bethya,' she turned quickly to her hostess who was standing apart from the other three. Sensitive Emma Jane guessed that Sydney's wife might feel left out of this reunion because the three of them were friends before Bethya and Sydney eloped and married.

Their host poured Madeira into delicate glasses and handed the first one to Emma Jane. She does look well, he thought, for Emma Jane was sleeker and plumper than he remembered and the radiance that shone from her seemed to light up the whole room.

'Here's to you, Lady Maquire,' he said, raising his own glass to his lips after he'd served the others. 'How does it feel to have a title?'

She giggled. 'You should know. I wish my mother could have been alive to hear about it. It would have helped her reconcile herself to the idea that I married a navvy! I'm most pleased for Tim's sake, though. It means that people recognise the work he's done. It's thanks to you too. If you hadn't backed us, we'd never have managed to take on the big commissions.'

With the help of financial investment from Sydney, she and Tim had started up their own building company after the first bridge was finished and they had been hugely successful.

'And it's thanks to him for more than that,' said Tim. 'I suspect he's behind the granting of this title. I'm right, aren't I, Sydney? You pulled strings, didn't you?'

Their host threw back the contents of his glass and poured another before replying, 'My dear chap, what's the use of sitting in the House of Lords if you can't do something to help your old friends? Anyway you deserve it. You've done more work abroad than any other contractor. You're very good for the name and reputation of Great Britain. As for investing in you, for once I knew what I was doing. You've repaid me very well. My money's increased ten times over. I hope you're going to stay at Bella Vista with Bethya and me when you go north. I invited you, didn't I?'

'Yes you did. Next week we're going to Camptounfoot to see Tibbie. We've not been there for several years and she's getting old.

Emma Jane's worried in case she's doing too much,' said Tim. Emma Jane had been Tibbie's lodger while she was finishing the bridge and they had grown very fond of each other. Tibbie had been genuinely delighted when her daughter's widower married her lodger a year after Hannah's death.

'Did you know that old Colonel Anstruther died and left Bella Vista to Bethya?' asked Sydney.

'That was good of him,' said Tim. Bethya had been married to Colonel Anstruther's son before she ran off with Sydney.

'He was a very nice man, very fair,' chipped in Emma Jane who had a soft spot for the old colonel, who had been her only supporter on the railway company's board when she insisted on finishing the bridge at Camptounfoot after her father died. If she hadn't, she and her mother would have been bankrupted by the other unscrupulous railway directors.

'He has indeed. Not only did he leave her the house but he left her his fortune as well – half a million in hard cash!' said Sydney with a laugh. 'My dear wife's a very rich woman, I'm happy to say. The only drawback is that people might think I married her for her money.'

Perhaps Sydney resents his wife's fortune although he's not a poor man himself, thought Tim.

Emma Jane rapidly changed the subject. 'But have you heard our greatest piece of news? We've got a baby. We'll bring him and his nurse with us to Bella Vista,' she said with a brilliant smile.

Sydney put down his glass and took her hands in his. He was well aware that for the first years of their marriage, Emma Jane's failure to conceive had been a great sorrow to them.

'A baby! That's better than a title! When was he born? What's his name!' he cried in unfeigned delight.

Tim answered proudly, 'His name is Christopher, after Emma Jane's father and he's eight months old.'

Their eyes met over Emma Jane's head and both were remembering the day that they watched Kate, Tim's infant daughter by his first wife Hannah, die of cholera in Dr Robertson's arms. Sydney was glad that the new child was not another little girl who might waken sad memories for her father.

Emma Jane turned her happy face to her hostess and asked, 'And how are your children? When we went away to France you had three. How are they?'

'Multiplying fast,' Sydney told her. 'We've increased their number by another two and there's a sixth on the way. I'll soon be knee-deep in children if my wife doesn't exercise a little restraint.'

Bethya snorted, 'Me! It's you who needs to exercise restraint!' To Emma Jane she added, 'After luncheon the nursemaid will bring the children down and you'll be able to see them.'

Emma Jane took her hostess's hand. 'You are lucky. They must be a great delight to you.'

Bethya beamed, for she was a doting mother too. 'They are. I like large families. I've got five sisters and we're all great friends.'

Emma Jane said sadly, 'I had only one brother and he was killed in an accident when he was twenty-four, but I'm still friendly with his wife Amelia. She's like a sister to me, though I don't see her often.'

Lunch was delicious and after the meal, the children were brought down from the nursery – a baby in the nurse's arms, two solemn-faced small boys with Sydney's blond hair and two delightful, dark-haired girls. They were all exquisitely well mannered, even the baby seemed smiling and polite.

When Tim and Emma Jane were walking back to the house in Half Moon Street which they'd taken for the duration of their stay in London, they talked over their impressions of the visit and she said reflectively, 'Didn't you think there was something strange about Sydney today?'

'There's always been something strange about him,' said Tim, looking fondly down at her.

'And you've always had a soft spot for him,' she riposted and her husband nodded. 'I suppose I have. He makes me laugh. I like him.'

She agreed. 'I like him too. He pretends to be hard and unfeeling but, of course, he isn't. There are so many levels to him, you're never sure that what he's saying is what he really thinks.'

Tim's face was sombre. 'Sometimes he doesn't know what he thinks himself… he acts on impulse.'

'I think he married on an impulse too,' said Emma Jane. 'I wonder if it's lasted. I hope it has. She obviously adores him. You don't think they're unhappy, do you?'

Tim shook his head. 'No, I *don't* think that. But Sydney's a strange fellow. There's a kind of madness in him that breaks out every now and again.'

Emma Jane sighed. 'Well I hope he keeps it under control now. If he says anything about it to you, Tim, tell him he's lucky to have a wife like Bethya and all those lovely children! When the nanny brought them down I could hardly believe my eyes, each one was more lovely than the one before it.'

He laughed. 'He won't listen to me, Emma Jane. He never did. The only time I tried to make him do what I wanted, I hit him... but he hit me harder.'

Before the Maquires started their journey to Camptounfoot, Sydney visited them at Half Moon Street. They were living in a cream-painted, flat-fronted building with flower-filled wrought-iron balconies fringing the windows of the first floor, and when the maid admitted him, he found Tim and Emma Jane sitting facing each other across an immense desk. This was how they always worked, both intent on the task in hand but conscious of the other all the time.

When their caller was shown in, the floor was covered with large sheets of paper and the scene reminded Sydney of the days at Camptounfoot when he'd watched Emma Jane poring over plans of the bridge in her wooden hut by the river.

'What are you doing?' he asked, sitting down and swinging his cane between his legs.

She smiled at him. 'It's a new contract for a bridge in America, near New York. We've a good chance of securing it. It's not unlike the one we did at Camptounfoot...'

Reaching down, she lifted up a sheet of paper, spreading it out on the carpet before Sydney and eagerly pointed. 'See, it's got twenty piers, not so high as our other one but just as difficult to build.'

He leaned forward and scrutinised the drawings which were meticulous and detailed, for she was the painstaking one of the partnership. Tim did the managing of the men and the building work; she did the planning and was as good at it as any man.

'It looks wonderful,' he told her and she beamed, her bright golden eyes sparkling as she said, 'Yes, I think so too, but nothing will ever look as good to me as the bridge at Camptounfoot. We're not counting our chickens on this one because we've got to win the contract first. We're up against the best of our competitors... And this'll amuse you, Sydney – do you know who one of them is?'

'I can't imagine,' he drawled.

Emma Jane laughed. 'You know him! It's Robbie Rutherford from Camptounfoot! You remember young Robbie who broke his leg on the bridge site? Dr Robertson said he'd never walk again but he didn't reckon for Robbie's determination. He's now one of the most important men with our biggest rival and rising fast. He took a good project off us last year in Germany. Tim was furious.'

Her husband raised his dark head from the desk and said, 'No wonder! You taught that lad all he knows about building bridges.'

She shook her head. 'No, he'd have succeeded in spite of me. Robbie's very clever and still young, so he's a long way to go. He can't be thirty yet.'

As he listened to them, Sydney was suddenly envious. They had purpose to their lives, goals to achieve, things to do… He wished the clock could be turned back ten years so that they were once again as they had been. But that, of course, was impossible.

He stood up and said, 'I see you're busy. I only dropped in to find out when you're going north so Bethya can write to the housekeeper at Bella Vista and tell her when you're arriving.'

Tim looked up from his papers and said, 'We thought we'd go up next week. When are you going?'

Sydney shrugged. 'Tomorrow, the day after, next week – it depends on Bethya. She always makes such a production out of travelling.'

A glance at his face made Emma Jane sharply aware of his aimlessness and she felt sorry that they should be so busy that they could not spend more time with him. She pushed the papers aside and said, 'You must take lunch with us… We're finishing now anyway…'

Sydney knew this was a lie, so he, too, rose and said, 'No, don't stop. I'm on my way to see Dickie Allandale. I want to hear his news.' As soon as he heard himself say it, he knew that he'd made a dangerous decision, as if he'd turned a corner and landed himself in a thick and menacing forest but, being Sydney, he would not back out.

Allandale House was a huge grey mansion overlooking Piccadilly. The old door-keeper knew Sydney and allowed him to pass into a cobbled semi-circular courtyard where another uniformed flunkey stood guarding the door. Once past him, the next obstacle was the butler, who directed the caller into an ante-room and said, 'I will enquire if His Grace is receiving.'

At last he was shown into the presence of his friend, who was drinking chocolate in a small parlour overlooking the road. 'My God it's easier to get into the Bank of England than see you,' laughed Sydney, throwing himself down in an easy chair.

Allandale, whose long solemn face and lugubrious air belied his raffish character, laughed back. 'Good to see you, Godders. The servants are careful because there's a lot of people I want to keep out. The butler didn't know you're not one of them.'

'Who do you close the door against?' asked Sydney curiously.

'Clerics and creditors mostly, chaps with bills.'

'Ah, the curse of the upper classes – chaps with bills. Get many of them, do you?'

'I get my share. If they don't stop, I'll have to go looking for an heiress to marry to give the bank balance a boost. I hear old Anstruther left your wife a cool half-million.'

'I didn't marry her for her money,' Sydney protested stiffly, for this was a sore point with him.

'But old Anstruther was always susceptible to a pretty face. Half a million's a lot. It'll pay the bills. And I hear you've been doing a bit of gambling recently,' said Allandale.

'I'd never touch Bethya's money,' said Sydney defensively.

'My dear chap, if husbands couldn't touch their wives' money, there'd be a lot of marriages that never happened. Don't be so pious, it's not like you,' drawled the duke.

Sydney was looking out of the window at the traffic rolling and jostling along the wide street. 'Where are you going to find your rich heiress?' he asked.

'Perhaps America. There's serious money there now and some successful businessman in pork sides or railway sleepers would be flattered to have a duke in the family. I'm surveying that market at the moment.'

'It all sounds very clinical. If you get married, what'll you do about Miss Beresford?' asked Sydney, still staring out of the window.

Allandale laughed. 'So you've seen Lucy? Quite a trophy, isn't she? Half of London's mad about her.' Lie sounded like a man who possessed a particularly fine horse and enjoyed showing it off.

'She's a good-looking girl,' agreed Sydney. 'I saw her in the Row the other day but I guessed you were strapped for cash because that isn't much of a horse you've mounted her on. Surely you could find her something better?'

His friend protested, 'But she likes them flashy. The more they prance about, the better she's pleased. She doesn't care if they're light in the bone as long as they're skittish.'

Sydney shrugged. 'Pity. She deserves better. Aren't you worried that some other man will snap her up when she hears you're heiress-hunting?'

Allandale was not worried. 'Lucy's more than capable of looking after herself. I suspect she's surveying the market too at the moment because she's not one to stay with a fellow till the bailiffs come round. You're uncommonly interested in her. You're not in competition with me, are you?'

Sydney turned round from the window and laughed. 'If I was, would I tell you, Dickie?'

On leaving his friend, he walked the short distance to his club where he took a few hands of cards and heard the gossip, in which Lucy Beresford figured. He found out that she lived in Curzon Street and her household bills were crippling Allandale.

Though Sydney's route home to Berkeley Square did not go by Curzon Street, he found himself walking along it at about four o'clock that afternoon and scrutinising the houses with a curious eye. Lucy Beresford lived at number eight, which turned out to be a smartly painted, discreet double-fronted house. A handsome young footman in livery guarded the door.

Sydney strolled past, swinging his cane and inwardly laughing. If I was Dickie, I'd be worried about that footman, he thought.

When he reached his own home, he found it in chaos with servants running here and there and Bethya issuing orders in her most unguarded half-caste voice.

He groaned because he knew that this was only the start of the complicated preparations that always overtook their household when they travelled. The arrangements for going to Bella Vista were commencing.

When he saw Bethya, her face was white and strained but there was no point in trying to calm her. She'd be in a state until they were safely settled at the other end – and then it would all start again when they prepared to return to London.

Events took un unexpected turn, however, because when they were at dinner, she suddenly gave a groan and slumped forward in her chair. Sydney, who was short-tempered with her, thought at first that she was playing for sympathy, but a close look at her pallid face convinced him this was no game. When he crossed from his place, she told him through gritted teeth, 'Something's happened to the baby… I'm losing it.'

She was carried to bed and a doctor summoned. Before midnight she miscarried and the grim-faced doctor told Sydney, 'Your wife is not a strong woman. She will require a great deal of care and consideration for some time if she is to be restored to full health. I would not advise another pregnancy for at least a year.'

Contrite and deeply concerned, Sydney stayed with her all next day. Their travelling plans were cancelled and he sent a note to Tim and Emma Jane telling them what had happened but insisting that they did not delay their departure. They were to stay in Bella Vista for as long as they liked.

When they protested he sent another note saying that Bethya was almost recovered and the Maquires would offend both him and his wife if they did not travel north as had been planned.

For their journey to Scotland Sir Timothy and Lady Maquire chose a train that would allow them to cross Camptounfoot bridge in daylight. As it drew near after ten hours of travelling, they jumped from their seats and stuck their heads out of the carriage window, straining their eyes in an attempt to see what lay ahead, recognising landmarks and exclaiming to each other like excited children… 'There's Falconwood, there's Camptounfoot, it'll come into view any minute now.'

At last the bridge could be seen rising over the river, a series of thin and elegant arches built of rose-red brick. It seemed to soar in the air like a graceful flight of birds. The excited pair in the train held hands and gasped, 'Isn't it wonderful, isn't it lovely!' while the nanny, whom they had brought with them to look after Christopher, wondered about their sanity.

Emma Jane and Tim did not even notice that she was upset. They were like children when they alighted from the train at Rosewell station, where a fine barouche was waiting.

As she settled into it, Emma Jane asked her husband, 'Is there somewhere you'd like to go before Bella Vista, my dear?'

He nodded. 'I'd like to visit the abbey, but you take Christopher to Bella Vista and I'll walk up.'

No explanations were necessary, for Emma Jane knew that her husband wanted to pay his respects at the grave of his first wife Hannah and their infant daughter Kate, who were buried in the abbey grounds. She patted his hand when he climbed down from the carriage and opened the iron gate into the abbey burying-ground. Its rusty creaking awakened a store of old memories for him.

He remembered carrying the bodies of Hannah and the baby down from the navvy camp – Sydney had shared the load with him. He remembered going to dig up an old Roman stone to mark their grave and Sydney had been there then too. His grief at that time had been terrible. It had burned within him like a raging fire and he'd thought that he would never recover, but here he was eleven years later, happy again, remarried to Emma Jane and a father once more.

The cholera mound where Hannah lay was covered with soft grass spangled with daisies. The white stone he'd put up at one end glittered in the fading sunlight, tilting slightly askew so that the figures carved on it looked as if they were walking downhill into the grave.

He passed a hand over its worn surface and whispered, 'Hannah, Kate, I haven't forgotten you. I'll never forget you.' But he hoped they knew that he had learned a great lesson: that love never ended, that it was unquantifiable and ever-expanding. He loved Hannah but he loved Emma Jane too. He was a very lucky and a very happy man.

He let the peace of the ancient burial ground fill him before he took the Prior's Walk to Camptounfoot. Every step of the path was familiar; every stone, every projecting tree root. The silver surface of the river glittering up at him from between its fringe of trees brought back memories of the times he'd walked it before.

When he reached Camptounfoot, some women standing in their open doorways recognised him, though they would have been little more than children when he was building the bridge at the end of their village. They nodded in his direction and said, 'Grand day,' as if he'd never been away.

He was glad that he was acknowledged because there had been a time when he was met with averted faces as one of the feared navvy gang.

He had deliberately not warned Tibbie to expect him, for he knew it would start her on an orgy of cooking and cleaning. Anyway, what he liked was to walk in on her and find her in her workaday apron with the cat sleeping on the chair.

Her front door was unlocked. He turned the handle slowly and tiptoed inside. The kitchen was dim and shadowy though the sun was still shining outside, and Tibbie was dozing in her wooden chair. Yes, the cat was in her lap.

Tim stood quietly in the doorway looking round the room. A drawing of Hannah in a maplewood frame occupied the middle of the mantelpiece; Bonaparte the parrot slumbered peacefully in its cage; a brightly coloured rag rug was spread out before the fire and a black kettle steamed gently on the hob. An immense feeling of belonging filled him.

He made a little knocking sound on the wood of the door with his knuckles and Tibbie started up, blinking, before she cried out, 'Oh, Tim lad, oh, Tim, I didn't know you were coming. I'm that glad to see you!'

She held out her arms and he went over to her, kneeling by the chair like a child to accept her embrace.

'It's grand to see you, Tim. You're looking awfy grand, sort of lordly,' she told him.

He laughed. His surprise was not spoiled. 'That's good. It must be because they've made me a Sir. Haven't you heard?'

She gasped, 'Made you a *Sir*! Oh my word, Emma Jane must be a Lady. Isn't that wonderful? Why did they make you a Sir, Tim?'

'I think Sydney arranged it.'

'They couldn't give it to a better man,' said Tibbie loyally.

He did not stay long.

'I'll have to get up to Bella Vista now. Emma Jane and Christopher went on ahead and she'll be wondering where I am. What about walking up to the big house with me?' he asked but she shook her head.

'Oh no, I'm longing to see your bairn but I couldn't do that!' She sounded shocked at the very idea.

'Why not?'

'It's a grand house. I've never been in it. I wouldn't feel right. Besides I've got Marie coming in for her tea soon. She went into Rosewell for a message for me.'

She was glad to have a definite reason for not venturing into the vast mansion that loomed up behind the village.

'Who's Marie?' he asked.

'Do you remember my friend Nanny Rush who ran the dame school in Rosewell?'

He nodded. 'I remember her. She looked after Mariotta's children when their mother died.'

'Marie's one of them. Nanny died and she's come to me. David, the laddie, is working in Maddiston and only comes back on Sundays, but Marie's at school and lives here.'

Tim stared at her, not entirely without disquiet. 'You've got Mariotta's children! How have they turned out?'

She shot him a sharp look and said, 'Nanny brought them up well. They're good bairns. David's a bit reserved but Marie's a sweet lassie and clever too. She can draw the loveliest pictures. She's settled down here well and she's made a friend, Kitty from over the road.'

He rose, grabbed his hat and said, 'I'm glad they've turned out well. Who's Kitty?'

'Wee Lily's bairn, the one she had after that Bullhead attacked her...'

Tim raised his eyebrows in surprise and said, 'And these two girls are friends? There's a coincidence for you! But I'd have thought Wee Lily's baby would have gone to a foundling home long ago.'

'Big Lily wanted her to give it up but she wouldn't. It might have been better if she had because the bairn's got a hard life and not much to look forward to except giving birth to another bondager's bastard in her turn. Life goes on like the seasons for folk like that and they have to make the best of it.'

Tim sighed. 'I expect you're right.'

On his way to Bella Vista, he passed the corner by the village shop, where a red-headed child was sitting on a stone jutting out of a grass bank. There was not a doubt in his mind that this was Wee Lily's child, for the most obvious thing about her was a recognisable inheritance from her father, whom Tim had cordially hated. She had his fiery hair.

This child was watching him curiously and smiled when he walked by. He smiled back, for her impish appearance amused him.

Kitty knew who he was too and when he drew level with her, she hopped off the stone to ask, 'Your name's Mr Maquire, isn't it?'

'Yes.' She obviously hadn't heard about the Sir either.

'You were one of the navvies working on the big bridge, weren't you?' she persisted, walking along with him and stared up at his great height with open admiration.

'Yes, I was, but that was before you were born.'

'But you'd know my dad. His name was Bullhead.'

'Yes, I remember him.' Tim's voice became cautious.

'What was he like?' she asked. She had a secret dream that her absent father might have looked like the man beside her. Tim had a dashing, piratical air. With his thick, curling black beard and his skin tanned by working in foreign lands, he looked like a hero from a storybook romance.

He had to search very hard for the right words. If he was to be truthful, he would have said, 'Your father was a bully and a brute, a coward, a drunkard, a murderer… I loathed him.' Instead he came up with, 'He was very strong. He was the best pulley man on any gang I ever had.'

She was delighted. 'What's a pulley man?' she asked.

'He hauls big blocks of stone up on ropes. Bullhead could haul bigger blocks than anyone else, right to the top of that bridge down there.'

'It's a high bridge! He must have been strong.'

Tim, filled with pity for this hapless by-blow of a brutal man, added, 'Here, wait a minute, I want to give you something.'

He carried little money with him nowadays, just a few coins rattling in his pocket to make him feel secure as they had always done in the days when he was poor. He pushed a hand in to find one and came up with it between thumb and forefinger.

When he handed it to the girl, she looked down at the coin lying in her dirt-encrusted palm with amazement.

'How much is it?' she asked, for she'd never held a gold coin before, never even seen one, come to that.

'It's half a sovereign, ten shillings and sixpence. Take care of it. Give it to your mother,' he told her.

She grinned like an imp. 'Thank you Mr Maquire, thank you very much.'

When he walked on she was still standing looking at the coin with her fingers curled up around it. She was so pleased that she could have eaten it. The wonderful Tim Maquire, the hero with the black beard and gleaming smile, had given her half a sovereign.

He must have liked her father. Maybe Bullhead wasn't as bad as everyone said after all.

There was no question of giving the money to Wee Lily because her mother would immediately pass it on to Big Lily. She'd have to hide it, and keep it until the day when she could spend it to good advantage. But where would it be safe?

With the coin clutched tight in her hand she walked up the road pondering the question. The hiding-place would have to be where there was no danger of Big Lily coming across it, so the farm buildings were out.

She went first to the village rubbish dump and found an old tobacco tin with a tightly fitting lid. Then she went to the field behind the farmhouse and pulled some sheep's wool off the hedge, stuffing it into the tin and making a little nest for her coin, which she laid reverently among the greasy folds of wool. When the lid was closed tight she ran to her favourite hiding-place beneath the thick hawthorns and squirmed down to reach her sanctuary. She was growing fast and it was getting harder to squeeze between the twisting trunks, but she succeeded at last and dug a hole with her hands in the soft, loamy earth. The tin was laid in, earth piled back on top of it and a flat stone put down as a marker. It would be safe there and in no danger of being turned up by a plough.

One day, when she really needed half a sovereign, she'd dig it up again.

-

Tim and Emma Jane went to Camptounfoot every day to see Tibbie. If it was dull or threatened rain, they travelled in a dogcart driven by Tim, but on fine days they went by foot, which was the way they preferred for they liked to be on their own with baby Christopher. This annoyed the nanny, who was a great snob and had already decided that, in spite of their titles, Sir Timothy and Lady Maquire were not the sort of people she preferred as employers, for they were far too informal in their ways.

Their favourite excursion was to the big railway bridge which they had built together. Christopher obliged them by staring up with wide eyes and raising his hands in an attempt to touch the massive arch over his head as his father carried him beneath it and exhorted him to admire his parents' mutual achievement. Though they knew it meant nothing to a child, they showed him where Emma Jane's hut had stood during the months of building and together remembered the long hard hours of bone-aching toil that they had endured there.

Their second stop was at Tibbie's and, on what was to be the last day of their holiday, they found her working in the kitchen with Marie. As soon as she saw them, Tibbie threw down the knife with which she'd been peeling potatoes and held out loving arms to Christopher.

'Oh come to your – Tibbie,' she cried, biting back the word 'granny' in the nick of time.

She was as fond of this child as if he were her own flesh and blood but when she realised how near she'd come to making a *faux pas*, she flushed. Neither Tim nor Emma Jane, who had heard the stumble and knew what it meant, minded. They were happy to share their beloved son with her.

While the women were conducting a session of baby worship, Tim went into the garden to smoke a cigar among Tibbie's roses. He was sitting in the sun with his eyes closed when the garden gate creaked open and Kitty walked in.

He looked at her through a curl of blue-grey smoke and said, 'Everyone's inside admiring the baby.'

She whipped round, about to leave again, but Marie appeared in the kitchen door with Christopher in her arms and called out, 'Kitty, come in and hold this adorable baby. He's so sweet.'

The red-headed girl was visibly shaken. 'No, no, I'm no' any good wi' babies. I'm feared I'd let him fall,' she said, backing away.

In truth babies were about the only thing Kitty was afraid of, for she felt acutely awkward under their penetrating stare and couldn't understand why sensible people made such a fuss about the little things. They frightened her far more than intimidating adults.

Soon the time came for Tim and Emma Jane to go. Before they left, Tim told Tibbie, 'We sail from Liverpool to New York at the end of next week and we'll have to be away from here tomorrow. I'm sorry it's so soon.'

She looked sad. 'How long will you be gone?' she asked. She was approaching the age when every departure frightened her, for she was afraid that she might not live to see the people she loved again.

'About eighteen months,' he said. She sighed and kissed his bearded cheek. It seemed incredible to her now how upset she'd been when Hannah ran off and married this fine man.

–

Marie and Kitty spent the rest of the day together and when she finally went home to Tibbie's Marie found that David had walked over unexpectedly from Maddiston and was impatiently waiting for her. As she came through the door, face flushed and eyes dancing, he burst ot with, 'Where have you been?'

'Down by the river.'

'Have you been with some boy?' he demanded.

She flushed scarlet. 'Of course not. I was with Kitty Scott!' It came out without a thought.

Then he rounded on her as if she'd uttered an obscenity. 'How can you be so stupid?' he shouted. 'I told you I don't want you to have anything to do with her. Her sort's the wrong company for you. Keep away from her.'

She rarely stood up to him openly but now she did. Her cheeks were scarlet and she felt a strange pounding in her ears as she faced him. 'I'll do what I want, David! I'll pick my own friends.'

He was extremely agitated. 'But you don't know about her!'

'I do. I know she's a bastard. It doesn't matter. I think it's terrible the way everybody looks down on her because of it.'

Her brother was stammering. 'It's not just that. It's other things…' He was staring at Tibbie as he spoke and she shook her head in warning at him. To Marie's surprise, he closed his mouth firmly, grabbed his cap off the back of the chair and stormed out of the door.

She was shaking when she looked from the doorway to Tibbie.

'What did he mean?'

Tibbie turned away. 'I think he must mean that Kitty's a bit ragged, dear. Something like that.'

'He's very stupid. She can't help being ragged. Her grandmother never buys her any clothes. I'd be ragged if you didn't get me dresses to wear,' said Marie in a wavering voice.

'Don't worry about it. He wants you to keep nice company. Just don't tell him that you play with her,' counselled Tibbie.

## Chapter Five

It was more than a year after her miscarriage before Lady Bethya Godolphin felt strong enough to undertake the journey from Berkeley Square to her vast estate in Scotland.

Although she was coddled and protected like a baby on the journey, she was on the point of collapse by the time she saw the minarets of her mansion, Bella Vista, rearing up from its embowering trees. The sight was like a glimpse of an oasis in a waterless desert and she tottered up to bed where she remained for three days without once going downstairs to see how the servants had taken care of her inheritance.

At last, conscious of her husband's dark glare and growing exasperation, she roused herself to descend to the drawing-room. Next day, she ventured out into the grounds on his arm.

She had forgotten what a lovely place it was. The rambling house, built by Colonel Anstruther in memory of some distant Indian palace, had little towers and turrets, an intricately carved portico and arcaded walk along the south-facing side. Lawns stretched before it and it was completely surrounded by trees, now turning to their stunning autumn colours of bright yellow, russet, dark red and gold. As a backdrop the house had three purple-flanked hills that stared over its roofs to the river in the valley floor.

She drew in deep breaths of air that tingled in her mouth like champagne and it seemed to work a miracle on her.

'I feel much better,' she told Sydney. 'I really believe I'm better at last.' She was grasping eagerly at the first sign of recovery and he backed her up for both of them were growing impatient with her intractable feebleness.

'You look better too. It's been a long time,' he told her and she smiled in delight.

When word reached Rosewell that Lady Godolphin was walking in the grounds, every delivery of mail brought cards of invitation, but

Sydney refused to allow her to accept any of them. 'We'll announce that you've come up here for rest and seclusion and that all invitations will have to be refused for the time being,' he said, grimly seizing the pile of deckle-edged cards and throwing them in the fire.

The one invitation she did accept, however, was to the school at Camptounfoot because as owner of Bella Vista she was its patron. It was arranged that she should pay a short visit one morning in company with the school governors, the Provost of Rosewell and Mrs Stewart, wife of the town's doctor.

On the day this visit was due to take place, the school was in a ferment of excitement. Its windows had been open since early morning to allow fresh air to blow through the classroom and Bella Ferguson, the oldest pupil and class monitor, had brought a small bunch of roses to put in a vase on Mr Arnott's desk and a larger bunch to make a bouquet for Lady Godolphin.

The pupils had all been warned to turn up in their best clothes, with clean faces and fingernails and were told that Mr Arnott intended to inspect them before the official party arrived.

Trembling at the thought of incurring his displeasure, they sat in their places, well brushed, stiffly starched and smelling of soap, anxiously anticipating his scrutiny as he walked round the benches, lifting locks of hair or eyeing hands that were spread open palmed on the desktops. When he found a set of fingernails that did not meet his rigorous requirements, he thumped his cane down on the back of the offending hand, saying, 'That won't do, Sammy! Go out and wash again, Tom.'

Eventually he came to Kitty Scott and rolled his eyes upwards with a heavy sigh. 'How do you expect Lady Godolphin to see you looking like *this*? he asked, standing back and swinging his cane in an arc around her, indicating that everything about the girl failed to come up to scratch. She glowered back at him from beneath tumbled hair but said nothing.

'You'll have to sit in the corner behind the blackboard and hope nobody sees you,' he said, for obviously there was no point in starting a clean-up operation on Kitty so late in the day.

Behind him Bella giggled, setting her friends off too, and Kitty flushed scarlet. It was unfair, she thought, because she'd made a special effort, untangling her hair with the pony's grooming brush and washing her legs in the burn, but that was obviously not sufficient.

She stood up and stalked to the stool reserved for dunces behind the teacher's board, conscious of Marie's eyes following her with unspoken sympathy.

The children did not have long to wait because a few minutes later Lady Godolphin wafted into the schoolroom on a cloud of scent. The fringed skirt of her taffeta gown made a lovely soft whispering sound as it swept across the bare wooden boards of the floor and her shallow-brimmed bonnet was trimmed with silk roses so realistic that they looked as if they had only just been plucked off the bush. Though her ladyship's face was pale, her graciousness matched her elegance. Mr Arnott was reduced to a stumbling, mumbling jelly by her adorable smile and the children sat hypnotised, watching everything that was going on in front of them as if it were happening on a stage.

Even Bella, who was sceptical about everything and everyone except herself and her immediate family, could find no fault with Bethya, who walked up the narrow aisle between the desks and bent over the books that lay open before the pupils.

In her sweet singsong voice she said nice things like, 'What lovely handwriting' or 'Can you really read that book? It seems so grown up for someone of your age.'

She never made any adverse comments and the people she congratulated flushed with pride. When she came to where Marie was sitting, she paused and looked at two drawings laid out on the desktop.

'Did you do these, my dear?' she asked in surprise.

Marie nodded, blushing bright red with confusion. 'Yes, madam,' she whispered.

Bethya leaned over and gazed again at the drawings for what seemed an age. Then she straightened up and stared over the children's heads at Mr Arnott. 'This girl is very talented indeed,' she announced.

He came hurrying up, exclaiming, 'Yes, I know, your ladyship. She's got great facility.'

'Oh it's more than that. She's really gifted. I've seen artists in London being fêted with much less justification.'

Bethya lifted up a watercolour of the hills that rose behind the schoolroom and told everyone, 'This one in particular is really beautiful.'

Then to Marie she said, 'Let me see what else you've done,' and spent a long time poring over the pictures, making enthusiastic noises and showering praise on the artist. Eventually, however, she realised that the class was growing fidgety and their teacher was throwing them threatening glances.

'I'm sorry if I'm holding things up,' she exclaimed. 'What other things do you want to show me, Mr Arnott?'

He had coached the children in a spelling bee and a mental arithmetic display so, while the visitors sat on chairs by the door, he fired questions at each pupil, who was expected to reply just as quickly. Things went reasonably well till, during the mental arithmetic display, he reached the front of the class where the dunces sat.

'What's seven times nine with three away?' he asked Sammy, son of the village carter. Sammy stared back at him with round blue eyes like marbles and muttered, 'Dinna ken.'

Arnott should have passed him by but he was swollen-headed with success and persisted, 'Come on, Sammy, what's seven times nine and then take away three?' Sammy continued to stare and his eyes slowly filled up with tears.

Suddenly a voice hissed out from behind the blackboard, 'It's sixty-three minus three, Sammy. Dinna greet. Say sixty.'

'Sixty-three,' said Sammy with triumph.

'Oh, Sammy!' said the voice.

Bethya laughed. 'Do you have a prompter behind that blackboard?' she asked Arnott whose face was like thunder.

'No,' he protested. 'It's one of the pupils who's been put in detention…'

'It couldn't have been for not knowing how to count,' joked Bethya. 'Bring out the mystery mathematician.'

Arnott nodded to Bella who ran forward and hauled Kitty from behind the board. Unfortunately, she looked even more dishevelled than before because she'd managed to get herself covered with chalk dust and spiders' webs as well as dirt.

Arnott felt rage rise within him at her for having brought shame on his school.

'She's a bondager's bairn and she'll be leaving school next year,' he explained to no one in particular.

'Well at least she'll know how to count,' said Bethya, who had not drawn away, smiling at Kitty.

But she was more interested in art than in counting and before she left she said to Arnott, 'We must try to do something about that girl who draws so well.'

He bent over her hand, making polite noises but he was thinking, 'What do you expect me to do? I'm here to give girls the basic skills of reading and writing. The best they'll ever be is an upper housemaid. The others, like Kitty Scott, will go on the land. Even Marie Benjamin, with her pretty drawings and nice manners, won't be able to step outside her class.'

Mrs Stewart was thinking the same thing. As the visiting party drove away, she said reprovingly to Bethya, 'It would be a pity to fill that girl's head with false ideas, Lady Godolphin.'

'But she's very gifted,' Bethya sounded sharp.

'My dear, do you know who she is? Her mother was one of those loose navvy women. The one who got herself murdered! A woman in the town took in her children but she's dead too and the girl's living in Camptounfoot with her foster mother's friend.'

Bethya hated to be thwarted. 'But there must be parish funds to provide a bursary so that she can study art properly. It shouldn't be impossible.'

Mrs Stewart looked at the silently disapproving Provost and sighed. It was all very well for Lady Godolphin to talk like that when she only lived in the district for a few weeks every second year or so. Someone should point out to her that money was hard enough to find without throwing it away on a girl who wasn't even from a local family.

After the visiting dignitaries left the school, Mr Arnott gave vent to his pent-up nerves by boxing the ears of both Kitty and slow Sammy for no specific reason except that he felt like hitting somebody. Neither of them minded very much because they were used to being the butts of his aggression.

Before they were turned loose, the class settled down to listen to self-important Bella reading them a passage from a book about a young Red Indian brave and a settler's son who sealed their friendship by mingling their blood and becoming blood brothers.

When they were eventually released, Marie and Kitty walked up the street together, a disparate couple – one excessively neat and tidy with flaxen hair falling as straight as a skein of silk to her shoulders; the other dusty and daubed with corkscrewed hair like a Medusa.

Kitty was the one who did most of the talking while Marie listened. 'That was great what Lady Godolphin said about you being a real artist. She liked your pictures a lot,' she exulted, for Marie's triumph delighted her as much as if it had been her own.

Her friend sighed. 'It was nice of her but it won't make any difference. David's got everything planned for me. As soon as he's able to rent a house, I'm to go and live with him. I'll not be doing much painting after I leave school.'

'He'll maybe get married and his wife won't want his sister living in the house,' said Kitty who was more aware of the possible conflicts of family life than Marie.

'He's promised me he won't. And he says I've not to get married either. It'll just be him and me. He's going to be very rich one day, he says.'

David's attempts to control his sister were unremitting. He hated the idea that she might have a life or interests of her own which he could not share. Even though he lived for most of the week in lodgings in Maddiston, he came back every Sunday to keep an eye on Marie and, from time to time, made unexpected visits, as if to catch her out in doing something wrong. When they were together he talked of little else but his plans for their future. Her destiny was intertwined with his as far as he was concerned, and he spared no time wondering if that was what she wanted.

She had tried suggesting that she might want a life of her own but he did not seem to hear what she said. It frightened her that she was so easily swept along by his stronger will and the prospect of living her life constantly in his shadow oppressed her, though she felt guilty if she allowed herself to contemplate escaping from him. She talked about this with Kitty, who could not see what the problem was… 'Tell him you want to be left alone. Tell him to mind his own business,' she advised. If talking didn't work, she thought, a punch on the nose would make him realise she was serious.

'But he's my brother, he loves me, we've only got each other… We must stick together,' said Marie. 'I don't have to worry about it all now. Tibbie says I can go on attending the school because David doesn't want me to go out to work. Mr Arnott's going to make me a monitor next year and I'll get to help with the wee ones. That'll be nice.'

Kitty pulled a face. She'd rather dig ditches than look after little children. 'I'll be leaving soon too. The parish won't pay for me to be schooled after I'm past eleven. I'm no' learnin' much anyway,' she said.

'Your counting's very good,' Marie told her.

Kitty shrugged. 'I won't need to count much when I go into the fields.'

'Do you want to work on the land?' asked Marie, who had seen the bondagers coming home on wet evenings caked with mud and soaked to the skin. Theirs seemed to be lives of unremitting drudgery.

Her friend was surprised by her question. 'Want? What's to want? When my granny dies, there'll only be my mother and me working at Townhead and I'll be the heid yin so that won't be too bad.'

'But that could be years and years away. Big Lily's as strong as a horse,' protested Marie, thinking of the years of being under her cruel grandmother's thumb that stretched before Kitty.

'I can wait,' said Kitty darkly. Then she brightened and said, 'Look, there's Rutherford's pig coming down the street. I ken it's their's by the black mark on its back. They'll be making it into ham and bacon soon. My granny kills it for them because Mr Rutherford's too soft-hearted to kill it himsel' and they give us sausages for her trouble.'

Marie shuddered. 'Poor pig,' she said. 'I hope I don't hear your granny killing it.'

'You won't. She's got a knife that's as sharp as a razor. I wish I had a knife like that.' Kitty sounded as wistful as any well-to-do girl talking about a pretty piece of jewellery.

'What would you do with a knife?' asked Marie.

'There's all sorts of things you can do with a good knife,' Kitty told her. 'I'd love that one of my granny's. It can cut through anything. If I had a knife I'd make us blood sisters like those twae lads in the story.'

Marie protested, 'But that would hurt!'

'No it wouldn't. It'd be easy. I'd cut my finger and then I'd cut yours and we'd mix the blood. It'd make us sisters.'

Marie frowned and Kitty nudged her with a sharp elbow. 'Are you scared?'

'No, of course not,' said Marie rashly but she felt safe because Kitty did not have a knife or any prospect of getting one.

Big Lily always carried the knife in the pocket of her skirt except when she was using it and she rarely forgot to fold it up and slip it back into its place immediately she finished any task in hand. Next day she was cutting open sheaves of hay while Kitty watched intently until Big Lily snapped, 'What're you doing standing there gogglin'? Away and feed the hens and mak' yersel useful.'

After that it seemed to the big woman that the pest of a child was always under her feet, eyes wide, taking everything in. She shouted and swore at Kitty but the little nuisance would not go away and Big Lily became suspicious of the continued attentions of her granddaughter.

'What are you aye hanging about me for? What do you want?' she demanded roughly.

'Nothing. I just want to help. I want to see how things are done because I'm leaving school soon.'

Big Lily frowned. 'I've been thinking about that. It would suit me if Craigie'll have you on the place because the work's getting harder for me. I'll ask him to take you. There's no point talking about it wi' his. They're thrawn bitches and they'd say no just for the joy of it.'

Kitty was surprised. 'But Craigie's in Edinbury. Will you send him a letter?' She knew that Big Lily could barely write her name.

Her grandmother roughly pushed her aside. 'I'll no' be writing any letters. I'll go to Edinbury to ask him about it.'

'You'll go there?' Kitty could scarcely believe that her grandmother would contemplate such a trip. She'd never been farther than Rosewell as far as Kitty knew and she did not like going there.

'I've been before,' snapped Big Lily.

'When?' asked Kitty.

'Nane o' your business. I've been, that's all that concerns you.'

Kitty refused to be rebuffed. 'Can I go with you?' she asked, eyes shining. The thought of a trip to Edinburgh enthralled her for she longed to travel.

'You! Get out of it. I wouldn't tak' you as far's Rosewell with me.' That reply was what Kitty had expected so she was not too disappointed.

Big Lily's trip to Edinburgh was planned for the day of the September Sheep Fair at Rosewell, a very special occasion when workers from all the farms round about were given a day off so that they could attend.

Because she was going away, Big Lily could not take any of Townhead's sheep to the fair and she did not think her daughter or Jake capable of undertaking the task. Even though she was so young, her granddaughter could have done it but Big Lily would not acknowledge her enough to suggest it.

Craigie's sisters, who stayed in the dimness of their house and never attended the fair anyway, were unaware that their farm would be unrepresented at this important local occasion and that their head bondager was going to visit their brother in the city. That in particular had to be kept from them.

Before she left, Big Lily lectured Wee Lily and Jake over and over again about what they must do in her absence. When she saw that she was only succeeding in confusing them, she was forced to turn to Kitty and ask roughly, 'Do you hear what I'm saying? I'll feed the animals before I go but they'll have to do it again at night. They've to milk the cows as well. Tell them not to forget anything. Before it's dark they've to go round every field and check that everything's all right. You see they do what I say or I'll belt your ear when I get back.'

On the morning of the fair a ghostly silver mist came drifting through the village. It was hanging in the corners of the bothy and carpeting its floor when Kitty opened her eyes. Her grandmother was standing in the middle of the room dressing herself up in clothes the child had never seen before and which had obviously been stored beneath the bed in a mysterious tin trunk that was always kept locked.

Big Lily looked even larger than usual in the misty light as she put on a white blouse and buttoned it over her huge bosom. Then came a long black skirt with rows of pin tucking round the hem and over that was draped a shawl of green silk with a deep fringe. On her head she perched a coquettish-looking, deep-brimmed cream straw bonnet with green ribbons. The bonnet was of a style that went out of fashion thirty years before and when its ribbons were tied under her heavy chin, she looked like a female impersonator.

Under her grandchild's fascinated gaze, she delved into the trunk and produced a dainty beadwork purse which clinked as she held it. Then she locked the trunk and put the key in her bag.

'That's to make sure you dinna touch anything when I'm away,' she told the child, for she knew that Kitty was awake and watching her.

What she overlooked was her knife. It was too big for the beadwork bag and she forgot that it was still in the pocket of her striped working skirt which lay in a heap on the floor by the fireplace. Kitty did not allow her glance even to drift in the direction of the skirt in case her grandmother remembered that the knife was there.

At last she was ready and strode out into the yard shouting instructions to Wee Lily and Jake in the cattleshed. Kitty lay still for a long time fearing that something would bring her back, but after a bit she felt safe enough to rise and hurried over to the discarded clothes.

The knife felt heavy and reassuring in her hand. Its curved bone handle fitted into her palm as snugly as a nut in the shell. When she pressed the little button that made the blade spring out, she found that it was razor sharp. A gentle stroke was all it would take to cut through skin.

Clutching it tightly she hurried out of the bothy, for she knew she had to hide it before Wee Lily came in for breakfast.

The best hiding-place was of course the hedge root and there she dug up her tin so that the knife could be laid in it beside the half-sovereign. When this task was completed she felt gloriously happy and very hungry. The day that stretched before her offered wonderful possibilities, for she and her mother had arranged to go to the fair together while Big Lily was miles away in Edinburgh.

Skipping, Kitty made her way back home knowing that she was free to eat whatever she chose for breakfast – thick slices of bread lavishly spread with honey from a jar jealously hoarded by Big Lily was what she chose and she consumed half a loaf sitting outside in the sun with the hens pecking for scraps around her feet.

–

Though Big Lily looked grim and forbidding to the outside world, she was inwardly quaking with nerves as she walked into the booking office at Rosewell station. Her heart was thudding as she fumbled in her purse outside the ticket office window.

'Where are you gaun?' asked the clerk, a spotty-faced youth with a supercilious attitude towards working-class passengers.

'Edinbury.' Her mouth was so dry she could hardly speak.

'Third class of course,' said he, staring at her hat.

She gathered something of her customary menace and asked, 'Hoo much d'ye want?'

'Ane shilling and threepence one way. If you're coming back it'll be half a croon.'

'That's a terrible price!' Five shillings was the weekly wage for Big Lily and her daughter together.

The clerk glared at her and said, 'You dinna have tae go. Ye can stay at home like a' the rest o' them.'

'I'm going and I'm comin' back,' she said, thumping an assortment of coins on the wooden shelf. He counted them out as if they were unclean and then handed her a ticket.

'Dinna lose it or you'll no' get back,' he advised.

This exchange temporarily calmed Big Lily's nerves. 'I'm no' in the habit of losing things,' she told him stonily as she stuck the little square of green pasteboard in her bag.

She needed all her bravado, however, when she arrived in Edinburgh. The hustle and bustle of the city completely intimidated her and for a few moments she fought against a panicky desire to get back on the first train leaving for Rosewell. The crowds seemed like creatures from another world; they even spoke to each other in a language that she could not understand.

From her only previous visit she remembered that the prison lay at the east end of Princes Street so she walked along staring up at the skyline hoping to see its grim outline. The new boots she'd bought for the outing nipped her feet. A blister was rising on her heel by the time she saw the prison, rearing like a citadel on top of a steep crag in front of. She trudged up the hill towards it only to find that the gatekeeper would not let her in without an official pass.

'Aw man, I've come an awfy lang wey,' she pleaded in her broad accent and this time she was lucky for he was a Borderer himself and recognised the dialect.

'Whereabouts are ye from?' he enquired.

'Camptounfit.' Miraculously he knew the village, for he was a Maddiston man who could tell at a glance that the woman in front of him could not afford to spend the time or the money travelling to Edinburgh unless for an urgent reason.

'Dinna tell onybody I let you in,' he whispered and held the pedestrian gate ajar. The inner courtyard was huge and grim, a sea of grey cobbles surrounded on all sides by high walls in which there were lines of little windows covered with iron bars. Faces peered between some of the bars and every now and again a shout rang out from one of the inmates.

The gatekeeper told Lily to go into the hall, which was floored with chipped black-and-white ceramic tiles. There she asked an attendant in a black uniform if she could see Craigie Scott.

'Are you a relative?' he asked.

'I'm his sister,' she said. There was no point revealing the Scott family secrets to people like him.

'I'll make enquiries. Wait here please.'

It was a relief for Big Lily to sit down on a wooden bench and rest her feet, but she did not have long to wait for soon the man was back with another, even starchier and more disapproving.

'We didn't expect any visitors for Scott today. You should have a pass,' he said in an accusatory tone.

'I lost it on the train,' said Big Lily humbly.

'Oh, I see, well, come this way. He's been quiet for some time now. It's possible he can have a visitor. We'll have to ask the person in charge of him.'

It seemed they walked for miles along corridors lined with more tiles. Their footsteps echoed as if they were in a vault but there was no other sound. At last they reached a door with a brass plate on it saying 'Interview Room', and she was shown into what looked like a cell, painted dark brown and containing a chair, a table and a little peephole window covered with an iron grille.

'Wait here,' she was told. Perched on the edge of her chair, she'd have given another week's wages for a cup of tea. Her eyelids were beginning to droop when she was brought sharply awake by sounds from the other side of the grille. She leaned forward and found herself staring at Craigie.

He'd hardly changed. Bristly red-grey eyebrows marked the ridge-like edge of his forehead above sceptical eyes. There were two long, deep lines drawing down each side of his mouth and the grizzled auburn hair sprang up from his brow like the comb of a cockerel. As always he looked sharp and sly, a man who liked to drive a hard bargain.

Her heart gave a strange lurch. 'Aw, Craigie,' she sighed, putting out a hand towards the grille.

He nodded at her, and his half-smile revealed broken teeth. 'It's you, Lily. They said it was my sister but I didnae ken which one.' His tone was neutral and it was impossible to tell if he was pleased to see her or not.

She sat back in her chair and became as gruff as he because she was very conscious of the listening man in uniform at his shoulder.

'You're fine I see,' she said through the grille.

'I'm grand, grand, and is everybody at Camptounfoot the same?' he asked.

She nodded. 'Grand too. Wee Lily's working hard. Your sisters are as thrawn and queer as ever but they're gathering in the money.'

He laughed his old bitter laugh. 'That's good. I hope they're hiding it in the right place.'

'They're putting it where you told them,' she assured him.

'Has anything else been found recently?' he asked, leaning forward in his chair and lowering his voice.

She whispered back. 'One or two bits. I found a sort of necklace in the neep field and Jake dug up a vase thing made of silver with a big handle when he was ploughing the big field last year. I gave it to your sisters. They hid it.'

Craigie's farm was on the site of a vanished Roman camp and the richness and variety of the treasures he and his ancestors had found while ploughing their soil was one of the village's secrets.

He seemed pleased. 'Right, right, good, good,' he said.

She let a pause lie between them for a moment and then plunged into the matter that had brought her there. 'I've come about Wee Lily's bairn. She's nearly eleven now and she'll be starting work soon. Can I take her in with us?'

'What's she like?' he asked.

'Like her father, red-heided and rough. I've done my best knocking the devil oot o' her but Wee Lily's ower soft. She's strong though and she'll be a good worker and not hard to pay.'

'What do the girls think?' He always called his sisters 'the girls' though they were both in their sixties.

'I didnae ask them. They'd just say "no" to anything I wanted.'

He did not protest at that. 'And you're sure this lassie's a good worker? We're no' wanting to take on any idlers. What about Jake? He's getting paid now too, isn't he? The farm cannae afford an army of workers. It's only a wee place.' Craigie always pleaded poverty though he had bags of gold and a treasure trove of silver in his cellar dug up from the old Roman camp.

Big Lily shrugged. 'Jake's an idle bugger. If you're wanting to save money I'll send him off,' she said.

Craigie's eyes glinted. 'Would the girl work for what Jake gets?' he asked.

'She'd work for less,' Big Lily told him and he agreed. 'All right, get rid of Jake and take her in his place. I'll write and tell the girls.'

She stood up. Their interview was at an end. Awkwardly, and without any open expression of affection, they took leave of each other and she started back on her journey home.

Meanwhile, Kitty was having the greatest day of her life. To be going out alone with her mother was such a joy to her that she did not even want Marie to go with them, though Wee Lily offered, 'You can ask Tibbie's lassie to come with us if you like.'

'Marie's going to the fair with her brother. He'd be angry if she didn't wait for him', Kitty said. It was only a guess and she was later relieved to find out that David did turn up for Marie.

The sheep fair was always held in a big field on the western slope of the second of the hills behind Rosewell. Dozens of pens full of sheep and half-grown lambs, all bleating away and setting up a tremendous din, were the real reason for the event which was to provide a place where local farmers could display and sell their stock.

When Wee Lily and her daughter walked through the gate it seemed as if everybody in the district was there, dressed in their best, greeting friends and family. Wee Lily was wearing her only cotton gown, which was patterned all over with sprigs of flowers and cut low at the neck showing the rarely exposed, creamy-white skin on her upper arms and breasts. Kitty had inherited her mother's skin because, unusually in a redhead, her complexion was a matt ecru colour, smooth and unmarked.

Both of their heads were bare because it was a hot day. Wee Lily wore her thick dark hair plaited in a knot at the nape of her neck and from a distance she looked handsome and imposing.

'This is my bairn Kitty,' she said to people she met, pulling the girl forward. Surprised to see her out without her mother, some of them asked, 'Where's Big Lily?'

'She's gone to Edinbury to see Craigie,' she said blithely and did not notice their surprise. Proudly Kitty grasped her mother's work-roughened hand as they walked to and fro, gazing at the sheep and the fairground hucksters who always turned up to coax money out of the pockets of rustics at local fairs.

They were walking along when Jake came stumbling out of a crowd of men standing at the door of the ale tent and grabbed for Wee Lily. His face was red, his hair tousled and he was obviously drunk.

'Lily, ah, Lily, walk round wi' me,' he babbled, gripping her arm. She literally jumped away from him, her face transformed from innocent pleasure to sheer dread. 'Dinna touch me, dinna touch me,' she hissed.

'Come on, Lily, get rid o' the bairn and you and I'll go roond thegither,' he pleaded, but she put an arm round Kitty and gathered her in.

'The bairn's staying wi' me,' she told him.

Jake would still not take no for an answer, however. Conscious of laughing men behind him he had to save his face. 'I'll buy you a beer,' he whispered, leaning closer to her. 'Then you and me can go and lie down up there on the hillside for a wee while…'

Kitty could feel her mother's arm shaking as she held on to her. 'I'm no' goin' to lie down wi' anybody,' whimpered Wee Lily like a frightened child.

Jake laughed. 'It's no' as if you've not done it before, is it? You've the bairn to show you know what's what. Come on up the hill wi' me. I'll marry you if you fall wi' another yin. It's more than that bairn's father did.'

'No, no,' sobbed Wee Lily, stepping back even farther to escape his grasping hand.

This was too much for Kitty. Wriggling out from under her mother's arm, she advanced on Jake and threatened him. 'Go away. You heard what she said. Leave my mam alone.'

He gazed down at her in astonishment. 'What's it to you? I'll gie you a saxpence and you can go and ride the swingboat.'

'I don't want your money. Leave my mam alone! If you don't, I'll tell Big Lily on you.'

That did the trick. Jake was terrified of Big Lily and knew how she'd react to the news that he'd been propositioning her daughter.

'You're all dafties anyway,' he sneered backing away. 'Dafties and bastards from way back. There's not a marriage line among you.'

Kitty didn't care about his insults. She grabbed hold of her mother's hand and pulled her away from the guffawing crowd.

'Come on, Mam, come on,' she said and together they ran to the other side of the field where Wee Lily spent her money on two mugs of dandelion beer from an old woman who had set up a trestle near the gate.

'Jake's aye bothering me,' she said as they sat side by side on a grassy bank to have their drinks. 'He's aye saying dirty things to me, but I don't want to go with him. I don't want to go with anybody. I'm feared of men after what happened that time with the navvy… Dinna ever go wi' a man, Kitty. It's terrible, terrible. It hurts such a lot.' She seemed to have forgotten that she was talking to a child and her daughter sat silent, staring at her.

'He smelt like a big boar when he grabbed me by the throat. He said if I didn't lie still he'd kill me. When he'd done it he kicked me in the side. I still get a pain where he kicked me. My ma and Tibbie said he'd broken my ribs.'

'How old were you?' whispered Kitty.

'I dinna mind. About fifteen I think. No' much older than you are now.'

'Did you know him?' was Kitty's next question.

Wee Lily looked shocked. 'Of course not. I'd never been wi' a man and I've never been wi' one since.'

Kitty patted the hand that lay on the grass by her side and said, 'Dinna think about it, Mam, forget it.'

Wee Lily wiped her hot face with the back of her hand and said, 'You stay away from men, Kitty. They're a' beasts.' Then she brightened, for distress never lasted long with her. 'Isn't it a braw day? Look down there at all the folk. Let's walk round the fair again.'

'Just once more,' Kitty told her. 'Then we'll have to get home because there's work to be done.' She knew that left to herself her mother would certainly forget her responsibilities back at the farm and Jake would probably not show up either because he was already reeling. In fact, it would be best if he didn't and she was determined not to leave Wee Lily in case he did. She knew what had to be done and she'd see to it that it was, not that she wanted to please Big Lily but she wished to avoid trouble falling on her mother's head.

All during the long and tiring journey back to Rosewell, Big Lily sat on the wooden seat of the third-class railway carriage and stared bleakly ahead like someone contemplating doom. Even though the sun had set, she still felt hot and marks of sweat stained her white blouse. The frivolous bonnet had been taken off and lay bent and disregarded on the seat beside her. Every now and then, she wiped her ruddy face with the edge of her green shawl, impervious to the disapproving looks of her fellow travellers.

Her head was full with a running thread of private thoughts, like a conversation with an unseen listener... There's Craigie shut up in that prison, away from the place he loves so dearly. I love him. He's the only man I've ever loved, though there were others after me when I

was a lassie, but I only ever wanted Craigie. He was strange then too…
even when he was fucking me he didn't say much. I don't know if men
do because I've only ever been with Craigie and he wasnae one for
fancy speaking, but I knew that I mattered to him.

He aye came back to me, didn't he? When Tibbie Mather's man
died I was worried because I thought Craigie wanted to get his feet
under her table but that passed. We'd have gone on like we were for
years if it hadn't been for that navvy grabbing hold of Wee Lily…

Big Lily's face darkened. If that navvy hadn't taken it into his head
to attack Wee Lily in the corn store, none of this would ever have
happened. Craigie wouldn't have shot him; he wouldn't have been
hauled up before the baillies and sent to the jail; he wouldn't be sitting
up there in that prison now, shut away from me. Oh God I wasn't even
able to put out a hand and touch him!

Big Lily did not imagine that anything would have changed radic-
ally if the murder had never happened. Craigie wouldn't have learned
to treat her with kindness or respect. He'd never work her less hard
or pay her more money, but all she wanted was for him to be there,
to see him every morning, to speak to him, to feel him grunting and
groaning on top of her whenever the mood took him.

Because of that Kitty, she thought angrily, I see him once in a
twelve year, through the iron grille of a prison wall. He shot the navvy
for interfering with his lassie. If that bairn had never been born this
wouldn't have happened.

She knew that Craigie's anger at the navvy was made up of many
more things than paternal affection. He was guarding his property,
fighting off the intrustion onto his land, revenging what he saw as an
insult and a disruption of their centuries-old way of life by the hated
railway. He was trying to hold back progress. But long ago she had
convinced herself it was the child's fault that Craigie was taken away.

Kitty's vibrant hair was a constant reminder of the man who'd
fathered her, the man who'd started all of the sorrow, the man who
was shot by Craigie, her brother, her lover and Wee Lily's father.

It did not strike her that she was being unfair to Kitty, for she
needed a scapegoat, a focus for her grief and rage. The very thought
of the child made a tide of rage rise in her.

I'm fifty years old, she thought. I'll soon be too old to work and
what's going to happen to us then? My lassie's simple. She cannae work
on her own. Craigie's sisters wouldn't keep her if anything happened

to me. They've aye known about me and Craigie; they ken find Wee Lily's his bairn and it's made them wild wi'jealousy. They'd send Wee Lily packing and the only place she can go is the Poors' House. Even if Craigie knew what was happening, he wouldn't be able to do anything about it. Or would he even try? You never know with Craigie. Till he shot the navvy, he'd never shown much interest in Wee Lily or acknowledged her as his child.

Big Lily knew there was only one way to safeguard her future and that of her daughter. She would have to make use of the bastard bairn and introduce her into the farm so that she could take over her grandmother's place when she was no longer able to work. Kitty would come in useful at last.

Darkness had fallen by the time she alighted from the train at Rosewell and exhaustion almost overwhelmed her as she walked the dark path towards the lights of Camptounfoot which glittered in the blackness ahead of her.

Though she was dog-tired she would not go to bed till she had checked the sheds and byre, where she found everything to her satisfaction. There was nothing to criticise, no matter how hard she looked. She knew very well that she owed this organisation to her granddaughter but felt no gratitude.

At last she pulled on the twist of rope that formed the latch of the bothy door and stepped into its smoky-smelling dimness. Her daughter had left a loaf of bread on the table beside a white pottery jug full of milk. She lifted the jug and drank straight from it without using a cup. Then she looked at the loaf and thought she'd have a slice.

Her hand went automatically to where the pocket in her working skirt should have been. Then she remembered that she wasn't wearing it. She looked around and spotted the old skirt lying folded up on the bed by Wee Lily's feet. She walked across to lift it and search the pockets but to her surprise the knife was not there. Her brow furrowed and she tried to remember where she'd left it but she was too tired to make a proper search.

Tearing off a chunk of bread from the loaf and dipping it in the milk, she satisfied her hunger. Then, without taking off her clothes, she crawled under the heap of covers on the bed and fell fast asleep.

Next morning she was first up and dressed in her working clothes before dawn broke. The noise she made searching the bothy for her knife woke the other two and Wee Lily sat up rubbing her eyes as she asked, 'What are you doing, Ma?'

'I'm lookin' for my knife. I've lost it,' was the gruff reply.

Kitty, hearing this, lay stiff with fear beneath her blanket and pretended to be asleep, but her mother got up and helped Big Lily rummage about among the tumbled bedcovers.

'I had it before I went to Edinbury. I remember using it...' the older woman was muttering.

'Maybe you left it in the byre or the dairy,' was Wee Lily's suggestion.

Her mother shot a look at her. 'Jake didnae take it, did he? He's aye liked that knife.'

Because of her encounter with Jake at the fair, Wee Lily looked sheepish but managed to shake her head. Seeing her confusion, her mother became even more suspicious. 'You've seen him with it, haven't you?'

'No, I haven't,' protested Wee Lily, but the seed of suspicion had been planted. Kitty, silent in bed, was grateful that the questioning had not been switched to her.

Later she heard Big Lily screaming at Jake in the cattle court, 'You've taken my knife, haven't you? It was my mother's and it's a grand wee knife. Gie it back, you thief you, or I'll clip your ear...'

Jake's protestations of innocence were ignored and Kitty lurked behind a gable wall to listen to what went on. 'If you don't gie it back, I'll send you packing oot o' here,' was Big Lily's next threat.

'Aw, mistress, I havenae taken your knife... honest. Dinna send me awa',' pleaded the distraught man.

'If that knife's not back here by tonight you'll be oot o' a job at term time,' threatened Big Lily.

Kitty walked to school with a solemn face wondering if she should give back the knife. Could she let Jake suffer for something she had done? All morning she pondered the problem, and at midday ran to her hiding-place to dig up the tin.

The knife lay enticingly in her hand, its worn, cream-coloured handle shining. She turned it over lovingly. The fact that it had belonged to her great grandmother made it even more precious. It was an heirloom in a family that had very little to pass on.

She decided to keep it a little longer and wait to see what happened with Jake. Putting the knife back in the tin, she buried her treasure again.

That night there was a thunderous atmosphere pervading the farm when she arrived home from school. Jake was acting like a beaten child and Big Lily shouted and stormed about the least little thing going wrong. Even the dogs slunk away with their tails between their legs if anyone as much as looked at them.

Wee Lily alone was impervious, going about her tasks with customary good humour, smiling lovingly at her child when her mother wasn't looking.

They were eating their supper when Big Lily suddenly glared at Kitty and announced, 'Tell your schoolmaster that you'll no' be back at the school after the end of the term. I'm taking you in here. Craigie said it was all right.'

Surprisingly it was Wee Lily who demurred, 'Are they going to pay her a wage, Ma?' she asked.

'Maybe, if she works well…' said Big Lily evasively. She knew it was hard enough getting money out of Craigie's sisters for Wee Lily and they were certainly not going to be keen to part with more cash for Kitty. What she was doing by getting her granddaughter onto the farm was literally buying herself security in her old age. 'We'll be feeding her off the land and she'll have this roof over her head. That's better than money at her age.'

'She hasnae any working claes,' protested Wee Lily next.

'I'll buy her some and she can pay me back when she's earning,' said Big Lily. Then she looked hard at Kitty and ordered, 'Mind and tell the teacher you're leaving. Jake's going away at the next hiring.'

Though neither Wee Lily nor Kitty had any affection for Jake, who was coarse and unlovable, he was part of their lives, almost one of their family and Kitty's remorse made her speak up for him. 'He'll no' get another place easily,' she said.

Big Lily shrugged. 'That's his lookout. He took my knife and he's no' brought it back.'

Kitty felt her legs trembling. Now was the time that she would have to own up if she was going to, but Big Lily was attacking her food like an animal, her brows lowered and shoulders hunched. The girl knew that her first reaction would be violence if she found out the truth. Fear kept Kitty's mouth shut.

Next day she hung guiltily about the farm so that she could eavesdrop and overhear her grandmother giving Jake his marching orders.

'Right, that's it. You've no' brought back my knife and so you're off at the spring term. You'll have to go to Maddiston hiring fair and find yourself another place,' she said brutally.

Jake's voice was trembling. 'Aw, missus, dinna send me awa', dinna. I'll do anything you want. You can have a shillin' a week oot of my money… I'll work harder, I'll… I'll… I'll marry Wee Lily for you,' he pleaded.

There was a silence after he said this and Kitty, peeping through the door, saw that her grandmother had stopped sweeping out the byre floor and was leaning on her brush thinking about his suggestion. 'What do you mean?' she asked cautiously.

'I mean I'll marry her in spite o' the bairn. Naebody else will, will they? Then you'll have a man in the house to do the heavy work when you get older.'

Inadvertently he'd hit on the fear that had been oppressing Big Lily's mind and she looked at him more carefully, as if considering that there was more to him than she'd suspected. But then she remembered the knife and hardened again. 'Well, maybe, but what about my knife?'

Jake thought he'd scored a point with her and decided to brazen it out. Drawing himself up he said roughly, 'I havenae got your bloody knife, woman. I've got a knife o' my ain. What would I want wi' an old thing like that?'

'That's it,' snapped Big Lily. 'You're off. I'll bring in the bairn to train up in your place. She's a cheeky little bitch but she's smarter than you by a long way.'

Kitty was still listening at the door when Jake came storming out shouting threats. He bumped into her, almost knocking her off her feet, and raised his hand, bringing it down on her head with a tremendous thump. 'Get oot o' my way, you wee bastard ye!' he yelled. She shook her head to still the ringing in her ears. To spite him she'd keep her mouth shut and keep the knife as well.

–

'I'm going to work soon, so we'll not see each other so much. I'll no' be able to meet you after school,' Kitty told Marie when they met next day.

'I'm sorry. Everything's changing, isn't it?' said Marie.

'What'll you do?' asked Kitty.

'I'll go on drawing and painting I expect. I like living with Tibbie and David's quite happy that I'm here because he's not able to have his own place yet. He's paying Tibbie for my keep though she doesn't want to take the money. She's told me she's putting it all in the savings bank and I'll get it as my dowry when I marry,' Marie told her friend.

She still spent many hours listening to her brother on the subject of their obligations to each other and was not at all sure that she would ever be allowed to contemplate marriage.

Her face, which had been childish when she first arrived from Rosewell, was now adult with a long, straight nose and a broad brow. Her blue eyes were large and innocent and her gaze still guileless. Though she'd soon be a woman she had not yet cast off childish things and what she most enjoyed doing was wandering around the countryside with Kitty, gathering flowers to draw and watching the birds and animals. They were clinging on to the last days of their childhood, knowing that changes would soon engulf them both.

'Do you remember what I told you about my granny's knife and how I could use it to make us blood sisters?' asked Kitty suddenly.

'Yes, I remember,' said Marie.

'Well, I've got the knife. I stole it from her. It's hidden. It's so sharp it can slice a blade of grass right down the middle.'

Marie stared at Kitty's eager face with dismay. 'Does Big Lily know you've got it?' she asked.

'Of course not. She'd go daft if she found out. She thinks Jake took it.' Kitty had the grace to sound a little shamefaced. Then she added, 'When we've mixed our blood together, I'll give it back to her.'

Marie was not anxious to start the bloodletting. 'I think you should give it back anyway. You know what she'll do if she finds out you've got it,' she said.

'I won't give it back yet. Not till we've used it for the thumb cutting,' said Kitty firmly.

'All right, but not yet. Let's wait till I leave school,' agreed Marie. Anything to put off the ordeal.

# Chapter Six

Six months of slaving on Townhead farm under her grandmother's cruel supervision almost broke Kitty's spirit.

Though she despised people who took refuge in tears, it was difficult to stay dry-eyed on bitter mornings when Big Lily drove her out into wraiths of hoar mist to gather turnips from earth that was iron-hard with frost. Without covering on her hands, and her feet without stockings even during bitter frosts, she struggled to complete her tasks. Sometimes her toes got so cold that she was sure they would drop off and it took hours of chafing them before the blood flowed back. When that happened, she wished she'd left them cold because then the chilblains throbbed and pulsed, a different kind of agony.

She was still dressed in rags, no protection against the bitter winter because, in spite of her grandmother's promise, no working garments had been bought for her. The only improvement in her wardrobe was that, instead of going barefoot, she was given an old pair of Big Lily's broken boots, but they let in the water. Because they were too big, she stuffed them with hay.

At Christmas, kind Tibbie gave her a black shawl she'd knitted and Kitty wore it every day.

The thing that angered her most was that she received no wages for her work. The little money Craigie's sisters were prepared to hand out for her was pocketed by Big Lily. Kitty's situation had changed for the worse.

By the time the grass began to grow again and snowdrops peeped up beneath the hedges, her peaked face had assumed a strange, austere expression that worried Tibbie and Marie. She looked as if she were burning up inside with hatred and Tibbie was afraid that if it burst out, she might do something very violent.

Marie was the only person to whom Kitty could talk about her misery, and whenever she could, she sought out her friend. One balmy evening they walked along the riverbank picking primroses and watching the birds building their nests. The scene was beautiful and tranquil but Kitty's emotions were in turmoil.

'I hate her, I hate her. She hit me with the pitchfork tonight...' She stuck out an arm and showed Marie a huge bruise on the soft flesh beneath the shoulder.

Marie's eyes were full of sympathy but there was little she could do except listen as Kitty went ranting on about Big Lily. 'I feel like a prisoner. Even Craigie in Edinbury's jail can't be any worse off than me. When I think that I could go on like this till I'm old, I feel desperate. I could kill her, Marie, I really could.'

'Do you want me to ask Tibbie to speak to her?' asked Marie gently but Kitty shook her head.

'That wouldn't do any good. She'd take it out on me for complaining. I never speak to her now because whatever I say is wrong. She hates having me around the place, but she needs my work so she's got to put up with me. She's never satisfied unless she sees me bent double under a heavy sack or doing a man's job. Look at my hands...'

Kitty spread them out to show her friend deep hacks on the knuckles and broken blisters on the palms.

'You should have a bandage on those,' Marie said but Kitty shrugged.

'What's the use? They'd open up again the day I took the bandage off. I wish I could run away. The only reason I stay is because of my mother. I'm feared that I'll still be here when I'm sixty, hard and cruel like my granny is now...'

Marie slipped an arm round Kitty's thin waist and hugged her. 'Don't give up. You should go away as soon as you can. Go to Maddiston hiring fair and get yourself another place.'

Kitty brightened a little. 'I was thinking I might do that next year. I could tell folk I was fifteen.'

'You'd pass for that now,' Marie told her, for Kitty was tall and her breasts were swelling, something that annoyed her a lot, for she wished she could always be flat-chested, like a boy.

Kitty cheered up a little at the idea of getting another place and asked her friend, 'What about you?'

Marie frowned. 'I wasn't going to tell you this yet because it might never happen, but Lady Godolphin came to the school yesterday and went into raptures about my pictures again. She said that I ought to have lessons from a real artist and I think she's going to find out about where I could go.'

Kitty was delighted. 'That's grand. There must be some good artists round here who could teach you. Lady Godolphin'll know them all. But will you be able to pay for lessons?'

Marie shook her head, warning against over-optimism. 'Tibbie said she'd pay for them but Lady Godolphin might forget to make enquiries... and David won't want me to go.'

Kitty snorted. 'If you get the chance, go. Don't let David stop you. It'll be your way out of Camptounfoot... Promise you'll go.'

'All right, I'll promise if you promise me that next year you'll go to the hiring fair,' Marie replied. They shook hands on their bargain.

While the girls were making this pact by the river, Lord and Lady Godolphin were entertaining the Duke of Allandale in their mansion a mile away.

A smiling Bethya was sitting in an armchair by the window with the setting sun's rays casting golden light around her. She knew she was still beautiful and was relieved to realise that she felt better than she had done for a very long time, for though she had been hiding the true state of her weakness, her malaise had lingered for so long that she was afraid it would always be with her, and Sydney was short-tempered with invalids.

'I went to the village school today and saw a girl there who really deserves help,' she told her husband, who grinned.

'Good works again. You're never happy unless you're doing something philanthropic.'

She frowned. 'Where I come from it's considered one's duty to give to the poor, but this isn't charity. This girl is an excellent artist. She should have proper tuition.'

Sydney said, 'And I suppose you want to pay for it. What does she paint? Kittens and wild flowers, I'll wager.'

'No, she does landscapes. She could be really good if she was taught properly.'

The Duke, who was an art connoisseur, leaned forward and asked, 'Is she a local?'

'I think so. She lives in the village anyway. Such a nice, well-mannered girl... obviously from a good home. Do you know of any painters in the district who might teach her?'

Allandale frowned. 'There's no one of any great merit round about at the moment. You'd have to go to Edinburgh for proper tuition. I could find out for you if you like.'

Bethya clasped her hands. 'How kind of you!' And she bestowed one of her sweetest smiles on their guest while her husband scoffed, 'That's a good mark on your slate, Dickie.'

The Duke was as good as his word. A few days later Bethya received a letter from him with the addresses of three painting academies in Edinburgh.

He had also gone to the trouble of finding out which was the best. 'I'd recommend that you send your protégée to Professor D'Arcy Abernethy in Princes Street. All the best Edinburgh families send their girls there for tuition,' he wrote.

Next day another letter was delivered to Tibbie's cottage by a uniformed flunkey from Bella Vista. In spidery black handwriting it was addressed to Miss Marie Benjamin. Both Tibbie and Marie stared at it as if it were liable to explode, before Marie carefully split the green wax seal and drew out a sheet of thick writing paper which was covered with the same handwriting.

She read aloud… 'Dear Miss Benjamin, I was so impressed by your artistic talent when I re-visited Camptounfoot school, that I would like to become your patron and pay for you to undertake a course of study.

'I have been given the names of suitable painting academies in Edinburgh which I would like to discuss with you to find out if you would be willing to attend one of them. Perhaps you will come to Bella Vista so that we can have a talk. I suggest that you come next Friday at three thirty o'clock…' Bethya's signature was scrawled over the bottom of the page.

Marie handed Tibbie the letter and said in amazement, 'She wants to send me to Edinburgh to learn painting!'

Tibbie was delighted. 'Isn't that wonderful!' she exclaimed.

Marie shook her head. 'Is it? I don't know. I've never been farther than Maddiston… I'm not sure I'm a good enough artist to go to a painting academy… What will David say?'

Tibbie snorted. 'Of course you're good enough. Lady Godolphin knows what she's talking about and if he's any sense, David'll see what a chance this is for you.'

Her positive attitude rallied Marie a little. 'I don't suppose it'll do any harm to go to the big house and talk about it,' she said doubtfully.

Tibbie was sure of that. 'If you refused the invitation it would be very rude. Friday's the day after tomorrow. Now let's find a bit of paper and write back to her saying you'll be there.'

—

On Friday morning, while Tibbie and Marie were fussing about which dress she should wear for her visit to Bella Vista, David was adding up columns of figures in the payments book of Henderson's Mill in Maddiston. His mind was not on his work, however, for he was dreaming of the day when he would be sitting in the next room, the manager's office, with some other clerk labouring to his command.

Mr Coleman, the mill manager, was looking out at him through the glass-topped door. David Benjamin, he was thinking, is the perfect employee. Meticulous in his work, in the office early every morning and always the last to leave. If there was ever any extra work to be done, David did it without complaint.

Coleman rose from his seat and went through into the outer office. 'Eh, lad,' he said in his broad Lancashire accent, 'I wish all the clerks in this place were as hard-working as you.'

David, perched on a stool before a high wooden desk, looked up and ran a hand through his long fall of fair hair. 'What's the matter, Mr Coleman?' he asked.

Coleman, who had been brought up from Manchester to run the Maddiston mill and still felt out of place and friendless in the Borders, did not reply but walked back into his own office where he bent down and fetched a dark-coloured bottle out of the bottom drawer of his desk. Uncorking it, he put it to his lips, took a long draw, sighed, wiped his mouth, recorked the bottle and put it back before saying loudly, 'That's better. Good for the nerves.'

David said nothing but his eyes were watchful. He knew the manager drank more than was good for him and one day he intended to use that knowledge to his own advantage.

Coleman, a tall, rangy man with a face like a hungry horse, went to stand in the big window overlooking the mill yard where the drays came in to load and unload.

'There's a lot of lazy buggers about,' he said. 'They don't realise you'll get nowhere unless you use a bit of graft. Graft, that's what's needed. They all say, "I'll finish it tomorrow, Mr Coleman." Tomorrow won't do, will it, David? I didn't get where I am by putting things off till tomorrow.'

David nodded. 'You're right, sir.'

'You don't put things off till tomorrow, do you, lad? But then you're not a local, are you? You weren't born here.' Coleman turned and stared at the boy on the stool in the outer office.

David had no idea where he was born but agreed, 'No, I'm not a local, sir. I was brought here when I was about three I think. I was born in London.' It might have been true.

As far as Coleman was concerned it would have been better if the lad had said he was born in Lancashire but London was at least better than Maddiston. He found the easy-going attitude of the local people almost unbearable. Anything he asked for they pretended to misunderstand and when they finally got the message, they put off doing it for as long as possible. He'd been waiting for a carpenter to repair the roof of one of the woolsheds for a month and the man had still not shown up. It was driving him crazy.

'That bloody carpenter's still not come and the woolshed's leaking. The winter's coming and the bales'll get soaked if he doesn't turn up soon. What'll Mr Henderson say if I let his bales get soaked?' he said mournfully.

Adalbert Henderson, the arbiter of all their fates, was the proprietor of Maddiston mill. He also owned another, smaller mill in Rosewell, and was locally respected for being both ambitious and crafty. This shrewd businessman had seen the potential of the rapidly growing weaving trade early and had sunk his fortune, made from cattle dealing, into it. He had prospered but did not allow the possession of great riches to change him, for he remained a working-class, rough-spoken fellow with no pretensions to grandeur.

Because he knew little about running weaving mills, he hired specialist labour from the south when he first embarked on the business. That was how Coleman came to be in Maddiston, living in the big mill house that Henderson had built for him and trying to turn people who were used to the slow and unchanging rhythm of the land into factory workers. He'd been doing it for ten years and it was a thankless task.

'Why do the people around here say they'll do a job and then never turn up?' he moaned.

'Would you like me to find another carpenter?' asked David.

'I've tried most of them and they're all slow,' groaned Coleman, wondering if it was time for another slug from his bottle.

'I was thinking that we ought to have our own carpenters in the mill. It's big enough for that now,' was David's next suggestion.

'Aye, big mills do that. It's the only way to get them to work I expect,' agreed Coleman.

'I could find a master carpenter and Mr Henderson might take him onto the payroll. I've got a man in mind,' said David.

Coleman looked at his assistant with respect. Only eighteen years old and as canny as a septuagenarian, he thought.

'You do that, lad. If you've somebody in mind, get your jacket and go to find him,' he ordered.

David looked down at his ledgers. 'I'll finish making these returns first if you don't mind, Mr Coleman, then I'll go.'

The mill manager was impressed but also impatient, for when David was out of the office, he felt easier about taking more little nips from his whisky bottle. He could tell from the expression in the lad's eye that he disapproved.

It was midday before David's clerking work was done and he set off for Rosewell where he knew there was a carpenter called Billy Black who would be glad of the offer of a job in Maddiston mill.

Billy lived behind the house where David and Marie used to stay with Nanny Rush. He had set himself up in business young, unwisely marrying at the same time, and his family grew yearly but he was still struggling to find enough customers to keep him fully occupied and pay his bills. The last time David met him, he'd talked of emigrating to Canada with his brood. The only thing that stopped him was the impossibility of raising the fares for them all.

The walk from Maddiston to Rosewell over the hills was about four miles but David thought nothing of it, striding along with his head up and the wind blowing through his hair. All the time he was scheming and planning, adding up sums in his head, calculating how long it would be before he had enough money put by to take a lease on a little house for Marie and himself. At the moment he lodged with the family of the mill gatehouse keeper and spent nothing apart from his board money and the sum to cover Marie's keep. Everything else he saved.

Billy Black was in his workshed, gloomily planing a long spar of wood, for someone had ordered a coffin.

'Hello, Davie. It's a while since I saw you,' he said when his visitor appeared in his doorway.

After a preliminary chat and exchange of news, David asked, 'How's trade?'

Billy groaned. 'Bad, bad. I cannae make enough tae buy boots for the bairns.'

'I was wondering if you'd like to come to work at the mill in Maddiston,' said David.

The carpenter brightened. 'Have you a job needing done?'

'We have. The woolshed roofs leaking but there's other things as well and all the Maddiston carpenters are too busy. The delay's driving Coleman crazy. He's thinking of hiring somebody full-time.'

The reception of this piece of news was ecstatic. 'I'm your man, I'm your man. I'll get my bag of tools directly… You're a good lad, a damned good lad. I'll no' forget this, Davie,' cried Billy.

The finding of a carpenter being so quickly over, David felt justified in taking some time off to look in on his sister and Tibbie. When he got to the cottage, he saw them through the window shelling peas in the kitchen and talking away fifteen to the dozen. He stood very quiet, listening to what was being said.

'I'll wear my grey dress, I think. It's the prettiest one I've got,' Marie was saying.

Then she looked up and saw her brother standing outside the open window. 'Oh I never heard you,' she cried. 'What a nice surprise. Tibbie and I were talking about what I should wear for my visit to Bella Vista.'

'You're never going there?' he asked suspiciously.

'I've been invited to tea today,' she said happily.

David looked at Tibbie and asked incredulously, 'Is this true?'

'Yes, it is. She's been invited by Lady Godolphin because of her bonny pictures. Her ladyship saw them in the school and asked Marie to the big house to talk about getting painting lessons.'

Tibbie sounded very proud but David's expression was an eloquent indication of how he felt about well-off ladies with nothing better to do than give tea parties for poor people. He was furious.

'She's meddling. Don't go,' he said shortly.

His sister flushed indignantly. 'Don't be silly. She wants to help me.'

He asked suspiciously, 'Why should she do that?'

Marie launched into her tale. 'Lady Godolphin came to the school twice and liked my pictures. Then she sent me a letter inviting me to meet her.'

'If she wants you to draw something for her, I hope she'll pay you a fair fee,' snapped her brother. Because he so sorely longed to move up in the world, he was jealous of and defensive against people who were his social superiors. His sister did not share these feelings, however, and she was already dazzled by the opportunity that was opening for her.

'I wish you wouldn't talk like that,' she told him.

'Come on, Marie, you know as well as I that the gentry don't entertain people like you and me unless they want something out of them,' he snapped.

Marie was bristling. 'Lady Godolphin doesn't want anything from me. In fact, she's offering to send me to Edinburgh for tuition.'

Her brother laughed, actually laughed and he was not given to laughing very much. 'She's playing games with you,' he told her, but her cheeks were flaming red as she asked him, 'Don't you think my pictures are good enough for her to like them?'

He hesitated. Ever since she was old enough to hold a pencil his sister had been drawing pictures and he looked indulgently on her interest as a harmless hobby.

'People like us don't become artists,' he said slowly.

'Why not?'

'Because we're poor. We're the sort of people who have to work for a living. Lady Godolphin doesn't understand that, Marie.'

'She does understand. She knows we're poor. She's offered to pay everything for me. She believes in me and that's more than you do!'

He spread out his hands in frustration. 'Don't be silly. Of course I believe in you. It's just that I don't see why she'd want to do something like that. I'm afraid that she might give you hopes that can't be fulfilled and you'll have to face disappointment later on.'

This change in his tone made Marie soften a little towards him. 'Why don't you come with me to Bella Vista and hear what she has to say? I'm sure she won't mind. It really means a lot to me. I love painting and I might never get another chance like this,' she said.

Her vehemence impressed him and he nodded. 'All right. I'll go up there with you. But I don't approve, you know.'

At three o'clock they were ready to go. Marie was dressed in her plain grey dress with a cream-coloured lace collar and her hair was knotted into a plait. She looked heartbreakingly pretty, as fragile as a wind blossom. Tibbie felt tears prick her eyes when she looked at the girl on the brink of womanhood and trembling like the first wild daffodil of spring.

David was dressed in his working suit of course but Tibbie brushed down his shoulders and told him, 'You look quite the businessman David. Be kind to your sister.'

With those words ringing in his ears, he offered his arm to Marie as they walked down the street and she laid her hand on it. It was not far to Bella Vista and from the top of the village street they could see the house's Indian-style towers sticking up from its belt of trees. David had passed the place many times in the past but he had never been beyond the little pepper-pot house which guarded the wrought-iron gates.

The gatekeeper swung open one gate as they approached and a long, grass-covered drive stretched before them like an endless ribbon edged with tall trees. They had to hurry because it was imperative not to be late and both of them were slightly out of breath when the house came into sight. It was huge, with three rows of glittering windows along its ornate front and two side wings that were not so high as the central portion. Beneath the ludicrously over-carved canopied portico was a massive double door with brass handles and two knockers in the shape of lions with their mouths open.

As soon as the visitors set foot on the bottom step, both doors were flung open and a bewigged manservant in livery stood within staring down at them. 'Her ladyship is waiting,' he intoned solemnly.

David tried to conceal how impressed he felt as they were shown into a vast room with long looking-glasses on the wall facing the garden. The windows echoed the shape of the mirrors and looked out onto a paved terrace. Because the day was bright, they were open and tendrils of yellow roses seemed to be trying to make their way inside.

They walked across an expanse of silken carpet patterned in pastel colours that reflected the colours on the ceiling. By a high marble fireplace carved with an exuberant scene of battling elephants bearing howdahs on their backs, their hostess sat waiting for them.

If she was surprised to see David, she made no sign when Marie said awkwardly, 'This is my brother, your ladyship. He wanted to come with me to discuss your kind offer.'

Bethya held out a hand to him and smiled sweetly. 'That's very thoughtful of him…' And to David she said as if he were doing her a great favour, 'How good of you to come to see me.' She indicated that her guests should sit facing her on her long sofa upholstered in figured silk. At her feet were two pugs and one hand was trailing idly over the head of the biggest of the dogs, which stared bleakly at the strangers from its great bulging eyes.

'I'm so glad you've come,' she said again and the distrust David had felt for her, simply because of who she was and what she represented, softened slightly, though he recognised that she was trying to make them feel at ease.

When the tea service was carried in, the immensity of the silver teapot made him defensive again. He could tell that it would cost far more than he would earn from many years' work and he was glaring at it when he heard his hostess saying to Marie, 'What do you think about my proposition, my dear? Would you like to go to Edinburgh?'

'I don't think she ought to go,' he said loudly, lifting his gaze from the teapot.

Bethya turned dark-fringed aquamarine eyes on him and he felt his resolve weaken under their soft regard.

'But why?' she whispered.

'My sister isn't used to travelling,' he blustered.

'I understand. It's very solicitous of you to worry about her safety. If you like, I'll send a maid with Marie till she's accustomed to the journey,' she offered.

'We're not the sort of people who have maids,' said David baldly.

Bethya leaned forward and handed him a cup of delicate china full of golden, steaming tea.

'I can tell by the look of you that one day you *will* have maids,' she told him. 'You seem like a young man with a great future. It's obvious too that you are a very caring brother. That's why I'm glad to have the opportunity to discuss my ideas about Marie with you.'

Her lovely eyes were on his face and he felt himself weakening even more. He'd arrived in her house determined to tell her that Marie did not need charity from her or anyone else, but now he could only smile like an idiot and sip the tea she'd put into his hand. He felt as if he were being enchanted and tried to fight against it.

When he did make his protest it was greatly watered-down from what he'd originally intended. 'I wouldn't like my sister to be thought of as an object of charity,' he said weakly.

Bethya looked at Marie, who was sitting silent, awaiting the outcome of this battle between her brother and her would-be patroness.

'Marie is an artist with immense promise. It's not charity that makes me want to help her, it's because I recognise her ability and know it would be a dreadful waste if it was not nurtured. I assure you that I've considerable experience looking at works of art, and I know your sister is very good indeed, but with proper tuition she could be even better,' Bethya told him.

David was flustered by her certainty. 'I'm sure you know what you're talking about, Lady Godolphin, but what is my sister going to do with this tuition after it's completed?' he asked.

She smiled. 'Your sister could teach art, or paint pictures that people would buy and hang on their walls. Her name could become known. A world of opportunity would open for her.'

He leaned forward and put the teacup on a table by his side. 'What if she isn't good enough for that?' he asked bluntly.

Bethya was just as blunt. 'She is, I assure you.'

David said, 'Male painters are always better than women. Women can't produce really great art.'

Bethya seemed unperturbed by this cavil. She tilted her head to one side and let the dark ringlets swing enchantingly against her shoulder as she smiled at him again.

'People do say that, I know, but there have been some very great women painters… Angelica Kaufmann and Elisabeth Vigée-Lebrun for example… and, of course, there are many others not so famous but equally well regarded among the cognoscenti. I'm sure you'd be very proud of your sister if she showed in big exhibitions.'

'Of course I would. It's just that I don't want her to be patronised…' He knew he was losing ground and, like a man falling over a cliff, scrabbled to keep a handhold, but the word 'patronised' sounded insulting even to him and his face flushed as he said it.

Bethya still did not take offence. 'I do understand how you feel. I think it does you credit, but I want to help your sister because it would give me great pleasure to see the work she will produce in years to come if she is brought under the influence of a good teacher now. It's not patronising in the sense you mean, though I would like to be her patron. Will you allow me that pleasure?' Here she smiled beguilingly at him and he stared back saying nothing.

Bethya went on, 'Let's try it for a little while. If Marie doesn't like Edinburgh or if you and she feel that she shouldn't go on painting, I will quite understand.'

She then looked at Marie and asked, 'What do you think, my dear? Would you like to try? I've made more enquiries about the painting schools. One is rather strict though good; the other is less strict but equally highly regarded. I think it might be better for you. I will pay everything. It'll be a pleasure for me to know I'm helping a genuine artist.'

Marie felt as if the world were expanding around her and had lit up with a glorious golden glow. All her reservations about leaving Camptounfoot, all her fears about displeasing David disappeared as she said, 'I'm very grateful to you, Lady Godolphin. I'd like to go to Edinburgh and I hope that I'll be a credit to you. I'll certainly try very hard.'

Bethya clasped her hands together in pleasure. 'Good, I'm so pleased. I'll write to Professor Abernethy and ask if he has a place for you in his classes starting this autumn.'

She looked at David and assured him again, 'Do believe me. This isn't charity. It's an investment. When your sister's famous, I'll want a very good picture painted specially for me.'

Awkwardly he tried to thank her but chagrin made him tumble over the words for he knew he'd been outwitted.

During their walk home, however, he chided Marie. 'It's not right that you should be getting mixed up with people like that. She'll put wrong ideas in your head. We'll never be able to equal that style of living, not ever.'

She didn't seem to be listening to him and kept on murmuring, 'All right, David, don't worry about it please…'

He grew more and more irritated. 'But of course I worry. I'm your brother. You're my responsibility. I don't want you to be put into a situation that can only cause you grief.' He didn't want her to slip out of his grasp, that was the truth of it.

Suddenly she stopped in the middle of the hedge-lined lane and said, 'You don't want me to go to Edinburgh, do you?'

'No I don't.'

'Well that's a pity because I'm going. If I don't like it or if I think it's the wrong thing to do, I'll stop but at least I'll have given it a try.'

The calm certainty in her voice silenced him. He knew there was no point going on about it any more. His tactics in future would have to be more subtle.

Three days later Bethya wrote again to Marie telling her that Professor Abernethy had agreed to take her as a pupil in his class and that she was to start on 25 September.

Waving this letter, Marie ran up the lane to where Kitty was cutting grass with a huge scythe in the orchard. She made a forlorn figure as she bent to her work with her glorious hair sticking sweatily to her face and neck.

Marie ran across and gasped, 'I'm going to painting classes in Edinburgh. Lady Godolphin's arranged it all for me.'

Kitty put down the scythe and leaned on it, wiping her glistening face with her forearm. Her pleasure was genuine when she said, 'That's wonderful. It's good of her.'

Overcome with remorse at being so full of her own news when her friend looked so wan, Marie put a hand on her arm and said, 'Now you must go away too. You promised.'

There was a fierce note in Kitty's voice as she said, 'I will. I'll go as far as I can. Today I've been looking out at the hills over there and longing to cross them… Just to go anywhere. I'm tired of slaving like this.'

Marie patted her arm. 'I'm sorry,' she said softly.

'Don't be sorry. That's good news about you and the painting class though. You'll be famous one day, Marie. I'll boast about knowing you. The only bad thing about your news is we'll not see each other so much.'

'I'm only going to Edinburgh on two days a week,' Marie told her but Kitty shook her head sadly.

'You'll make new friends there and forget Camptounfoot.'

'I won't. I really won't!' Marie was vehement.

Suddenly Kitty grinned. 'Do you remember when I stole my granny's knife so that we could be blood sisters? We should mix our blood now if you're going away.'

Marie's heart sank at the idea but she did not want to hurt Kitty's feelings. 'When will we do it?' she asked doubtfully.

'Why not now? I'll go and get the knife and be back here in a couple of minutes. Wait for me.' Dropping the scythe on the sweet-smelling grass, Kitty dashed off.

She hadn't been to her hiding-place for a long time and weeds had grown up over the marking stone but the tin was still there, tightly closed. The knife and her half-sovereign were quite safe.

When she came back her eyes were dancing and she pulled the knife from her skirt pocket to show it to Marie, who was slightly disappointed to find that this famous treasure was so small and insignificant-looking, little better than a penknife, she thought.

'It's not very big,' she said, for she had expected something more ferocious-looking.

Kitty snapped out the blade and told her, 'But it's really sharp.'

Though the gleaming weapon was only about four inches long, it was honed to a vicious-looking point.

'Do you want to be cut first?' asked Kitty.

Marie spread out her fingers and looked at them carefully as she asked, 'Will it hurt? Which finger will you cut?'

Kitty was examining her own hands which were, as usual, none too clean.

'The thumb I think. There'll be more blood there.' Without flinching she drew the knife blade down the pad of her thumb and a thread of blood welled up behind it. They looked at the scarlet line and Kitty shook a drop of blood off her hand. It fell on the cut grass at her feet and lay gleaming like a ruby.

'I never felt anything. Do you want me to do it to you? I promise it doesn't hurt,' she said.

Marie held out her white hand and the cool steel was laid against her thumb. At first she felt nothing. Then came the sting, sharp and searing like a burn, but, remembering Kitty's stoicism, she bit back a cry of pain. A narrow red scratch quickly welled to a steady flow of blood and the two girls watched it with fascination till Kitty held out her own bleeding thumb and solemnly rubbed it against Marie's.

'Hold it still, hold it still,' she whispered and they stood with their thumbs pressed together for about two minutes till the sharp pain died away.

'Now we've got the same blood,' said Kitty solemnly. Then she giggled. 'It did hurt a bit, didn't it?'

She reached down and pulled a large dock leaf out of the cut hay, handing it to Marie. 'Wrap one of these round it. Dock leaves take the sting out of nettle burns so they should help a cut.'

Tibbie was surprised that evening when Marie came home with a large green leaf bound round her finger. 'What've you been doing?' she asked.

'I cut myself down by the river,' was the reply.

'Let me dress it with some of my marigold salve on a clean cloth. If you get it dirty, it could be dangerous,' said Tibbie and bustled off to find her medicine chest which contained cures for every domestic ailment and emergency.

No one asked Kitty why her finger was wrapped up in a dock leaf. Next morning her thumb was throbbing but she thought little about it and went out to work. The throbbing grew worse, however, and by the second day, her thumb was so badly swollen it looked like a big carrot. She could hardly lift her hand, she could not work, the injury was impossible to hide.

Wee Lily noticed it first. 'Has a wasp stung you?' she asked.

'Aye, a wasp, that's what did it,' said Kitty, attempting to hold her hands behind her back, but Wee Lily grabbed for the injured one and said, 'Let's have a look. My God, there's yellae stuff coming oot o' it. Look, Ma. Look at this. Isn't it terrible!'

Big Lily cast an indifferent eye over the red and swollen thumb. 'I've seen a man lose his finger when it looked like that,' she said. 'I hope you can still do your work. You needn't think you're getting off it.'

'Maybe she needs a doctor,' suggested Wee Lily.

'We havenae the time nor the money for doctors,' was Big Lily's reply. 'Tak' her over to Tibbie and see what she can do.'

Tibbie wrinkled her brow as she gently held Kitty's hand in hers.

'What a queer thing!' she said. 'Marie cut her thumb in the same place as this. I dressed it for her the day before yesterday and it's nearly healed now, though I think it'll leave a scar. What have you two been playing at? Were you touching broken glass or a sharp knife or something down there at the river?'

Kitty shook her head. She was feeling feverish and light-headed and her thumb hurt worse than ever. All she wanted to do was to lie down and go to sleep. Tibbie treated her kindly, washed the thumb and made her steep it in a bowl of warm water in which she dropped oil of lavender. The fumes were very soothing and Kitty felt her head swim while Tibbie anointed and dressed the thumb.

'It'll no' fall off, Tib, will it?' asked Wee Lily anxiously.

'No, Lily, but she'll have to try to keep it clean. In a couple of days I'll look at it again.' Then Tibbie turned to Kitty and told her, 'Don't go playing with knives, that's my advice to you. You're too old for that sort of carry-on.'

Back in the bothy Big Lily eyed Kitty's white bandage and asked Wee Lily, 'What did Tibbie say?'

'She said it'll be all right if we keep it clean. She told Kitty no' to play with knives.'

The innocent words rang out in the room like a clarion call and Kitty felt her whole body freeze in terror as she saw her grandmother stiffen. Big Lily was sharp and never missed anything that interested her.

'She said what?' she asked.

'Tibbie told Kitty no' to play wi' knives. She said she must have been messing about with a knife to get a cut like that.'

Big Lily turned to her granddaughter, who was sitting very still with her heart beating in her ears like a hammer. 'How did you cut your finger?' she asked.

'A bit o' glass… a bit I found on the riverbank…' Kitty stammered. She did not have the time to get out any more words, for her grand-mother's hand caught her along the side of the head and sent her flying from the chair.

'You bloody little liar you. You're the one that took my knife, not Jake. You're the thief, aren't you?'

'I'm not, I'm not,' Kitty protested but she was wasting her breath. Big Lily was on to her with terrible fury, hands slapping, boots kicking. She lay huddled on the floor and covered her head with her bent arms while punishment rained down on her. She was saved by her mother, who jumped between them and pushed the furious attacker away from the girl. 'Leave her be. You'll kill her,' she cried out.

'She deserves to be killed. She's a bloody thief. She took my knife and blamed it on Jake. She's like her father, a rogue through and through. Where's my knife? Give me back my knife!' Big Lily's last shouts were addressed to Kitty who lay gasping on the floor.

'I havenae got your knife,' she protested. It would have taken torture on the rack to get the truth out of her. The knife represented all the hatred between her grandmother and herself and she was determined to be the winner of the war between them.

At first she thought that she had got away with it because for several days Big Lily retreated into a state of silent antagonism and stalked around the farm not speaking to the others. Her presence in the bothy was like a black, overhanging cloud but, fortunately, she took to leaving them alone in the evenings after the work was over, disappearing without saying where she was going.

On the fifth evening she came back before nightfall but she was not alone. When she pushed open the bothy door, a dark figure was standing at her back and she said loudly, 'In ye go, Jake. Mak yersel at hame.'

To the astonishment of her daughter and granddaughter, she pushed the ragged, figure of Jake into the circle of firelight. After he was sent away from Townhead, they'd heard he was taken on as a labourer at the Rosewell abattoir, not a job for the squeamish. To anyone who would listen he related his grievances against Big Lily, but now it seemed as if he and his persecutor were on friendly terms again because she actually offered him a mug of ale, which he accepted.

Then she turned to Wee Lily who was sitting with her jaw hanging in astonishment and said, 'Get up and fetch ale for Jake. You'd better get used to lookin' after your husband.'

Wee Lily's face went red and then white. She shook her head slowly and said, 'Aw no, Ma. I'm no' getting merrit.'

Big Lily's reply was very definite. 'You're marrying Jake and that's an end o' it.'

Kitty sprang to her mother's defence. 'But she doesnae like him. She's feared of him,' she cried as she ran across the floor and put both arms round Wee Lily's shaking shoulders.

Big Lily charged over and grabbed the girl by the hair, jerking her head back cruelly. 'This is no business of yours. You'll no' even be here to see it happen. You're oot o' here tomorrow. I've fixed that up too.'

Kitty stood her ground. 'I'm staying here to look after my mam.'

Big Lily laughed. 'She'll no' need you to look after her when she's got a man in her bed and another bairn in her arms. You're going to

Falconwood. I've fixed up with Tom Liddle to take you as his bondager lassie. Now we've got Jake back, you're no' needed here.'

Wee Lily, huddled stricken in her chair, seemed to come to life. 'No' Tom Liddle, Ma, dinna send her to Tom Liddle. Ye ken what he's like wi' lassies.' For all her simplicity, she relished gossip and never forgot what she'd been told.

Big Lily answered her daughter without looking at her because she was staring ferociously at Kitty. 'What does it matter with her kind? That's all they're good for,' she said gleefully.

Jake, who'd been standing in the middle of the floor twisting his cloth cap in his hands, suddenly turned and made for the door but Big Lily grabbed his sleeve and held on to him. 'You're staying here. It's her that's going,' she said nodding in Kitty's direction.

Wee Lily burst into loud tears. 'I dinna want to get merrit. I'm fine the way I am.'

'Nonsense. It's time you were wed. You're twenty-eight years old and you can have other bairns,' said her mother briskly.

Kitty, made brave by anger, stepped between the two women. 'You can't marry her to him…' she said pointing scornfully at the shambling figure of Jake.

Big Lily stared bleakly at her. 'It's got nothing to do wi' you. She'll do what I tell her. She hasnae ony choice and when I hand you over to Tom Liddle I dinna care if I never see you again.'

Early next morning, before dawn broke, Kitty was marched the mile and a half over the hill to Falconwood by her grandmother. Neither of them spoke a single word on the way. All the girl took with her was an old work skirt and a frayed staw hat that Big Lily had hauled out of the trunk beneath the bed. On her feet were the broken boots. She hadn't even had time to dig up her precious tin box.

The farmyard at Falconwood was deserted but she could see that it was excessively neat and tidy with fresh paint everywhere and not a single weed daring to grow between the cobblestones in front of the stable door.

Big Lily knocked on the door of a cottage standing at the end of a line and facing a little burn. A grey-haired woman answered and all Big Lily said, with a sideways thrust of her chin, was, 'This is her.'

A hand came out and beckoned to Kitty to enter the cottage while her grandmother turned on her heel and marched off without a word of farewell. The cottage kitchen was dark but Kitty soon became aware that two pairs of cold, hard eyes were staring at her.

Both of the Liddles were in their fifties, a childless, pious, sour-looking pair. Mrs Liddle always wore black, which gave her the appearance of a professional mourner and she was renowned locally for her God-fearingness because she attended church in Rosewell twice every Sunday in spite of the handicap of severe rheumatics which made her walk like a slow crab. Her husband Tom had a mean, narrow mouth, tiny suspicious eyes, and a red-mottled complexion. His grey hair was always greasy and marked in runnels by the comb he used to tidy it; his shoulders were narrow and his legs bowed.

While his wife stood surveying Kitty with her arms crossed over her breast, he sat at the table slurping up porridge with evident relish. Then, as if to emphasise his superiority, he handed his wife his empty plate and said, 'I'll have some more of that.'

She hobbled to the fire and ladled out another large helping. Nothing was offered to the newcomer whose stomach was rumbling with hunger and whose mouth watered, but she kept her expression impassive because she did not want them to know how much she longed for something to eat.

Her eyes scrutinised Liddle and she thought, What an ugly little man. He must have been ugly even when he was young. The fear of him, which had oppressed her ever since she saw her mother's reaction to his name, lightened. I'm capable of coping with that little whelp, she thought scornfully.

Her gaze disconcerted him and he spoke. 'I hope you're no' yin of them idlers. We havenae ony time for idlers here.'

'I'm not scared of work,' said Kitty.

'Your granny's a good worker but your mother's a daftie. I hope you dinna take after her or you'll be no use to me and I'll have to send you back,' was his next remark delivered in a sneering voice.

Kitty hated it when people made disparaging comments about her mother. 'My mam's a good worker too,' she protested.

Mrs Liddle chipped in with, 'That kind work well enough when they're told what to do. She was dropped on her head when she was wee, wasn't she?'

Kitty glared at the woman. 'I dinna ken. She's just a little bit slow, that's all, but she's able to work well enough.'

'What'll happen to her when your granny goes?' said Mrs Liddle sanctimoniously.

'I'll take care of her,' said Kitty fiercely.

Seeing that she wasn't going to gather any gossip from the girl, Mrs Liddle became brisk. 'When my man's done eating,' she said, 'you can take the dishes out to the back door and wash them. Then fill the coal bucket and sweep the hearth.'

There was a bucket of scummy-looking water outside the scullery door in which Kitty dipped the plates and cutlery. The sun was up now but a chill mist was drifting up the valley. Her fingers tingled with cold as she dipped them in the water and she felt herself shuddering, for her grandmother had omitted to buy her a jacket and the shawl she'd got from Tibbie had been left behind. She had only the thin covering of her cotton blouse to protect her from the cold.

She went back inside and soon warmed up because she was kept busy. Mrs Liddle sat at the side of the fire, watching her do their chores. When she finished she was told, 'Now you'd better get yourself across to the yard as quick as you can. Liddle's waiting for you.'

It was half-past six and the Falconwood workers were all lined up in the farmyard, waiting to be inspected by the steward, Mr Laidlaw. When he arrived Kitty was surprised to see that he looked as if he might be a lawyer or a minister. He held a sheet of paper from which he solemnly read out the tasks of the day, detailing some men to field work, some to carting and others to cleaning out the sheds. The women he left to the last.

When Liddle and his co-workers hurried away, Laidlaw turned to Kitty, who was standing on her own.

'You're a new face. Who are you?' he asked.

'I'm Kitty Scott. Liddle's new bondager,' she said. She could not bring herself to call Liddle 'mister' or use his first name.

Laidlaw nodded. 'Oh yes, I remember. He spoke to me about you. You're from Camptounfoot, aren't you? I knew Craigie before he was sent to Edinburgh.'

Kitty nodded. She'd never seen Craigie but had heard plenty about him throughout her life. His presence seemed to brood over the district though he was forty miles away.

Laidlaw went on, 'We'll find you something to do. MacPhee can take you in hand.' He turned on his heel and called out, 'MacPhee, come here.'

Kitty was to discover that nobody ever called the bondager fore-woman at Falconwood anything but MacPhee. If she'd been given a first name it had been forgotten long ago. MacPhee was very tall, as tall as Big Lily who was nearly six feet, but she was thin instead of heavy. In fact, she looked as if she'd been put together from the broken, gnarled branches of a tree – even her fingers looked like tied-together bundles of twigs. Her face beneath the tied-down bondager's bonnet was deeply wrinkled, pale and lugubrious. Kitty felt a nervous giggle rising to her lips when she saw this tall, gaunt apparition advancing towards her through the early-morning mist.

'Take this lassie in hand. Find her something to do,' said Mr Laidlaw.

MacPhee gazed at Kitty and asked, 'Do you no' hae a jaikit, lass?'

Kitty shook her head. 'No.'

'You'll need a jaikit. I like a' my woman to be well turned-oot.'

Kitty nodded, wondering how this piece of news could be sent to Big Lily, but MacPhee seemed to have the power of reading her thoughts and obviously knew a lot about the bondager's bairn.

'I doot your granny will nae gie you one. I'll see what I can find. Come on,' she said and Kitty followed her across the yard to where the other bondagers were waiting.

There were seven of them altogether counting Kitty and MacPhee – two girls not much older than Kitty; two young women in their twenties and an older woman with russet-apple cheeks and a sweet smile. It was the last one to whom MacPhee spoke. 'Rosie, you must have an auld coat in your hoose. Will you give it to this lassie? She's Liddle's new girl, you know.'

The woman called Rosie nodded and smiled at Kitty. 'Och aye, of course. There's plenty of jaikits in oor place. My lassie left yin behind when she got married last year. Wait here and I'll go to get it.'

While she was away, MacPhee gave out the work orders for the day, detailing some of the women to cleaning out the cattle court; sending others to hoe turnips and telling Effie, one of the younger girls, to take Kitty and clean out the hen-houses.

When Rosie came back with a bundle in her arms, the bondagers all gathered round Kitty and helped her into a black jacket that was a good deal too big for her. They rolled up the sleeves and buttoned it up, then stood back and congratulated themselves. 'That'll do just grand. It'll keep you warm anyway. If you went out wi'oot a coat in the winter time you'd soon dee of the galloping consumption,' they told her.

Kitty was surprised at their kindness. She had not been treated that way by many people during her short life and wondered why they were taking so much trouble with her.

As they hurried to the field where the hen-houses stood, Effie grinned at her and said, 'You're lucky. MacPhee's taken a shine to you.'

'How do you know?' Kitty had thought MacPhee very grim.

'Because she's given you an easy job. If she didn't like you, you'd be in the cattle court shovelling shite.'

Kitty laughed. 'Cleaning a hen-house isn't an easy job either.'

'It's naething to oor cattleshed,' Effie told her. 'When you do that you're up to the waist in glaur and it takes days to get rid o' the stink.'

They worked well together, Effie wielding a brush and Kitty the big shovel. When they'd amassed a big pile of chicken droppings, Kitty was sent for a barrow into which the droppings were piled and she had to wheel them to the dung heap. By this time she'd taken off her new jacket because the sun had risen, promising another fine day. In its warm rays the dung heap steamed virulently and the smell seemed to hang around it like a miasma, a veil of stench.

At mid-morning Effie threw down her brush and sat on the grass with the hens pecking about her legs. 'Come on an' eat your piece,' she said to Kitty.

'What piece?'

'Dinna tell me that old bitch Annie Liddle didnae gie you a piece? You'll have to steal one from her tomorrow. Come on, share mine. I've plenty.'

She handed out a slice of bread and cheese to Kitty, who took it gratefully for her hunger was prodigious by this time.

'I'll give you a tip,' said Effie. 'What you have to do is warn Liddle that if he doesnae treat you right you'll tell Mr Laidlaw. He's mortally feared o' the steward because he's on his last warning with him. After the business wi' the last wee lassie, Laidlaw said if there was any more trouble he'd put Liddle off the place.'

'What wee lassie?' asked Kitty curiously.

Effie pulled a face. 'His last bondager. He takes in charity bairns. Nobody else'll give their lassies to him… he's funny wi' them if you know what I mean.'

Kitty's heart felt cold in her chest. 'What happened?' she asked.

Effie was eager to tell her. 'The poor wee soul was only ten years old. Her name was Bessie Maddiston. She was a foundling and they called her after the place her mother left her. She was that terrified of Liddle she'd start to cry if he as much as looked at her.'

'What happened to her?' asked Kitty.

'She died. Something went wrong with her inside the women said. She'd been bothered by Liddle and she was bleeding. She never said a word against him, though. She was too scared I think. The Liddles didnae send for a doctor soon enough and she died... She wasnae the first one that had trouble. The lassie before her ran away. You look out for yourself, Kitty, and if there's any trouble, run for MacPhee. Liddle's almost as scared for her as he is for Laidlaw.'

'Do you think there'll be trouble for me?' asked Kitty.

'It's as well to expect it. Folk like Liddle dinna change,' was Effie's reply.

Work finished on Falconwood that night at seven o'clock and because it was still light, Kitty decided to risk her grandmother's wrath and go back to Townhead to see her mother. There was no one in the farmyard when she got there and she tiptoed quietly over to the dairy door to see who was working there, for she could hear the banging of crocks coming from inside. Wee Lily, sleeves rolled up, was working alone, skimming the cream off the morning milk.

'Mam,' she called softly through the dairy window. 'Mam, it's me.'

Wee Lily whirled round and her face lit up with joy. 'Oh, bairn, come in so's she doesnae see you,' she whispered.

'Where is she?' whispered Kitty looking round.

'She's gone to Rosewell to fix up the wedding.'

'Your wedding?' asked Kitty and Wee Lily nodded miserably.

'Aye.'

'When is it?'

'I dinna ken.' Kitty saw that her mother's face was quivering and desisted from more questions which would only upset her. There was obviously nothing to be done. Wee Lily wasn't capable of taking a stand against her mother and it was a miracle that she'd fought back enough when her child was born to be allowed to keep it. The girl put an arm round Wee Lily's waist and said, 'Don't you worry, Mam. When I'm big enough I'll take you to live with me. I've got to get back now but send a message to me by one of the wee laddies from the village when you're to be married and I'll try to be there. Don't forget.'

Wee Lily nodded. 'I'll no' forget. I'll send you a message. I dinna want to marry Jake.'

'I know, I know,' whispered Kitty hugging her again. 'But don't worry. You're bigger than him. If he gives you any trouble just knock him down.'

Wee Lily gave her childish laugh, throwing back her head, 'Aye that's right. I'll knock him doon…'

When she left her mother, Kitty ran across the road to Tibbie's cottage and tapped on the back door. Marie answered and smiled. 'I was wondering what had happened to you. I haven't seen you for days.'

'I came to say I've been sent away.'

'Where to?'

'Falconwood.'

Marie laughed. 'Falconwood! But that's just over there. I can see the roof of the big house up among the trees.'

Kitty eyed her bleakly. 'I'm at Falconwood farm. It's behind the house, farther down the valley.'

'But not far, not any farther than a mile. You'll be able to come home every day if you want to.'

'My granny won't let me. She's turned me out. She says my mither's got to marry Jake so's she can have more bairns.'

Tibbie appeared at Marie's shoulder and both of them looked shocked. 'Your mother's getting married to Jake?' asked Tibbie in disbelief. She was going to say he was a halfwit but thought that might not be too tactful.

Kitty nodded fiercely. 'She doesnae want to marry him but my granny's fixed it up. She needs another hand on the place and she's taking Jake instead o' me.'

Tibbie shook her head slowly. 'It's maybe not a bad thing for you to get away, Kitty…'

The girl nodded. 'I know, but she's bound me to work for Tom Liddle.'

Tibbie's face revealed that she knew the stories about Liddle. 'That wasnae very sensible of her,' she conceded.

'She did it for spite,' said Kitty.

Two days later she was working with MacPhee and the other women when an urchin from Camptounfoot came running over the field shouting, 'Yer ma's gettin' merrit in Rosewell this mornin'. She sent me to tell you.'

Kitty looked at MacPhee with a silent plea in her eyes, so the tall woman nodded and said in a kindly tone, 'Awa' ye go. But dinna stay all day.'

She ran all the way to Rosewell Abbey, part of which served as a parish church for Rosewell and Camptounfoot. This church was in a walled-off section of the ruined nave, which was makeshift and dingy. The whitewashed walls were streaked with green mould and damp but there was one beautiful stained-glass window high in the wall overlooking the burial ground. A strong smell of rot and decay pervaded the whole place and it was hard to believe that this had once been a magnificent medieval building where God was worshipped with pomp and great richness.

A few traces of past glory still remained for those who cared to look. Delicate sandstone arches soared overhead, branching up and knotting together in sculpted roses. At the tops of the supporting pillars were elaborately carved finials of flowers and fruit, musicians, angels, devils, even a pig playing the bagpipes. These carvings were darkened by hundreds of years of soot and smoke from the candles used to light the cavernous interior.

It started to rain as Kitty ran through the fields and a steady drip, drip, drip of water could be heard running off the broken arches that rose on each side of the approach to the door when she reached her destination.

There were only three people and the minister inside the church. Wee Lily, face blotched and lips trembling, did not look round when Kitty burst in. The minister was not bothering to hide the fact that his mind was on his midday meal which awaited him in the manse standing on the edge of the burying-ground. He had little sympathy with the poorest and least-educated of his parishioners and took little trouble when ministering to them.

As he asked them their names, he was planning to attend a meeting of the richest and most influential parishioners to discuss raising funds for the construction of a new parish church in a different site on the other side of the town. For Rosewell was growing rich and he wished it to worship its God in more salubrious surroundings than the broken-down ruins of the abbey.

The couple in front of him looked far from inspiring. Jake was trying to pretend that he understood what was being said… 'Procreation of children… cleaving unto no other… you may now kiss the bride,' gabbled the minister with his eyes raised to the church ceiling. The last bit was the only part of the service that was not completely incomprehensible to the participants and when the word 'kiss' was spoken Jake turned towards Wee Lily with his lips obscenely puckered but she drew back as if stabbed and gave a heart-rending sob.

Her mother, standing by her other side, gave her a jab in the ribs that sent her reeling into the chest of her bridegroom and the kiss was finally achieved but the minister was already walking away, drawing the band off his neck and thinking, I might as well read the marriage service over a couple of sheep for all that pair understood of it.

Disconsolately the bridal party trailed out into the rain ignoring the red-headed girl standing in an alcove at the rear of the church, but she ran after them and threw her arms round the bride crying, 'Oh, Mam, I'm sorry.'

Wee Lily sobbed even harder. She was dressed in a floppy cloth sun bonnet with a deep frill and the same cotton dress she had worn to the fair. Its tight puff sleeves made her upper arms look like mottled hams under the chill of the rain. The dress was too long and wet round the hem with water off the soaking grass, so she hitched it up and showed her heavy boots.

She clung to her daughter with tears running down her face and Jake took one look at them, jammed his cloth cap onto his head and walked away in the direction of the Abbey Hotel by the churchyard gate. The only thing for him to do now, he reckoned, was to celebrate his wedding day with ale and it looked like he would be celebrating alone.

Big Lily didn't try to stop him for she was grabbing the intruder by the shoulder and hissing, 'What're you doing here? You should be at work.'

Kitty wriggled away. 'MacPhee said I could come to my mother's wedding. She gave me time off for it.'

'She should have more sense. All you'll do is cause trouble,' snapped Big Lily.

Angrily Kitty broke away from her grandmother and turned to hug her mother, who was wiping her nose with the back of her hand and gulping hysterically.

'Dinna greet, Mam. When I'm able I'll come and take you away,' she told her.

Big Lily was furious. 'You'll do naething of the kind. You leave her be. You're just jealous in case she has any more bairns and then your nose'll be put oot o' joint,' she fumed, roughly hauling the girl back again and trying to push her off along the path, but Kitty was wiry and determined. She fought back.

'Leave me alane,' she shouted, her brown eyes flashing fire.

'Leave you alane. I'll flatten you!' threatened Big Lily, lifting her hand and opening the palm to give a stinging slap to Kitty's face. But she had miscalculated. Her granddaughter was growing up.

Big Lily only managed one blow. Before she could draw back her hand again, a balled fist connected with her chin. Her head snapped back, her eyes rolled and she fell over like a pole-axed stirk.

Kitty and Wee Lily looked at the body lying senseless in the middle of the path and then at each other.

'Oh my gosh, ye've kilt her,' gasped Wee Lily, stopping crying and kneeling by Big Lily's side, chafing the huge hands and calling anxiously, 'Ma, Ma, get up, Ma.'

Big Lily groaned and rolled her head about a little.

'She's not dead – worse luck,' said Kitty and turned to walk away. Behind her Wee Lily was helping the older woman to sit up and Big Lily gathered enough strength to shout, 'I'll kill you, you wee bitch. I'll kill you, by God I will. Don't let me see you again if you don't want a hammering.'

Kitty did not turn round but the minister, coming out of the vestry and heading across the wet grass to the manse, stopped in his tracks when he saw the tableau being enacted in the middle of the path.

'What do you think you're doing?' he shouted at Wee Lily who, totally confused, was trying to help her mother up and answer him at the same time.

'It's my ma, I'm helping my ma,' she stammered.

He was furious. 'What do you think this is? It's a holy place, not an alehouse.' He was sure they were drunk, for their faces were flaming red and the older woman was staggering.

'Where's the man?' he demanded. Wee Lily wordlessly pointed in the direction of the Abbey Hotel.

'I might have guessed as much. People like you shouldn't be allowed near a church. Get away home this minute and don't cause any more trouble,' he ordered.

Kitty had not seen their humiliation, for she was running across the fields which she knew so well. As she ran, tears poured down her cheeks and she let them flow unchecked, finding a strange relief in giving way to them. She gulped and sobbed till the pain of her fury of grief made her ribs and chest ache but still she could not stop. Through the many hardships she had endured in her life, she wept rarely and now it seemed as if all the pent-up tears were pouring from her at once.

At last she felt cleansed, wiped her face on her sleeve and stood very still thinking about her life and wondering what lay before her. The hatred she felt for her grandmother was something that she was beginning to treasure. She could feed off it. It would fuel her and armour her.

She wondered if she was really jealous of her mother marrying. She acknowledged that she did not want Wee Lily to marry Jake but her dislike of him was not jealousy, it was more fastidiousness and she hated the idea that he would force himself on her innocent and unwilling mother. It would not have been so bad if she had been married off to someone with whom she could have enjoyed married life because she probably had the capacity to relish that in the same way she relished her food, but Jake was little better than a rutting boar and Kitty was afraid that all her mother would experience would be unfeeling re-creations of the rape that still haunted her confused mind.

As far as Kitty could see, nothing lay ahead for any of them but misery, work and a blanking-out of the mind. If she was to escape the degradation of her mother and grandmother, she would have to get away... she'd have to walk and walk, over the hills that rimmed her horizon. She'd have to find out what lay on the other side.

'Hoo did it go then?' asked MacPhee when she saw Kitty coming through the field.

'Grand, grand, they got married and then they went home,' said the girl in what she hoped was a light voice, but the forewoman noticed there were tear marks on her face and said consolingly, 'Weddings aye mak me greet too.'

'I've no' been greetin',' said Kitty defensively.

'All right, if you say so, but you should be glad your mother's married. There'll be somebody to look after her when your granny's gone.' MacPhee had worked in and around Falconwood all her life and knew Big Lily and her daughter well.

'I just wish she hadnae married Jake, that's all,' said Kitty.

'But there's no' much choice for her and she wouldnae want to leave Townhead, would she? It's her father's place after all and she's got a right to be there, though Craigie's sisters would deny it.'

As soon as she'd spoken MacPhee realised from Kitty's surprised expression that she did not know the secret of Wee Lily's paternity and wished that she'd been more discreet, for she was a kindly woman in spite of her forbidding exterior.

Kitty was onto the slip like a terrier after a rat, however. 'What do you mean? My granny has aye told me that she couldnae mind who my mother's father was.'

'Oh well, maybe she cannae. Maybe I'm wrong.' MacPhee was hurrying across the field with Kitty on her heels.

'Who did you hear it was? You must know if you said his place was at Townhead,' she persisted.

'I cannae mind,' mumbled MacPhee but she was lost and knew it.

Kitty put a hand on her arm and held her back. 'Please, MacPhee, please tell me. I've a right to know, haven't I? After all, he was my grandfather whoever he is... Please tell me the name.'

'What I heard is maybe no' true. It's maybe just gossip. But folk say that your mother's father was Craigie Scott.'

Kitty stopped dead and felt as if the breath had been driven out of her body by a huge blow. 'Craigie! Our farmer, our boss! It cannae be Craigie,' she gasped.

'Folk say it was. It wouldnae be unusual – except...'

'Except what?'

But MacPhee had been sufficiently indiscreet already and wasn't going to say any more.

'Farmers often father bairns on their bondagers. You'd find plenty of them round here if you knew the truth,' she hurriedly added.

'There's something else, isn't there? What else do you know?' asked Kitty standing her ground, but MacPhee drew herself up to her formidable height and snapped, 'I havenae time to stand here blethering wi' you. Get ourself a spade and go back to the field. Effie's there and she needs a hand.'

Kitty took her place beside her friend and started working close enough so that they could speak to each other without shouting.

'Did your ma get merrit then?' asked Effie.

'Aye, she did.' Kitty sounded glum and the other girl glanced over her shoulder to say, 'Dinna mind. It's no sae bad being merrit. I wish I could find a nice lad to take into my bed instead of having to lie with them under the hedge when I feel like a bit o'comfort.'

Effie liked talking about sex and would go with any man who asked her. She had become Kitty's chief source of information on the subject and while they worked Effie regaled her with graphic accounts of her couplings with various members of the Falconwood staff.

'MacPhee said a funny thing just now,' Kitty suddenly told her.

Effie laughed. 'MacPhee funny. I dinna believe it. That woman's never made a joke in her life.'

'I don't mean that kind of funny. She said something strange. She said that Craigie Scott's my mother's father.'

'What's strange about that? Somebody had to be her father and there wasnae all that many laddies around Townhead. Anyway, folk said Craigie shot that navvy that couped your mother because she was his lassie. He admitted to the polis that he was her father. Folk knew about it before that of course, but no one said anything because of him and your granny…'

'What about him and my granny?' asked Kitty, stopping working and looking fiercely over at Effie who said, 'I dinna mean to insult you or anything, honest I don't.'

'Go on, tell me, dinna beat about the bush. I want to hear it.' Kitty was speaking through gritted teeth.

'I've aye heard that Craigie fathered Wee Lily in spite of him and your granny being brother and sister.'

Kitty could say nothing because she felt sick. A terrible spasm seized her stomach and she threw down her spade and cried out, 'Oh God, I'm going to vomit.' She ran to the edge of the field to throw up. When she came back a few moments later her face was paper-white. 'Is what you said true?' she asked Effie, who was working away with a will.

'About Craigie and Big Lily you mean? Aye, so they say, but who can tell really? The only folk who know for sure are your granny and Craigie Scott and he's up in the prison so we cannae ask him.' Effie laughed.

'But I thought you werenae meant to do it with your brother,' asked Kitty bemusedly.

'Nor are ye but some folk do. They get daft bairns though and the line's rotten after that,' said Effie complacently.

Kitty felt sick again, for the unthinking words rang in her ears... 'Daft bairns... the line's rotten after that'.

My mother's simple. That means that I'm rotten. If I have children they might be dafties too, she thought. She felt as if a door had been opened revealing secrets which she had never suspected. She was being told things that she would rather not know and they made her hate her grandmother even more for being the cause of such horrible revelations.

Evening was drawing in when she and Effie returned to the tool-shed to put their spades in the long rack. Effie began flirting with a couple of ploughboys and Kitty offered to stack her tool for her and carried the two of them into the shed, glad to go into a quiet place where she would be alone and able to think. She was standing in the shadows when the door opened behind her and a voice said, 'Your ma'll be getting bedded the night then.'

Liddle stood there with a leer on his face. It was not possible to get to the door for he was blocking her way out.

'She'll be seeing one o' these again,' he said next and pulled open his unbuttoned fly to reveal a grey penis in a state of semi-erection. Kitty stared at it dispassionately.

'You're a dirty old man and if you try anything on wi' me, I'll tell Mr Laidlaw on you,' she warned him, but at the same time taking the precaution of lifting a sharp sickle off the wall and holding it menacingly in her hand.

He backed away. 'You'll be like the rest o' your family, keen enough on it when you're a bit older,' he jeered as he backed away.

'I'll never be that keen that I could fancy you,' she snapped.

'It's no' a question of what you fancy. Wi' your family it's a case of who you can get – like your granny and her brother,' he shouted as he made his escape, tucking himself into his pants as he went and leaving her shaking with anger.

# Chapter Seven

The corn was ripening to a brilliant golden colour on the morning that Marie walked to the station at Rosewell with Tibbie on her way to her first art class in Edinburgh. They were both as excited as they would have been were she going to Timbuktu.

Marie felt very smart in the new clothes that she and Tibbie had bought from the best draper's in Rosewell. They'd chosen a soft blue dress, a Paisley shawl with a deep fringe and a maidenly little bonnet with artificial violets tucked into the rim. Everything smelt, and felt, new, which added to the feeling of adventure.

'You look real bonny,' Tibbie said as the train was about to leave and Marie smiled her thanks. She was in need of all the reassurance she could get. Going to Edinburgh was the boldest thing she'd ever done and she wished Kitty could have been there to see her off, but the harvest was beginning and it was impossible for her to get away from Falconwood.

Bethya's maid was already seated in the corner of a second-class carriage, looking bored and indifferent. Mindful of David's expressed concern about his sister braving Edinburgh alone, Bethya had detailed a housemaid called Ellen Merrilees to go with her. The girl was Edinburgh-born and boasted of her familiarity with the city. Unfortunately, she was also disdainful of country people and resented being told to take care of a girl who was unused to travelling.

The train was slow in starting and Marie, leaning from the open window, thought her heart would burst with nerves before it finally pulled away. Her nervousness was not only because she'd never been to a city before, she was also uncertain that she was doing the right thing. She was afraid that as soon as the art master saw what she could do, he'd send her straight back to Rosewell and this uncertainty had been fuelled by David who'd been steadily undermining her for weeks.

First of all he suggested that her nervous disposition would not be able to cope with the hustle and bustle of a city; then he switched to the tack that she would be scorned by the other students, girls who came from a very different social background to her own. He did this by advising her how to cope with them.

'Don't let those upper-class girls frighten you,' he told her over and over again. 'They're not really any better than us. They just think they are.'

If she protested that she was going to learn how to paint and not to meet other girls, he smiled. 'Of course you are. And you mustn't be put out if the master says cruel things. He'll be used to really good painters. You mustn't let him sap your confidence.'

At last they chugged out of the station, leaving Tibbie waving frantically on the platform. Maddiston was the first stop and when they drew into the station, Marie saw her brother on the platform.

'David, David,' she called leaning from the carriage and he came running along to take her hand.

'Be brave. And remember you don't have to keep on going if you don't like it,' he said earnestly.

Behind her, Marie heard Ellen Merrilees sniff scornfully and when the train started again, she said, 'I've never known folk to make such a fuss about a wee train trip. Haven't any of you been anywhere before?'

Marie shook her head. 'I certainly haven't and neither has David. Our father was one of the workers who helped to build this railway line though, so he must have travelled a lot.'

'Might have guessed as much,' said Ellen, who shared the general condescension towards navvies. The knowledge made her treat Marie in an even more cavalier way.

It took all Marie's pride not to clutch the maid's arm when they stepped off the train at Waverley station, for the noise, the hustle and bustle were overwhelming. The city brought out a new aspect in Ellen too. She seemed to become taller and more bold than she was in Rosewell and intent on showing Marie how familiar she was with urban chaos. Shouldering her way through a crowd of other travellers, hauling Marie behind her, she headed for the steep flight of steps leading to Princes Street. It was a breathless climb but when they'd completed it, they found themselves in a broad thoroughfare packed with carriages, people on horses, men pulling handcarts and horse-drawn tramcars.

Marie quailed. Her heart began to beat very fast and she drew back into the mouth of the stairs, wishing she could retreat into the station, but Ellen had other ideas.

'The place you're going to is number ninety-three Princes Street,' she said consulting a piece of paper she held in her hand. 'This here's Princes Street and it can't be far. I'll take you there and come back for you at a quarter past three.'

Though she resented being sent to look after a yokel, it was good to be back in her native city and free to spend half a day visiting friends and relations in the High Street, where she'd been born. She intended to get rid of Marie as soon as possible and make the most of her freedom.

She set a good pace, striding along the pavement and pushing loiterers aside till they found ninety-three, an elegant town house facing directly across to Edinburgh Castle, which sat high on its crag on the southern side of Princes Street.

A flight of broad white steps with black railings on each side led up to the front door from the pavement and Ellen stopped at the foot of them.

'This is it,' she said indicating the number painted on the door. 'You'll surely be able to manage to get yourself in? All you've got to do is rap the knocker.'

Marie flushed, angered by the assumption that she was a total incompetent. 'Of course I can. I see you're in a hurry. Please go.'

The maid didn't protest but swept off down the crowded pavement like a sea cutter.

Marie lifted the enormous knocker and dropped it in its bed. The noise it made was so loud that she stepped back in alarm. Almost at once the door was opened by a middle-aged woman wearing a mob-cap and carrying a feather duster, who took one look at Marie and said, 'Up you go, my dear. He's waiting for you.'

A wide stone staircase with elegant metal banisters led to a broad landing off which a half-open door showed a long room overlooking Princes Street. It had vast, uncurtained windows to the front and the rear and the floor was polished wood that shone like glass. Dotted here and there across its wide expanse were tall wooden easels and canvas stools. There was no sign of anyone, however, and Marie hovered uncertainly on the threshold till the woman in the hall called up, 'In you go. I'll tell him you've arrived.'

As soon as she stepped into the salon, something wonderful happened. It might have been the smell of paint; it might have been the sight of the easels and the clarity of light flowing into the gleaming empty space, but her fingers suddenly itched to pick up a brush and start painting. Dazzled she walked down the middle of the floor staring at half-finished canvases propped on the easels and did not turn her head when there was a footfall behind her.

'Do you like anything in particular?' asked a warm voice and she whirled round to see a plump little man with an upstanding frill of grey hair and gold-rimmed eyeglasses. His clothes looked as if he had stepped out of the past, because he was wearing black silk stockings, black pantaloons and shoes with silver buckles, a high-necked white shirt and a black waistcoat that buttoned over his round stomach. The thought that flashed through Marie's head when she saw him was, He looks like Humpty Dumpty.

This pleasing little vision came prancing towards her, walking on his toes. His hand was outheld and he cried, 'Good day, my dear, good day. You are Lady Godolphin's young friend, aren't you? She wrote so glowingly of you, I've been looking forward to meeting you. My name is D'Arcy Abernethy.'

All Marie's nerves and misgivings were dispelled by the stimulating atmosphere of the studio and the warmth of this greeting. 'Yes, I'm Marie Benjamin, Mr Abernethy,' she said.

'*Professor* D'Arcy Abernethy,' he corrected her in a kindly way before taking her arm and leading her up to a window. 'Just look out there. Isn't that a wonderful view? What other city in Europe has a view like that?' he asked her.

'I've never been anywhere else,' she told him and he laughed.

'But you will, my dear, if Lady Godolphin is right. I hope you've brought some of your work to show me.'

She was carrying a small document case bought for her by Tibbie and raised it in his direction. 'Yes, they're in here,' she told him.

He frowned. 'Not very big, are they?'

She didn't explain that she had never had access to large sheets of paper and practised her art on scraps or single sheets. Her nervousness returned.

Bending down she opened the case and brought out a sheaf of watercolours of the countryside around Camptounfoot and some of wild flowers that she'd done during her wanderings with Kitty.

He held them up in front of his face and peered closely at them, one after the other. This took a long time, for after he'd looked he laid them down on a tabletop and bent over them, finger on plump chin.

Marie felt as if she were going to faint, for the suspense was almost more than she could bear and her self-esteem was falling with every moment that passed. David's warnings about the high standard of art in Edinburgh resounded in her mind.

'I'll go back to the train and forget all about this,' she said at last, watching the Professor's solemn face.

He shook his head and asked, 'Have you any others with you?'

'No, I'm sorry, that's all I brought. And anything else I've got isn't better I'm afraid.'

'Don't be sorry, my dear. These are delightful. Lady Godolphin's right. You have an amazing talent, although it's quite unpolished. This flower picture has a Dürer-esque quality about it, and in the landscapes, the skies are good and skies are very hard to paint. Yes, you've mastered that. Remarkable in one so young. The perspective's a little out in places... that needs work. And your range of colour is unsophisticated. You need to widen your palette.'

'Do you really like them?' she whispered, only half-believing him.

'Like them? They're delightful. It will be a pleasure to teach you, my dear, a real pleasure. We'll start with drawing practice. The class does not begin till half-past one but I'll fetch you a chair and a table and you can do some charcoal sketches. Wait here a moment till I get things organised.'

While Marie was gathering her sketches together again and putting them back in the case, the woman who had opened the door to her, came into the studio and asked, 'Have you eaten? I'm sure you haven't and Papa is so silly, he'd never ask. When he's talking pictures, he doesn't think about food.'

She'd called him Papa and Marie had thought she was the maid! Her face flushed scarlet with embarrassment at her mistake, but the woman did not mind. She was obviously used to being taken for the servant.

'I'll get you something,' she said sweetly to Marie. 'Sit down there on the window seat and I'll bring it up.' She brought bread and cheese, an apple and a glass of red wine, the first Marie had ever tasted. She was brushing breadcrumbs off her skirt when a group of young women came into the studio, laughing and chattering among themselves. They were all beautifully dressed in clothes and jewellery that made Marie's gown look insignificant.

One of them looked across at her and asked, 'The new girl? The Prof said you were coming today. Lady Godolphin's friend, aren't you?'

Marie nodded and one by one they smiled at her, saying their names which she immediately forgot because she was so flustered. The only one she remembered was a girl with very black hair swept tightly back from an elfin face with a pointed chin and sparkling dark eyes. Her figure was slight and wiry and she looked like a sporty young boy.

'I'm Amy Roxburgh,' she said with a wide smile before walking over to the far window and hiding herself behind a large white canvas propped up on an easel.

Before long the Professor came back, followed by his mob-capped daughter, who was struggling to carry a fold-up chair and a table at the same time.

'Put them down there, Milly,' he said indicating a spot by the window. 'Then go and bring George.'

George turned out to be a huge plaster-cast head of a Roman emperor wearing a wreath of laurel. He was laid on the window ledge and adjusted to just the right angle by the Professor, who then indicated that Marie should sit down in front of him.

'Make a drawing of George, my dear. Note his fine nose and the nobility of his brow. Make him look like the ruler of a vast empire. Go to it!' he exclaimed, clapping his hands and skipping off into the middle of his other students.

As he made his rounds, Marie could hear him making comments on their work. 'Oh no, Sibyll, your flowers look dead. They're alive, paint them as if they are living and vibrant. I want to be able to *smell* them!'

When he came to Amy Roxburgh at her stance in the far window he stood back and sighed, 'My dear Miss Roxburgh, everything you paint is larger than life and three times more coloured. Do try to tone things down a little.'

Gradually, however, as Marie pored over her drawing of George, the world around her withdrew and she became oblivious to the talk and laughter of the other students, who, as three o'clock approached, left off their painting and gathered again in chattering groups. It took a hand on her shoulder and the Professor's voice in her ear to break her concentration.

'It's ten past three, Miss Benjamin. Your maid has come to take you to the station. That's a good drawing you've done but when you come back I'll show you how to master charcoal in order to give depth. You're coming back on Friday, aren't you?'

She stood up, wiping her charcoal-stained fingers on her handkerchief. After concentrating so long on the plaster cast of the Roman emperor it took a few seconds for her eyes to adjust and she staggered a little.

She did not fall because a hand slipped under her elbow and a laughing voice said, 'You work too hard. You mustn't do that or you'll show all the rest of us up. Most of us are only here to pass the time, you know.'

It was Amy Roxburgh. Marie recovered quickly and said, 'I'm sure you're not!'

Amy nodded solemnly. 'But we are. It's good to be able to paint little pictures. It gives us a nice hobby for when we're respectable married ladies. But it wouldn't do to be too serious, would it?'

Unsure if she was joking or not, Marie stared at her and Amy grinned like a cheeky urchin. 'The Prof said your maid's waiting. You'd better hurry. I know what maids are like. Positive tyrants. I'll see you again, won't I? I always come here on Tuesdays and Fridays.'

'Yes, I'll be back on Friday,' said Marie. All her dread about the painting class had disappeared and she could hardly bear to tear herself away from George.

The maid, Ellen, was waiting at the front door. Her face was scarlet and she smelled strongly of drink, for she'd spent three hours in one of the taverns of the Old Town among the cronies of her youth. When she saw Marie coming down the stairs, she ran forward and grabbed her arm. 'Come on, hurry up, we'll miss the train if we don't run.'

Amy, descending the stair behind Marie, laughed and said, 'Just like I said, tyrants. I'd get another maid if I were you, my dear.'

Ellen was pulling Marie out into the street, dodging in and out between strolling people like a rabbit making its getaway from a hungry dog. Marie had no choice but to run after her.

When they got to the station, Marie said angrily, 'What's all the hurry about? The train doesn't leave for another ten minutes.'

Ellen didn't bother to answer but dashed straight into the station buffet and ordered herself a glass of gin.

'I need a drink before I can face that journey with you again,' she said rudely, throwing it back and pushing the glass across the polished wooden top for a refill. By the time they boarded their train, she was staggering and two old women, already seated in the carriage, drew back from her in distaste.

When they alighted it was Marie who was looking after the maid. She took her into the ladies' waiting-room and poured cold water on her face. 'Can you manage to get back to Bella Vista on your own?' she asked.

Ellen bridled. 'Of coorse I can. Awa' ye go and leave me be. I'm weel able to tak care o' mysel', no' like some folk.' In her cups she had abandoned the carefully modulated accent she adopted when at work and reverted to pure Edinburgh.

Marie left, determined that she had no need of a chaperone any longer. Friday could not come fast enough as far as she was concerned.

One important thing had to be done before she could return to Edinburgh, however. She must go to Bella Vista and report to Lady Godolphin about her first visit to the painting class.

Bethya was lying on the sofa with her eyes closed when the butler announced the arrival of Miss Marie Benjamin.

Marie, shyly entering the room behind the imposing man-servant was surprised to see the change in Lady Godolphin since their last meeting. She was no longer a figure of glamour in a rose-bedecked bonnet but a thin invalid lying on a sofa with the funny-looking dogs snuffling beside her. Her lips were tinged blue and her glorious hair seemed to have become less vital, for the long side tresses lay limply on her shoulders. However, her voice and manner were as vivacious as ever.

'My dear Miss Benjamin!' she exclaimed. 'How kind. Have you come to tell me all about Professor Abernethy's class? I've been dying to hear how you got on with him. He's very quaint, I believe.

Marie took the chair that was indicated to her and said awkwardly, 'Yes, your ladyship. He's kind and he said he could teach me a lot – about colour and perspective in particular.'

Bethya said, 'I do hope that means you've decided to continue going to Edinburgh.'

The girl nodded. 'Oh yes, I want to go on attending the classes. The atmosphere of the studio makes me want to work. I'm so grateful to you, your ladyship.' Marie was concerned at Bethya's wan look, however, and soon rose from her seat, saying, 'I don't want to tire you out. I only came to say it was a wonderful experience and that I'd like to continue going to the classes...'

But Bethya gave a little gasp and gestured to her to sit still. 'I'm only a little tired. Though I wonder what I've got to be tired about. I don't seem to have to do anything but lie here. My husband is quite exasperated with me. No wonder he's gone to London again! I want to hear everything from you today because I'm going back south tomorrow.'

Marie was genuinely disappointed. 'So soon! I'm sorry to hear that,' she said.

Bethya smiled. 'But I'll only be away till next year. When I come back I want to see all the pictures you've painted.'

Marie blushed. 'I hope I don't disappoint you, Lady Godolphin,' she said.

'You won't,' said Bethya confidently. 'I've great hopes for you.'

She had no idea what a deep impression she made on Marie, who left Bella Vista that afternoon absolutely determined to justify Bethya's faith in her, no matter how much hard work it took.

And she did work hard. She worked from the moment she set foot inside the painting studio till the moment when she had to clean her brushes and return home. At Camptounfoot, she continued to work, drawing and sketching from morning till night and all the time her skill was increasing. Her application and eagerness to learn was greater than that of any other student in Professor Abernethy's experience and when he wrote to tell Bethya so, she, in her turn, glowed with the feeling of having done something useful. She looked on Marie as her private project. Somehow it was very important to her that the girl should do well.

There were other effects on Marie, however, apart from making her more skilled with brush and pencil. By the time six months had passed, she began to feel as if she were two different people.

At home in Camptounfoot, she was the same girl that she had always been – sweet-natured, shy Marie who was anxious to please everyone. She still looked forward to the occasions when Kitty was able to slip away from work and they could go for one of their old walks along the hedge-lined lanes that radiated out from the village. They tried to talk as closely and confidentially as they had always done but little by little their worlds were drawing apart and Marie unconsciously began looking at her old friend with more sophisticated eyes, to see her from a different perspective.

For when she went to Edinburgh Marie became a different person. There she was no longer a navvy's abandoned child, a penniless orphan. In the art class she was a star, a person of mystery, a girl who held her own among the daughters of lawyers and judges, landowners and men of property. They assumed that she came from the same background as they did and, though she hated herself for the deception, she did nothing to disabuse them of that idea.

That meant she drifted into an uncomfortable situation in which she did not have the courage to make her true circumstances known. She should have told the truth from the beginning but the opportunity never seemed to come. Because she had been accepted into the art class under the auspices of Lady Godolphin, who was paying her bills, it was assumed that she must be some irregular relation to the Godolphin family. Many of the well-to-do girls had relations born on the wrong side of the blanket who were absorbed into their families in a sideways manner. If they were girls, they were educated and, hopefully, married off well or, failing that, provided with a post as governess in some superior family.

Marie's fellow students assumed that she was one of those illegitimate sprigs of a lordly tree. They did not think less of her because of it.

Amy Roxburgh was always the most friendly of Marie's fellow pupils and when she finished covering her own canvases with daubs of colour, she would come wandering over to see what Marie was doing and always expressed deep admiration.

'You're very clever. How do you do it? You must show me because I'm really quite serious about wanting to paint well, you see,' she enthused. In fact, Amy was a vigorous and original painter but she lacked the discipline to concentrate on her work.

It was different with Marie, who was obsessive and painstaking. Whatever the Professor told her, she absorbed eagerly and put into practice. In a short time she finished with George and progressed to drawing other plaster casts taken from the Professor's store. He brought out a succession of posturing nymphs, armless torsos and, one day, a large statue of a male discus thrower wearing nothing except a strategically placed fig-leaf, which caused a lot of girlish giggling.

One afternoon, when they were leaving the class Marie and Amy walked down the stairs together and Amy said, 'No maid today, I see. That girl you brought on your first day was a complete bully.'

Marie smiled. 'I only had her with me on the first day to make sure I found the house and because my brother thought I wouldn't be safe alone, but I prefer being on my own.'

'Your brother sounds like my parents. I wish they'd let me out without a servant but they always worry if I'm alone. You've obviously won your brother round. How did you do it?' said Amy mournfully.

The coachman, who delivered her to classes and collected her when they were finished, was waiting impassively at the door while she stood making conversation with Marie.

'My brother doesn't live at home any more so he doesn't know I'm going out without a servant,' Marie told her.

'Don't you have parents – a mother or a father?' Amy sounded surprised.

Marie shook her head. 'Both of them are dead. My brother and I were brought up by Nanny Rush and when she died, we went to Mrs Mather. That's where I live now.'

'Orphans! How romantic.' Amy clasped her hands in admiration.

'You're lucky to have a mother and a father. I don't remember either of mine,' said Marie sadly.

'But your relative, Lady Godolphin, and your nanny have looked after you, haven't they?' asked Amy and Marie realised that Amy assumed 'Nanny Rush' was a servant who looked after children and that Bethya's philanthropy was not caused by charitable admiration but by blood links. That was her chance to tell the truth but she let the moment pass. She was afraid of how Amy, with her liveried coachman and privileged life, would react to the news that her new friend was the daughter of a navvy and did not even know her father's real name.

Then the real deception began. Marie was quick-witted and a fast learner, so, by listening to the chatter of Amy and the other girls in the painting class, she quickly absorbed their mores and mannerisms. She watched how they behaved, she listened to their descriptions of what happened to them when they were away from classes and, little by little, she began to feel as if she belonged to their world.

She hated herself for her silent lies but having let things go for a long time, it was too late to back out.

One cold winter day when the train had been very late in arriving at Edinburgh because it had encountered snowdrifts on the top of the hills that cut the capital off from the Borders, Marie arrived shivering with cold and found the girls all crowded round a blazing fire and doing no work as the Professor was sick with an ague.

Amy immediately noticed that Marie's fingers were blue and wrinkled on the tips with cold.

'My dear, look at your hands. Don't you wear gloves?' she exclaimed.

Marie did not own a pair of gloves, only fingerless mittens like those worn by women working on the farms, and she did not want to own up to them though they were in her pocket. 'I forgot them,' she lied. To change the subject she told the girls about the tremendous snowdrifts that had held up her train and how wonderful the world looked in its cloak of pure white. 'I wanted to paint it there and then,' she said.

Amy, however, was not thinking about painting. 'You'll never get home tonight. Look, it's started to snow again,' she said, pointing at the southern-facing window. A curtain of drifting snowflakes like big goose feathers was sailing past it.

Marie was upset. 'But I must go home! Tibbie'll be so worried about me. I'll have to go now...' She was pulling on her cloak again in a great hurry to get back to the station but Amy stopped her.

'Don't be silly. You don't want to be in a stranded train all night, do you? You'll come home with me and we'll send a telegraphic message to your Tibbie.'

'But Tibbie's never had a telegraph message,' protested Marie. In her experience no one in the whole of Camptounfoot had ever received such a thing. It was quite an occasion when the postman delivered a letter to anyone's house.

'Then she's going to get one today,' laughed Amy. 'My man's outside. I'll send him to the railway station to despatch it. I think I've enough money to pay for it.' She shoved a hand into the pocket of her skirt and came out with a green morocco purse that she emptied into her other hand. Several guinea coins glittered there and she said casually, 'Oh yes, I've enough. I'll go down and tell him what to do. Come with me Marie and give him the address for the message. I think it should be something like, "Don't worry, am staying in Edinburgh till the snow stops with Amy Roxburgh, who is very respectable." Will that do?'

I shouldn't be doing this. I should try to get home, thought Marie but the lure of staying the night with Amy was too strong so she obed-iently wrote down Tibbie's address... 'Mrs Mather, Camptounfoot', which implied that she dominated the village and not that it was so small that everyone there knew everybody else.

When the coachman went off with the message, Amy clutched Marie's arm and cried, 'Isn't this fun! My family will love to meet you because I've told them all about you. My mother loves art. That's why she sent me to the classes. She thinks that I'll turn into a female Leonardo da Vinci or something but I'm afraid there's not much hope of that. Bring some of your drawings to show her.'

The Roxburgh carriage was snug because the attentive coachman tucked the girls in beneath fur-lined rugs and placed a copper pan of warm charcoal at their feet. Through its little windows they could see that snow was already piling up in the streets of the city and Marie felt as if she were in a fairy story as they drove along. She had never been in such a grand conveyance before because her road travelling had been on the exposed top of the cart of the Camptounfoot carrier who sometimes gave her and Tibbie a lift to Rosewell or Maddiston.

The pair of horses pulling Amy's carriage slithered and slipped along Princes Street and headed out of the city in a westward direction. They passed lines of houses and shops with lights festively blazing in the windows. The shops were all crowded as if people were rushing out to spend their money because of the bitter weather. Amy sensed her companion's excitement and laughed. 'You're acting as if you've never been on a busy street before!'

'Well I haven't. Rosewell's only like a little corner of Edinburgh. And it's much more old-fashioned, another world.'

Amy said, 'I suppose it is, but this part of the town's too new for me. I preferred our old house to the one we live in now. We used to have a place in George Square and there was constant coming and going on the pavement outside the front door, but Mama wanted a house with a park so now we live in Murrayhill. She named it after her family... she's a Murray and very proud of it. She even named one of my brothers Murray, too!'

Marie had heard enough of the conversation between the art class girls to realise that family names were of paramount importance and could guess that the Murrays set themselves higher than the Roxburghs.

It took half an hour and a hard haul for the horses to cover the three miles to Murrayhill, which, to Marie's amazement, turned out to be a vast Palladian-type mansion sitting on the side of a south-facing hill and staring out over lawns, all covered with snow.

The gates were open in anticipation of Amy's arrival and when the carriage drew up to the front door a male servant ran out and hurried Amy in through the snow, exclaiming, 'Come in quickly, miss, your mama's been worried about you in this terrible weather.'

'I'm all right, but I've brought a real storm victim with me. Miss Benjamin can't get home to the Borders. Prepare a room for her please,' ordered Amy.

'I don't want to be any trouble,' breathed Marie, which made both the servant and Amy look at her in surprise.

'It's no trouble. We've got dozens of empty bedrooms. You're welcome to one of them,' said Amy.

Mrs Roxburgh was sitting in the library before a blazing fire and she certainly didn't behave like someone who was worried about her daughter's journey through the storm. When the girls walked into the room she looked up without surprise and kept her finger in the book she was reading to mark her place.

In appearance she resembled Amy a little, though there were grey streaks in her hair and her face was deeply wrinkled. To Marie she seemed as old as Tibbie, which was a disappointment because she'd visualized Amy's mother as young and smartly dressed, rather like Bethya.

What she lacked in looks, however, Mrs Roxburgh made up for in confidence and assurance. She behaved as if the introduction of an unknown girl as a house guest was an everyday occurrence, smiled at Marie, shook her hand and then said, 'You must be the Miss Benjamin my daughter has been talking so much about. I believe you're a very talented girl. The only one of Professor Abernethy's present pupils with genuine talent, according to Amy.'

Marie flushed. 'I don't think I'm as good as that.'

Amy chipped in, 'Now, now, Marie, don't act false modesty. You know perfectly well that the Prof's in a wax of delight about having you in the class. You're the only real painter among us.'

'You're a good painter too,' protested Marie.

Mrs Roxburgh shot the stranger a sharp glance over her eye glasses and said, 'Amy could be better if she tried. Perhaps your example will make her change her ways.'

Amy laughed. 'Mama, you only want something to hang on your walls and tell your blue-stocking friends that it's by your daughter.'

'That's true,' agreed her mother unabashed. Then she looked at Marie again. 'Perhaps one day you'll show me something you've done, Miss Benjamin.'

Amy giggled. 'I knew you'd ask that. I told Marie to bring some of her drawings with her so's you could see them. She'll show them to you after supper.'

The finger came out of the book. 'I'm interested now. Bring them in. I want to see what my daughter's been raving about for weeks.'

The reception of Marie's drawings was sufficiently enthusiastic to make her embarrassment even deeper.

'How old are you?' Mrs Roxburgh asked after she had leafed through the drawings several times.

'I'm sixteen.'

'Who taught you to draw?'

'No one. I've been doing it since I was very small. My first teacher was Nanny Rush. She taught me to copy pictures out of books and when I wanted to do something with colour she bought me a little box of paints.'

'How old were you then?'

'About five I think.'

'Mmm. Like Mozart or Thomas Bewick,' said Mrs Roxburgh, handing the sheets of drawings back. 'You're obviously one of those freaks of nature. Be careful that too much teaching doesn't spoil what you've got.'

Marie took her work and put it back carefully in her case. She didn't know if she'd really been complimented or not and Amy saw her confusion. 'Who was Thomas Bewick, Mama?' she asked.

'An eighteenth-century wood engraver who did wonderful countryside scenes, quite untaught. When he was only a child he made drawings with a stone on the hearth of his home in Northumberland.'

Amy looked at Marie and said, 'My mama has more information in her head than encyclopedias have between their covers. She should have been a university professor.'

'If I was a man that's what I would have been,' said her mother bleakly, taking up her book again.

This was obviously a signal for the girls to leave and Amy took Marie's arm saying, 'Let's go. I'll show you the room you've to sleep in. We'll see Mother at dinner.' Mrs Roxburgh only waggled a vague hand in their direction as they were leaving the room, for she was deep in her book again.

Outside the door Amy laughed. 'Isn't she funny? She liked your pictures, though. I could tell she was impressed and it takes a lot to impress her.'

When she was left alone in the bedroom assigned to her by a maid, Marie wandered around gazing at the heavy furniture and the oil paintings that adorned the walls. The paintings were of the 'impressive mountain landscape' school with shaggy cattle and rushing streams which did not appeal to her but she appreciated the luxury and comfort of the room. A fire blazed in the hearth, the bed was deep in blankets and a feather quilt, and a pile of books lay on a table by the bedhead.

When the maid came back and asked if she would be required to help the guest dress for dinner, Marie shook her head, for she had no baggage except her drawing case and the thought of going down to dine in her travelling clothes with a collection of strangers terrified her.

'I feel a little ill. I don't think I want any dinner. Please give my apologies to the family,' she said.

'You're ill? I'll fetch the housekeeper,' said the maid and hurried away.

The housekeeper asked what was the matter and Marie croaked, 'My throat hurts.'

'I'll tell Madam,' said the housekeeper.

Eventually Mrs Roxburgh arrived with her glasses still on her nose. 'I'm told you're ill. What's the trouble?' she asked.

'My throat is sore,' said Marie, wishing that this whole charade had never started.

'Let me look at it,' said Mrs Roxburgh. When she had peered down Marie's open mouth she sat down on the bed and said, 'It looks perfectly all right to me. Are you nervous of us? Is that what's wrong?'

'Yes, I'm nervous. I'm not used to strangers...'

'You don't dine out much, do you?'

'No.'

'Well, my dear, I've found in life that sometimes the things you dread turn out to be not so terrifying if you face them straight on. You've got to start being sociable some time. I often don't feel like taking dinner with a crowd of people but even if I dread it, it's often very enjoyable. Come down to dinner and sit by me and you'll be all right. There's not many of us, only seven at table tonight, and Amy does most of the talking so you won't need to exercise your vocal chords too much.'

Marie sensed that this woman guessed a good deal more about her than she was saying and she longed to be able to unburden herself of her secrets, to tell all about Tibbie and Bethya and Kitty and David and her dead father and mother, but she was far too overwhelmed, so instead she nodded her head and said, 'Thank you. I'll come down to dinner.'

In fact, as Mrs Roxburgh had predicted, the dinner party was not so terrifying after all, though Marie quailed when she saw the table gleaming with silver and laden with glittering glassware. Again her hostess seemed to know what was worrying her. Whenever a new course arrived, she took up the requisite spoon, knife or fork and held it still for a few seconds before she started eating.

Amy did indeed do most of the talking, teasing her three handsome brothers and her indulgent father, who laughed at every sally she made. She was obviously the spoiled darling of the household and only her mother seemed to look on her without utter infatuation.

The brothers, all as dark as Amy, were called George, Murray and Albert and they dazzled Marie by their poise and handsomeness. They were all older than their sister and went out of their way to be charming to her friend, but Marie was particularly taken with the middle brother, Murray, who had the most brilliant smile and most dancing eyes of them all. Between the attentions of Murray and his mother, she lost her nervousness and began to enjoy herself.

The dinner party broke up after a lot of family banter and laughter. When she went to bed she felt as if she had been reborn; another new world had opened up before her and was welcoming her in.

# Chapter Eight

When his wife and children arrived back from Bella Vista with the minimum of warning, Sydney was taken aback and suspicious because he thought that Bethya might be spying on him or trying to catch him out.

He had two major things on his conscience. The first was heavy gambling which he always turned to when he was bored and which Bethya had several times made him promise to give up. During her stay at Bella Vista, however, he had been gambling every night and already his debts were so large that he was planning to sell some property in order to pay them.

His second secret was a growing obsession with Lucy Beresford. When he first saw her he had been amused that his friend Allandale should have fallen prey to such a girl but, from time to time, he had found himself wandering to Rotten Row with the specific purpose of watching her.

Over a period of several years that habit of watching gradually became an obsession, one which he could neither break nor explain. She was conscious of him too and he knew that when he was watching, she put her horses through their paces with more flamboyance than was absolutely necessary. Though they never spoke to each other, there was a strong current of mutual attraction flowing between them.

It was not as if he compared Lucy with Bethya whose beauty never failed to delight him. There was a coarseness about the young courtesan that, instead of detracting from her appeal, actually added to it for him. He liked the thought that she would not smell of camellias but of straw and sweat, her hair would not run through his hands like silk but would tickle like tow. She did not seem so fragile and delicate that her bones would snap. She was strong and vigorous, noisy and ebullient. No one could be more different to his elegant wife.

The confused state of his mind made him extremely ill-tempered and one morning, soon after she returned, he charged Bethya with becoming a neurotic hypochondriac. She burst into tears and said, 'How can you say that when I'm really ill? I'm having another baby and I'm so afraid that I'll lose it like the last one.'

'My God, that's awful,' he gasped.

She stared at him through tear-filled eyes. 'But I thought you'd be pleased! I've been waiting till I was sure about it before I told you... I'm nearly four months now.'

He groaned and she began sobbing heartbrokenly. 'It won't make any difference to your life. I'll not force you to spend time with me. I knew you were getting bored with me being ill all the time so I've written to my sister Miriam and asked her to come to stay and keep me company. I don't want you to feel trapped by my illness or by this pregnancy.'

'I don't feel trapped,' he told her but both of them knew that he was telling a lie. Nevertheless he was glad that Bethya would have her sister with her, for he realised that she was lonely and sadly in need of a confidante. He was no longer sufficient company for her because what she needed now was someone to talk to about him.

'When is your sister coming?' he asked in a gentler tone.

'I told her to take the first passage she could get. She should be here soon. It'll free you from staying with me so much.'

He snorted. 'Free me! You make it sound as if I'm in prison. That's nonsense.'

Bethya was the one to step back from confrontation. 'I'm sorry, I'm probably only being fanciful. It's my condition,' she said softly. She was afraid to open the pit that lay between them in case it proved to be full of writhing snakes. Better to walk round it and look the other way.

After the argument he went to the park, though he knew he shouldn't. In fact, he started off walking in the opposite direction, but his feet would not carry him there. They would only go to Rotten Row.

The Duke of Allandale was sitting beside the ride in a huge barouche watching his mistress disport herself and he waved his whip at Sydney inviting him to climb into a seat beside him.

'You're looking glum, Godders,' he said.

'Am I? But you know I'm not one for going around with a grin on my face,' was Sydney's reply.

His friend put a hand on his shoulder. 'You need some diversion. I'm going to the theatre tonight. There's a French company at the

Haymarket. It's a long time since we went out together. Come with me. I'll call for you at seven. Bethya won't mind, will she?'

Sydney looked hard at his friend. 'No, she won't mind. That sounds tempting. Yes, I'll come, Dicky.'

That night they did not go out in either of their crested private carriages but walked onto the street and hailed a hansom cab, for both knew that they were trying to re-create one of the old adventures they had shared when young and wild.

The broad thoroughfare outside the Haymarket Theatre was crowded with carriages and its brightly lit foyer packed with people wearing the most fashionable clothes, but there were no modestly dressed ladies, no respectable middle-class wives and daughters among the crowd.

All the women parading in the open space behind the glass doors were women of pleasure, powdered and painted, corsetted and gowned in silks and satins that cost the equivalent of a year's wages for a working man and sometimes even more. These were the *poules de luxe* who had graduated from the streets into the protection of rich men. Some were young, little more than children, while others were well past their prime though making up for that by the magnificence of their apparel and the assurance of their behaviour. Every woman knew to a shilling how much the others' gowns had cost.

The most famous young woman of them all deliberately made a late entrance into this throng. Her smart little barouche drew up in front of the door of the theatre with a clatter and her handsome footman leaped down to lower the steps so that she could alight and pass through the gaping crowd. Heads turned to watch her approach, as she smiled and waved a folded fan at the favoured few she deigned to recognise. A wake of whispers followed her.

She was wearing a pink gown with an immense stiffened skirt that took up a huge area of floor. The bodice was cut very low showing the division between her milk-white breasts that rose up very high on each side of an immense pink rose tucked between them. For a woman who took so much exercise riding in the park every morning, she was, surprisingly, as round and plump as a dairymaid.

Lucy Beresford, or Minnie Clough as she was born, rarely allowed her heart to rule her head. Since she'd set herself up as a woman of pleasure at the age of fifteen one principle had ruled her life and that was 'nothing for nothing'. Even if a man wanted only to hold her hand, he would have to make it worth her while. Her aim was to make a fortune before she was thirty and then retire. She had seen too many raddled old women frantically staving off age and decay in order to pay their bills. She was grimly determined that would never happen to her.

She spotted her current lover – or one of them – standing in the shadow of an overhanging balcony watching her parading through the admiring men. With him was the man who had been haunting the park to watch her. She waited every day for him to turn up; she put on her best show for him. He interested her because he never made any attempt to approach her and Lucy did not like to be passed over.

Allandale took Sydney's arm, 'Come on, I've taken a box. Let's go and sit down.'

Lucy did not share the box with them but sat downstairs in the stalls with a collection of eager male admirers. She never glanced up in Allandale's direction.

In the interval, the door of the box opened and she walked in, sitting down in a chair vacated by Sydney who stood up at the sight of her. Close to, she was even more delicious than from a distance. Her complexion was as smooth as satin and unmarked by any flaw. She looked as if she was made from spun sugar, good enough to eat. She even smelt like a piece of confectionery. What made her most arresting, however, was the aura of sensuality that seemed to emanate from her, contrasting oddly with her milkmaid appearance. She had thick, pleasure-loving lips, heavily lidded, sleepy eyes and a roguish smile.

'You've not been to see me for a week, Allandale,' she said, tapping his cheek with her fan.

'I'm trying to wean myself off you,' he told her.

She flirted her head aside making the golden curls brush over his hand. 'Lucy'll get you back. She always does. Come tomorrow at half past three.'

Then she looked at Sydney and her eye ran up and down his lean frame. 'You're the man who watches me in the park,' she said.

'I live near there,' he told her.

'So do I. Within walking distance,' she said as she flounced out of the box.

When the play was over Allandale said, 'Let's go and dine. We could play some cards if you like.'

Sydney shook his head. 'I don't think so. You go to your club but I'll go home.'

No blandishments would make him change his mind and when Allandale set off in a cab, Sydney turned and strode along St James's. It was a surprise to him when a small carriage came out of a side road and drove along by his side. As it passed him the footman on the box leaned down and opened the door. A white-gloved hand waved out at him from inside and Lucy Beresford's voice called, 'Come in.'

'Are you in the habit of picking up strange men?' he asked as he climbed in and sat beside her.

'You're not strange. I think we know quite a lot about each other,' she told him. It was difficult to see her, for she was sitting in the darkest corner of the carriage with a dark hood drawn over her head. Then she leaned forward and put a hand on each side of his face pouting her lips at him.

He kissed her, putting an arm around her shoulders and pulling her towards him. He could smell her vanilla-like scent and feel the satiny texture of her skin.

'Won't your footman be jealous?' he murmured.

'Why should he? He's my brother,' she said with a giggle and kissed him again.

'Family enterprise,' murmured Sydney tasting her lips with his tongue.

'That's right,' she said pulling him towards her. Her breasts were like full-blown roses and they tasted of vanilla too.

Her house was in darkness when they reached it and after the footman opened the door, he disappeared. Their lovemaking was violent and angry. Sydney plunged into passion with a kind of despair and when sated lay back on her satin-covered bed and groaned in anguish. She was lying beside him, totally naked, pink-flushed and sweat-glazed.

'Wasn't it good? Don't you like me?' she asked, raising her head from the satin pillow.

'It was too good. I like you too much. I can't afford you, though,' he told her.

She sat up, her breasts upright and challenging. 'Did I ask you for any money?' she demanded.

He propped his head on his elbow admiring her. 'No, but you're not a charitable society for the relief of depressed gentlemen, are you?'

She giggled. 'I certainly am not. You can pay me extra next time.' She was quite sure there would be a next time. They always came back.

Next morning his wife told him that her sister Miriam was arriving on the mail-boat due in a week's time.

'That's very good, my dear,' he said enthusiastically. 'She'll be company for you.'

On the day that the ship carrying Miriam from Bombay was sched-uled to arrive at Tilbury, Bethya was too unwell to go to meet it, but Sydney was waiting on the quayside.

A sharp feeling of wanderlust gripped him as he watched the crewmen and stevedores rushing about tying up the vessel. When Bethya's child is born we'll travel again, he told himself, and not for the first time resolved to mend his errant ways, to give up Lucy Beresford and stay away from the gambling tables.

The first passengers were flooding down the gangplank to be met with cries and embraces from waiting friends and relatives. He had no idea what Bethya's sister looked like so he fought his way through the crowds to grab the sleeve of one of the officers and tell him, 'Find Miss Miriam Jordan for me, old chap.'

The man was sufficiently impressed by Sydney's commanding manner to do as he was asked. In a short while he came off the ship ushering a small woman in front of him.

The sight of her was a complete surprise to her brother-in-law, who had been expecting a pretty woman like Bethya. What he was presented with was a wraith in a white dress and plain bonnet whose bird bones and anxious face made him remember the sari-clad women he'd seen begging on the streets of Bombay during his only visit to the sub-continent many years before.

The trouble was that Miriam resembled Bethya in the same way as a caricature resembles the sitter and it only took one glance for him to be sure that they were sisters.

Miriam was shy and visibly shaking as she was presented to Sydney so he went out of his way to reassure her, taking her hand and welcoming her to England. She smiled then and said, 'You must be my sister's husband. She's described you so well.'

'And you're as beautiful as she is,' he lied gallantly. Where Bethya was ivory skinned and her half-caste breeding only showed in the lambent beauty of her dark eyes and her strange, high cheekbones, this young woman looked pure Indian. Her skin was very dark and her body bony. She had a wide mouth with a broad jawline and prominent white teeth. Her velvety brown eyes seemed to beseech him to think well of her, which made him compare her to an endearing puppy dog, the kind that goes on wagging its tail till it falls over.

If Bethya tries to introduce this sister into her London circle of friends, she will be committing social suicide with most of them, was his first thought.

Sydney had never felt any shame about his wife's mixed origins. He liked the fact that she was so different from the milk-and-water prettiness of English misses but now, faced with Miriam, he suddenly realised that his daughters might be looked down on because of their mother's background, for they were the ones who looked most like her. The boys were all blond, like himself. People who had only suspected that Bethya was of mixed blood, would be in no doubt of it after they met Miriam.

He was angry at himself for thinking this way – it went against everything he had ever believed – and as recompense, he went out of his way to be even more charming and attentive to the stranger. He took her arm, gave orders about her baggage, whisked her off to his carriage and had the hood lowered so that she could have a good view as they drove along. He entertained her during their drive back to London with amusing stories about his family and tales about the places they passed through. He even told the coachman to make detours so that she could see special sights. Before they reached Berkeley Square, she was his slave, totally enamoured of him.

The plainest and youngest of five sisters, Miriam had always yearned for the ideal lover but none came along for her as one by one her prettier siblings married and left home.

Bethya, the second eldest, had been the first to go, marrying fat and red-faced Gus Anstruther. Miriam had not envied her Gus except that he was an Englishman who would take her away from India and a society that looked down on them all for being half-castes.

The other sisters all married men from their own community, merchants and traders with money in the bank and big mansions on Colaba Causeway, but Miriam remained with Mama and Papa till news came of Bethya's illness. The family were horrified to learn that she was sick and lonely. One of them would have to go to help, they decided. The one they chose was Miriam.

She had no real idea of what she was coming to, because although Bethya's letters were glowing and enthusiastic about her faraway life, she had always been prone to exaggeration and her family took her descriptions of the glories with a pinch of salt. She couldn't really be a lady with all those fine houses, could she? Not their Bethya.

On the drive to London, Miriam's tongue was loosened by Sydney's affability and she talked about this and much more as they drove along. She had a very marked singsong Eurasian accent and a way of saying things that he found amusing, so he laughed at her sallies, which encouraged her even more. The sight of the Berkeley Square house, however, silenced her.

Staring at it and then at him, she asked, 'Is this your house? Do you live in all of it? Don't you share it with other families?'

Highly entertained, he escorted her inside. 'It's all ours, but you'll have your own apartments. Bethya's had a lovely time picking the furnishings for them.'

'Arrey, glory be!' said Miriam, eyes round with amazement as the butler opened the door and revealed the glories within.

Sydney felt for her as if she were one of his children. 'Your sister likes to live well, but then she's a very rich woman,' he told her.

She looked questioningly at him and it struck him that Bethya's family may not be fully aware of how kind fortune had been to her when Anstruther died. His wife, he knew, had a secretive streak and it amused him to think that she'd kept her family in the dark though she was generous to them, sending crates of expensive gifts to Bombay three or four times a year. He wasn't going to be the one who broke the news that she possessed a magnificent country estate; enough silver to fill a vault; paintings by Tilly Kettle and George Chinnery, Alfred Stubbs and even a couple of Raeburns; not to mention capital of more than half a million pounds. He'd let Bethya do that herself if and when she chose. Miriam had endured enough excitement for one day, he decided.

The sisters' meeting after more than sixteen years was affecting. Bethya stood up from her place on the sofa and wordlessly held out her arms. Miriam rushed towards her and they clasped each other tightly, heads bent together and weeping so hard that it was impossible for either of them to speak for a long time. If one recovered herself a little, the other would start crying again and they clutched each other close once more. Sydney was embarrassed at the sight and walked out of the room, firmly closing the door and leaving them to their reunion.

He did not return till he heard Bethya ringing the bell for the butler. 'Send the children down to meet their aunt,' she told him. Miriam's artless delight won the younger members of the family over as well, though Sydney could see from the expressions of his older children that they were surprised by the Indian appearance of their aunt.

They soon mellowed to her, however, as she knelt on the carpet and showed them the simple wooden toys, jumping jacks and rattles she'd brought for them from India. She was like a child herself, full of wonder, unabashed in her praise of everything she saw, obviously devoted to Bethya and eager to help her in any way she could.

For the next couple of days, the sisters spent all day together in Bethya's boudoir gossiping and giggling as they used to do long ago. When Sydney interrupted them, they looked up startled as if he were an intruder. That made him feel less guilty about his adventures with Lucy, which he told himself he was not going to repeat. But, of course, he did. He could not stay away.

He tried to be uxorious, however, and when Bethya was too tired to go out because she had over-stretched herself in her enthusiasm at seeing Miriam again, Sydney took his sister-in-law on sightseeing tours during which she gasped and enthused over everything from Trafalgar Square to St James's Palace.

Encouraged by her enthusiasm he took her to art galleries, to the pleasure gardens along the river and even to the theatre, choosing Shakespeare's *King Lear*, a more respectable play than the Haymarket farce and not frequented by the demi-monde, so there was no danger of seeing Lucy there. *Lear* moved Miriam to tears and she sobbed all the way home in the carriage.

Next morning, when they were alone at breakfast, Bethya seemed to be brooding. 'What's the trouble?' he asked, seeing her downcast face.

'It's Miriam,' she said.

Ah, he thought, the problem of her colour has struck Bethya at last. What's she going to do about it?

'You mustn't let it worry you,' he told her.

She stared at him, her lovely eyebrows raised. 'Why not? Shouldn't I feel a little jealous because my husband is spending so much time with my sister?'

'My dear girl, I'm only taking her out to help you,' he protested.

Her eyes were swimming with tears. 'I know I'm being silly but I can't help being jealous. I'm not able to go out and you're off jaunting with Miriam every day.'

'You're being ridiculous,' he told her. 'Your sister is a sweet person and it's a pleasure to entertain her, that's all. I thought you were worried about prejudice.'

'What prejudice?' he asked.

He felt that he had wandered into a dangerous area. 'The prejudice people might feel about her colour... our daughters... you...' For once he faltered.

She was watching his face intently and nodded slowly. 'I know. I'd forgotten she was so dark. It's unfair if people think less of her for it.'

'I know it's wrong but people are strange, especially in society,' he told her.

Bethya stood up and walked to the window. 'I think I'll take Miriam and the children to Bella Vista for a while,' she said without looking round. He knew that she was removing her sister from her London circle and he knew why.

'That might be a good idea. You like it there and you can rest more easily than you can in town. Dr Robertson from Maddiston will look after you and if you want any other doctors, one could travel up to you,' he said carefully.

'Yes, that's what I'll do,' she said, turning round and smiling at him. Then she added, 'I hope you behave yourself while I'm away.'

He looked outraged. 'Of course I will. What do you mean?' he asked.

She was touchingly anxious not to annoy him. 'I only meant that I hope you don't go gambling. I know you've been doing a lot of that recently. Your steward down in Shropshire wrote to me about you telling him to sell off three farms. Those farms are part of our girls' dowries. You mustn't sell them!'

Relief overwhelmed him that this was all she meant. 'I'll not gamble. I'll go to Shropshire and sort out the farm business and then I'll join you at Bella Vista for the hunting season,' he promised.

When at last he waved his family and Miriam off from the station on their way to Scotland, he told himself that he would stand by his promise. More than that, he would not go near Lucy. It took a day before his resolution snapped and he once more found himself at her front door.

This time she very sweetly asked for five hundred pounds, which he gave her.

# Chapter Nine

Marie Benjamin was in love, very much in love, but she harboured no real hopes of being loved back by the object of her affections. It was delightful just to feel love because its influence made the whole world look different; the sun shone more brightly, every morning dawned full of promise; her work improved; even the scowls of her brother failed to spoil her happiness.

The object of her affections was Amy's second brother, Murray. Since the night of the snowstorm when Amy had taken her back to Murrayhill, Marie had become a pet of the Roxburgh family, particularly of Mrs Roxburgh, who told her daughter to bring her friend home as often as possible. She enjoyed examining Marie's work, noting the improvements in it and making suggestions about what she should do next.

On several occasions Marie had been persuaded to spend the three nights between Tuesday and Friday at the Roxburgh home so that she need not make the tiring journey between Edinburgh and Camptoun-foot. On these days Murray was usually at home and Marie thought she had never seen anyone so handsome or so charming. She hung on every word he spoke, cherishing it like a jewel so that she could lie in bed later and think about him, going over what he said, remembering his opinions on the matters discussed at the family dining-table. She cherished every scrap of information she could glean about Murray like a magpie picking up glittering baubles. Her devotion to him shone from her eyes and she was unaware that all the family noticed it and teased him about it.

She lived for the time when Amy would come up to her as classes finished on Tuesday afternoons and say, 'Don't go back to Camptoun-foot tonight. Why waste money on so many train fares when your bed's waiting for you at Murrayhill?'

There were weeks, however, when this invitation was not offered, weeks when the Roxburghs were going away or entertaining and then the days dragged for Marie until she could see Murray again. Yet when she did, she was barely able to utter a word to him and feared that he would be able to spot her confusion, for her legs turned to water and she felt the colour flood into her cheeks. Fight as hard as she could to control those reactions, they always overwhelmed her when he was nearby.

As well as loving Murray, she was besotted with the whole family and their magnificent home. Though she was ashamed of her feelings, going home to Camptounfoot was an anticlimax after Murrayhill and though she tried to hide how she felt, her abstraction and dissatisfaction with the way of life she had always known was growing obvious to those who loved her.

To Tibbie, the cottage seemed very empty on the nights when Marie stayed in Edinburgh. Once more her only companions were the cat and the parrot and ruefully she remembered how she'd agonised about taking in David and Marie in case her life would be disrupted by them. Now she missed Marie's chatter and longed to have someone to care for. Having another person in the house had made her feel useful and when Marie was not there, the ticking of the little clock on her mantelpiece seemed very loud in the empty room.

'Eh dear,' she sighed and walked out into the garden to survey her vegetable plot. She was standing there, staring up at the mist-wreathed hills, when a voice hailed her over the garden gate.

'Mrs Mather, aren't you going to say hello to an old friend?' it asked.

A man in fashionable and expensive clothes was standing with his arms on the top rail of the gate, smiling at her. On his head was a tall hat and his gloved hands carried a cane.

Tibbie blinked in surprise and said, 'My word, it's Robbie Rutherford! It's a long time since I've seen you. What are you doing here?'

'I'm home on a visit to see my father and mother. I've been away working in Italy for the past few years but it's grand to be back!' cried Robbie, who had not lost his Border accent and whose grin was as wide and infectious as it had been when he was a cheeky little lad running messages in the village.

Tibbie remembered that he had been the best message runner of all the little lads, for he never forgot anything you sent him for. It had been no surprise to her to hear from his proud mother that he'd become a great success in business and worked as a chief engineer with a big company that built tunnels.

She held her gate open and welcomed him in. 'Come inside, Robbie, come in and tell me all your news.'

As he walked in she noticed that he still had the limp caused by the breaks in his legs when he was working on the Camptounfoot bridge with Emma Jane.

'Are you married yet, Robbie?' she asked as she bustled about getting out the best teapot and china cups.

He shook his head. 'Not me, I'm not ready for marriage.'

She smiled at him. 'But you're over thirty, lad. Most men are married by the time they're that age.'

'I've never met the right woman, or if I have, she's married to somebody else,' said Robbie very solemnly and she remembered that he'd been badly smitten with Emma Jane though she was several years older than he was. I hope he's not pining after her still, thought Tibbie.

'Your mother must be pleased to have you back,' she told him.

He laughed. 'Yes, she is. She's never stopped talking since I arrived yesterday. I've heard all the gossip of the past few years in one go. This village has been as busy as ever, it seems… all those new bairns born, all the same men getting drunk and running after other folk's wives, the same scandals. Joe's still up to his old tricks, frightening the women at night I hear, and Bob's lassie, Bella, is setting her cap at the new schoolmaster. When I left the village Bella was only a wee thing in pinafores.'

Tibbie laughed. 'She's a madam is Bella. Mr Arnott hasn't a chance if she's got her eye on him.'

Robbie looked at her over the edge of his cup. 'What news is there of Craigie Scott, Tibbie?' he asked. He'd been there the day that Craigie shot the navvy called Bullhead. He saw it happen, he saw Bullhead's skull explode like a smashed apple and he never forgot it.

She shrugged. 'Just the same. He'll never be let out. Big Lily went up to see him a while ago. She was very quiet and subdued when she came back but she told me that he was fine.'

'My mother told me Wee Lily's married to Jake and hates him. I didnae think she was fit for marrying,' said Robbie.

'Neither is she,' agreed Tibbie. 'Big Lily should have left her alone but they needed another hand on the place and that was one, way of keeping Jake I suppose… It's a terrible business. Many a night Wee

Lily runs out of the bothy and sleeps in the haystack or the cowshed because of the rows that there are over there! It's something awful.'

'What happened to her bairn?' asked Robbie, who remembered seeing Wee Lily going out to work in the fields with her baby tied into her shawl.

Tibbie brightened. 'You mean Kitty? Big Lily sent her over to Falconwood to be bondager to Tom Liddle. She's growing into a big strong lassie, a fine-looking girl, but she and her granny are like flint and tinder, they strike sparks off each other. Kitty could go to the bad or she could turn out all right… It's in the balance at the moment, I think.'

'Her father was bad enough. He was the cruellest man I ever knew and I've met some rough ones since then, believe me,' said Robbie slowly.

'Dinna blame the lassie for her father,' said Tibbie, surprised that Robbie should show such prejudice.

'It's just that Bullhead's hard to forget,' said Robbie uncontritely.

When he'd drunk his tea he walked across the road to his parents' cottage that sat in the middle of a lovely walled garden on the other side of the street from Tibbie's. He was opening the gate when a terrible din started up in the steading next to the cottage garden. A woman's shrill scream rang out followed by a man's rumbling bullying.

'Hey woman, come here woman, come when I tell you, dinna run awa' frae me like that!' he was shouting.

Curses and obscenities followed this, and the man could be heard slapping the woman, who kept on pleading with him to stop. Robbie was a chivalrous fellow and he could not turn away from a woman in such trouble so he ran in his awkward gait to the shed that the din was coming from and burst in through the door.

Jake, both fists clenched, was hammering away at Wee Lily's body while she cowered with her arms up over her head and her back half-turned to him. She was sobbing and gulping pitifully.

'Stop it, stop it, you brute,' yelled Robbie and threw himself onto Jake's back. He was bigger than the labourer and though he was lame in one leg, he was far from being a cripple.

Jake was sent flying. His head collided with a wooden pillar holding up one of the roof beams and he slid to the ground with a surprised expression on his face. Then he toppled over silently and lay still.

Robbie dusted his hands with satisfaction and said, 'Lily, go home to your mother and lock the door. He'll not bother you any more tonight. Go on now like a good girl.'

Surprisingly she remembered who he was. 'Thank you, Robbie, you're a good laddie,' she sobbed and ran away without as much as a glance at her unconscious husband, whom Robbie pulled up and set on his feet.

'Come on you. I'm going to stick your head in the water trough and try to talk some sense into you, though I don't suppose it'll do much good,' he said angrily.

Jake's head was ducked in a trough of cold black water and he emerged spluttering and swearing, 'Hey, what d'ye think you're doing. That wumman's my wife. I can do what I like wi' her.'

'You shouldn't beat her like that. You're a man and she's a woman. That's not the way good men behave,' Robbie told him severely.

Jake wiped his face with his hand and attempted to exonerate himself. 'But she'll no' let me fuck her. She runs awa' frae me every night and screams like a stuck pig if I get on top of her. It's no' fair,' he complained.

Robbie sighed. He'd grown up with them and knew that any child born of an association between them would almost certainly be subnormal. He wondered why Big Lily was so anxious to bring another one of that kind into the world. Then he started talking patiently to Jake. 'Listen, if Lily doesn't want you, there's not much sense forcing yourself on her. It won't make her feel any better about you and it'll be no fun, if you know what I mean. Why don't you go into Rosewell and find yourself one of the women that hang about the square at night? Here's two shillings, that'll buy you one tonight and another one tomorrow.'

Jake seized the money with delight, crying as he ran off, 'Thanks, Robbie, you're a good laddie.'

Robbie laughed. It was the second time he'd been called a good laddie in five minutes and he felt as if the clock had been turned back and he was wee Robbie Rutherford, the village message boy, again. That night he was rewarded by the peace of the steading being completely unbroken.

Next day he walked from house to house calling on old friends and talking about his life in distant places. Although what he said was true, he was afraid that he sounded unbearably boastful, as if he were deliberately rubbing in that he had got away and they were all still in Camptounfoot.

He wished that he could stop but some devil inside pushed him on, making him sound more and more cocky and assured. He knew the villagers well enough to realise that they would not be over-impressed. They may not have travelled far but they were shrewd observers of human nature and they'd known him for a long time.

'That Robbie's got awfy fu' o' gas,' was what they'd say when he turned his back. It was what he'd say if one of them tried it on with him. The thought made him laugh.

On his way home from paying a call on the family who lived in the corn mill at the western end of the village, he saw a tall, slim girl walking ahead of him. Her back was very straight and she strode along like a soldier, very upright, head high and feet planted firmly on the ground with each step she took. She carried a black hat in her hand and a mass of tousled bright red hair cascaded down her back in a waterfall of colour.

Robbie knew that this was Bullhead's daughter. Nobody else could have hair like that, a shade of red that was rarely seen; not the beautiful auburn beloved of painters, but a burning, vibrant red as if the person from whose head it sprang was either tremendously passionate or furiously angry – perhaps both.

'Are you looking for your mother?' he asked when he was close to her. She spun round and he saw a guarded look come into her brown eyes.

'Who are you?' she asked abruptly.

'Robbie Rutherford. That's my family's house over there.' He pointed at their garden wall.

She nodded. She could place him now, though she did not at first recognise the dandified fellow who stood beside her.

'Oh that's who you are. Yes, I'm looking for Wee Lily. My granny's in the big field ploughing and I thought she might be on her own just now.'

'I've not seen her today but last night Jake was hitting her and I told her to go home and lock the door,' said Robbie.

'Did he hurt her?' she asked angrily.

'I don't think so,' he said.

'One of those days I'm going to kill that bastard if he doesn't stop knocking my mam about,' said the girl. Though her tone was almost conversational, Robbie could tell that she was completely serious.

'I don't think that's a very good idea,' he told her.

'What does it matter to you?' she asked.

'Nothing really. I just think that if you killed him, they'd hang you and that must be an unpleasant way of dying.'

'They didn't hang Craigie,' she said.

'Craigie was insane. Besides he had a good reason for killing Bullhead. He had it coming to him.' For a moment Robbie forgot who the girl was.

She glared at him. 'Did you know him?' she asked.

'Know who?' He was defensive now, having recognised his slip.

'The man they called Bullhead.'

'Yes.'

'What was he like?'

He stared at her. She looked intelligent and resourceful. There wasn't any point in telling her lies. 'He was a pig, I'm afraid.'

She said nothing, just kept on staring into his face.

'I'm sorry,' he said slowly.

'Don't be sorry. Why should you be sorry? Nobody else is,' she said and strode into the steading just at the moment that Wee Lily appeared in the dairy door. It was plain from her expression of delight and the way she threw out her arms how much she loved her child.

'Aw, Kitty,' she cried as they embraced.

Robbie watched the girl put a hand on her mother's face. 'Has Jake been hitting you again, Mam?' she asked.

'No' much. Robbie over there stopped him. He's a grand lad is Robbie.'

Kitty did not turn her head towards Robbie but went on looking at her mother. 'Where is he?' she asked.

'He's over there by the byre.'

'No, I mean Jake. Where's Jake?'

'I dinna ken. He's never come out to work this mornin' and my mother cannae find him. She's hopping mad.'

'You tell him when he does come out that if I get my hands on him, I'll mark him like he's marked you,' said Kitty in a voice of menace. Robbie could guess that she was well capable of it.

When Robbie went off shaking his head, Kitty and her mother fell into their usual kind of childish conversation which Kitty had long ago grown out of but which was all that Wee Lily could sustain.

'What are you doing here, lass? Won't they miss you at the ferm?' she asked.

'MacPhee sent me into Rosewell to give an order to the haberdasher for her. She's no' expecting me back for a bit yet. I thought I told you to hit Jake if he tried anything on wi' you, Mam.' Kitty's voice was angry.

'It doesnae matter. I'm having a bairn soon and Big Lily says if it's a laddie we can get shot o'Jake yince and for a'.'

Kitty stared at her mother. 'You're having a bairn? When? Is it Jake's?'

'Of course it's Jake's. And I dinna ken when but I'm having it. I'll no' need to let him in my bed again and that's why he was mad yesterday.'

Wee Lily sounded very happy at this turn of events, but the feelings that rose up in Kitty almost overwhelmed her. First of all there was disgust that her mother had slept with Jake at all in spite of hating him.

'How could you let him into your bed, Mam?' she asked angrily.

Wee Lily only shrugged. 'Big Lily told me to. She said I had to get another bairn. If it's a laddie, we can get rid o'Jake.'

'I know, you said that already,' snapped Kitty. What she was feeling now was terrible jealousy because she realised that any child born to her mother would be loved with unquestioning affection, the same love as Wee Lily had always given to her.

She wanted to cry, to howl and scream and was furious to realise that Big Lily was right, she did not want her nose put out of joint with her mother. Already, though the next child was not even a noticeable swelling in Wee Lily's belly, she felt displaced.

She turned away and walked towards the door. Wee Lily watched her going and asked sadly, 'Where are you going? Do you no' want a cup o' milk?'

'No, I don't. I'm going to see if I can meet Marie off the train. It's about this time she comes home,' said Kitty shortly. She could not bear to listen to her mother telling her again that if the child she was carrying turned out to be a boy, all her hopes would be vested in him.

There was a fine mist drifting up the river and trailing its ghostly fingers among the leafless trees of the Prior's Walk. Kitty strode over the rutted track without noticing the stones.

She was furious and hurt. If Wee Lily had not been so childish, Kitty would have rounded on her and accused her of lack of love but there was no use saying anything like that to her mother. It would not be understood.

Halfway along the path she saw a figure coming through the mist towards her. Marie was not as tall as Kitty but she had filled out and lost her girlish look. As she drew nearer, Kitty saw that her friend had become a woman of some style dressed in smart city clothes, a long grey jacket that buttoned up neatly to her chin, a matching skirt that swept the top of her good-quality boots and a little grey hat with a green feather sticking up from the ribbon. On her hands she wore black leather gloves and she carried a shallow leather case containing her pictures.

Kitty felt ill-dressed and slovenly as she walked towards this vision. She was conscious that all the clothes she wore were hand-me-downs from other women on Falconwood. Even her bondager's hat was an old one thrown out by MacPhee. She had never in her whole life chosen something she wanted to wear.

She was unstinting in her praise of the transformed Marie, however. 'My word you look grand, like a duchess. Edinburgh's made a differ-ence to you,' she exclaimed as they came near to each other. Marie smiled, pleased to see her friend, for in recent months their meetings had been rare. During the summer months Kitty was kept working late on the farm and since the painting classes began again, Marie had been spending more and more time with the Roxburgh family. She knew she was drifting away from the old life in Camptounfoot and only came back reluctantly. She did not want Kitty to realise this, however, and anxiety to cover up made her very effusive in her greeting.

'Kitty, how wonderful to see you! What a lovely surprise,' she exclaimed. Even her voice had changed, Kitty noticed.

They linked arms and walked back along the path. Having Marie with her again cheered Kitty up and she was able to thrust the pain of Wee Lily's news to the back of her mind at least for a short while. Marie was telling her about the work she was doing and about the other girls in her class, carefully glossing over Amy for she did not want to wax too enthusiastic about her new friend to her old one.

Kitty listened and when it was her turn, talked about Falconwood and especially about Effie, the bondager who most often shared her work.

'Effie's getting married soon. She's got a man at last and it's no' without trying. I think the only men in Falconwood she's not slept with are Laidlaw and Liddle,' she said baldly.

Marie, who had become used to the gentility of Edinburgh girls, was shocked. 'That's awful. Does the man she's marrying know?'

'He doesn't care. She'll work along with him and they'll take a herd's place on some farm. Poor Effie, it'll be bairns and hard work, and hard work and bairns for the rest of her life, but she's daft, she's as pleased as a dog wi' two tails,' said Kitty.

'Well if that's what she wants, it isn't so bad,' suggested Marie.

The memory of Wee Lily kindled a spark in Kitty. 'Of course it's bad, it's terrible. She'll be an old woman before she's twenty-five. You won't catch me getting married. I'd rather go to jail like Craigie,' was her stout reply.

Marie thought she was joking and laughed. 'I'm sure you'll get married one day and I certainly hope you don't go to jail. Some man'll come along and sweep you off your feet.'

Kitty noticed there was a yearning note in Marie's voice when she said this. She looked sharply at her, wondering if she was about to lose her friend in the same way as she was losing her mother, to someone else.

'Thae daft lassies in Edinburgh are filling your head wi' rubbish,' she snorted.

'Oh no, Kitty, I believe in love. I really do,' said Marie fervently, thinking of Murray. She wished she could tell Kitty about him, about his wonderful dark hair and soft brown eyes… about the lovely way he spoke and how he looked soulfully at her when he sang to Amy's accompaniment on the Murrayhill piano.

But Kitty was obviously not in the mood for that sort of confidence. She stopped in the middle of the path and said scornfully, '*Love*… It's a lot o' shit. It's a swindle put oot by men to convince women they should do as they're told. The boots are a' on the men's feet. Look at my mam and Jake. He sits doon and gets fed. He never lifts a hand to help. He does as little work as possible but they keep him because he's a man and they need a man to keep their place. Now he's got her in the family way and she's as pleased as a dog wi' two tails.

'And look at Craigie, come to that, up there in the prison. He writes letters to his sisters telling them what to do and they do it. If he told them to go down and jump off the big bridge, they'd do it, I'll be bound. So would my daft granny come to that.'

There was a note of fury in her voice that startled Marie. 'Oh Kitty,' she said, patting her friend's arm. 'Has Jake been giving your mother trouble again?'

'Not just him. Every man means trouble as far as I can see. Liddle keeps trying to creep up into the attic when I'm asleep. It's getting to the stage I'm scared to close my eyes. He's put some o' the farm lads up to bothering me too. Two of them are aye jumping out on me and trying to feel me up. I'm sick of it.'

Marie had been guarded from troubles like those. 'That's awful. You should speak to the steward about it,' she said.

Kitty turned on her. 'What good would that do? Laidlaw's no' going to give them their marching orders because they bother a lassie and say dirty things to her. Besides, he looks at me in a funny way now. I think he'd be the same as them if he got the chance.'

Marie stared at the tall figure walking by her side and realised that the tousled tomboy Kitty had grown into a statuesque Amazon. Her head of glorious hair meant that she would stand out in any crowd. No wonder men took an interest in her. She knew better than to say this, for Kitty would not have been flattered by such a comment.

'Come into Tibbie's with me,' she suggested instead. 'She'll have tea ready. You've not been in for a long time. She'll be pleased to see you.'

The cottage was warmly lit by paraffin lamps with big glass shades in warm colours of pink and ruby-red. The fire was blazing and the whole place had an atmosphere of comfort and ease that was not usual for such a humble home.

Tibbie wisely spent the money that Tim sent her and it was she who'd paid for Marie's fine clothes because she wanted the girl to hold her own in Edinburgh society. Even then there was still plenty left over for bags of coal and the best of food.

When Kitty stepped inside the cottage door she paused as she always did and cast an admiring look all around. Everything sparkled and shone, from the gleaming table to the brass fire irons and there was a mouthwatering smell from golden pancakes cooking on a black griddle over the fire. This must be how the gentry live, she thought, for she did not know any better and Tibbie's way of life was so vastly superior to anything else she'd ever seen.

'Kitty, it's grand to see you. Sit down and I'll mask the tea,' cried Tibbie, lifting the cat off its nest on the chair to make way for the guest. Then she looked at Kitty again and asked, 'Aren't you grown up? How old are you now, lass?' It seemed as if Kitty had matured in only a few days.

'I'm nearly fifteen,' said Kitty shortly. She was tired of people making comments about her transformation from child to woman. She wished she could go back to being the barefoot urchin who hid under hedges. At least no one bothered about her then, no men gave her evil looks or made lewd suggestions to her.

She looked across at the ladylike Marie and thought that men would be more polite to her. They wouldn't grab for her in the hayshed because she was only a bondager's bastard and ripe for the taking.

It was very important to her, however, that she and Marie remained friends. That bond must not be broken because it was a bond made when they were children and it mattered a lot to Kitty, who had no other real friend.

'I was wondering if you'd like to go to the Rosewell dance on Saturday night with me', she said suddenly.

Effie had been telling her about how all the other young women went on Saturdays. Kitty had never been to a dance and now she thought it might be some place that she and Marie could go together.

As soon as the words were out of her mouth, however, she knew she'd made a terrible mistake. Marie's eyes showed total shock but she covered it up almost at once. Not quickly enough though, because Kitty saw it.

'It doesn't matter,' she said hurriedly. 'It doesn't matter. I don't really want to go.'

There was nothing that Marie wanted to do less than dance in Roseweil's public hall, because her experiences in Edinburgh had introduced her to a very different world. But she thought Kitty had set her heart on it and did not want to hurt her, especially after the peculiar way she was behaving and the terrible description she had given of her life on Falcon wood.

'What a good idea,' she enthused. 'I'd love to go. I've never been to a dance.'

'There's always grand music,' said Tibbie wistfully, thinking of the times she and Nanny used to go dancing together. In her kindly way she smiled on the girls, imagining that they would be following in her footsteps. So it was arranged. Kitty and Marie were to go dancing on the following Saturday.

There was no one in the farmyard or in Liddle's cottage when Kitty arrived back at Falconwood. Mrs Liddle, she knew, was in the habit of attending prayer meetings held in other cottages in the evenings and Liddle took advantage of her absence by drinking with the unmarried men who lived in a communal bothy at the back of the hayshed.

Relieved to have the place to herself, Kitty set about bringing life to the fire and preparing a meal. She ate and, barefooted, was about to mount the stairs to her comfortless bed, when the door creaked open and Liddle staggered in. He was drunk, drunker than she had ever seen him, and when he saw her standing by the hearth, he slammed the door shut, turned the key and shoved it in his pocket.

'Now I've got ye. Now you canna get oot. Now I'll show ye, cheeky little besom that ye are!' He hissed and swayed towards her, hauling at the neck of her blouse with both hands and ripping it down the front.

Kitty shoved frantically at his chest and cried out, 'Get away from me, you pig.'

'I'm a pig, am I? Let's see about that,' muttered Liddle, roughly ripping the girl's clothes. She hated the touch of his hands on her skin; she loathed the sour smell of his breath on her face.

As she fought against him, a strange red tide was rising within her. It was a tide of fury swollen to terrible force by all her pent-up resentments and angers. Her struggles increased.

Liddle was angry too, violent and dangerous in drink. He put both hands round Kitty's neck and pulled her head down towards him, half-throttling her.

'Come on, ye've no' had a man yet. It's about time ye started. I'll show ye,' he was muttering as he fought with her. She pummelled him with her fists, kicking at his legs with her bare feet, regretting the fact that she'd taken off her heavy boots. The grip that he had on her neck threatened to immobilise her and she knew if she did not get away from him soon, she would pass out.

The situation was desperate. She was being pushed back against the wall and Liddle was groping under her skirt with one hand while he held her head back with the other. The only weapons she had were her strength and desperation. With a superhuman effort she turned her face towards his hand and bit viciously into it. Bone crunched beneath her strong teeth and he gave a horrible yell as he let go.

That was all she needed. With every ounce of her muscle power, she aimed her fist straight at the contorted face so close to hers. The punch exploded, throwing him back like the kick of a horse. He staggered against the table edge and fell to his knees with blood pouring from his mouth.

Kitty stood over him, both fists up like a prize fighter, but he did not rise. He rolled around on the floor, clutching his bitten hand to his chest and groaning, 'You wee bitch. I'll get you for this. I'll get you, see if I don't.'

She pushed at him with her foot and ordered, 'Give me the key. I'm not staying here with you another night.'

He was still wiping blood from his face and muttering curses so she said it again, louder, '*Give me the key.*' She could not bear to search him for it because that would mean she had to touch him.

Without looking up, he slipped his fingers into his waistcoat pocket and brought out the big iron key, which he threw on the floor in front of him. She was too wary to bend down for it, but pulled it towards herself with her curled toes. Then she stuck her feet back into her boots, grabbed her shawl and made her escape.

Outside the only sounds came from hooting owls hunting in the stubble fields. The wild rage left Kitty as suddenly as it came and she felt strangely drained and empty as she stood panting and shaking with nerves in the yard. Now she realised how terrified she had been during the encounter with Liddle.

'Where will I go? What will I do?' she asked herself aloud. Then she spotted a light shining in the window of the bothy that MacPhee shared with Effie and a younger bondager called May. She ran awkwardly across the yard in her unlaced boots and rapped on their door. It was Effie who answered.

She took one look at Kitty and screamed, 'Oh my God, what's happened to ye? You're in rags.'

'Let me in, Effie. Liddle did it. He tried to rape me,' groaned Kitty.

MacPhee appeared behind Effie. She looked even taller than usual in a long white nightgown and an incongruous cotton mob-cap. Even in her distress, Kitty was impressed at the sight of the headgear because most bondagers slept in their underclothes and few owned a nightgown, far less a nightcap.

MacPhee was cool in crises. 'Come in at once,' she said, pulling Kitty inside.

It was only when she stood in the sanctuary of their room that Kitty realised her blouse was hanging in shreds from her shoulders and her skirt was half-pulled down from her waist.

'He'll be drunk,' said MacPhee calmly.

'Yes, his wife's out and he aye gets drunk when she's away,' Kitty told them. Effie was exclaiming about the damage to Kitty's clothes, both hands over her face. To her that was of more significance than loss of virginity, but MacPhee was more matter-of-fact.

'He didnae get you, did he? He didnae manage anything?' she asked. Kitty shook her head.

MacPhee then silenced the still gasping Effie with a shove in the ribs. 'Shut your mooth. She'll get anither blouse. What're we going to do about this lassie tonight? She cannae go back to Liddle's place.'

Kitty agreed. 'I'm no' going back into that house. Never. I've had to fight him off almost every night since I've lived there and now he's really out to get me because I bloodied his face,' she told them.

MacPhee looked pleased. 'Did you now!'

'I hit him with my fist.' Kitty held up her hand. There were bloodied cuts on the knuckles from Liddle's teeth.

'Well done,' said MacPhee. 'He's had that coming for a long time.'

'I'm no' going back,' said Kitty again. 'And I canna go home to Townhead because my granny'd just send me back to Liddle.'

'You can stay here so long's you dinna mind sharing a bed wi' Effie,' said MacPhee with decision, 'but I'll make Liddle pay for your keep because you'll still have to be his bondager. You're bound for this year, aren't you? I'll speak to Laidlaw about it. He'll fix it up.'

Next morning MacPhee looked formidably angry when she marched over to the gang of men waiting in the semi-darkness of dawn for their tasks to be assigned to them.

'Hey, Liddle, let's have a look at you,' she cried, pulling him out of the shadows where he'd been standing. His face was swollen, his lips split and bloodied and one of his teeth was missing in the front.

'Kitty packs a good punch,' said MacPhee admiringly. 'That's what you get for forcing yourself on a lassie. You should have got it years ago if truth be told. Especially over the last wee bairn you hurt.'

The other men crowded round staring and some of the younger ones were laughing.

'Did a lassie do that to you, Tom? My word, I wouldnae like to admit to being knocked doon by a woman,' they crowed.

'She's a bitch,' he muttered through swollen lips. 'She's an animal, no' a woman. She should be a navvy like her father.'

The men laughed even more and some of them looked across at Kitty with approval, for Liddle was not popular.

MacPhee was not finished with him, however. 'I've something to say to you before Laidlaw comes oot,' she hissed, pulling him towards her. 'I'm keeping the lassie in my hoose from now on but you'll pay me twae shillin's a week for her keep because she'll still be your bondager, at least till term time. If she bolted, you'd no' have a lassie and Laidlaw would get rid of you. He's fed up wi' your antics anyway.'

There was nothing Liddle could do but accept this ultimatum. Then MacPhee walked back to her women and said to Kitty, 'Don't go near him. I'll collect your wages and give them to you. How much does he pay you a week?'

Kitty told her, 'He gives me a shillin'. He gives the rest to my granny, or so he says.'

Bondagers on Townhead earned around five shillings a week when there was full work so she was obviously being underpaid, but Big Lily had made a private bargain with Liddle and the amount paid was not told to Kitty. She had literally been sold into slavery because, by the terms of her bond with Liddle, she could not leave him until the time came round for workers to make new bargains in the spring.

'Huh,' snorted MacPhee. 'You're a good worker, so I'll no' be givin' anything to your granny. I'll pay you what's due if you work as well as you've been doing till now. Look out, here's Mr Laidlaw coming. I'll speak to him about this later.'

The work of the agricultural year was almost finished. Ploughing for next season's crops had started and the cattle were being brought in from the fields to spend the winter in warm, steamy, smelly cattle courts. Sheep were being driven down from the slopes of the Three Sisters hills where they had summered. For the bad months they would be pastured in meadows by the river.

The business with Liddle was soon forgotten in the urgency of this work and Kitty settled down to the tranquillity of living with Effie, MacPhee and May. The accommodation was spartan but it was companionable and, above all, safe. She saw Liddle only in the distance now, for he was giving her a wide berth.

When Saturday morning came round, she told Effie about her plan to go dancing in Rosewell with her friend Marie.

'Have you never been dancin' before?' asked Effie.

Kitty shook her head.

'What are you going to wear?'

This was a problem that had not occurred to Kitty. 'My skirt and blouse, I suppose,' she said, for she owned nothing else. Her ripped blouse had been replaced by an old one of kind Rosie's daughter.

Effie squawked, 'You cannae go dancin' in your working claes. I'll lend you a dress. I've a bonny green yin I used to wear to the dances when I was thinner. You can have it.'

Like many young bondagers, Effie was intensely dress-conscious and spent most of her wages on clothes from the pedlars who came round the farm towns with full packs of garish finery to coax money from the lassies.

The gown she hauled out of her box that evening was viridian green, a colour so bright that it almost hurt the eyes. Kitty stared at it in disbelief. Instantly she knew that it was the worst possible colour to go with her hair. At school, Bella and her friends used to chant a verse, 'Red and green should never be seen, except upon a gypsy queen.' Gypsies were even more disdained in Camptounfoot than bondagers' bastards.

'I think I'll just wear my old clothes,' she said to Effie, who bridled.

'What's wrong wi' it. It's a braw goon.'

'Yes, it is, but I'm afraid I might spoil it. What if I spilt something on it?' said Kitty hurriedly.

Effie was generous. She thrust the dress at Kitty and said, 'I'll no' mind. You can have it to keep. Go on, take it. You'll really catch the lads' eyes if you wear it.'

The dance was to be held in Rosewell Public Hall, a large red sandstone building overlooking the square. When Kitty arrived at Tibbie's at about half-past seven to collect Marie, she found her friend waiting in a pale-coloured, high-necked dress that was the very model of discretion.

The shawl that Kitty had draped over herself to hide the green gown as she left Falconwood was not sufficiently concealing for Tibbie's eagle eye, however.

'What's that you're wearing, Kitty? Let's see it,' she asked sharply. Reluctantly Kitty lifted the corner of the shawl to show a part of the dress's ruched skirt and she could tell from a momentary flash of consternation on Tibbie's face that she looked as garish as she feared.

'I was lent it by a lassie on the farm,' she explained hurriedly. Tibbie collected herself and covered up her surprise at Kitty's finery by asking, 'Have you girls got enough money to pay yourselves into the dance?'

Kitty stuck her hand out to show a medley of carefully hoarded coins and Tibbie laughed, remembering the times she went dancing with Nanny.

'I'll give you the entrance money and you can keep all that for the refreshments. Here you are,' she said, reaching up to her mantelshelf and bringing down an old tea caddy. When it was opened Kitty saw several golden coins and much silver lying inside it and Tibbie presented them each with a florin, which was a fortune to Kitty. Then they went on their way arm in arm.

During the walk to the hall, Kitty kept herself draped in her working shawl and wished with all her heart that she'd never thought of the idea of going dancing in the first place.

By her side Marie was thinking the same thing, for she dreaded the evening that lay ahead. Her shyness, and the aspirations she had been given by her visits to Murrayhill, would make it almost unendurable. For Kitty's sake, however, she pretended to be excited and succeeded so well that the young bondager truly believed her friend was looking forward to the evening.

Halfway along Prior's Walk they saw Bella and the schoolteacher, Mr Arnott, coming towards them. Bella was clinging to his arm in a proprietorial way and smirked when she saw her old schoolmates. It was obvious that she intended to stop and talk to them.

'Isn't it a fine evening?' she asked, stopping in the middle of the path and effectively making it impossible for them to pass by without talking.

'It's a fine night,' agreed Kitty, trying to sidle by.

'Going to the dance, are you? We saw crowds of young folk going in when William and I passed, didn't we, William?' said Bella sweetly.

'Yes,' he agreed. He was anxious to move on for Kitty's satirical eye still upset him. Bella, however, had more to say.

'It's nice for young lads and lassies to have a place where they can meet each other,' was her next remark. She sounded as if she were about fifty and condescending though she was only a year older than

Marie. Squeezing William's arm, she went on, 'Of course, we don't have to go. We're getting married next month.'

'Fancy that,' said Kitty in a meaningful voice.

Bella's eyes flashed with her old dislike and she sounded falsely sincere as she said, 'You're looking very grand tonight, Kitty. Is that green you're wearing. It's the right colour for you.' Kitty flushed as she remembered Bella's verse about gypsy queens.

Mr Arnott's fiancée was not finished with them, however. She turned to Marie and said, 'And you're looking well too. I hear you spend a lot of time in Edinburgh now. I always say to William that I'm surprised how friendly you girls are – when you've got good reason not to like each other very much, especially you, Marie.'

'What do you mean?' asked Marie in genuine surprise.

'Because of your mother and her father of course,' said Bella sweetly.

Marie and Kitty looked at each other and Kitty jumped in to say, 'My father has nothing to do with Marie.' She pulled at her friend's arm.

Bella's voice was like honey. 'But he *has*. Marie's mother was living with him after Benjamin died. And he killed her in the most brutal way. It was terrible. Everybody knew he was the murderer but they couldn't prove it. Your father killed Marie's mother, Kitty. That's the connection I'm talking about.'

'That's not true,' said Marie weakly.

'Oh but it is,' cried Bella as she and William walked away. 'Everybody knows about it. Everybody but you apparently. I'm amazed your brother's kept it from you for so long.'

The girls left alone on the path stared at each other in consternation and Kitty saw there were tears in Marie's eyes.

'Is that true?' she whispered.

'Aye,' said Kitty grimly.

Marie gave a terrible gulp. 'Why didn't you tell me? You should have told me if you knew. You shouldn't have let me find out like that. I always knew there was a mystery about how my mother died. David has dropped hints from time to time but I just thought he was jealous of our friendship... Oh my God, what a horrible man that Bullhead must have been!' she whispered.

Kitty could not bring herself to plead, 'But it's not my fault. Don't hold him against me.' Her soul was crying it out in silence, however.

Marie said it for her but she sounded unconvinced. 'Of course, it's got nothing to do with you,' she assured her friend, but she did not take Kitty's arm again.

'I don't want to go to that dance,' said Kitty bluntly, standing still in the middle of the path. 'I didn't want to go from the beginning. I was just trying to think of something you'd enjoy. You've been so strange recently, so taken up with these folk in Edinbury.'

Dispassionately Marie noted how Kitty pronounced the name of the capital. It seemed to make the gulf between them wider.

'Because of my classes, I have to spend a lot of time there,' she said, but they both knew that wasn't entirely true.

The anger that she always found so hard to control had taken Kitty over. She turned round and headed back to Camptounfoot.

'You do what you like but I'm not going to that dance for folk like Bella to laugh about us,' she said.

Marie felt a rush of relief as she turned with her. 'I don't want to go either. I never wanted to go in the first place. I only said I would because you seemed so keen and you made me feel guilty about going to Edinburgh so much. That's why I said I'd come with you,' she said.

'Why should I want to go dancing?' asked Kitty, glaring fiercely at her. 'I hate men. I've never met a good one except that Tim Maquire and poor old Jo. Get yourself back to your friends in Edinbury. I'm going to Falconwood to give Effie back this horrible dress. Goodbye, Marie.'

Lifting her green skirts with both hands she took off at a sprint and was soon swallowed up in the darkness.

Marie called after the disappearing figure, 'Don't be silly, Kitty. This is what Bella wants.'

'She's won then,' came back Kitty's voice.

Kitty did not go straight back to the farm. She slipped down the narrow alley between two of the cottages on the village main street and into the field behind Tibbie's cottage. Once again, her objective was the hiding-place in the hedge. Hurriedly she dug up her tin, tied the half-sovereign in the corner of her shawl and stuck the knife in her boot. The first chance she got she'd run away, she decided.

## Chapter Ten

At the beginning of February, the cold was more intense than the oldest people in the village could remember. Hoar frost gripped the world, turning it to ghostly white. Even at noon, the temperature never rose above freezing point.

The houses in the village seemed to huddle, deeper into the ground and grey streaks of smoke rose from the chimneys making defiant trickles in a gun-metal-grey sky. There was little traffic in the streets and when people had to go out they were wrapped up against the biting wind with only their eyes showing above scarves and mufflers.

Early one morning a galloping horse went through the village street and half an hour later it returned in company with another. Tibbie saw them pass her window and told Marie, 'There's Dr Robertson with the groom from Bella Vista.'

Marie, who was eating breakfast leisurely because she could not get to Edinburgh along the snow-blocked line, glanced up anxiously and said, 'I hope Lady Godolphin's all right. She's been looking terribly ill and sad recently.'

Tibbie was reassuring. 'Robertson's a good man. He'll look after her and it's not as if she's not been through it before. This is her sixth, isn't it?

Marie nodded, but for the rest of the day her thoughts were with her patroness. She tried to tell herself that her concern was not selfish. She had grown devoted to the beautiful and gracious Bethya, but it was impossible not to wonder, 'What will happen to my painting classes if she dies?'

The thought of having to give them up, to come back to Camptounfoot and wait for David to get his house, and, worst of all, never to see Murray and the rest of the Roxburghs again devastated her. 'I mustn't think about it. I'm being selfish,' she scolded herself, but whenever a rider passed the cottage window, she rushed to see who it was. There were not many riders that day and none of them was Dr Robertson.

In fact, Lady Bethya Godolphin very nearly died giving birth to her son. It took all the skill and effort of Alexander Robertson to keep her alive and there were times when even he despaired. The problem was that the patient was so weak that she was unable to put in sufficient effort to deliver the child.

Robertson bent over her, exhorting her, encouraging her and eventually, after two days of labouring the child was delivered. When the midwife took charge of the baby, the doctor hovered anxiously over the mother, marking her laboured breathing, listening to her faltering heart, prescribing a variety of drugs, some of which helped while others did not.

Sydney and Miriam had been with Bethya through the whole ordeal, taking turns sitting by her bed and holding her hand. Her lovely silken eyelashes lay flickering on her white cheeks and her husband whispered to her, 'I'm sorry, Bethya. Don't die, my dear. Don't die.'

She could not answer him but she heard and the intensity of his voice gave her strength to go on fighting.

When Miriam watched over her, Bethya was only conscious of a brown hand holding hers and thought she was back in India, at Kandala in the hills above Bombay where her family used to go in the hot weather and where she had once had a severe bout of fever, her first brush with death. Their bungalow in Kandala was rambling and ramshackle, dusty and needing paint, but always full of the people she loved – her parents and her sisters, the old servants who had brought her up, the three-legged pye-dog that used to come to the verandah every morning and beg for scraps. In her mind she was there, while her body fought for breath.

At last, on the fourth day, she recovered her strength sufficiently to ask about her baby and whispered faintly, 'Is the baby all right? Where is it?'

Miriam leaned over and told her. 'The baby's with a wet nurse. He's a fine boy.'

They brought in the child and Sydney was summoned so there was a crowd round the bed when she held her son for the first time.

Miriam pulled back layers of white wool to show his face and he yawned widely like a sleepy kitten showing a pink tongue and Bethya managed a little laugh as she looked up at Sydney.

'Oh my dear, he's your living image. Look at that nose!' she exclaimed. Even though he was so young, the baby had his father's prow-like beak but the stubble of hair that covered his head was jet-black. He looked like a little pirate.

'We'll call him Alexander because he looks like a conqueror,' she said and her hand went up to Sydney's face, patting his cheek. Then she closed her eyes and drifted back into her dream-world, but they knew now that she was going to live.

The news that she was out of danger soon reached the district and among the letters that poured into the house was one from Marie Benjamin. 'I prayed for your recovery', it said. And indeed Marie had prayed both for Bethya and for herself but her prayers for herself asked that she clear her mind of self-interest.

When she read Marie's letter Bethya made a little note in a pad that lay by her on the bed. The note was to remind herself to make provision in her will for Marie Benjamin's painting fees for two more years. By that time, she reckoned, the girl would have launched herself on a career.

It worried Sydney and Miriam that she had such a fixation with making a new will, but she told them, 'A brush with death such as I've had makes you realise what can happen unexpectedly. I'm not planning to die soon, my dears, I'm just tidying things up that's all.'

There was something on Sydney's mind and when he and Bethya were alone together he said to her, 'When you make your will, my dear, I don't want you to leave anything to me. I want you to divide your fortune among the children. I've enough for myself and I remember that when I was growing up money was the cause of the trouble with my father. I don't want that obstacle to come between me and my children because I realise that there's enough of my father in me to make the same mistakes as he did…'

She did not argue. 'If you think you have enough, I'll leave everything to the children, to the girls as well as the boys because women should be independent, I think.'

'I have enough,' said Sydney.

When she was asleep, Dr Robertson came in and told Sydney, 'I'm sorry to have to tell you that over-exertion, or over-excitement could kill your wife. The utmost care must be taken to keep her quiet and happy. Her cardiac insufficiency is marked, I'm afraid.'

'And how long has she got?' asked Sydney stonily.

'It could be a long time. These things are very unpredictable.'

The two men looked at each other and Sydney said at last, 'Thank you, Robertson. You didn't say anything to her sister, did you?'

The doctor shook his head.

'Good, good,' said Sydney. 'We'll keep it to ourselves then, shall we?'

To beguile himself at Bella Vista he passed his time hunting with the pack of his friend Allandale, who was still in London.

While she worked in the fields below the lower slopes of the Three Sisters hills, Kitty often heard the sound of his horn and watched him dashing headlong over rough country as if he was daring Fate to break his neck.

The cold was intense and even though she was young, Kitty's bones ached with the bite of it. At last the frost broke and the rain came, which meant that the problem was no longer cold but mud. The bondager women wound ropes of straw into leggings which they wrapped round their calves above the boot-tops. All of them except Kitty knitted thick woollen stockings and she was presented with two pairs because she could not knit. No one had ever taught her.

As the end of February drew near, the talk on the farm was all of Maddiston Fair, which was due to take place on the 28th. It was the biggest event of the year, the annual hiring fair where farm servants went if they wanted another place or if their current employer was not keeping them for another year.

Laidlaw went round the cottages on a chilly evening, rapping on the doors of the people he was prepared to take on for another term. Anyone whose door was not knocked at knew they would have to go to the fair, carrying some symbol of their expertise – a hayfork, a carter's driving whip, or a shepherd's crook. Bondagers in search of a new place went arrayed in their traditional costume, in petticoats starched like boards, hats newly varnished and boots blackened till you could see your face in them.

MacPhee took Kitty aside one morning and said in a kindly voice, 'It's no' that we dinna want you on the place, but I think you should go somewhere else at the hiring fair. Laidlaw's keeping Liddle because he's good with the horses. He doesnae care about the trouble between you and him, so it's best if you go.'

Kitty nodded. The news did not upset her because for some time she had been fretting to get away. Every time she stared southwards at the blue outline of the line of hills that formed the border between England and Scotland, she longed to see what was on the other side. Her feet itched with her desire to travel. Wanderlust was a legacy from her father, had she but known it.

'I'll put in a good word for you wi' folk I ken at the fair. I'll see you get a good place and a better house to live in than Liddle's,' said kind MacPhee.

'Thank you,' Kitty replied. 'I was thinking of going anyway.'

That night, when her work was finished, she went back to Townhead and found Wee Lily making straw ropes for herself and her mother to wear in the fields. Big Lily sat silently smoking her pipe by the side of the fire. She saw Kitty enter the bothy but said nothing, for a wonder.

The girl sat down beside her mother and kissed her cheek. Wee Lily's belly was grossly swollen and Kitty hated the idea of the child inside it. 'Are you all right, Mam?' she asked softly.

'Grand, grand,' said Wee Lily.

'Where's Jake?'

'Oot shutting up the hens.'

'He's not hitting you now, is he?'

'No, my ma doesnae let him. He's gey quiet. Jo says he's got another woman in Rosewell.'

Kitty lowered her voice even more, sharply conscious of Big Lily's listening ears. 'Mam, if I was to go away, would you come with me?' Wee Lily looked astonished. 'Go, where to? I've never been off Townhead except to go to Rosewell noo and again.'

'I don't know. I'm going to be looking for a place at Maddiston Fair next week.'

Big Lily spoke up with satisfaction in her voice. 'So you're being sent off then. Has Falconwood got rid o' ye?'

Kitty did not answer, just kept on asking her mother, 'Would you come with me, Mam? I'd look after you. You wouldnae need to stay here with Jake.'

Big Lily loomed up at the side of them. 'Get out of here. Your mother's staying where she is. Her bairn's due any day now and then we'll be safe, we'll have another pair of hands to do the work when I'm old.'

Before she went away, Kitty turned to her mother for one last appeal. 'When I get a place, I'll come back for you.'

But Wee Lily shook her head and whimpered, 'I cannae leave, bairn. I cannae leave here. I'd be feared…'

'You heard what she said,' shouted Big Lily, pointing at the door. 'Get oot o' here before I throw you oot. And dinna come back.'

Kitty thought about going over to Tibbie's and making it up with Marie but anger over the fall-out on the night of the dance still rankled with her. Marie had made no effort to contact her, so why should she be the one to make the first move? If she found a place at Maddiston, she'd tell Marie, but in the meantime, she'd wait.

Back at Falconwood, she was surprised to see a man standing in the lee of the cattleshed. His presence was given away by the glow of the cheroot he was smoking and the smell of it drifting across the yard to the girl told her that the lurker was not one of the labourers, who all smoked clay pipes. She drew back, for the trouble with Liddle had upset her more than she realised.

To avoid him she walked round the outside of the yard and headed in an oblique way for MacPhee's cottage but a voice called out her name. 'Kitty!' it said.

She stopped and looked round, ready to run if she had to. Laidlaw the steward came out of the gloom and walked towards her.

'Kitty,' he said again, 'wait a minute. I want a word with you.'

She stood very still and said nothing.

'I hear from MacPhee about the trouble with Liddle and that you won't be staying on for the next term,' he said when he was closer.

'That's right,' said Kitty.

'I'll be sorry to lose you,' said Laidlaw.

'I feel like a change,' Kitty told him.

'Maybe I could offer you another change,' he said.

She looked at him in surprise, wondering if he had another farm in his charge.

'What sort of change?' she asked cautiously.

He was smiling. 'A change for the better. A very comfortable place with not much to do.'

'I'm not scared of work,' she said.

'I know that,' said Laidlaw. 'I've been watching you. I'm looking for a girl for the house.'

Kitty shook her head. 'I've no house skills, Mr Laidlaw. I wouldnae ken where to start in a house.'

He smiled again. 'I've maids to do that work. I'm looking for a girl for myself, for my bed.'

She stepped back. Of course, that was what he was after. She knew that until a few months ago, he'd had a mistress living in, an ex-shopgirl from Maddiston, but she'd upped and run away to get married. Now he was looking for a replacement.

'I couldnae do that job either, Mr Laidlaw,' she said stiffly.

He wasn't put off. 'I'd give you money for yourself and I'd buy your clothes. You could have your folk over to the big house any time you liked. You're a bonny lassie and you and I would get along grand, I think.'

'Would you marry me?' asked Kitty boldly.

He threw the stub-end of the cheroot onto the cobbles and trod on it with his booted foot. 'You're anticipating a bit, aren't you? We'd have to see how we get on first.'

She knew perfectly well that marriage had never entered his head. If he ever did wed, it would be to the daughter of some respectable farmer who could bring him a dowry in money or land.

'I'll go to the hiring fair,' said Kitty.

Laidlaw was not too put out. 'Think about my offer. It's the best one you're likely to get,' he said as he walked away.

Kitty watched him go and knew that she'd burned her boats. Even if she wanted to, she couldn't stay at Falconwood now.

She had never been to the hiring fair because her mother and grandmother did not need to attend them and Big Lily would not take a day off work even for a major event like that, though all the other farms gave their workers holidays.

When MacPhee talked about the fair, Kitty told her, 'I've never been to it. I've been to the sheep fair at Rosewell but no' to Maddiston.'

'My word, lass, Rosewell's nothing! You'll be dumbstruck when you see the hiring fair, such a crowd o' folk and all the stalls and sideshows. It's an entertainment, I can tell you. You meet folk you havenae seen for years.'

If staid MacPhee went starry-eyed over the fair, it must be something special, thought Kitty.

The bondagers were all saving their money for the big day and spent hours discussing what they intended to wear. Because she was looking for a new place, Kitty had to wear traditional uniform and her friends all contributed something towards this so that she could look extra-smart – she was to wear MacPhee's new hat, Effie's best boots and May's cotton blouse because the one she got from Rosie was faded.

Effie was in a great state of excitement because the man she intended to marry would be looking for a new place at the fair and their future depended on what he found. She talked about this endlessly and what was worse, speculated on and on about the dress she should wear in order to back him up, until MacPhee's tolerance snapped.

'That's it, not another word about fancy claes. Get on wi' your work, Effie, or I'll give you a bad character and your lad'll never get a place with you in tow,' she shouted.

So Effie was reduced to whispering to Kitty in bed at night… 'What do you think, Kitty? Should I wear blue or green? Maybe I should dress very plain so's not to make any farm wife jealous. I'm going to have blue satin for my wedding dress. That'll make up for not looking grand at the fair…'

'I'm no' a specialist in dresses,' Kitty murmured as she drifted off to sleep and her dreams were haunted by memories of the dreadful green dress that she'd worn on the night she'd had her break-up with Marie. She spent a lot of time wondering what was happening to her friend and wishing she had gone to see her when she was last in Camptounfoot. Before she went off to her new place, she resolved, she'd seek out Marie and make up the trouble between them.

By 1872, Maddiston Fair had been in existence for six hundred years. Until thirty years previously it was a very small affair, for the hiring of agricultural workers only, but the prosperity brought to the town by the railway and its booming mills had caused a one-hundred-per-cent rise in the population in less than twenty years. The fair, which was traditionally held on the last Thursday in February (when it usually poured rain), became a mill holiday too.

On fair day, weavers, loom mechanics, spinners and darners turned out with their families, all dressed in their best, to spend money at the side shows, roundabouts and shooting ranges which came to Maddiston from all over the country.

On the eve of the fair David Benjamin took himself down to Camptounfoot to invite his sister to attend the festivities with him. He found her in the kitchen with Tibbie, preparing for an early departure to Edinburgh next morning.

'Surely you're coming to Maddiston Fair?' asked David, eyeing her leather case and travelling cloak lying on a chair by the fire. There was another small portmanteau with it and that made him very suspicious.

Marie looked guilty. 'Oh, dear, I'd forgotten about it. I said I'd go to Perthshire with Amy's family.'

Her brother's expression darkened. 'Perthshire?' he asked incredulously. 'What are you going there for?'

'The Roxburghs usually go to the country for a break at this time of the year,' she said.

David sneered. 'They all go to the country? What do you want to go to the country for? This is the country. Don't you get enough of it? According to you, the city's much better.'

She flushed as she always did when she was trying to stop herself from showing anger and said reasonably, 'They've invited me to go with them so that I can do some drawings. The scenery is spectacular near their house at Killin, I believe.'

He knew he should have been pleased that his sister had been taken up by people with a house in Perthshire and the leisure to enjoy it, but he wasn't. He was bitterly jealous and terrified of losing her. He almost shouted, 'I think those people are leading you astray. They'll make you want things you'll never have.'

Marie's tolerance ran out. 'What makes you so sure I'll never have them?' she snapped.

As he stared at her a horrible suspicion took root in his mind. Someone was trying to take her away from him.

'I don't want you to go. I want you to come to the fair with me,' he said with a quaver in his voice. But Marie was no longer so easy to manipulate. She shook her head and said firmly, 'I'm going to Perthshire with the Roxburghs. I'm sorry I forgot about the fair. I'll go to it with you next year.'

'You might not get the chance!' he yelled and stormed out of the cottage door.

All that night resentment festered in his mind as he lay in bed, building and embroidering on his suspicions until he could almost see the villain who was enticing his sister away from him.

'And I've worked so hard, I've planned so hard for us to be independent! I'm doing everything I can to make a home for her. How can she be so ungrateful?' he told himself over and over again.

Next morning he knew that he could not bear to go into the fair alone, to watch the crowds of happy people wandering around with their families. Mental anguish drove him to the counting-house where he could submerge himself in work.

Henderson's Mill was deserted as he sat at his desk with his head down over a sheaf of order forms, laboriously checking and rechecking that everything had been sent out correctly. One of the things that had brought increased prosperity to mill in the past few years was his insistence that orders be fulfilled as quickly and as correctly as possible. He devised a system for making sure that parcels and even big bales of tweed were despatched by train to the south on the same day as the order landed on his desk. No other local mill could match this speed of turn-round and delighted customers passed the word that you couldn't beat Henderson's for speed and efficiency.

The upsurge in business, at a time when his other mill in Rosewell was not working to full capacity and had to struggle to find orders, was noted by Adalbert Henderson, who woke on fair day also determined not to waste his time on festivities. He intended to take advantage of everybody being away to go to Maddiston and scan David's books in order to find out exactly how the fortunate upturn in business had been achieved.

If he asked Coleman about it, the manager was fair to David and sang his praises unreservedly, happily unaware that he was putting another nail in his own coffin, but he could not really explain the despatching system to Henderson's satisfaction and canny David kept his secrets to himself, for he did not want it to be poached for Rosewell too.

Imagine Adalbert's surprise when he walked into the counting-house and found his chief clerk there.

'Hey, hey, what's this? A young lad like you would be fairing, I thought!' he exclaimed as he stood with his hand on the jamb of the door.

David looked up and rubbed his stinging eyes wearily. 'No, Mr Henderson. I don't like fairs. They're just a waste of money if you ask me. I thought I'd take the chance to check on the orders when there's no distraction.'

Adalbert was a crafty and suspicious man, so for a moment he wondered if this lad was up to some fishy business of his own. His eye immediately went to the safe but it was locked and he knew that

Coleman kept the key. Assuming a pleased expression he walked to David's desk and leaned over his shoulder. 'I'm glad I found you here, young Benjamin. You can show me how you've tightened up the procedures in this place.'

David smiled, a rare thing these days. 'It's quite simple really. I found out that orders sometimes lay in the counting-house waiting to be carried out for days at a time. The clerk we had in charge then was very dilatory. So I took his work over and Mr Coleman gave him his notice...'

Henderson clapped his shoulder. 'Well done, well done. Hurry them up, eh? Put the fear of God into them; Lazy buggers.'

Encouraged by his employer's interest, David decided to explain his bright idea more fully. Turning back the papers before him, he said in explanation, 'I worked out this system, you see. When the order forms go down from the counting-house, they are stuck on a big spike by the door. Each man has a number and he takes the form with his number on it. When he's packed the order, he stamps the front of the form and puts it in a box by the exit. The spiked order goes to the carriage department that I've set up in the big shed by the gate. It has to be stamped on the back when the order is put in our cart for going out. Then it's driven to the station and the carter returns another form when he returns to the mill. The forms end up with me again after that and I can trace the progress of any order from this office, through to the station, even to the train it goes out on. If it's delayed, I know who to blame.'

When he got all that off his chest, David leaned back in his high stool and looked up at his employer whose eyes displayed respect that one so young could have such a grasp of the essentials of business.

'By jings,' he exclaimed, 'you're a smart one, aren't you? But that system wouldn't work unless there was somebody like you checking it, would it? I'm impressed. I think you should forget about work for one day. Come on, I'll take you to the fair and buy you a drink.'

David shook his head. 'I don't drink, Mr Henderson. I think it causes a great deal of hardship for poor people.'

Adalbert liked his grog, however, and did not go along with teeto-talism. 'Oh, come off your high horse. Your father was a navvy, wasn't he? They drink plenty. If you and I are to get along together, you'll have to take a glass of something with me even if it's only ginger wine. Get your jacket and we'll go to the Red Lion. There'll be a big crowd there now. None of your temperance friends'll see you in the crush.'

David obediently got his jacket. He wasn't going to jeopardise his chance of a good relationship with Henderson for the sake of his anti-drink principles. He could take a stand on things like that later when he was in a position of power.

As they walked up the rutted road from the mill that was built on the riverbank to the town's square where the clamorous stalls and sideshows were set up, Mr Henderson greeted acquaintances with a wave of the hand and a shouted invitation to join him in the Lion. He acquired a following of hopeful drinkers but it was to David that he spoke. This priggish young man with the pale face and impressive brain intrigued him.

He was holding David's arm as they pushed their way into a crowd of people filling the saloon bar of the Red Lion Hotel, which faced the cobbled square. The noise was deafening and the smell of spilled beer sickening (at least to David) but he had no alternative other than to go with Henderson, who shouted to the barman, 'Get the drinks up, man. Ask them what they want. It's on me.'

David's function was to run to and from the mahogany-topped bar and have Mr Henderson's glass filled and refilled. Whenever his employer downed a glassful, David was expected to do the same and he knew Henderson's eye was on him. After his fifth glass of beer he began to feel very strange. The smoke-filled air of the bar seemed to be lit up with thousands of sparkly lights, people's faces swam in and out of focus as he spoke to them but what they said did not make sense, though single words reverberated in his brain. His legs felt feeble but that did not stop him thinking he was as strong as an ox, capable of taking on the world. It was while he was thinking this that he fell backwards and hit his head on the edge of the table. David passed out cold.

Mr Henderson regarded the collapsed body of his counting-house clerk dispassionately. 'That's what he gets for not drinking. If he took a glass every day, he'd carry it better,' he said and indicated that another of his acolytes should help David to the door.

Fresh air did the trick. David found himself sitting with his back against the hotel wall while a stranger gazed down at him, 'All right, young fellow?' this man asked.

Shamefaced, David struggled to his feet and attempted to brush down his trouser legs. 'Of course. I'm fine,' he lied and wished that by some miracle he could be lifted out of the square and deposited in his own bed a quarter of a mile away, for he did not think he had the strength to walk there.

His good Samaritan was walking away and saying, 'All right then, if you're fine, I'll go back inside.'

Left alone, David reeled through the press of people standing around the stalls, bumping into several, who drew away from him in distaste. His head was throbbing and his mouth felt sandpaper-dry. He put a hand on one of the wooden stalls and leaned heavily on it trying to recover his equilibrium. Then he felt a hand on his arm and a voice saying in his ear, 'It's David, isn't it? Are you sick? You're awfully white.'

He looked up and saw his sister's schoolfriend, Kitty Scott, dressed up as a bondager with her bright hair flowing down her back, standing beside him.

'I'm perfectly all right,' he slurred and she laughed, obviously not believing him.

'Where are you going?' she asked sympathetically. She was not puritanical about people who had too much to drink but she had not expected to find Marie's strait-laced brother in such a state and her reservations about him softened. He must be human after all.

He shook his head. 'I don't know. I think I'll go home.'

'To Camptounfoot? You'll never make it,' she said.

'Not to Camptounfoot, to the mill. I live in lodgings at the mill.' The world was whirling around him and he wished he could lean on her, for she looked as strong as a young tree.

She took his arm firmly and said, 'Anyway you cannae stay here like this. You'll get your pocket picked. I'll take you back. Just tell me where to go.'

Turning her head she called to a group of girls behind her, 'I'm taking this laddie home. I'll meet you later.'

One of them screeched back, 'That's what you say! He's a good-looking lad. We'll no' see you again the day.'

Kitty laughed back, 'We're not all like you, Effie.' Then she tugged at David's arm and said, 'Come on, let me help you. Where's this place that you live?'

He went without a murmur, staggering slightly and letting her lead him. As they walked, she talked, asking him about Marie and saying, 'She seems to be enjoying herself in Edinburgh. I doubt we've lost her in Camptounfoot. I miss her a lot.'

At this David gave a strangled gasp and words came pouring from him, the words that had been going round and round in his lonely, bitter mind. 'You miss her! What about me? I'm her brother. I love her. She's all I've got and I'm all she's got, but she's taken up with strangers... They'll drop her but she needn't think she can come crawling back to me... She can starve for all I care. She's my sister! There was only her and me after our mother went away. I remember her telling me to look after Marie... But she doesn't care, she doesn't want to come and live with me and I've worked so hard...'

Kitty had to steel herself against dropping his arm when he launched into this tirade. There was something in his words that chilled her, that made her remember the terrible story about Big Lily and Craigie Scott.

'You can't stop her making friends. She'll probably meet somebody in Edinburgh and get married one day,' she suggested but that was very far from being the right thing to say.

David stepped in the middle of the road and shouted at her, 'Don't you realise that's what I'm worried about?'

Kitty opened her mouth to protest, 'But—'

He interrupted her with another shout. 'But nothing. I promised I'd take care of her. I told her that. Why should she want to go to Edinburgh in the first place? It's that interfering Lady Godolphin's fault. People like her should stay in their big houses and mind their own business and not interfere in other folk's lives. They only cause trouble. I ought to write to her and to those friends of Marie's in Edinburgh and tell them to leave her alone.'

Kitty was perturbed by his state of agitation, for he had gone from the stage of being staggering but quietly drunk to what looked like dangerous fury. His fists were balled as if he might strike her. She stepped away from him and said, 'You mustn't write letters to Marie's friends. That's not fair. She's happy. Let her be. I've lost her too, but I'm glad she's happy.'

He threw himself away from her. 'Go away. You're a fool like all the rest. What's happy? A fool's paradise, that's what it is. All the happy people are fooling themselves.'

Kitty sighed. 'Oh come on,' she said, taking his arm again. 'I'll walk you home. You'll forget all about this tomorrow.'

'I will not forget. I'll never forget. Go away and let me be. I don't want your company. You're a ragamuffin, always have been. Your father killed my mother… You must be after something but you won't get it from me. Go away.'

She dropped his arm as if it were red-hot and turned abruptly round to march away from him. She did not look back and he did not call after her but went on reeling down the road muttering imprecations to himself.

Effie was surprised to see her back so soon. 'That didnae take long,' she said.

'He was drunk' said Kitty shortly.

'Drunk and incapable,' giggled Effie. Her friend did not reply but linked her arm into one of the other girl's and said, 'What will we do now?'

'I'm off wi' my lad,' said Effie. 'We dinna get a lot of time on oor ain… What are you lassies going to do?'

'I've got to find myself a place. Nobody's spoken to me yet though,' said Kitty mournfully as the remembrance of why she'd come to the fair came back to her mind.

May piped up, 'MacPhee was looking for you a minute ago. She had a man with her and he was looking for a good lassie. If you run back into the square you'll maybe see them.'

Kitty found MacPhee standing by one of the candy stalls with a fresh-faced young man and his pretty wife. She waved when she saw Kitty and called out, 'Here, lass, this is Henry Goodson and he's wanting a bondager because his wife's having a bairn. I said you'd do.'

Kitty looked carefully at the man. He was clean and decent and was holding his wife's hand as if he really cared for her. They were a very respectable pair.

MacPhee whispered in her ear, 'I can vouch for them. They're good folk. You couldnae find a better place.'

The bargain was made. Kitty undertook to go to work for the Goodsons at the May term in a farm five miles beyond Duns. It seemed half a world away to her but she was told that a cart would be sent to collect her.

Henry paid her a shilling in token of their bargain and she gave him her word that she would turn up on the appointed day. Then they went into the Corn Exchange hall and she signed a paper confirming that this was what would happen. It was a good bargain. She was to be kept in the Goodson's house and be paid five shillings a week. At last her luck seemed to have turned.

After the formalities were concluded Kitty took off her hat and went in search of her friends, May and another young bondager Emily, who lived with Rosie at Falconwood.

There was no lack of things to do at the fair for girls with a few coins in their pockets. Kitty had Henry Goodson's shilling as well as the florin Tibbie had given her to go to the dance but which had never been spent. Tied in the corner of her petticoat she also had Tim Maquire's half-sovereign and the precious knife was tucked down inside her boot. She never left her treasures in the farm cottage for fear they would be stolen.

The first attraction for the girls were the travelling hucksters who displayed their wares out on sheets spread over the cobbles and they wandered around examining the goods for sale.

Kitty was beginning to enjoy herself, for she was long accustomed to thrusting her worries and annoyances to the back of her mind and taking best advantage of the passing moment. David's outburst was almost forgotten. He'd shown he didn't like her but then he never had so she'd lost nothing, only gained an unsettling insight into his mind and the relationship between him and his sister.

Behind the stalls were a line of sideshows and a big roundabout on which children and three drunken youths from Falconwood were riding. They shouted to the girls, 'Come on, have a ride, haw haw, haw… Come on carrot top, have a ride wi' us.'

The other two girls were inclined to linger but Kitty walked away on her own and found herself in front of a table on which was perched a large brass birdcage containing a sleek black bird with a bright orange beak. It eyed her speculatively and chuckled to itself as if at a private joke.

Kitty had always been fascinated by Tibbie's parrot, which lived in a similar, though smaller, cage, so she lingered by this bird till its owner, a tall, rangy-looking woman with a tanned, mannish face and high cheekbones like a Red Indian asked her, 'D'ye want to feed him, dearie?'

'What does he eat?' asked Kitty.

The woman pointed to a small tray behind the cage on which lay tiny cubes of apple. 'He likes that,' she said. 'Only a penny a piece.'

'But a whole apple doesnae even cost a farthing!' protested Kitty, child of a village where apples were so plentiful in autumn that they couldn't be given away.

The woman smiled. 'But this apple's special. When he eats it, he'll tell your fortune.'

Kitty was still young enough to be capable of belief. She looked from the imposing woman to the strange bird that was unlike any she'd ever seen before. 'How does he do that?' she asked.

The woman lowered her voice and leaned nearer. 'This is an Indian bird, my dear. It belonged to a great prince out there and it's called a mynah. It has special powers. Not only can it talk but it can see into the future as well. Give me a penny and I'll give you a bit of apple. When he's eaten it, he'll tell you something that'll be of great importance to you. I can tell that you're at a watershed in your life and you need advice.'

This was a line that always impressed young girls and Kitty fell for it. She handed over a penny and took a square of green apple between finger and thumb. 'He won't bite, will he?' she asked, gesturing at the cage from which the bird was watching her with its head cocked to one side and its eyes glistening.

'Bite? He's as gentle as an angel,' protested the bird's owner. 'Just put the apple on the edge there and then tell him your name. He'll do the rest.'

Kitty did as she was told and when the mynah hopped across to pick up her offering she said to it, 'I'm called Kitty Scott.'

It looked up at her, winked and said quite clearly, 'Beware of men!'

Kitty stepped back, astonished. 'It spoke! It said, "Beware of men",' she exclaimed.

Her two friends had caught up with her by this time and they clutched each other in astonishment. 'That's Liddle!' they exclaimed.

Kitty could think of several other candidates for the caution but nodded in agreement. 'Aye, so it could be. That's a wonderful bird you've got there, missus,' she said.

'It is and it cost me a king's ransom. There's not another bird as wise as this one in the whole of the Queen's realm,' intoned the bird's owner solemnly. Seeing that the girls were ready to believe her, she went on, 'He can give you a more detailed fortune if you like... a better guide to the future.'

'How?' asked Kitty, who was thoroughly hooked.

'He picks out one of these bits of paper,' the woman held out a sheaf of tightly folded notes, 'and gives it to you. Can you read?'

Kitty nodded. 'Yes.'

The woman went on, 'On the paper the bird gives you are written predictions for your future.'

Her listeners were entranced, eyes wide and lips parted. 'How much does it cost?' asked Kitty.

The bird's owner eyed the girl and estimated at one glance what she was likely to have in her pocket – she couldn't guess about the half-sovereign, however. 'It costs a silver sixpence,' she said.

'Sixpence!' the girls all breathed together. It seemed a fortune.

'A silver sixpence isn't much to pay to see into the future, is it? Kings and princes would give thousands of pounds for the chance,' said the big woman.

Kitty counted out two copper pennies and a silver threepenny piece. 'Will this do?' she asked holding it out.

The woman pretended to ponder and then nodded. 'Oh, all right, I'll take that because you've got bonny hair and I can tell from the bird's eye that he's got an important message for you.' She cupped her large hand and the money was poured into it. Then she produced her sheaf of grubby papers, riffled through them like playing cards and, opening the door in the side of the cage, shoved them inside. The bird hopped onto her index finger and idly pecked at it with its bright bill, while the girls watched entranced, their faces close to the bars of the cage. The mynah played up to the papers, dithering about pushing its head in among them. Sometimes it seemed to be about to take one but always drew back at the last minute making its audience give a sharp intake of breath at each essay.

'Tell him your name again,' whispered the woman to Kitty, who breathed in an awestruck tone, 'I'm Kitty Scott from Camptounfoot…'

The bird opened its mouth and gave a little croak, then ducked its head down and firmly grasped one sheet, hauling it out of the woman's fingers. It drifted down onto the floor of the cage.

'That's it, that's your fortune,' cried the bird's owner and reached inside to retrieve the piece of paper that would reveal Kitty's destiny.

It was well folded and grubby but the writing was in clear copper-plate in very black ink. What it said was, 'Good luck will attend you at the full moon throughout your life. You will be blessed in many ways and loved by many men but you will only feel love once in return. Women betray you often but you will meet some who are true to you. Cherish your friendships. Your family plays a large part in your destiny. You must never forget them. You will travel far and be richly clothed.'

'Believe what that paper says,' said the woman.

Kitty nodded. 'I do, I really do. There's a lot in it that's true already, you see.'

By this time it was four o'clock and the girls were tired and thirsty. They sat in the shelter of a wooden booth, for the wind was cutting though the rain had stayed away, and drank a bottle of ale which May bought in the jug bar of the Red Lion. That made them feel better and they decided to go in search of MacPhee, who could tell them when to rejoin the farm cart which had brought them from Falconwood early in the morning and would take them back again.

Money was running short – Kitty's funds were down to ninepence, having laid out for her fortune, the ale, a bag of treacle sweets and a small and nasty meat pasty sold for twopence a time by an old woman with a tray suspended round her neck.

MacPhee was sitting with a couple of other women on a bench beneath the leafless elm trees that encircled Maddiston square. This was a position of vantage from which they could see all the people passing through the fair and make comments while they ate an assortment of food which was laid out on a bit of red-and-white-chequered cloth beside the woman at the end of the line. When they saw the girls approaching, they all moved along the bench and made room for them to squeeze on at the end.

MacPhee leaned forward and introduced her companions. 'These are my sisters,' she said. 'They're a' bondagers like me and we meet here every year. Ellen brings the food and we catch up on each other's news.'

Ellen, the only one of the three who had any spare fat on her bones, grinned cheerfully and offered the girls the remains of a loaf that had been cut down the middle and filled with cold meat. They fell on it gratefully.

'When does the cart go back?' asked Kitty.

MacPhee looked up at a big clock facing out from a turret on top of the Corn Exchange on the other side of the square. 'In another three hours, at half-past seven. See and no' miss it or you'll hae to walk to Falconwood and that's a good four mile.'

She grinned directly at Kitty and said, 'I'm glad you took the place wi' Henry Goodson. He was saying to me he'd take you sooner than the term if you like. I'll ask Laidlaw to let you go when we get back tonight.'

Kitty was pleased. 'I'll have to say goodbye to my mam then,' she said.

'Go and see her tonight. The cart can drop you off at Camptoun-foot Road end,' said MacPhee, who could be relied on to arrange everything.

By this time it was five o'clock and the fair seemed to have taken on a second lease of life. A roar of music burst out on the far side of the press of people. It was a catchy tune with the thud, thud, thud of a big drum running through the sound of trumpets and euphoniums, the sort of music that set people marching. The source of it, the girls saw, was a wooden stage set up in front of a tent with a banner along the front proclaiming, 'Gentleman Joe and His Boys… World-Famous Fighters Under the Management of Grandma Kennedy.'

'It's only a boxing booth,' sighed Kitty in disappointment.

Her friends and she were about to turn away when a big man in a stained singlet and black tights shouted down to them from the platform, 'Don't any of you lassies fancy yourselves as lady boxers? I'll give half a guinea to any girl that goes into the ring with Joe tonight.'

May shouted back at him, 'How much is a ticket?'

'A shilling.'

'We've nae money.'

'If one of you fights, I'll let you all in for nothing,' he said, leaning down and pointing at Kitty. 'What about you? You look like the fighting sort.'

May and Emily giggled. 'Aye she is!' and fell about laughing at the memory of Liddle's bloody nose, but Kitty shook her head. 'I can only fight when I'm mad,' she said.

The promoter was interested. He knew that the crowds would turn out to see a girl fighter, especially one with hair like blazing fire. 'Go on, get mad then,' he advised. 'It's worth getting mad for half a guinea.'

She shook her head. 'I'm feared I'd get hurt.'

He put a hand to the side of his mouth and whispered, 'You'll no' get hurt. It's all a fix-up. Joe'll not hit you. How do you think Grandma Kennedy does it? A real big punch would go through her.'

'Who's Grandma Kennedy?' asked May.

The man looked astonished. 'You've not heard of Grandma Kennedy! The most famous woman boxer in the world. She's on here tonight fighting Joe. Come on through and meet her. She'll tell you that you'll not get hurt.' He lifted a flap in the canvas, inviting them to go into the shadowy world beyond the stall façade.

They hesitated, but not for long. Taking comfort in each other's presence, one after the other they climbed onto the platform, through the canvas door and into another world.

Grandma Kennedy turned out to be a wiry little sprite of a woman with a wrinkled face and greyish hair which was twisted tightly back from her hook-nosed face into a straggly bun. She stood with her hands on her hips staring at the girls as they walked in behind the busker.

'What's this, what's this?' she asked in a tone that would have scared a sergeant of the Dragoons.

'It's some lassies that might fight tonight if you tell them they won't get hurt,' said the man.

Grandma Kennedy stared at the three in front of her. She pinched May's arm and said, 'Too flabby.' She ran an eye over pale-faced Emily and merely snorted. Then she turned her attention to Kitty and looked at her for much longer. 'This one'll do,' she said eventually.

'But I dinna want to fight,' protested Kitty. 'I'm feared of getting hurt.'

'Feared?' asked Grandma Kennedy with raised eyebrows as if Kitty had expressed a belief in dragons.

Kitty nodded. 'I might get a broken nose or something.'

'What's so special about your nose?' asked the old crone peering at it.

'Nothing, but I dinna want it broken,' said Kitty, who felt she was losing this argument before it really began.

'It'll not get broken. Joe canna box his way out of a paper bag any more. I've got to make it look as if he's hit me, groan and stagger about like this…' The redoubtable old dame staggered back from them, threw a hand over her face and fell flat on her back as if she'd been pole-axed. After a second she raised herself up on one arm and asked Kitty. 'Could you do that?'

Kitty was amused. 'Yes, I think I could,' she said.

'We'll give you ten silver shillings and a sixpence if you do,' said the busker and Grandma joined in with, 'Get her a breastplate, Bill lad. There must be one to fit her.' In seconds someone appeared with a metal contraption like a solid corset with leather straps that was put over Kitty's head and buckled round her waist, though she protested, 'But I haven't said I'd do it. I don't really want to fight anybody.'

May and Emily were no help to her. Giggling they said, 'Go on, Kitty, go on, you've got a punch on you like the kick on a horse.'

They were eager for her to fight because Bill the busker had promised them a shilling each if they could talk her into it.

Now he added his argument to theirs, 'And mind it's a half-guinea for you even if all you do is get into the ring and run about a bit.'

Another half-guinea, thought Kitty. Added to what she had already that would make her worldly fortune one pound and one shilling... two hundred and fifty-two pennies. It seemed like a fortune. If she wasn't happy at Duns, she could take the train to Edinburgh and look for work there.

She clanged the metal breastplate with her fist and liked the hollow sound it made. No blow could penetrate it.

'If you're sure he won't hurt me,' she said and they all shouted, 'Of course he won't.'

'Hey Joe,' called Grandma Kennedy to the back of the tent, 'Come and meet your opponent for tonight. Tell her you'll miss with every punch.'

Joseph Maloney Brady was over six feet tall and heavy with it. He rolled slightly when he walked as if the ground was shifting beneath his feet like the deck of a ship and, in fact, he had spent a lot of time on board during a stint in the Royal Navy from which he'd deserted to travel with the Kennedy family.

'This lassie'll come up from the crowd tonight and offer to fight you, Joe. Don't hurt her and don't hit her on the face. Do it the same way as when you're fighting me,' Grandma explained in the tone of one talking to a small child.

Joe nodded and smiled seraphically, his small hazel eyes shining. 'Right, Grandma,' he agreed.

Satisfied she turned back to the girls. 'All right, now be out there in the crowd when we start at six o'clock. And you,' she said pointing at Kitty, 'keep that breastplate on but make sure it doesn't show.'

Kitty was still not sure she was doing the right thing. 'If he's not going to hit me why do I need it?' she asked.

'Just a precaution,' Grandma Kennedy assured her.

There was still half an hour to go before the boxing began and the girls walked round the attractions again.

'I think I'll just go back to that tent and give her back this thing,' Kitty said, shifting uncomfortably under the weight of the metal breastplate that hung from her shoulders like a leaden yoke.

The others wouldn't hear of it and urged her to think of the money, theirs as well as her own.

'It'll all be over in a couple of minutes,' they assured her. 'Just pretend to fall down like the old woman did and lie there.'

When the Corn Exchange clock was striking six they found themselves in the middle of a crowd of people pushing their way into the boxing tent. Bill the busker, in a clean singlet, was shouting out the attractions…

'Five shillings for any man brave enough to go one round with Gentleman Joe!

'A chance to see the amazing woman fighter, Grandma Kennedy, seventy-five years old and as tough as any man!

'Ladies and gentlemen, this is the best boxing booth in the world. Roll up, roll up, to see fighters who'll go on fighting till they drop dead!'

When she heard this Kitty turned round and was about to head for open country but May grabbed her skirt and held it tight.

'Come on, Kitty, this'll be a laugh,' she whispered.

'For you maybe, but what about me? I'm the one who's going to be hit,' she moaned, but she couldn't get away because the crowd had closed behind her like a human wall.

The first bout, a contest between two stable lads, ended quickly with one of them carried off on a stretcher; then a burly man with a red face climbed into the ring and was sent flying by Joe's second punch. Joe was cheered to the echo every time he made a hit and the crowd grew more and more hysterical.

Bill climbed through the ropes again, held up a hand and yelled hoarsely, 'Now for the bout we've all been waiting for. Is there a woman in this town brave enough to fight Joe?'

Silence.

'Half a guinea for the woman who'll stand up to Joe,' yelled Bill again.

No one moved, though May and Emily were trying to shove Kitty forward.

'What a pity the women o' Maddiston are all feardies,' said Bill sadly when there was a shout from the back, 'I'm no' feared' and a fat woman in rough working clothes came waddling through the crowd. Her face was purple and she had obviously been drinking.

She glared up at Bill the busker and though he looked puzzled, he bent down and extended a hand. She was so heavy that she almost pulled him over the ropes when she took his hand and it took three of them to haul her into the ring. The crowd was howling with delight… 'Let her get a punch at him. Go on, missus, punch the hell out of him!'

She advanced on Joe and swung a punch that sent his head back and made his eyes roll in shock. Then she lowered her head like a maddened bull to charge at his stomach but he saw her coming and stopped her with an uppercut that stiffened her limbs and sent her flat on her back on the canvas. They revived her by pouring a bucket of water over her head and she was helped away to the Red Lion bar where she spent all the money Bill had given her on treating her friends to drinks.

By this time Bill had pinpointed Kitty's flaming head in the crowd and was yelling directly at her, 'Is there another brave woman in Maddiston? This is a last chance to prove lassies are as brave as laddies!'

It wasn't the challenge and it wasn't the money. It was because she had said she'd do it and he was shouting directly at her. She stepped forward with her friends at her back and found herself by the ring, where she was met by a stifling smell of sweat and embrocation.

'I'll take him on,' she said and the crowd went wild, yelling and cheering, 'It's Carroty Kate from Camptounfoot. It's Wee Lily's lassie!'

Bill was delighted when he heard her nickname. 'Carroty Kate's our challenger then. Give her a big hand.'

They hauled her onto the square of taut canvas, someone tied her hair back with a strip of linen and a bell gave a fierce little tinkle. The crowd roared like a surging sea as she stepped up to face Gentleman Joe, an impressive sight in a skin-tight vest and buckskin breeches.

She felt as if she had stepped into a horrible nightmare. Joe's fists went whooshing past her ears and he leaned towards her grunting, 'Pretend I'm hitting you. Pretend it hurts.'

She tried and next time he threw a punch at her, drew her head sharply aside and gave a horrible groan that elicited a delighted yell from the bloodthirsty spectators. She felt the round would never end but at last the bell rang and people began jumping round the ring with their hands above their heads shouting, 'She stayed one round!'

In the corner Bill handed her a sponge and said, 'Go another round. Joe's going to take a fall for you.'

'What?' she asked bemusedly.

'Hit him as hard as you can.'

'But I don't want to hurt him.'

'He's been hit by bigger folk than you. He'll be all right. In you go…' and she was pushed into the middle of the ring again. When Joe came towards her she drew her arm back as she had done when she hit Liddle and punched him full on the chin. He shook his head like a stalled ox, reeled a little and toppled over sideways.

The silence was shattered by yells of disbelief. 'She's knocked out Gentleman Joe. A lassie's knocked out Joe!'

She had little time to enjoy her triumph, however, because Grandma Kennedy came bursting through the ropes, dressed like a man in breeches and vest that did not conceal the fact she, too, was wearing a metal breastplate. Her taut little body radiated energy although the skin was loose and wrinkled like the skin of a tortoise.

'Knocked out my Joe did you?' she snarled, advancing on Kitty. 'Then you'll have to knock me out too.'

She swung a fist at Kitty's head and it connected, making the startled girl see stars. This, she thought, is serious. Grandma Kennedy is fighting mad. She backed away but the little woman kept coming on, bandaged fists pummelling away without mercy.

'Stop it, stop it,' she managed to whisper but Grandma was not listening.

'Take that and that,' she was saying as she punched and each blow hurt more than the one before. Finally it was too much for Kitty. Back went her fist, she found her balance and the blow connected with Grandma Kennedy's jaw.

The old woman went over in a heap and ended up on the ground like a broken doll. Kitty dropped to her knees by the body crying out, 'I'm sorry, I'm sorry, I just got angry.'

As she looked into her opponent's face, however, one eye flickered open and the lid dropped in a definite wink before the old woman was carried away on the shoulders of her men.

Bill gave her a whole guinea in front of a cheering ecstatic crowd. 'No one's ever knocked out Grandma Kennedy before,' he bawled.

At this the tent exploded with loud cheers and a bemused Kitty saw May and Emily jumping up and down, embracing each other and shouting like lunatics.

She grasped her money and was about to leave when Bill took her arm and whispered, 'Go out the back way. My mother wants to speak to you.'

Grandma Kennedy was sitting on an upturned box by the door with an open bottle by her feet, apparently none the worse for her fight. She proffered the bottle to Kitty and asked, 'Want some?'

The girl shook her head. 'No thanks. Are you all right? I was afraid I'd hurt you but you made me so angry.'

'I had to make you angry. You were fighting Joe as if it was a put-up job. The crowd would've lynched us if they guessed. I told him to lie down and I'd take over. It worked, didn't it? They loved it.' She was obviously highly pleased with herself and with Kitty. Taking another swig from the bottle she said, 'We could build up a good piece of business between us, you know. People would think you were just one of the crowd like tonight. Sometimes I could win, sometimes you could. We'd share it.'

Kitty shook her head. 'I don't think so. I don't want to be a boxer.' The old woman said, 'It's good money. We rake in twenty or thirty pounds a night at a big fair and we all take a share. If you were on the bill we'd make even more. That hair's a big draw. They'd come to see it flying about all over the place. Think about it. I'd take you with us and I'd look after you well. Ask your mother what she thinks.'

Kitty stiffened. 'I dinna need to ask my mother. I make my own decisions. I'm on a farm at the moment and I think I'll stay there.' She wanted to travel, that was true, but not with a boxing show.

'Your choice,' said Grandma philosophically, 'but it's a good offer. Life on the road's grand. You never get stale. I'd be good to you. My old man's dead but my sister and I travel together and we wouldn't let any of those bucks get at you if that's what worries you.'

She waved a hand at her listening entourage, who all shuffled their feet. She obviously had them under strict control. Kitty would not change her mind, however.

May and Emily were waiting at the tent door when she emerged and they threw their arms round her neck and kissed her, crying out, 'Well done, Kitty, well done. That man gave us two shillings each because of you. He promised us a shilling but he doubled it!'

At that moment the clock struck the half-hour and Emily screeched, 'The cart, the cart, it leaves at half-past seven.'

People were converging on Kitty, wanting to shake her hand and congratulate her, but she pushed them away so that she and the girls could take to their heels and run across the emptying square as if they were being pursued by the Devil. They caught up with the cart as it was negotiating the corner out of Maddiston's main street and heading down the open road for home. There were only five people on board, all quiet-living people off the farm. The rowdy boys were still at the fair and would make their own way home. MacPhee pulled the girls aboard and started to scold them. 'You nearly missed us and then where would you have been? I told you it was leaving at half-past seven.'

'It was Kitty's fault,' gabbled May. 'She knocked out two people in the boxing booth. It was marvellous.'

MacPhee thought they were joking and laughed. 'Don't be daft, May,' she said.

Kitty gave her friend a sharp jab in the ribs as she said sharply, 'That's rubbish, May. Be quiet.' She didn't want to talk about her triumph, or about her bounty of a guinea, and it was unlikely that anyone on the cart would have been in the boxing tent. The boys might have been there and seen it but they wouldn't be able to spread the news till tomorrow and that was early enough as far as she was concerned.

The cart dropped Kitty beneath the big railway viaduct and she walked up the hill to Camptounfoot, led on by its lights twinkling in the distance.

Unfortunately, the bothy was in darkness and she knew better than to rouse her grandmother from her first sleep, but Tibbie Mather's lamps were lit and she was sitting knitting in a glowing circle. Yearningly Kitty stared through the window from the dark garden. The scene was like an idealised painting of old age.

Gently she tapped on the glass, not wanting to frighten the woman inside but Tibbie did not scare easily and without looking up she called out, 'Go away Jo. I'm too old to be feared for you.'

'It's not Jo. It's Kitty,' came the voice from outside and when Tibbie let her in she was smiling.

'Come in lass. You're out late. Marie's not here. She's gone to Perthshire with her Edinbury friends.' Marie had obviously not told Tibbie about the trouble between herself and Kitty.

'I just came to tell you that I've got a new place, on a farm near Duns,' Kitty explained.

Tibbie nodded. 'That's good. Does your mother know?'

'I wanted to tell her but they're asleep and I didn't want to wake them up.'

'I'll tell them if you like,' offered Tibbie. 'I think it's good that you're going away. You need a new start.'

Kitty nodded. 'I know. I love this village and the orchard and all the places I know but I want to see the rest of the world as well. I'll give you the address of the place at Duns I'm going to and if anything goes wrong with my mother, will you please let me know?'

'Of course I will, lass,' said Tibbie kindly. 'And I'll tell Marie that you came to say goodbye to her.'

The walk across the fields to Falconwood was a pleasure for the frosted stubble crunched beneath her boots as she hurried along. White owls swept over her head like ghosts; little animals bustled about in her path; beneath the trees that surrounded Falconwood from the back, drifts of frosted dry leaves rustled as she kicked her way through them like a child. The moon was up and it gilded everything with an eery light but she was not afraid, for she enjoyed being alone with only the birds and animals for company.

As she walked over the back field she heard the geese cackling under the apple trees. In the excitement of returning from the fair, they had been forgotten and if they were not shut up, a fox would almost certainly get them for this was a perfect night for hunting. She broke a stick off the hedge and went towards the sound, intending to drive them to their little house. The stick was for protection because the gander was fierce.

'Come on, come on,' cried Kitty as she walked towards him. 'Come in. You don't want to be eaten by the fox tonight, do you?' She was quite unaware that she was being watched by human eyes.

Tom Liddle had not gone to the fair because of his wife's religious convictions against drink and pleasure-taking, which he pretended to share. Now he stood in the lee of the cart shed with Walter and Tommy, the toughest of the young lads who'd come home very drunk from the jollifications and were telling him about Kitty's exploits in the boxing tent.

He listened sourly, fingering his chin, which was still sore from the thump she'd given it.

'She packs a punch that little bitch,' he agreed. 'She needs teaching a lesson but nane o' you lads are up to doing it. You're a' feared o' her.'

The biggest of the two, Walter, straightened his shoulders. He'd had enough drink that day to make him very brave indeed. 'I'm no feared o' her,' he said. 'She's just a woman, isn't she?'

'You're feared o' her tongue, that's what you're feared at,' sneered Liddle.

'I'm no',' protested Walter weakly.

They were about to go to bed when they heard her calling to the geese. Liddle put his fingers to his lips telling them to keep silent. 'Now's your chance,' he said.

'I'm awa tae ma bed, man,' said Walter.

Liddle sneered. 'I kent you were feared for her. But she's just like any woman, lie on top o' her and you've got her. You'd be feared to do that though, wouldn't you? You're no' man enough for her.'

Walter was a lady's man, and a coarse one at that, who'd had his way with most of the girls on the farm, especially with Effie.

'There's no' a woman alive I'd be feared to fuck,' he snapped, nettled by Liddle.

'Go on, show me. Catch the carrot top. There she is out in the field now. Away and grab her. Tommy here'll help you if you need any help, won't you, Tommy?' Liddle's voice was like poisoned syrup.

Tommy, staggering drunk and not really aware of what was going on, slurred, 'Aye, I'll help you, Walter. Whit's it ye need doin'?'

Liddle was pushing Walter on, saying, 'She's a hard wee bitch. She needs a lesson. Will you be the yin to teach her?'

'Just you wait and see, wait there and see,' hissed Walter, and Liddle and Tommy watched as he slunk round the wall heading for the field gate.

Kitty did not hear him approach because her normally sharp reactions were dulled by weariness. The geese were safely in their hut and she was yawning as she bent over the gate to slip its chain into the hook when, suddenly, two hands went round her waist and threw her forward over the gate's top bar. Her arm was twisted beneath her and she could feel the weight of a man's body pressing her down.

'Got ye, got ye. Stay there till I show you what's what,' came a voice that she recognised as Walter's. He was a man that she particularly disliked because of his treatment of Effie and she knew that by the way he was handling her this was no mild piece of horseplay. This was serious.

With a superhuman effort she arched her back and threw him off her. Then she turned to face him and screamed, 'Get away from me, get away from me!' But there was nobody round about to hear her. Everyone except Liddle and Tommy had gone to bed.

Walter put his hands on her shoulders and shook her to and fro till she thought that her neck would snap.

'You do what I want and you'll be all right. If you don't, I'll damned well kill you,' he told her.

She smelt the beer on his breath. Somehow she managed to get upright with her back against the spars of the gate and grappled behind herself in the hope of finding the stick she'd thrown down, but it was too far away. In the shadows beneath the overhanging roof of the cart shed she saw two people and shouted to them, 'Help me, help me! Get him off me.'

When she heard Liddle's mean laugh, she realised that there would be no assistance coming from that direction. If she was to be saved from Walter, it would be by her own efforts.

My knife, my knife, I've got to find my knife, was her chief thought as she fought against him, biting and scratching like a wildcat, kicking with her booted feet. She must have hurt him for he yelled and hit her across the face with the back of his hand, dazing her.

'Stand still, stand still,' he gasped while he struggled with one hand to undo the button of his fly. Though her head was swimming she knew that this was her chance and kneed him hard in the groin. When he bent over gasping, she reached into her pocket and grasped her knife. Miraculously her fingers found the blade catch as Walter threw himself onto her with his erect penis jabbing at her belly.

Though it had lain in the tin box for such a long time, the knife blade was very sharp and it slid into his chest as if it was cutting butter. He went limp, stood stock-still for what seemed like a hundred years, then put a hand on his shoulder and gasped, 'You bitch, you've stabbed me.'

'The bitch has stabbed me!' he yelled out to the watching men.

Kitty was in shock. She edged away sideways holding the knife up in front of herself like a talisman to ward off evil and told the men running towards her, 'Don't come near me or I'll stab you as well.' They stopped short at the sight of the blade gleaming in the moonlight, staring from her to Walter, who was leaning his arms on the top bar of the gate with his head laid on them.

Kitty was near enough to see a red stain spreading over the breast of his white shirt. She backed away further and ran to the other side of the yard while Liddle went up to the wounded man and saw the stab wound.

'You've killed him. You've killed him. They'll hang you for this!' he yelled at Kitty as Walter slid down the gate and lay groaning on the ground. Still holding out her knife, she turned and ran towards the wood that marked the boundary between Falconwood and Townhead.

She was in a complete panic and had no idea of where she was going. Instinctively, like a hunted animal, she headed for the ancient orchard at Townhead. She almost didn't get through the stream tunnel but made it after a tight squeeze and found herself among the ghostly, silver-branched trees where she huddled, shaking and gulping in hysteria.

She stayed there for what seemed like a long time with both arms wrapped round her body as if in an embrace, her right hand still holding the open knife. When her first outburst of terror passed she tried to think coherently.

It was impossible to stay in Camptounfoot, for anyone looking for her would go straight there. And they would be looking for her if Walter was dead... She didn't doubt that she'd killed him. Liddle's words, 'They'll hang you for this...' echoed in her brain. What chance would she have in any trial with two witnesses against her? Liddle would stand up in the witness box and give damning evidence.

She stood up in the moonlight and looked around. Trails of silver smoke rose to the midnight-blue sky from fires that had been left banked up to burn overnight; the oil lamp on the corner of Jo's wynd guttered feebly as it had always done; the bulk of the farmhouse loomed in front of her. She crept over to the orchard gate and gently eased it open. Down the street feeble lights showed in a couple of windows where candles were burning within – perhaps because an old person was sick or a child was frightened of the dark. Across the road she could see the roof of the bothy where she had been born and where her mother lay asleep.

She knew she had to go away, as far and as fast as she could, but it gave her terrible pain not to be able to tell her mother what had happened. Tears poured down her cheeks as she took her farewell of Camptounfoot and the people in it. Sobbing heartbrokenly she ran down the street, dodged into a narrow lane and headed for Bella Vista where the thick woods around the house would provide a temporary hiding-place.

Where will I go? What will I do? she was asking herself as she ran. There was no chance that she could remain in the district, no chance of taking up a new place even as far away as Duns because her red hair made her too easily recognisable. She would have to put as many miles between herself and Falconwood as possible. She'd have to hide in a city.

London, that's where I ought to go, she decided.

A train left Rosewell station for London early every morning. She'd often watched the smoke puffing out of its chimney as it negotiated the bridge over the Tweed. But how to get on it without being stopped by the authorities who would almost certainly be looking for her.

Not owning a watch she had no idea of the time. It could be five o'clock in the morning for all she knew. As she hid beneath the trees in Bella Vista woods, however, she heard the tolling of the abbey bell… the midnight bell. The people of the town allowed it to be rung for the last time then but, after that, it was silent till six o'clock in the morning when it summoned them from sleep.

If it was midnight there were another five and a half hours to spend before the London train left. She wondered if it was possible to hide in the station without being seen and jump aboard the train when the postmen were loading the mailbags? She couldn't take the risk of buying a ticket because the booking-office clerk knew her. In fact, most of the people in Rosewell knew her.

From her hiding-place she could see the dark swell of rising ground that cut Rosewell off from Maddiston. That was where her salvation lay, she realised. She'd go over the hills to Maddiston in the hope that Grandma Kennedy and her crew had not left yet. Speed was essential if she was going to catch them.

The way over the hill was a rutted track used by drovers herding cattle from farther north in Scotland to London's Smithfield Market. Though the drovers' road was heavy going, it had the advantage that there was little chance of meeting anyone else on it at this time of night.

She forded the river at a place Jo had shown her long ago and ran up the hill to where the drove road began. In places it was so boggy and overgrown that it almost disappeared and there were deep ruts that took her unawares in the darkness, but other parts were paved with huge stone slabs that showed the road had been laid originally by the Romans. Gates cut across it where farm boundaries ended but Kitty did not wait to open them, for she was in such a hurry that it was quicker to shin over and keep on running, stumbling in her heavy boots, panting and gasping and holding her hand against a stitch in her side. Sometimes she fell over a stone not seen in the dark but always picked herself up immediately and started running again. The palms of her hands and her knees were scratched and raw with abrasions from her falls but she did not notice the pain.

It was ten minutes to two o'clock in the morning when she reached Maddiston Square. Most of the pedlars had gone, though some of them lay sleeping in darkened corners, using their packs as pillows. The stalls were disassembled and lay in piles on the cobbles waiting to be loaded onto carts when dawn came. The boxing booth had disappeared too and all that remained of it were spars of wood wrapped up in a roll of canvas. It was amazing that so big a structure could shrink to such small size.

There was no sign of any of the boxing booth people and Kitty groaned aloud in disappointment. Grandma Kennedy had represented an escape for her. If the old woman had already taken the road, where could she go? The police would catch her; she'd be sent to prison like Craigie – that is if she was lucky. If she wasn't, she'd hang for the murder of Walter.

Who would believe that she was only trying to defend herself? People would think she should have lain down and let him rape her… She could just hear them saying, 'After all, being taken by force isn't such an unusual thing in the bondager community. She probably led him on and, anyway, look at her mother and her grandmother…'

The Red Lion Hotel was closed and its door barred against importunate late drinkers, so there was no one who could tell her where Grandma Kennedy might be. She sat down heavily on the bench used by MacPhee and her sisters during the afternoon – was it only a few hours ago? – and stared bleakly over the rubbish-littered square. Then, in spite of her determination to stay awake, she fell asleep.

It was cold and still dark when she woke with a shudder. The town clock chimed, telling her the hour was five. A few desolate-looking people were drifting over the square. Oh, thank God, one of them was Bill the busker.

She ran over to him and took his arm, 'Where's Grandma Kennedy?' she asked.

His eyes were bleary and bloodshot and he smelt of drink but he recognised her. 'Carroty Kate! My mother's down in her van in the field by the river. What do you want with her?'

'I want to come with you. I've changed my mind about her offer.' Kitty was shivering with cold and fear. Bill, a kindly man, took his woollen muffler off his neck and draped it round hers.

'You'd better not wake her up so early. She'll take your head off. We're planning to be on the road by six. You can speak to her then.'

There was no point beating about the bush. 'Bill,' she said urgently, 'I've got to hide. Somebody's after me. Please don't make me stay where I'll be seen. Let me go to where she is. I can hide beside her van till she wakes up. Just take me there, please.'

There was no mistaking the urgency of her appeal and Bill did not waste time asking the whys and wherefores.

'Come on,' he said, taking her arm.

They walked quickly down a broad road to a field that stretched along the riverbank. In the far corner, beneath a grove of sheltering trees, six dray horses were grazing beside a cluster of caravans painted with big letters advertising the boxing booth.

The only one that was not garishly covered with slogans was Grandma Kennedy's. Hers was dark plum-red with gold trimmings and fancy curlicues painted around the door and window.

Bill was tiptoeing when he approached it. 'She's not awake yet,' he said softly to Kitty, indicating the closed door.

'I'll wait,' said the girl. For shelter she crawled under the van and lay down behind one of the huge wheels that were also decorated with swirls of gold leaf.

Bill bent down and whispered to her, 'You'll hear her getting up but don't be too hasty. She's always in bad fettle in the morning.' Sleep overwhelmed Kitty again as she lay on the grass and in the event it was Grandma Kennedy who heard her snores and wakened her. A stick was pushed under the van and jabbed into Kitty's ribs.

'What d'you think you're doing in there?' asked a hoarse voice. 'Come out and let me have a look at you.'

When the girl's head appeared out of the shadow beneath the van, Grandma cried out in surprise, 'The red-headed lassie! What are you doing in there? Have you changed your mind?'

Kitty clambered to her feet and said, 'Yes, I want to go with you. When are you leaving?'

'Huh, you're in an awful hurry all of a sudden, aren't you? What've you done? Stolen your mistress's silver? I don't want to be bothered with thieves or people chasing after them.'

Grandma Kennedy did not seem as eager to recruit Kitty as she'd been the previous evening.

Kitty said stoutly, 'I'm no' a thief. I've never stolen anything in my life…' Except my knife, she thought.

Her vehemence softened the old woman a bit, and she asked in a gentler tone, 'Well, why are you so keen to come with us now when you wouldn't consider it yesterday?'

Kitty decided to tell the truth. 'I'm running away because last night I stabbed a man who was attacking me,' she said.

'How do you mean? Was he going to force you into letting him fuck you?'

'Yes, he was trying to rape me – and his friends were watching. One of them put him up to it. It was awful. I fought hard but he was stronger than me… I could hear his friends laughing…' The full horror of what she might have endured if she had not found the knife in time, struck her with awful force and she shuddered at the memory of Liddle's horrible laugh when Walter grabbed hold of her.

Grandma Kennedy looked sympathetic but not particularly shocked or surprised. 'Men, they're a lot of dirty devils,' she said coolly. Then she added, 'You stabbed him you say. What with?'

Kitty reached into her pocket and produced the bone-handled knife. 'With this,' she said, handing it over.

The old woman took it into her hand with respect. 'That's a neat little thing, handy to have about you. Did you hurt him?'

'He fell down groaning and Liddle, that was the man who put him up to it, shouted at me that I'd killed him and they'd hang me for it. Then I ran away.'

'Quite right too,' said Grandma Kennedy briskly. 'But there's no proof he's dead, is there? Where did the knife go? Into his guts? Into his chest?'

Kitty tried to re-enact the scene in memory and held up a hand to show Grandma Kennedy what happened. 'He was leaning on me while he opened his pants. I used my right hand like this but I couldn't get much space so I jabbed at him this way…'

She made a short jabbing action, watched with interest by Grandma. 'You jabbed straight at him?' she asked.

The girl nodded. 'Yes, straight. I couldn't turn. He was pushing against me with his... thing...'

'Was he taller than you?' was the next question.

'No, heavier but not taller. His face was against mine too and he was sweating... ugh...'

Grandma Kennedy was matter-of-fact. 'That's all right. Don't go on any more. I think you probably hit him in the shoulder. That wouldn't kill him providing they got help to him in time. Unless he bled to death of course... But don't worry too much, there's a chance he'll be all right.'

She was discussing it in the same way as she'd talk about a black eye given to one of her boxers. Kitty felt some of her terror seep away to be replaced by a little of her habitual optimism. Maybe, just maybe, everything would be all right.

Grandma Kennedy saw the lightening of the girl's expression and hurriedly added, 'Not that I think you should bank on it. I wouldn't advise you to go back to find out. You've done the right thing coming to me. I'll take you with us when we leave here. Get up into my van and stay out of sight till I come. I'll tell you when it's all right to show yourself again.'

Kitty was overwhelmed with gratitude. She wanted to throw her arms round the old woman's neck and hug her but desisted because of Grandma's formidable aspect. 'I'll never be able to thank you. But won't you get into trouble if the policeman finds you're helping me to get away?' asked Kitty.

The wiry old woman was halfway up the van steps by this time and she looked down at the girl. Her eyes were sympathetic as she said, 'When I was about your age I was raped. I remember how terrible it was. I remember how much I hated the man, how I wanted to kill him. If I'd had a knife, I'd have stabbed him too. I know you're telling me the truth because you were telling me my own story. Come on, get into the van and stay hidden. We're on our way to Carlisle and must be off early. We still travel slowly, not like the trains.'

Inside, the caravan was painted dark green and there were more gold leaf scrolls running along beneath the roof. Wooden shelves flanked little windows at each side. Candlelight showed shelves filled with colourful pieces of china, not the rough earthenware figures that Kitty had seen in Camptounfoot houses, but fine china painted all over with sprays of flowers. She particularly admired an elegant teapot with a curving spout and bouquets of roses painted on its side. The bed was a high bunk with cupboards beneath it and there was a table hinged to the wall beneath the window. On the opposite side to the bed ran a long bench with cushions on which a scruffy-looking little black dog was sleeping in the middle of the biggest and softest cushion of all.

When they entered, it looked up and wagged its tail at Grandma but snarled at Kitty.

'It's all right, Toby. She can come in,' said the old woman and the dog laid its head on its paws but its golden eyes were watchful.

'Will he bite?' asked Kitty, indicating the dog when she saw that Grandma was about to go out and leave her alone in the caravan with Toby.

'Only if you touch anything that belongs to me. Just sit quietly and he'll not bother you. Lie down and go to sleep if you like. You look as if you need it.' Then the old woman bustled off leaving the two occupants of her caravan suspiciously eyeing each other.

Kitty sat very still on the bed, hardly daring to move, but in time she toppled over sideways sound asleep and when that happened Toby closed his eyes and went to sleep too.

They were wakened by the noise of a horse being backed into the van shafts. Then someone jumped into the box and they went lurching and swaying out of the field. Toby ran to the window and stared out wagging his tail. It was obvious that he liked being on the road and travelling changed his mood, for when Kitty got up and stood beside him so that she could see from the window too, he didn't bother to snarl at her.

They went in cavalcade at walking pace down the road to the south, crossing over the bridge at Rosewell, across the town square and through the village of Camptounfoot.

Kitty stood back from the window so that no one could see her as she was carried past familiar cottages where people were rising for another day. There were already children in Camptounfoot's street and she caught a glimpse of Jo walking down to the river.

'Goodbye, goodbye,' she whispered. If she'd seen her mother or Tibbie Mather, she probably would not have been able to contain herself and would have jumped down to hug them.

The line of vans made a slow pace going up Camptounfoot Hill but when they reached the top, the going was easier and the horses began to trot as they rounded the corner past Falconwood. From her vantage point at the window Kitty saw the land she'd helped to work. The bondagers were in the turnip field with MacPhee at their head, bending over in the back-breaking work of gathering up the roots to feed to the sheep during the winter. In the distance she could see three ploughs, each pulled by a pair of horses with a man holding onto the handles as they travelled up and down over the field and the broken earth unfolded behind them like the waves of a sea. It was too far, however, for her to make out which of the farm men were ploughing. Everything looked normal and it seemed that no one had missed her or that anything out of the way had happened. It was as if she'd dropped into the river like a stone and the water had closed over her.

# Chapter Eleven

It was some time before people realised that Kitty Scott had disappeared. At Falconwood and Camptounfoot it was thought she had gone to work in Duns; at Duns her new employers thought she had postponed her arrival until the normal hiring day change in May.

When it was eventually discovered that she had vanished off the face of the earth, there seemed to be no explanation for it because Walter Thompson put his stabbing – a flesh wound it turned out – down to an incident at the fair and Tom Liddle kept his mouth shut about the attempt to rape Kitty.

She won that money in the boxing booth, said everyone, and just took off with it without telling her mother or anyone else where she was going.

When Tibbie heard this story she furrowed her brow remembering the last meeting she'd had with Kitty. 'I can't understand it,' she told Marie. 'She told me she was going to Duns. She sent you her love and asked me to keep in touch about her mother… It's not like her to say one thing and do another. I hope she's come to no harm. Wee Lily's worried about her but Big Lily doesn't give a fig.'

Marie rubbed the scar on her thumb reflectively. 'I think she'll be all right, Tibbie. Kitty's a survivor,' she said. It was a lovely day and her heart was singing because the previous day she'd seen Murray, for he'd stood watching while she sketched in the Roxburghs' garden. At one point their hands brushed when he bent to pick up her painting box and her skin still prickled where he'd touched it.

She was counting the days till she could see him again. Next Tuesday evening perhaps, four long days to put in dreaming about him. In a strange state of mind, half bemused delight and half suspended animation, she mooned around the village, making little sketches, talking to Tibbie, helping with the housework, stroking the cat, listening to the gossip… The only excitement was when her brother came over from Maddiston.

On Sunday afternoon he appeared at the door unexpectedly. It was raining and the women rushed towards him, fussing while he took off his coat and unwound the muffler from around his neck.

'You'd better have a wee dram to get the cold out of you,' said Tibbie, bringing out the whisky bottle.

David hadn't touched alcohol since his experience with Mr Henderson at the fair, so he primly refused but he did not seem his usual melancholy self. He had something special to tell them, he said.

They both looked at him expectantly, wondering what sort of surprise he was about to spring on them. 'Something very nice happened to me yesterday,' he said.

Tibbie hoped he'd met some nice girl he wanted to marry but had the sense not to voice this wish. Marie racked her brains to think of something her brother had always wanted and could not come up with a thing. Their failure to guess his secret did not displease him. It meant he could drag out the suspense.

'I've just been given the best present I'll ever get, I think,' he told them.

They looked back at him with smiles on their faces till Marie's tolerance broke and she said, 'Do tell us, David. What is it?'

'I've been made manager of the Maddiston mill,' he announced with a note of great pride.

The effect was everything he desired. His sister and Tibbie gaped at him in astonishment, exclaiming together, 'Manager! How did this happen?'

'Coleman got drunk again yesterday morning and fell down in the yard when Mr Henderson was there, so Henderson sent him off and made me manager. I take up my new position on May the first and as soon as Coleman and his wife move out of the big house, I'll move in.' This was what he had been working and planning to achieve ever since he stepped into the mill office but it had come sooner than even he expected.

'That's wonderful for you, David,' said Marie. Then she shook her head a little and added, 'But what about poor Coleman? You always said he was a nice man. What's going to happen to him?'

Her brother shot her a hard look. 'He'll go back to where he came from I expect. He's a nice enough man but he drank and that meant he couldn't do his work properly. He was too soft. The workers made a fool of him.'

It was obvious that when David was in charge things would be very different. All he wanted now was for the ex-manager to get out of the way as quickly as possible, and he longed to move into the mill manager's big house. He was literally counting the hours and praying that there would be nothing to hold up Coleman's departure.

'But you're so young,' gasped Tibbie.

'I'm not... I'm twenty-one,' protested David. In fact, Mr Henderson had been told he was twenty-four and he could pass for that easily.

His sister and Tibbie were over their first surprise by this time and told him how clever he was. They both said they were proud of how well he'd done.

'That Mr Henderson must think a lot of you,' said Tibbie admiringly.

David smiled and looked across at his sister as he said, 'Well, you know what this means, don't you? You'll have to start packing your things, Marie. I should be moving into the big house in the next few days and so there's no need for you to go back to Edinburgh because as well as getting the house, I'll be earning two hundred pounds a year!'

Tibbie gasped again, showing the admiration he yearned for, but Marie's reaction was not what he'd expected. She did not seem at all pleased.

'I'm glad you've done so well, I'm happy for you but I'm not going to Maddiston,' she said coldly.

'But you're almost finished with this painting business. You must have learned enough. Now you can settle down. I need you to look after me,' he spluttered.

'I'm not going to live in Maddiston and I'm not going to stop attending my classes,' she repeated, clenching her fists, infuriated because he treated her painting as a trivial pastime, like fancy needlework.

He leaned forward and said angrily, 'I think it's time my sister stopped taking charity money. I'm earning enough to keep you now.'

Her face was scarlet. 'I don't take charity money. Lady Godolphin sponsors me because she recognises my talent. One day I'll repay her by painting a lovely picture for her.'

He snorted derisively. 'Some payment. What she wants from you is the feeling that she has some simple country girl dependent on her bounty. You make her feel generous and kindly. You're a fool to stand for it, bowing and scraping to her, "Yes, Lady Godolphin" this and "No, Lady Godolphin" that. It makes me sick. Don't you realise what you're doing? Haven't you any pride?'

Marie stared at him with a feeling of sickness rising in her throat. 'I don't bow and scrape... I only treat her with the respect that I'd give to anyone of her class.'

David launched himself into a tirade now. 'Why's she better than us? Just because she married a fop with a title, that's why. We're as good as she is, better because she's coloured, or hadn't you noticed that? She gives money away and you think she's marvellous, but she's got so much that she doesn't miss it. It's like you giving a crust of bread to a tramp at the door. For God's sake, don't make yourself into an object of charity. I don't want you to be beholden to anybody.' Dim, long-banked-down memories of his downtrodden mother came sharply into his memory, making his fury stronger.

Marie shouted back at David, 'You only want me to be beholden to you. That's what you mean. You don't want me to get free of you, to have a life of my own. Lady Godolphin doesn't ask anything of me but you do, you're the one who wants a slave and I'm not going to give up the chance I've been given for you or anyone else.'

He jumped up from his chair and towered over his sister. He'd grown very tall, Marie noticed. She also saw that he was adopting the stance of a man of power, the pose of Adalbert Henderson whom he unconsciously copied.

'I'm telling you that you're to come to Maddiston and live with me. I'm your guardian,' he ordered.

She was on her feet too, eyes blazing. 'I will not come and you're not my guardian. If anyone is, it's Tibbie.'

Tibbie had never seen her so animated or determined and longed to cheer her on but held her tongue.

David turned to the watching woman. 'Tell her she can't stay in your house any longer,' he said sharply.

Tibbie shook her head. 'I can't do that. She's welcome here for as long as she wants to stay.'

'I won't pay for her unless she's with me,' he said.

'That doesn't matter. I don't need the money,' said Tibbie calmly. Marie was watching her with eyes full of gratitude.

David thumped his fist on the table. 'You're both against me. But you'll find out I'm right. She'll need me in the end. She'll come begging to me to take her in.'

He grabbed his coat from the chair where it was drying in front of the fire and struggled his way into it again. Neither of the women tried to stop him as he stormed out of the door into the rain.

—

It was a relief to Marie when the weekend was over and she could take the train back to Edinburgh. She actually ran along Princes Street in her haste to reach the studio. She was eager to be back with her friends and her work, eager to shake off Camptounfoot, David and all of her past.

In the big studio she sniffed the heady aroma of turpentine mixed with linseed oil. It was a smell she loved, a smell that made her want to throw off her jacket and start painting immediately. She could hardly spare the time to say more than 'Good morning' to anyone.

Amy looked up, waved and grinned as she came running in, some of the other girls waved too and the Professor bustled over to say, 'I want you to go across to the gallery on the other side of the road and look at the Dutch flower pieces there. You might like to try your hand at copying one of them.'

Time passed like magic when she painted. The hours flew by like seconds and it felt as if she had only started when Amy stood beside her wiping her brushes on a cloth and saying, 'You're coming back to Murrayhill with me tonight, I hope. We've arranged a dancing party and lots of people will be there.'

Including Murray! was Marie's first thought but she demurred half-heartedly. 'I'd love to but I'm always in your house. Your mother must be tired of the sight of me,' but she hoped with all her heart that Amy really meant to take her home.

Though she'd stayed at Murrayhill often, she never presumed that she would be asked back. There was no problem with Tibbie, for if Marie was not off the half-past seven train, it was accepted that she would not be home that night.

Amy laughed. 'My mother's got to the stage that she doesn't know whether you're one of her own children or not and sometimes I think she prefers you to me. She's always boasting to her friends about this wonderful artist she knows and that, my dear, is you,' she said.

'Your mother's an angel,' said Marie in a heartfelt tone.

Amy raised a sceptical eyebrow. 'Don't be deceived. My mother's only an angel so long as you're doing what she wants. Anyone who crosses her sees a very different side, I assure you.'

'Well, she's never shown her different side to me,' said Marie loyally.

'Not yet,' said Amy, 'but then she might never. You're her darling and I know she'd be furious with me if I didn't bring you home tonight.'

They drove in Amy's carriage as usual. The coachman knew Marie by now and smiled when he handed her in. She loved the luxury of the carriage. That was the way people ought to live…

Murrayhill was a buzz of activity when they turned into the drive. To Marie's amazement there were flames leaping from oil braziers on each side of the front door. She turned and asked Amy, 'What's happening?'

'It's Mama's birthday. We always have a ball to celebrate it. I didn't tell you because you'd have gone off fussing about buying her a present and she wouldn't want that. But she wanted you to be there,' Amy told her.

Marie almost wept. 'But I want to give your mother a present. You should have told me, oh, why didn't you tell me. I'd have brought her one of my drawings from the studio. And what will I wear? I haven't anything grand enough for a ball.'

Amy laughed. 'Stop fussing, we've thought of that. Mama asked her dressmaker to send a couple of gowns that would fit you. You've to pick the one you like best. It's to be a present from her to you.'

There was no use protesting, no use refusing the gift. How wonderful it was, thought Marie, to be so comfortably off that you could buy a gown for a strange girl without thinking twice. But she worried about not having a present for the kind Mrs Roxburgh.

'Would you give me some charcoal and a sheet of paper? I want to make a drawing for your mother,' she said to Amy.

'What will you draw?'

'I don't know… I could do flowers…'

'She thinks flower pictures are rather prissy,' said Amy.

'Then I could draw the house…'

'You haven't time,' was Amy's objection to this.

'I know, I'll do a portrait of you,' said Marie in sudden inspiration and this time Amy did not object except to say, 'I'll find it hard sitting still for long enough but I'll try.'

They ran upstairs to Amy's big bedroom overlooking the lawns and Marie began her work, but it was harder going than she'd expected. Amy's face was too mobile to settle into one expression. It took two hours and the maids were ringing the dressing gong by the time she finished.

'I'm not satisfied with it, but it'll have to do,' she said morosely looking at the sketch. 'Oh, I wish you'd told me about your mother's birthday. I'd have done her a really good drawing if I'd known.'

Amy did not spare more than a glance at her portrait. 'That looks good to me. Cover it up and present it to her after dinner. She'll be thrilled.'

Marie was not so sure, for there was something she did not like about the portrait but she could not pinpoint exactly what it was. However, she rolled it up in a neat scroll and tied it with a ribbon that Amy found for her. It was too late now to do anything else.

When she at last went into the room that she was always given when she stayed at Murrayhill, there was a froth of colour on the bed, where two very pretty ballgowns had been laid out for her. The first was sky-blue with ribbons fluttering from a bow in the middle of its low-cut bodice but the second made her draw her breath in admiration, for it was the colour of Kitty's hair, a lovely amber-red, with a panniered skirt of velvet interlayed with taffeta. The bodice was modestly scoop-necked and two ribbon rosettes crowned the shoulders.

While she was looking at the dresses, a maid came in and offered to help her dress. Such attentions always embarrassed Marie, who was not used to them, so she sent the girl away. She did not even try on the blue gown but lifted the skirt of the glowing amber-coloured one and slipped it over her head. The silk lining slid over her body with a satisfying rustle.

She was so slim that she required no corsetting or lacing but the dress was designed to be fastened up the back and she was forced to ring for the maid, who came in and expertly secured twenty hooks and eyes which made the bodice fit tightly to Marie's breasts and clasp her waist so that it looked even narrower than its actual eighteen inches.

'It suits you very well, miss,' said the admiring maid and offered to curl the tendrils of Marie's fine hair with a pair of curling tongs that were already heating over a small candle-holder on the dressing-table.

Abstractedly Marie said, 'No, my hair's naturally straight and it looks best that way. I'd feel like a doll with it curled.' She stood gazing with disbelief at her reflection in the mirror. It was the first time she'd ever worn anything so beautiful and it made her feel like a beggar-girl transformed into a princess.

The maid saw how delighted she was and offered, 'I'll run through to Miss Amy's room and borrow some of her cologne to make you smell nice.'

When the cologne was sprayed on, the dinner gong rang and Marie hurried downstairs holding up her panniered skirts. She was greeted by cries of delighted admiration from the entire Roxburgh family, but the one who gave her most pleasure was Murray, who jumped from his chair and held out his arm, saying with a charming smile that made her knees go weak, 'I claim the honour of leading this beautiful stranger in to dinner.'

Her heart was beating so fast that she feared he would see the pulse leaping in her neck. The wine that was served with the delicious meal helped her to calm down and soon she was laughing and talking as convivially as all the others round the table.

At the end of the dinner, the handsome Roxburgh children stood up with their father, champagne glasses in hand, to toast their mother at the top of the table. She was dressed in ruby-red velvet and the diamonds in her hair and around her neck made her glow in the candlelight. She looked like a queen.

Uncertain what to do during this family tribute, Marie sat still, but Murray gently reached across and pulled her to her feet, saying, 'You must join in too. You're practically one of the family by now.'

Her heart was bursting with love, gratitude and unalloyed admiration as she stood up and raised her glass to the woman in the high-backed chair. Tonight she felt part of their privileged world, not just a wistful onlooker from the outside, not a waif brought in from the cold.

When her gaze sought Murray's he smiled, making little crinkles of laughter lines crease in the corners of his eyes. Marie sighed, sending him unspoken words, 'I love you, I love you…'

Before the guests arrived for the ball, the Roxburgh children presented their gifts to their mother. Her husband, she told them, had already given her the magnificent diamond parure which she was wearing as she sat enthroned, receiving her family's homage.

Amy gave her mother a china cottage that had tiny flowers round the door and creepers up the walls. It was greeted with cries of delight and a kiss on the cheek, which was also the tribute paid to the elder son's Paisley shawl, Murray's gold brooch with a quartz rose in its heart and youngest son Arthur's crystal perfume spray with a large rubber bulb encased in silver mesh.

When she received this last gift, his mother aimed the nozzle at him and sprayed him with tuberose that scented the whole room.

'Ugh,' cried Amy. 'Why did you buy that scent, Arthur? It's shopgirl scent, very vulgar.'

Arthur went scarlet. 'I thought mother would like it because it's the kind you wear, Amy,' he said.

'Not any more,' said his sister lightly. 'I've grown out of such tastes.'

Marie, listening to this, was uncomfortably aware that she was reeking of tuberose too, because that was what the maid had borrowed from Amy. The first faint cloud appeared on her happy horizon. What a terrible mistake, she thought, for to her Amy was the setter of fashion and the expert on everything that was *comme il faut*.

Finally it was Marie's turn to hand over her gift. She had laid it under her chair and bent to pick it up and take it across to Mrs Roxburgh, who protested, 'My dear, not you too. I expressly forbade Amy to tell you it was my birthday because I didn't want you spending your money on me.'

'I've only done you a drawing. It's a portrait of Amy,' said Marie, handing it over and, greatly daring, bending low to kiss Mrs Roxburgh's cheek. Then she added, 'I want to show you how much I appreciate everything you've done for me, how kind you've been... even this lovely dress...'

With a quaver in her voice she held out the rustling skirt that shimmered in the firelight as if it had been brushed with gold. Mrs Roxburgh beamed at her, 'You look so beautiful that the sight of you is sufficient reward. I knew that colour would make your hair look lovely and it has. Blondes have such an advantage when it comes to dressing. Amy thought you'd take the blue but I knew that your artist's eye would tell you this is better.'

She unrolled the drawing and held it out, gazing at it with her sharp and perceptive eye. For a while she said nothing but then gave a little laugh. 'You've caught my daughter's sharp look, haven't you? You don't flatter. That's why you'll never make a fashionable portraitist. People like to be flattered.'

Marie was disappointed but not surprised that Mrs Roxburgh did not like the picture because she had not cared much for it herself.

She began to explain, 'I wanted to do you something else but there wasn't time. I'll start something else for you tomorrow, though.'

Mrs Roxburgh smiled. 'Please don't. I'll treasure this because it's a very good character drawing, masterly in fact… You're too good for portraits, that's what I meant to say.'

Arthur rose from his seat to look at the drawing over his mother's shoulder.

'It's little Miss Do-As-I-Say to the life,' he said looking at Amy with a laugh. Amy coloured and bit her lip.

The drawing was passed round and when it reached Murray, he was tactful. 'The handling of charcoal is masterly. Look at the clever way Marie has toned the skin. It reminds me of a Raphael cartoon,' he said. Amy still said nothing and kept her eyes fixed on her plate. She was obviously far from pleased.

Marie's heart was like lead and it took all Murray's blandishments to prevent her quietly slipping away and spending the rest of the evening in her bedroom.

When he saw that she was upset, he crossed the room to stand behind her chair and lead her out on his arm when the family prepared to go into the hall to receive the ball guests.

There was hubbub there. When the host and hostess started shaking the hands of the first arrivals, Murray whispered in Marie's ear, 'Save me the first waltz. I think you look beautiful.'

There was a singing in her ears and her eyesight seemed to be somehow affected, but delightfully so, for everything was suffused with light and colour. Her embarrassment over the drawing of Amy was forgotten as she went into the huge drawing-room which had been transformed. Furniture had been pushed back or carted away and the carpet unrolled to reveal an expanse of parquet that shone like ice and looked equally slippery. The grand piano and harp that always sat in a corner were still there, but there were people sitting by them as well as a trio of string instrumentalists and a stately-looking gentleman in a tailcoat with a baton in his hand.

Pots of ferns, flowering plants and bamboos from the conservatory had been brought in and were massed behind the little orchestra. When the host and hostess stepped into the room, the music began and would not stop till midnight.

Marie Benjamin was to remember Mrs Roxburgh's birthday ball for the rest of her life. Many, many times, she was to relive it in memory.

The only dancing she had ever done till then was when she and Kitty had pranced about as children to the music of a fiddle in the main street of Camptounfoot where, on warm evenings, the villagers came out of their houses and one of the men played. The younger folk would start essaying a few steps and soon everybody, even Jo and Tibbie, would be hooching and hopping about in an impromptu display.

It was very different at Murrayhill. When the music struck up, Murray bowed before her and took her hand to lead her onto the floor. Her heart was thudding so fast that she was really afraid that she might faint. His hand holding hers, however, was cool and reassuring and his wonderful brown eyes were looking at her with unguarded admiration. 'I never thought you could look so lovely,' he whispered.

She stammered, 'I'm not… I'm not a good dancer, I'm afraid.'

He laughed. 'Of course you are. I can tell by the way you walk,' and saying that he put a firm arm around her waist and swept her into the middle of the eddying crowd. Feeling as if her bones had turned to rubber she yielded herself to him and was swept along like a bobbing cork on the top of water. It was so lovely to let him guide her, to be as light as a feather and feel her feet barely touching the ground, to be in Murray's arms. If I were to die now, she thought, I wouldn't really mind.

Miraculously, she found that if she listened to the music, she could dance… it was as easy as that! Everything was easy when she had Murray to share it with her. When the final chord was played, she looked up at him with her cheeks pink and eyes sparkling. He held her tight for longer than was necessary and breathed softly in her ear, 'Did you hear me when I said that you look lovely tonight?'

To her own amazement she actually managed to flirt. Dropping her eyelids, she whispered back, 'Yes, I heard you and I thank you for the compliment, but does it mean you don't usually think so?'

He laughed. 'Don't fish, Miss Benjamin. I'll think about that question and let you know.'

Deliriously, happy, she danced after that with the other Roxburgh brothers and a crowd of their friends who clustered round her and whose names she instantly forgot, for all the time she was making conversation with them, she was acutely conscious of Murray. She noticed every person he danced with – his mother, Amy, his aunt, three girls in pastel-coloured gowns, a bouncy, plump girl in scarlet whose laugh was like the Maddiston mill hooter, and a tall, dark-haired girl in a dress of dark green plaid. These last two he danced with twice before he finally returned to Marie.

This time the music was sweet and sentimental and he seemed solemn as they circled the floor. They hardly spoke but when they were dancing at the back of the room out of sight, he dropped a quick peck on her cheek and whispered, 'I've been thinking about your question. You're always lovely.'

She was too overcome to speak and they danced on in silence till the music stopped. He was still holding her hand as he watched the happy crowd beginning to depart. 'The end of a party is always sad,' he said. 'I wish it could go on for ever.'

Marie shook her head. 'Oh no, if that was the case, we'd have nothing to look forward to, would we?'

He smiled. 'That's very wise. What are you looking forward to?' he asked quietly.

She thought for a moment. 'Painting well. After that I don't really know.'

'Most young ladies look forward to getting married,' he said.

She was flustered! 'I suppose I do too, but I've no one in mind. At the moment painting is more important.'

He did not relinquish her hand as he said, 'I hope we don't lose touch though the ball is over, Cinderella. I don't intend to let that happen.' Colour flooded into her face and again she was lost for words. When he gently let her hand go, she hurried off to join Amy, who was saying goodnight to people at the front door.

It was only afterwards, lying in bed, that she thought of several things she could have said to him in reply but, of course, she hadn't and she was afraid that she'd not get another chance.

Next day she rose late and he had gone off to the university by the time she sat with Amy at the breakfast-table, going over the events of the previous evening. Amy was in one of her teasing moods. 'I think my brother is smitten with you,' she said.

Marie tried to appear casual. 'Which brother?' she asked.

'Oh don't be silly! Murray, of course. I saw his adoring look when he was dancing with you. I saw him holding your hand at the end. You mustn't break his heart. He's very susceptible is poor Murray. He's been in love at least three times already.'

Marie's heart gave a cruel lurch but she managed to ask, 'Who with?' Amy was eating bread and butter and had to mumble through crumbs. 'Various girls, some nice, some dreadful, but none of them has lasted more than a fortnight. He's a bit of a flirt, I'm afraid, very susceptible to girls.'

Marie smiled. 'I'll remember that. Who was the plump girl in scarlet he danced with last night, the one with the loud laugh?'

Amy loved to gossip. 'Alexandra Adamson. Her father's so rich it's obscene and she's his only child, Alexandra's simply *mad* about Murray but he keeps her at arm's length, though it's difficult as you must have seen. She throws herself at him. I think she's sure that her money'll get him in the end and she might be right. He's quite keen on money. He's studying to be a lawyer and most of them are very money-conscious.'

Marie went on to ask, 'And who was the dark girl in green plaid? Your father and your other brothers danced with her too. She seemed very dignified.'

The girl in green had sailed through the party with a poise that suggested nothing in life would ever discomfit her and although she was not pretty, she exuded a strange attraction, an indifference that drew men to her and meant she was never short of dancing partners.

'That,' said Amy portentously, 'is our cousin Julia, a very different case from poor Alexandra. We're all terrified of Julia – even my mother treats her with respect because Julia's parents are both dead and her only brother was killed in the Indian Mutiny, so she owns a castle in the Highlands and has a vast fortune – Alexandra's in triplicate I believe. My father is her trustee because she was his brother's child, but she tells him exactly what to do. We all keep in with her because she might leave her money to us or our children.'

'Why do you think she won't marry? I thought she was very impressive-looking,' said Marie, who remembered the cool way the tall girl had circled the floor with Murray. They were the same height and made a striking pair.

Amy scoffed, 'My dear girl, her tongue could cut cast iron. She doesn't suffer fools – or anyone else come to that – gladly and it would take a brave man to ask her to marry him.'

They didn't go to Edinburgh to classes that day but stayed in Murrayhill, gossiping, giggling, amusing each other. The *froideur* that had come between them over the portrait seemed to have disappeared and Amy was going out of her way to be as delightful as possible.

When the men came home, they spent another delightful evening with Mrs Roxburgh playing the piano and everyone singing. Amy was a skilled performer of comic songs, some of them quite risqué, but Murray had a deep baritone voice that made Marie's toes curl with desire. When he sang sentimental ballads, he looked at her with his dark eyes and she would have died for him if he'd asked her.

After the parents retired upstairs, the young people remained in the drawing-room playing cards. While they were sitting out, Murray took Marie's hand and pulled her gently towards the conservatory. Inside its door, among the tropical foliage and with the smell of damp moss filling her nostrils, she was kissed for the first time.

'I think I love you,' he told her.

'You think?' she asked in a faint voice.

'Yes, I really think so. You're so pretty and such a clever artist. If I was able to propose to a girl, I'd ask you to marry me but I've nothing to offer you…'

She shook her head. 'I'm not fortune-hunting, Murray.'

He kissed her again and sighed, 'I know you're not but I have to have some decent prospects to put before your father, haven't I?'

'My, father's dead,' she told him.

Again another kiss. 'Then perhaps one day you'll consider marrying? Will you?'

She did not want to appear too eager but she would have married him there and then if given the chance… 'Perhaps,' she said. It was an effort to make her voice as light as his.

Then she slid her arms round his neck and, without artifice or thought of keeping him in suspense, kissed him full on the lips, not one of the brushing little kisses they'd exchanged so far but a full-blooded, enthusiastic kiss that obviously took him by surprise. He clutched her tightly to him and kissed her back.

'We're ideal for each other,' he murmured as he sank his face into her hair.

She had no chance to agree with him because at that moment the pixie face of Amy peered round the corner of the door. 'Just as I thought, two lovebirds billing and cooing. Come out you silly pair. It's a good thing the parents have gone to bed because Mama would have a fit if she saw you,' she said mockingly.

Murray was short with his sister. 'Go away, Amy. You're a little snooper.'

She laughed, 'Don't worry. I won't tell. But come out before the servants see you because they might not be so discreet.'

After that she and Marie had a secret that they referred to obliquely. Amy always referred to Murray as 'the swain' and often wandered across the Professor's studio in the middle of a class to say things like, 'The swain asked me to say he and his friends will be waiting for us when we finish.'

They met in a recently opened tea parlour where Marie and Murray clasped hands under the table while their friends laughed and gossiped around them. From time to time they managed to snatch a kiss, but the lack of opportunity for this only increased her passion, though he seemed to take the flirtation more lightly.

Marie went to Murrayhill as often as before but Murray was rarely there and when he was, Mrs Roxburgh contrived to keep them apart by seating him at the far end of the table Or sending him off on some errand that took him out of the house for hours.

Amy told Marie that the time for his examinations was coming round and his mother was anxious that he was not diverted from his work. For evening after evening he was closeted in his room and she hardly saw him at all.

When summer came, Murray went to France with a group of friends. He did not write to her and Marie spent the fine days at Camptounfoot fretting. When classes began again in September, Amy appeared with a very glum face.

'There's been bad news about Murray,' she whispered to Marie when she came into the studio.

'What's happened to him? He isn't hurt or ill, is he?' she asked anxiously.

'Oh, no, nothing like that. The silly fellow has failed his exams. He'll have to do them all again next year. Mother and father are furious. They say he didn't work hard enough.'

Marie pretended to take this news philosophically but she was desperately disappointed, for this meant that another year would have to go by before Murray was in a position really to ask her to marry him.

Her own prospects, however, seemed to be brightening as his waned. Professor Abernethy was loud in his praise of her copies of the Dutch flower paintings.

'This is wonderful. You've found your *métier*. You could sell these. I think we should have an exhibition next spring and display your work. It's time my school had a show and you'll be a star to draw the crowds,' he enthused.

He brought his friends to look at Marie's paintings and they were equally complimentary, calling her a 'rare talent' while she blushed under their praise.

One society painter, who swept around Edinburgh in a long black cloak like a swashbuckler, put his hand on her arm when he'd looked at her work and said, 'You're remarkably good for a woman. But let me give you a piece of advice, my dear. When you sign your work, don't write Marie Benjamin.'

She looked at him in surprise and asked, 'Should I use another name?'

He smiled superciliously. 'Of course not. What I mean is, don't use the name Marie. Sign your work by your initial only... M. Benjamin. Then it's more likely to sell.'

At first she did not understand and he had to explain. 'If you only use an initial, the buyers and the critics won't know you're a woman, my dear. Pictures by women don't sell, I'm afraid.'

'But that's dreadful. It's unfair,' she protested.

The painter shrugged. 'So it may be, but it's a fact of life. If you want to sell, use your initial. If it doesn't matter, stand by your principles by all means...'

Ruefully she painted out Marie on the canvases she had already completed and signed herself as M. Benjamin. She wanted to sell.

# Chapter Twelve

With Toby sitting beside her, Kitty perched on the top step of Grandma Kennedy's wagon.

She and the dog were good friends now but it had taken over a year to win him round, for suspicion of strangers was part of his nature. She slid an arm round his neck and felt his spiky hair against her skin as she stared out over a vast landscape of rolling hills that awed her by their emptiness.

They were on the way to Alston, high on the Cumberland moors, and the landscape was forbidding, spread out for mile upon mile of bare windswept hills covered with reeds and cotton grass. Not a house, not a tree, not a living soul could be seen apart from the slowly creeping wagons of the cavalcade.

Kitty's passion for travelling, for keeping on the move, which had made her so unsettled at Falconwood was fired by the variety of places she had seen since she joined the boxing show. They trekked the roads from the hop fields of Kent to the dour grimness of Lancashire mill towns, avoiding big cities apart from seaports and concentrating on smaller towns where people were avid for entertainment.

She loved setting up the booth in a new place, but even more she loved dismantling it and setting out for another destination. Now she was wondering about Alston. What would it be like; how would the people react to the show?

They were still a long way from their destination when they stopped for the night in a hollow between two hills. Tomorrow they'd wend their way on up, up, up till they reached the town where they'd be one of the attractions of the annual fair.

Grandma Kennedy came hurrying over. She never seemed to move at normal walking pace but scuttled like a crab.

'It's going to blow a gale tonight. We'll have to tie the wagons down in case they get blown over,' she shouted in the teeth of a rising wind.

226

Kitty grinned. She enjoyed rough weather and to be blown over would only be another experience to add to all the ones she'd had in the past eventful year. She joined the men throwing thick ropes over the roofs of the caravans and securing them to the ground with big U-shaped metal pegs that were driven in with a huge wooden mallet wielded by Joe. The women's job was to grab the ends of the ropes when they came snaking over the roofs and hold them down till they were securely pegged. When everything was finished, Bill the busker, who was supervising the operation, wiped his brow and stared at the leaden sky as he said, 'All right, blow all you like now. We're safe enough.'

As she passed by, Grandma patted Kitty on the back, saying, 'Well done, Kate. Come on in now, it's suppertime. We'd all better get bedded down before this storm starts.'

As usual they were sharing their supper with Grandma's sister Sophia, the big woman who kept the fortune-telling mynah. Tall and stately, copper-skinned and craggy-faced, she bore no physical resemblance to little Grandma and Kitty found it difficult to believe that they were sisters but they assured her they were, though by different fathers.

'It's the mother who counts, not the father,' said Grandma solemnly and Sophia nodded her great head in agreement.

'You're right. It's the women who count. It's the women who carry on the family. It's the women who rear the children. It's the women who hold things together.'

The sisters were fond of each other and when suppertime came, Sophia always arrived at Grandma's wagon with her contribution to the meal in a wicker basket covered with a pristine white cloth. On the night of the high wind she brought a meat pie, three red apples, a spherical yellow cheese like a cricket ball and a black bottle of wine. As a finishing touch she fished out three tightly furled pink roses and stuck them in a little glass jar in the middle of the table. She must have picked them many miles back, for the travellers had passed no gardens or rose bushes for a long, long way.

When everything was laid out, the table looked like a picture and Kitty gazed at it with admiration. Everything in the wagon was always attractive, clean and tidy, luxurious in fact, although the space was cramped. The contrast between the lives of the travelling folk and those of the farm-workers she had lived with at Falconwood, and her grandmother's bothy, was very marked. Some farm wives kept clean and tidy houses but they had no money to spare for inessentials like pretty china and the embroidered and tasselled cushions that covered the bed and the bench beneath the window where Kitty slept at night.

She had also discovered that the travelling people were a good deal more decorous in their behaviour than farm folk. With them she never heard the foul language that she had been accustomed to on the farm, where men did not bridle their tongues in the presence of women or children. Nor did she hear any of the earthy and crude jokes that both men and women at Falconwood bandied about among themselves. Grandma hated what she called 'vulgarities'. Her language was forthright and simple – she always called a spade a spade – but it was never smutty. Kitty felt far safer with the travelling folk than she had ever felt at Falconwood.

Grandma's first name was Beattie and she had brought Sophia up from childhood because their mother died when the younger sister was six years old. Their mother owned the entourage and on her death, the business was passed down to the eldest daughter, Grandma.

Kitty sat on the bench with her chin on her hand and asked questions. 'Did you both get married?' she wanted to know. 'I know Bill's your son, Grandma, but what about Sophia?'

Grandma nodded. 'Oh aye, we got married. I married our star boxer, the Tornado he was called. He was a bonny man! You and I nearly fell out over him, didn't we, Sophy?'

'But he liked you best, Beattie. I married his brother, the big idiot,' said Sophia.

Grandma stood up and began tidying the debris on the table. 'It's all past now. They're both dead. And we're still here.'

'So we are,' agreed Sophia. 'And so's our sons, your Bill and my Henry.'

She looked at Kitty and said, 'Henry's in the Navy. He's too smart to go on the road is my Henry.'

Grandma bridled at this. 'It's a good job some lads stay on the road or where would we be? We couldn't manage without Bill,' she told her sister who hurriedly agreed. It was obvious that no matter how formidable Sophia appeared outside, the tiny sister ruled over her.

When their meal was finished, Kitty took the dishes outside to wash in a little burn that ran past their camping site and the gathering force of the storm surprised her, for the wind was tearing at her hair and making her skirt swirl around her legs. It was already difficult to walk against it, so she did not take long over her task and was back with the two women very quickly. She was happy in their company, they amused her with their stories, and she never once considered leaving them.

The only shadow in her life came when something made her remember her mother. She wondered if the baby had been born safely, but it was impossible to find out because she was afraid to let anyone in Camptounfoot know where she was in case the policeman was looking for her.

Next morning the wind had blown itself out and Kitty sat on the driving box of the wagon beside Bill as they drove into Alston.

'Do you think there'll be a big crowd tonight?' she asked.

He nodded. 'It's always good here. Everyone turns out for the fair. There's not much else to do on the top of these hills. They're nice folk though, the old-fashioned kind.'

She nodded. She had been with the show in similar towns where the railway had not yet penetrated and where the people were simple and unaffected, content with the way of life that their forefathers had led, not hankering after cities or foreign parts. It was always a pleasure to put on a big act for them, to draw howls and screams from the spectators.

Their routine was easy. When Kitty, pretending to be a girl from the crowd, knocked down Joe, Grandma jumped in to avenge him. Sometimes she won and sometimes victory went to Kitty.

In order to get away with it, they had to be sure no one saw the red-haired girl arriving with the show wagons, so when they were still quite a way from the town she jumped down from her seat beside Bill and stood by the roadside watching the cavalcade disappear towards their campsite. She would meet up with them after the show, on the road out of the town as they left.

The storm of the previous night had left the air fresh and the sun was shining brightly. She jumped into the road, Bill waved his hand to her and touched his whip to the broad backs of the pair of horses in the shafts, and she bent down to take off her straw bonnet and boots and wandered slowly towards the town. She liked going barefoot, for the soles of her feet were still as tough as leather from years of being without shoes.

When she'd been walking for about ten minutes she heard the clip-clop of horse's hooves coming up behind her and stood back against a stone wall to let the rider pass. It was a young man dressed in a rough brown corduroy jacket, with a red kerchief knotted round his neck.

His dark head was bare and when he drew level with her, he lifted his riding stick and saluted her gravely, saying, 'G'mornin'. Fine mornin'.'

She smiled and agreed, 'Yes, very fine.'

He pulled on his horse's reins and slowed it to a stop. 'Going to town? Going to the fair?' he asked.

'Yes,' she told him.

'Hop up at the back then. Ride pillion with me,' he offered, looking down at her bare feet.

'Why not?' she said and he drew his horse towards the wall which she clambered onto and from it onto the broad back of the horse. She was clinging round his waist when they set off again and he called back to her, 'Have you come far? I don't recognise you.'

She made a wide gesture with one arm, saying, 'From way back there. I've come to live with my uncle Jo and his family.' Jo was the first male name that came into her mind.

'Jo who? I don't know any Jos and I know most of the folks in these parts. I've lived here all my life.' He had a pleasant, deep voice with something like a laugh in it, no matter what he said.

Kitty frantically tried to think of a neutral surname but had no notion of what names were common in those parts. She gazed around and saw an old brown haystack in a field. It gave her inspiration.

'Jo Brownrig,' she said and added hastily, 'he's new to these parts though. He's only just come.'

'Where is he living exactly?' persisted her new companion.

She giggled. 'Wouldn't you ask that and I don't know the answer? I forget the name of his place but I know how to find my way back… I've to walk straight along the road back there for about a couple of miles and then branch off to the left for another two and then take a little lane up a hill for a mile and a half or so till I see a hill shaped like a sugar loaf…'

She succeeded in confusing him utterly and he was still worrying about the sugar-loaf hill when they reached the field that was to be the showground for the day and she jumped down from the pillion, thanking him.

He was reluctant to let her go and reached down to catch her hand, saying, 'Don't go yet. Stay with me. I thought we might go round the fair together. There's lots to see.'

She looked up into honest brown eyes and saw that they were flecked with little dots of gold. She instinctively knew that this was a man she could trust.

'What's your name?' she asked.

'Gerald Greatstone. Folk call me Gerry. I'm twenty-two years old and I'm not married. I've a farm on the other side of the hill with my father. We graze sheep mostly.'

She nodded. She knew enough about farming to tell that it would be hard work tending sheep in those hostile hills. His life could not be easy. She nodded her head.

'All right, I'll stay with you for a bit,' she told him.

He jumped down from the horse and stood smiling at her. 'You're not the Queen of Faeryland, are you? Coming walking out on a bright morning with your hair glowing red and then disappearing when darkness comes...'

His imagery delighted her and she laughed. 'Maybe I am. Let's see. Are you prepared to take a chance on it?'

'I'll take a chance. I'd love to be enchanted by you,' he told her. His smile crinkled up his face making his eyes dance.

Physically he pleased her, for he was as tall as she and well made with broad shoulders and a tapering waist. His face was long with a wide, mobile mouth and peaked eyebrows; his hair was dark and waving and it reached down almost to the collar of his coat at the back. He looked like a gentleman and spoke like one too, though she could tell by his hands that he did not leave the manual work of his farm to other people.

'My name's Kitty,' she said, taking his arm after he'd tied up his horse. The jostling, noisy fair crowd swallowed them up and they walked from stall to stall, not really seeing the goods displayed there, for they only had eyes for each other.

It was not the fair that delighted Kitty, for she was used to fairs by this time; it was not the little town which was small and backward; it was not the inn where they went at midday for something to eat and drink because it was crowded and noisy; it was not the weather which was mild but not brilliant... it was his company. He turned the day to gold.

Never before had she felt so at ease with a man, never before had she wanted to please one so much. When they paused in front of the boxing booth, she saw Bill looking suspiciously at her and obviously wondering about her companion but she gave back no sign of recognition or reassurance. She was being someone else, a farm girl out to enjoy herself with handsome beau.

It was impossible not to give something of herself away to him as they talked, for he was so honest and forthright. In an outburst of confidence he told her how his beloved mother had died the year before; he told her about the loneliness he and his father endured in their house on top of the moors; he told her of his love for the inhospitable land and how it held him through good days and bad.

In return she told him that she was an illegitimate child born to a bondager. Amazingly, she heard herself telling him about Bullhead and how she'd dreamed that he would be handsome and dashing but found out he was an ugly villain. He listened with sympathy and held her hand.

When evening was drawing near and she knew they must soon part, she told him about Marie and her mother, how she'd lost her friend and was worried about Wee Lily. It was the first time she'd talked about that to anyone since she left Camptounfoot.

'Perhaps they both miss you as much as you miss them,' he offered as a consolation.

She nodded. 'That doesn't help. It makes me feel worse. Sometimes I can feel someone is thinking about me. I'll be busy doing something and not thinking about it when I get a feeling that I'm not alone. It's very odd.'

'You should go back to them if you feel like that,' he said but she shook her head. 'Oh no, I can't go back.' She did not tell him why.

'You're a mystery woman. I'm sure you are the Queen of the faeries,' he told her with a laugh and she looked up into his face. When their eyes met she was overcome by the most peculiar sensation. Her head swam, her stomach tightened and she felt as if she were about to faint. She had to put her hand on his arm to steady herself and when she did that he laid his own hand on hers and gave a sigh which told her he felt the same way as she did. They were enchanted.

In the distance she heard the thud, thud, thud of the boxing booth band. She shook her head. The time had come to leave him. She stood back and said, 'I have to go now.'

He looked sad. 'Not yet please. The fair goes on till dark. Don't go yet.'

But the distant music was calling her. 'I have to go.'

'Why? Is someone waiting for you? Have you a husband somewhere?'

She shook her head. 'No, I've no husband.' She could not tell him that she was a plant from the boxing show. She did not want him to know about that part of her life. It was better to be thought of as an enchantress.

He was bitterly disappointed but still tried to detain her. 'Don't run away like this. It'll soon be dark and you've a long way to go. I'll take you back to your uncle's place on my horse,' he offered but she shook her head.

'No, that's not possible. I must go now.' It was nearly half-past seven and her appearance on the show was always the last item on the bill, which had started at seven o'clock.

She did not want him following her; she did not want him to see her playing out her charade with Grandma.

He clasped her hands in his and held them against his heart. 'I don't know why you've got to go, but please change your mind. Please stay with me, just for another hour, that's all,' he pleaded. 'If we've only got one day together, let's make it as long as possible.'

Kitty stared at him. How handsome he was, how admirable in every way. He deserved a day that he would remember all his life and so did she. What he said about them only having a short time with each other impressed her for it was true. They would never meet again. One day in the whole of their lives for two people to meet and then part.

All of a sudden it struck her that there was nothing to stop her staying in Alston with him. It would be very easy. She could walk away from the boxing show, leave it behind and go back to his farm. They'd get married and live together…

The thought almost made her draw her hands back. No matter how attracted she was to Gerry, she did not want to marry him or anyone else. She did not want to end up as a farm housewife with a family of children. Instinctively she knew that many different adventures lay ahead of her and if she gave up the chance now, she would regret it for ever.

Yet the touch of his hands on hers was having a very peculiar effect on her. She looked into his face and she melted with desire. 'I want to kiss you,' he said softly.

She had never kissed anyone. He bent his lips to hers very slowly and gently and she felt his arm tighten round her waist and pull her towards him. The world went velvet-black but not for long because suddenly it was shot through with brilliant coloured lights, flashing and flowing in all directions.

'Don't go away yet,' he whispered when he let her go.

He didn't need to ask any more. Kitty Scott was not going anywhere. Not yet. I want this man, she told herself. It was part of Kitty's nature to make decisions by instinct and then rationalise how she had come to her conclusion later.

She was almost seventeen years old and ready for love. For some time she'd been aware of the effect she had on the men of the boxing show, for they crowded round her and courted her carefully but no one approached her directly because they were all afraid of Grandma. She could have had her pick of them but there was no one she wanted.

Now in Gerry she'd met a man that she did want; now she'd come across her perfect physical partner. The blood in her veins ran fast, she had a passionate nature and was avid for experience.

She would not be taken by force like her mother. She'd fought off Liddle and Thompson but she knew she would not die a virgin. She would be the one who did the choosing and this was the first man who pleased her.

She gently kissed his cheek. 'All right, I'll stay a little longer but I'll have to go eventually,' she told him. They walked like people in a trance along the lines of paraffin-lamp-lit stalls. She was very conscious of him beside her and all the time her passion mounted.

Their wanderings led them to the field where his horse had been turned out to graze and hand in hand they walked over the grass in search of it.

At the far side of the field there was a little rocky gorge making a channel for a fast-flowing waterfall. Without speaking they sat down beside it and started kissing each other again. The die was cast. They could not stop. It was all so natural and easy when they began to make love, as natural as a nymph and a shepherd in a pastoral.

When they drew apart at last, Gerry was apologetic. 'I'm sorry, I'm sorry. I couldn't help myself.'

She laughed. 'Neither could I. Don't be sorry. It was lovely.'

He leaned over and took her face in his hands. 'Please don't go away. Stay with me. I'll cherish you all my life if you do. I love you.'

She shook her head. The music was loud in the distance. She could hear it again. It was calling her back. 'I have to go. I can't stay with you but I'll never forget you, never.'

'You'll have other lovers,' he sadly told her.

She did not deny it. 'But I'll always remember you,' she said, 'because you're my first.'

He put his arms around her and leant his head against her flat belly. 'I love you. You've cast a spell on me.'

She stroked his hair. It was really hard to go, hard not to let him see what a war was being fought inside her. One part wanted to stay with him and make love for ever but the bigger part, the stronger part, said, 'You've things to do, places to see, you can't stay here in Alston.'

'I have to go. Please don't try to stop me. It's hard enough as it is.'

He groaned. 'I can't understand this. Are you bespoken to someone else? Is that what this is about? I never believed the story about the sugar-loaf hill...'

She shook her head. 'I'm not promised to any other man and I'm not married. I chose you and I'll never forget you. If I stayed here with you it would be like that poem about the mermaid woman, the one who came out of the sea and got married and then one day she had to go away again... I heard it at school and I thought it was very sad. I wouldn't want to make you sad. Be happy but don't forget me.'

He sat up and told her, 'I'll never forget you. I love you. Wherever you go, remember that. One man, up here in the hills, will always love you.'

She knelt by him, put her arms around him and kissed him gently as she said, 'Thank you, thank you very much. You can't know how much that means to me. No one has ever said anything like that to me before.'

It was harder than ever to go but she forced herself although her eyes were filled with tears as she turned away from him.

When she ran off into the darkness, he did not try to follow her but sat with his head resting on his knees for a long, long time.

# Chapter Thirteen

Gerry was not the only one who'd been enchanted. When Kitty reached the middle of Alston, she was amazed to see from the church clock that it was nearly midnight.

A hand of fear clutched her belly. What if they'd gone off without her! She started to run to the field where the fair was held and on the way she met a disconsolate little crowd of men beating the bushes by the roadside with sticks. They were looking for her – or at least for her body – because Grandma was sure that she'd been murdered.

Bill looked up and saw her coming, pelting up the lane with her bonnet in her hand and threw down his stick with a muffled curse.

'By Hades you're in for it. The old woman's spitting mad about you!' Kitty grabbed his arm. 'I'm all right. I was – detained. I'm sorry I didn't come for the fight tonight, though. Is she really very angry?'

'She's furious. Some woman from the crowd fought Joe and half-killed him. Grandma wouldn't go into the ring with her.'

Kitty sighed. 'Oh that's bad. Is Joe all right?'

'A black eye, that's all, but his pride's hurt.'

He walked beside her to Grandma's wagon and Kitty could see the lights inside shining out through the little window. 'I'll go in on my own. I'll explain what happened,' she told him.

'You'd better make it a good story,' he replied as he walked away to call off the hunt.

Grandma and Sophia were sitting facing each other over the table on which playing cards were laid out. Sophia was trying to find out where Kitty was by reading the cards. They looked up expectantly when the door opened and their expressions changed from anxiety to astonishment and anger when they saw her.

'What time do you call this?' demanded Grandma.

The girl stood in the doorway and hung her head. 'I'm sorry. I meant to turn up for the fight but I couldn't. I met a man, you see.'

She told them the truth, for she thought they were women enough to appreciate it.

They looked at each other in astonishment. Grandma spluttered in fury but Sophia laughed. 'A man, eh? That's not like you, lass,' she said.

Kitty told her. 'He was marvellous, really marvellous. Now I know what all the fuss is about.'

Grandma was muttering furiously, 'Slut, you're just like all the rest... I expected better of you. You'd better take your stuff and go, that's what you'll be wanting to do, isn't it?'

Kitty sat down beside her and took her hand. 'Please forgive me, Grandma. I don't want to go away with him, though I liked him a lot. I want to stay with you. I sent him away.'

The sisters looked surprised and Sophia said, 'You're a strange lassie. Are you sure you want to go on travelling? Wouldn't he take you with him?'

'Yes, he wanted to take me but I wouldn't go. It was my first time. I told him how good it was but I never pretended I was going to stay with him.'

Grandma shook her head and said sarcastically, 'It's usually the men who act that way. But what if you've fallen with a child? Have you thought of that?'

Kitty hadn't and her face showed disquiet. 'But it was my first time, and only once. You can't fall the first time, can you?' she protested. She'd forgotten about her mother and Bullhead.

'Oh yes you can,' hissed Grandma. 'And you needn't think we're going to burden us with a bairn on your behalf.'

Kitty stood up from the table. 'Then I'll go off on my own. I can look after myself.'

If she was pregnant, she'd get rid of it, she decided. She wasn't going back to find Gerry, and the thought of having a fatherless child to rear was too reminiscent of her own childhood to be borne.

Sophia seemed to understand her thoughts because she said, 'Don't worry, you'll not fall with a child. I've got a draught that'll do the trick if you take it immediately. You've just come from him, haven't you? You must take it now if it's going to work.'

Grandma was still not won round and she turned on her sister to say bitterly, 'Trust you to take her side. You weren't any better at her age.'

Sophia straightened in her chair. 'That's how I can understand what she's going through. She's a woman now, not a lassie any more. She can make her own choices and I'm pleased she's not going to run off with the first man that takes her fancy. I'm glad this lassie is proud of herself tonight. It's better than being scared all the time.'

'Scared! Who's scared? You wouldn't go into the boxing ring with men like I do, would you?' Grandma shouted.

Sophia was scornful. 'That's not the kind of scared I'm talking about. You're not scared of taking a punch, I'll give you that, but you're scared of living, of taking a chance. And now you're too old. But this lassie's not scared. Don't punish her for it.'

Grandma glared at Kitty, who stood in the doorway about to leave for she was sorry to have raised this row between the sisters. 'I'm sorry,' she said.

'Where do you think you're going at this time of night? You'd better come in and Sophy'll mix up that potion of hers. For God's sake be more careful in the future,' Grandma said sharply and Kitty ran across the floor to hug her.

'I know I was wrong to let you down. I won't do it again… but he was so lovely. I knew I'd never find such a good man to be my first so I took him. Was that so bad?'

Sophia laughed, a gurgling laugh that seemed to well up from deep inside her. 'That wasn't bad at all. It makes me very jealous,' she said.

The draught worked. Next morning Kitty felt slightly ill but she did not become pregnant and deliberately did not wonder about it. She had an enviable ability to put disturbing ideas out of her mind.

The boxing booth's next stop was Newcastle where they set up on the dockside. The crowd there was very rough.

Challengers who climbed through the ropes were heavy stevedores and drunken sailors offships tied up alongside the crowded quays. The show intended to stay for a week but on the fourth night Joe had his jaw broken by a devastating blow from one of the challenge-takers and they closed down immediately.

Groaning, Joe was carried off to his wagon where, once he was attended to and given a bottle of brandy to kill the pain, Grandma, Bill and Sophia, with Kitty listening in, held a discussion about what they should do next.

'Joe's finished. He's getting too old anyway,' said Bill sadly. 'He's all right for little village fairs but not for a place like this. We should break camp and get out of here tonight before something worse happens.'

'What could be worse?' asked Grandma morosely. 'We've got no big fighter, only a lot of sparring partners. None of them are any good really. We need a strong man to take on all comers.'

'This is the sort of place we'll find one,' chipped in Sophia. 'Joe joined at Portsmouth, didn't he? We need a tough deserter. Let's put the word round… How much will you offer, Beattie?'

Beattie pondered the problem. 'Well, a good man's worth a hundred guineas to us. We could offer that I suppose.'

Kitty was astonished to hear this vast sum talked of. She knew that Grandma kept money in a box sunk into the floor of her van but had no idea it could contain so much.

Bill shook his head. 'That's too much to start off with. Let's have a running knockout contest for the next three nights… the winner to receive a purse of forty guineas and the chance to travel with the show. How about that?'

They all thought his idea a good one and next day handbills were printed for distribution around the neighbourhood announcing the contest.

On the first night a crowd of men stormed the tent door at opening time demanding to fight, so it did not look as if there was going to be too much trouble finding a replacement for Joe.

Only Grandma remained gloomy. 'The good thing about Joe is his gentle nature. He's not mad and he's not wild and that's unusual with those fighters. Some of them are killers. We'll have to watch who we take,' she warned the others.

While they were in Newcastle she and Kitty did not do their put-up routine because the crowd there was too volatile and if they suspected a fake contest, they would wreck the tent. So in order to be of some help, Kitty went round with Bill distributing leaflets, for they wanted to drum up as much interest as possible. The sight of her was another inducement for men to come to the booth. Although she was not aware of it, she had a knowing, sexy air that turned heads in the street.

Men and boys presented themselves as possibles and in the afternoons, Bill weeded out the unsuitables, leaving only the best behind for the evening show. Kitty and the two older women watched from behind a canvas curtain that cut them off from the howling crowd as fighter after fighter went on, fought his heart out and was finally carried off. One man went through all his bouts unscathed, however. No matter which opponents were presented to him, he brutally demolished them, knocking them down and had to be restrained from hitting them while they were lying at his feet. He was a killer and everyone soon learned to treat him with respect, for he was universally feared. His name was Samuel Poole.

Grandma watched him perform with admiration but also distaste. 'He's what I mean when I say we've got to watch who we get. He's a dirty fighter and a bad lot that one,' she said.

'He might not win in the end,' Sophia told her. 'Somebody usually turns up at the last minute and confounds all expectations.'

'I hope you're right,' was Grandma's rejoinder.

The dirty fighter was an Australian off a merchantman that had recently docked in the harbour. During the day he walked around the quays with a little group of cronies who spent their time flattering him and buying him drinks. When he fought, they wagered heavily on him and, so far, he had not been beaten so they had done well. Physically he was unprepossessing, being short and very squat with huge muscled shoulders and upper arms that he held out stiffly from his body as he walked. His head seemed much too small in proportion to his torso and when he stripped for a fight, it could be seen that his upper arms and legs, his chest and his back were covered with tattoos, great convoluted circles and coils in deepest purple.

By the last night of the contest, he was expected to win and it was difficult to get a bet against him. Even the people who were not wagering were eager to see him fight, for his fame had spread all over the city and swells drove down from their clubs and smoking-rooms to join the spectators. Bill charged a five-shilling entrance fee that night and stood at the tent door with a metal bucket into which they threw the money.

There were four contenders – a young man from Newcastle city; a sailor off a Royal Naval vessel in the roads; a huge black man with a brilliant smile who was off a vessel that plied between the Tees and Lagos, and the terrible Poole. All of them had demolished their opponents in previous bouts but none so cruelly as Poole.

The Newcastle lad and the black man were matched against each other first and their contest did not last long because the negro's lightness of foot and superior reach soon overwhelmed his opponent, who was carried off to catcalls and jeers.

Poole climbed into the ring next and stood with his hands clasped over his head acknowledging the plaudits of his cronies. His opponent, a tough-looking man with his hair in an old-fashioned pigtail, stood watching this display with crossed arms and a sneering smile. He put up a good fight, scoring several hits on Poole's jaw, but he could not match the Australian's weight and soon he was literally bowled over. When he was down, Poole kicked him in the guts and that put him out of the running for good.

Kitty and the two old women were breathless with excitement when the bell rang for the final bout.

'I hope that black man wins,' said Grandma but they all knew such an outcome was not very likely. The man from Lagos seemed too good-tempered to defeat Poole. And so it turned out. Within three minutes, he lay spread out with blood pouring from his nose while Poole pranced around him with his arms in the air.

'Bastard!' hissed Grandma and it was the first time Kitty had heard her use such a word. But she was smiling benignly when she walked into the ring to present the winner with his purse of forty guineas.

When he took it, she told him, 'I hope you'll team up with us and tour the country, Mr Poole.'

He grunted, 'I'll think about it.' Grandma smiled sweetly but when she got back behind the scenes again, she shouted at Bill, 'Doesn't he know that part of the deal is that he joins the show? What does he think he's getting forty guineas for?'

Her son threw up his hands. 'I told him before it started. He's only playing hard to get.'

Grandma looked dangerous. 'He'd better not play games with me or he might find he's taken on more than he can cope with,' she said.

Half an hour later Poole and his gang came sauntering through from the front of house to speak to her. He was dressed in a bright blue jacket with brass buttons and tight trousers that showed the muscles of his upper legs and calves. His little eyes, beneath the curled brim of a tall hat, shone with cupidity and guile.

'Well, missus,' he began, 'what'll you offer me to join up with you? You need a fighter now that your old man's crooked.'

'There's plenty of fighters around,' said Grandma coolly. 'We're thinking of taking on the black man you fought tonight.'

'Huh, not much of a punch on him. He won't get into the big money,' said Poole. 'But if you get me, you could make money, a lot of money. I could be a champion.'

Grandma was, rolling up hand bandages and she didn't even bother to look up as she said, 'We're not looking for a champion, just for a good steady fighter who'll put on a good show.'

Poole laughed. 'So your fights are fixed, are they? I thought as much. You need a good man. You need me, missus.'

Grandma's eyes were large and innocent as she asked, 'Do I? How much more will you cost? You've already had forty guineas off me.'

Poole drew down his brows. 'I'll need a wagon of my own and twenty pounds a week…'

Grandma and Sophia laughed disbelievingly and the older sister said, 'Twenty pounds! We don't take twenty pounds in a good week all told. You'd better get back to your ship if that's what you're wanting.'

He reckoned he'd overstated his case and climbed down a little. 'All right, I'll take ten a week but I'll make that back for you because I'll be fighting the big names in the business within a year.'

Bill leaned forward and whispered something in his mother's ear but she made no sign whether she agreed with what he suggested or not, only directed herself at Poole as she said, 'When you fight a big name we'll give you ten a week. In the meantime I pay five – top rate. Take it or leave it.'

He went off with his friends to discuss this and half an hour later he was back. 'I'll take it,' he told her, 'but there's something else I want if I sign up with you.'

'I'll give you a wagon and a pair of horses,' said Grandma bleakly.

'That's all right but I also want a woman.' Poole was leering at her, showing stubby little teeth with dark lines down them.

'A woman? Can't you get your own woman, a big strong man like you? How do you expect me to get one for you?' she asked in genuine surprise.

'Because you've got the one I want. I want the tall girl with the red hair. That's the woman I want. Throw her in and you've got a bargain,' said Poole.

It took a couple of seconds before the significance of what he'd said sank in with Kitty but when it did, she felt as if all the blood left her in a huge ebb, only to come surging back again like a tide of anger. She could not restrain herself from giving a derisive snort but Grandma glared at her ferociously and she knew better than to say anything.

The old woman was smiling sweetly at the pugilist and saying, 'You've got good taste in women, Poole.'

He preened himself like a fighting cock.

'That's the one I want,' he said arrogantly.

Grandma smiled again and said, 'I'll have to speak to the girl in private but we might be able to come to some arrangement. All you've got to do now is sign up to come with us and be here tomorrow morning early so that we can get on the road.'

'Where are you going first?' he asked.

'Berwick-upon-Tweed and then Edinburgh. We plan to be there in time for Leith Races. There's a lot of good fighters there. You'll have your work cut out with them,' she told him and he bridled. 'There's no fighters in Edinburgh who can put me on the floor, missus,' he boasted.

'Oh well,' she said mildly, 'that's what we all hope, isn't it? Just be here tomorrow and then we'll see.'

Kitty managed to control herself till he left but when he was out of earshot, an angry torrent of words burst from her… 'If you think you're going to give me to that ugly brute, you can think again. I'd sooner throw myself into the harbour. I'm telling you I don't care what you say, I won't do it. Not even for one night will I do it.'

Grandma, who had begun counting the takings from the bucket while this outburst was going on, looked up and said calmly, 'I never said I'd give you to him, did I?'

'You said you'd be able to come up with some arrangement – not with me, you won't, not with me!'

Kitty's face was red and her voice trembling. She couldn't believe Grandma was doing this to her.

'Calm down,' said the old woman. 'Calm down and listen to what I've got to say. We need that pug. With him we'll make a lot of money. He's drawn more tonight than we've taken in six months. People pay to see a dirty fighter more than they'll pay for a clean one, I'm sad to say.'

Kitty opened her mouth to protest again but Grandma held up a hand to hush her. 'Listen, I've worked it out. Here's some money. Take it and get your things together. Bill'll take you to the station. You'll have to be well away from here before Poole comes back. If you stayed, he'd get you in the end. We'd never have a moment's peace. His kind don't court girls, they take them and they don't take them gently, not like your Alston lad.'

Kitty looked at the pile of silver coins that had been pushed in her direction. There was about ten pounds there and she wondered if her ears and eyes were playing tricks on her.

'You're paying me off?' she whispered. 'But where will I go when I get to the station?' Tears were stinging at the back of her eyes.

Grandma's face was sympathetic. 'Don't worry, lass, don't cry. I've thought of that too. You'll go to London. Sophy and I have another sister there, in Whitechapel. We'll give you her address and a letter. She'll look after you.'

It didn't take long to gather her meagre possessions together. Her precious knife and the gold half-sovereign from Tim Maquire went into her pocket and the rest of her money into a carpetbag that Sophy provided.

On the verge of tears, Kitty patted Toby on the head, embraced the sad-faced sisters, who did not, of course, shed any tears though it was obvious that they were sorry to lose her, and shook hands with all her friends from the boxing show before she hopped up on the pillion of a big draught-horse that Bill was using to take her up to the station.

The coins in her bag clinked as she heaved it aboard and one of the men shouted, 'Shove some clothes in beside all that money or you'll be knocked on the head for it the moment you set foot in London.'

Grandma provided an old shawl to act as a muffler for the money and at last Kitty was ready to leave, waving back to the people standing round their wagons as she rode away. She wondered if she'd ever see any of them again and tears stung her eyes. She could not believe in the suddenness of the parting.

The station was cavernous and gloomy in the darkness of the night. Porters in green livery were pushing heavy carts to and fro but there were few passengers to be seen, for the next train was scheduled to leave at midnight, not a popular departure time for ordinary people.

Her head was swimming and her eyes stinging with tiredness but she knew she had to keep awake and alert, because she was carrying so much money.

Bill stayed with her till the train was ready to leave and she asked him, 'How will you get Poole to go with you when he finds out I've disappeared?'

'He won't find out till we're well on the road and by that time Grandma will have worked on him. She's good at that. She'll convince him that he has to go with us and anyway, his kind like to fight. He'll soon pick up another woman, some of them go for men like that,' he said.

When the train came clanking into the station he saw her into a window seat, put her bag at her feet, hugged her and stood waving on the platform as she was borne away. She dropped her head and let the tears flow again because it seemed that what had been the happiest time of her life was coming to an end and she did not know what lay ahead.

For several hours no other travellers shared her carriage and she was able to rearrange her bag in order to make sure the money did not clink and also to read the letter Grandma had given her.

By the flickering light of a small oil lamp above her head, she saw that it was addressed to Mrs Cora White, by the Plume of Feathers, Whitechapel High Street. It was unsealed so she was able to read what Grandma said…

> *My dear Cora,*
>
> *Both Sophy and I hope that you continue to be in good health as we are ourselves. Sometime soon, God willing, we might be in London and can all meet again. By this letter I am sending you a good girl who has travelled with us for nearly two years and never put a foot wrong but one of my pugs is after her and we have to get her out of the way. You know what trouble that sort of thing can cause. Look after her and keep her away from those jockeys. Your loving sister, Beatrice.*

The letter, which sounded so like Grandma, cheered Kitty up and she laughed aloud. So Beattie was a shortened version of Beatrice. Beattie certainly suited Grandma better than her given name. She was very far from being a prim and proper Beatrice.

The prospect of a welcome at the other end of her journey from someone like Sophia or Grandma brightened her and she was lulled into sleep by the rocking of the train as it chugged through a dark world. She stretched along the bench with her head resting on the carpetbag and slept for several hours.

When she woke it was dawn and from the window she saw street upon street of closely built houses; grim-looking factories; grimy workshops; inns and alehouses on every corner and more horse-drawn traffic than she had ever seen in her life. Carriages, carts, lorries, horse-drawn trams jostled and collided at intersections and around corners.

She leaned forward and watched entranced, longing to be out among such excitement and energy.

When they finally drew into the terminus, she heaved up her bag and was one of the first out onto the platform, striding along towards the metal gate.

A line of hansom cabs stood in the forecourt and, remembering her bounty of silver, she went straight for one and called up to the cabbie, 'The Plume of Feathers, Whitechapel High Street...'

Her assurance made the man in the box think her city-bred and he asked, 'Is that the Plume at the east end or the west?'

'The west,' she hazarded, hoping she was right, for she did not want him to revise his opinion of her. What she wanted most of all now was to be accepted as one of the confident-looking people who walked along London streets as if they owned them.

The city thrilled her. All her life she had been waiting to be thrust into this mêlée. The shouting of the cabbies and the wagon drivers; the rattling of wheels on stone-paved streets; the din of voices rising like an undercurrent beneath it gave her a surge of excitement that made her fingertips tingle. She stared eagerly at the clothes of the people on the sidewalks and the goods displayed for sale in shop windows.

It seemed that London was the richest city in the world, for everywhere there was finery, luxury, ostentatious expense. Eagerly she clasped her hands together in her lap as she was borne along through the sea of traffic.

The journey took more than an hour because of the heavy press of cabs and carts at every junction, but time did not hang heavily on the passenger because she was so enthralled with everything on the route. When at last they drew up before the ornate front door of the Plume of Feathers public house, she asked the cabbie, 'How much?'

'Two bob,' said he and she fished in her bag to extract three shillings which she presented to him.

'*Two* bob,' he said, handing one back but she waved it away.

'Keep it, that's for you,' she said grandly and he looked surprised, for he had not expected even a penny tip from a girl so plainly dressed.

The door of the bar was half wood and half frosted glass engraved with lions, flags and a huge plume of Prince of Wales feathers. She pushed at it but she did not know her own strength for it went back with a wide swing leaving her standing in the open space with her bag in her hand and her hair wildly escaping from its combs.

Some men at the bar gazed at her in astonishment before the bartender said, 'Women in the snug only, miss. Next door…'

With a bare arm he pointed to the left but she shook her head. 'I don't want a drink. I'm trying to find Mrs Cora White.'

'Might have guessed,' muttered one of the drinkers, sinking his face into his glass.

The others laughed and the barman said, 'That's next door too, next to the snug. You'll find the door two up.'

Can this be the place or were those men playing a joke on me? Kitty wondered when she stood at a black-painted door bearing a shining brass plate engraved with the words:


## EXCELSIOR CLUB
## MEMBERS ONLY


There was a bell-pull at the side and she yanked it, hearing its tolling far back in the building. After a few moments the door was opened by a manservant in a dark tailcoat and a green-and-gold-striped waistcoat.

'Ye-es?' he asked, eyeing her up and down.

'I'm looking for Mrs Cora White,' she said, proffering her letter.

He took it in finger and thumb (he was wearing white gloves, she noticed) and told her, 'Wait there.' Then he closed the door and left her standing on the pavement.

A curious head was poking out of the Plume of Feathers' door and she heard the men laughing. She turned her back and stared at the sky but, fortunately, she did not have long to wait. Soon the black door opened again and the footman told her, 'Mrs White will see you.'

Inside there was a curious smell, not unpleasant and somehow reminiscent of her childhood. Then she remembered what it was. Tibbie Mather's washhouse used to smell like that on Mondays when she did her weekly laundry in the big iron boiler.

Kitty wondered if Mrs White ran some kind of upper-class laundry, for the fittings of the long, deep hall were sumptuous. The floor was carpeted in deep red patterned with blue and green and the furniture was massive carved mahogany with heavy legs and ornamented fronts. The side tables were covered with dozens of studio photographs in ornate silver frames and a huge looking-glass hung on one wall. It showed Kitty's bedraggled reflection and she made a belated attempt to tidy her hair with her hand as a tall, thin woman in a dove-grey gown with a high bustle at the back swept into the hall.

Jet-black hair was piled high with a curled fringe along her forehead and she wore long golden earrings that tinkled as she walked. She bore no resemblance to Sophy or Grandma and Kitty wondered if she had been fathered by yet a third man.

She was carrying Grandma's letter in her hand and waved it at Kitty as she asked, 'How are my sisters?'

'Very well. Grandma's got a touch of rheumatics but nothing too bad.'

'She's given up boxing I hope – at her age. She's seventy-seven, you know. I expect Sophy's still got that awful bird, mangy thing.'

'Yes, yes.' One yes for each question, thought Kitty, though Grandma hadn't given up boxing.

'They seem to think well of you, but you know that, don't you? You'll have read the letter,' said Mrs White.

It was obvious that she would have considered Kitty lacking in enterprise if she hadn't, so she nodded. 'Yes. I thought a lot of them too.'

'What's the story then? Why did you have to bolt?'

Kitty put her bag down on the floor and said, 'They wanted a new boxer and he wouldn't come unless he got me as well as the money.'

Mrs White nodded. 'Huh, boxers. Beattie was always daft about boxers. I couldn't see it myself. They're all punchy by the time they're thirty. Jockeys are much better. Give me jockeys every time. You take my tip, dear, stick to jockeys.'

Kitty nodded, slightly bemused by this talk of jockeys but amused at the same time.

Mrs White smiled slightly and said, 'I think we'll get on, you and I. What can you do?'

'I worked on a farm once. I don't mind hard work. I'm very good at counting, though I've not done much of that recently... I know quite a bit about birds and wild flowers... I can pretend to box and take a fall... but I'm not much of a cook or anything like that and I'm no good at ironing, I'm afraid.'

'Ironing! Birds and wild flowers!' exclaimed Mrs White, looking at the manservant, who raised his eyebrows. 'We've not got much call for that in Whitechapel. The counting might be a help though. Are you a virgin?'

By the tone she used she might have been asking if Kitty could do fancy needlework. The girl shook her head. 'No, I'm not.'

'That's good. I like my girls broken in. I don't hold with some of those places you find round here. Disgusting I call it,' Mrs White's face assumed an expression of outrage.

Kitty felt a surge of panic. 'I'm not a prostitute, Mrs White. I won't sleep with a man for money. That's why I came away from the boxing show. I was happy there but I wouldn't go with Poole and Grandma never asked me to!'

'That's all right. My girls make their own decisions. If they set up with a client or not, it's nothing to me. They can make a bit on the side so long as they're discreet, but I don't sell them... I sell the bathhouse and if there are pretty girls working in it, the customers are pleased.'

'The bathhouse?' That explained the soapy smell. 'What exactly would I have to do?' Kitty asked suspiciously.

'Whatever you fancy. You'll catch the eye anyway. Some girls fetch and carry soap and towels, glasses of wine, things like that; some keep the appointments book or tally up the chits, but it's men that do the washing and the massages. More discreet you know. Saves embarrassment on both sides.'

Kitty thought rapidly. 'I could tally up. I'm very quick at counting.'

Mrs White nodded thoughtfully. 'Maybe. We'll give you a try and see how you do. I don't suppose you've anywhere to stay. Take her up to the attic and find her a bed, Laverty. Then she'll have to get a decent gown. Show her where to go and charge it to me. I like my girls to look smart. You can pay me back out of your earnings.'

The last remark was addressed to Kitty, who knew she looked anything but smart. Grandma had bought her dark grey gown when she first joined the boxing booth and she'd worn it ever since. It was faded by now.

To her surprise she found that not only was Laverty, the footman, going to tell her where to buy a gown but he intended to accompany her. He was still wearing his livery as they walked out into the street and everyone they met seemed to know him, nodding and exchanging greetings as they went along.

They did not have far to go and soon stopped in front of a large shop in which gowns were displayed in the window. Laverty pointed at one of lavender silk and said, 'That'd suit you. Just your colour, dear.'

He had a funny, lisping way of speaking that amused Kitty.

'I like brighter colours myself,' she said but he shook his head vehemently. 'Oh no, not with that hair. Take it from me, dear, lavender or pale blue, leaf-green or primrose-yellow. Madame will send anything else back. Pale colours are more discreet, not so tarty.'

'Oh, all right. Will I go in and try it on?' asked Kitty.

'I'll come with you,' said Laverty.

'You don't have to,' she protested, flustered by the idea of parading before him in her petticoat, which she was sure would not come up to his standards.

He grasped her elbow and said with a laugh, 'Don't worry about me. If the Venus de Milo walked in stark naked, I wouldn't even twitch. The Boy David, though, that's a different matter!'

They bought the lavender dress, which did suit Kitty very well. It had a bustle at the back like the gown Mrs White had been wearing, and Kitty loved herself in it, turning to and fro in front of the long mirror, admiring the way it made her look tall and elegant.

Laverty sat watching with an amused smile on his face. 'The sparrow turns into a peacock, eh?' he said. 'I wonder how long it's going to be before some customer snatches you up from under Madame's nose. The good ones always go quickly.'

Kitty frowned at him in the mirror. 'Nobody's going to snatch me unless I want to be snatched, I can assure you of that.'

'Ha ha,' said Laverty. 'Just you watch out for those little men then. There's nothing so dangerous as tough little men and you're going to meet plenty of them at Mrs White's.'

The rustling parcel under her arm, which she would not allow Laverty to carry, gave her a thrill of excitement. Sophia's mynah had hit the spot when it pinpointed Kitty's weakness for fine clothes because after her ragged childhood, it was an indescribable thrill to have a new dress, and not a hand-me-down. She could have danced along the Whitechapel pavement, for she felt sure that another adventure was about to happen, and she knew that she could look after herself whatever it was that Fate threw at her.

'What exactly is the Excelsior Club?' she asked Laverty as they strolled past busy shops selling everything from fruit to lengths of lovely materials.

He looked at her with arched eyebrows. 'You mean to say you came to Madame's and don't know that?'

'Her sisters sent me.'

'Oh them. They're the only people Madame's frightened of. That explains this. I was wondering why she was so keen to spend money on you…' he said, rapping the parcel with his knuckles. 'She'll look after you if you're from them. You're not a member of the family, are you?'

'Adopted,' said Kitty shortly, recognising that Grandma's influence was worth a lot even in Whitechapel.

'And they didn't tell you about the club?' asked Laverty.

'They didn't have time. A boxer was after me and they got me away as quick as they could.' This seemed quite ordinary to Laverty, who nodded.

'Those boxers are the very devil. Did he get you?' he said slightly enviously.

'Of course not! What happens at the club?' persisted Kitty.

He laughed. 'What doesn't happen at the club! Seriously, it's a bathhouse for London's sporting men, especially jockeys who have to lose weight fast. They come in and sweat in our hot rooms, have a massage, drink champagne and play cards or spend time with the girls. We're the best bathhouse in London. We get all the big names. You've heard of Freddy Farrell? He's a regular with us.'

Kitty shook her head. She'd never heard of Freddy Farrell and Laverty was shocked.

'Where have you been? Freddy Farrell's the Prince of Wales's favourite jockey! He's won forty races this season already. And we get more than Freddy, we get all the others as well – Sam Malone, Tom Titmarsh, Tod Anson, the American jockey. And because they come, we get the nobs too. Madame Cora's place is famous.'

'It's not a brothel, is it?' She'd soon find some other way of earning a living if it was.

Laverty pursed his mouth. ''Course it's not. Nothing sordid like that. It's a bathhouse, like I told you, a men's club, but some of them like girls – though some don't, I'm glad to say – and Madame makes sure that the girls working in the house are all eye-catchers. They carry the drinks around, things like that but all the massaging and soaping's done by men. Very proper. The girls make their own arrangements with clients. They pick and choose… and some of them move on to comfortable berths, I can tell you. We've had three married into the gentry and another's set up in Curzon Street earning a fortune. If you don't know about Freddy Farrell, I don't suppose you'll ever have heard of Lucy Beresford?'

Kitty shook her head and expressed suitable amazement when told that it cost five hundred pounds a night to be entertained by Lucy, who, said Laverty, had spent six months learning how to be a lady at Madame Cora's when she was fifteen years old and still a hoyden from the haysheds of Newmarket racing stables where her father worked. One of Cora's jockeys brought Lucy to London with him.

'She comes back to see us now and again,' he said proudly. 'She's not got too grand though dukes and lords are running after her. The Duke of Allandale and Lord Godolphin pay court to her now and you can't go much higher than that, can you?'

Kitty kept quiet about the fact that these were names she did know. Lord Godolphin of Bella Vista with the beautiful dark-haired wife, and the Duke, the greatest man of Camptounfoot and Rosewell! She could hardly believe what she was hearing. How Tibbie and her cronies in Camptounfoot would love that bit of gossip.

The more she heard about the Excelsior Club, the more she thought it would be amusing to be there for a while, at least till she found her feet in this exciting city. Next she went to a bank and deposited her bag of silver, which she was surprised to find amounted to nine pounds and eight shillings. Madame Cora had given her a bed in an attic with three other girls and she did not think it safe to keep her money there. The knife and the gold she always carried with her.

Then she wrote to Tibbie to tell her where she was, but asked her to keep the information to herself. Into the letter she slipped a money order for five pounds.

'I want you to keep this money for my mother and give it to her bit by bit. Not all at once because she'll either waste it or give it to Big Lily. She must have had her baby by now and she'll need things for it. I hope it's not being brought up in rags the way I was. Buy what's needed from this money and when I can, I'll send you more. If you have a moment, perhaps you could write and give me news of my mother. I think of her often. I also think of you and Marie and send you both my love,' she wrote.

# Chapter Fourteen

When the letter arrived from London, Tibbie was very excited because it was the first definite news of Kitty. It was a relief to find out that she was not dead but living in Whitechapel and thriving sufficiently to send money orders to Scotland.

Kitty will always bob back up, she thought. It would not be kind to let Wee Lily go on thinking her daughter was dead but on the other hand, if Big Lily heard about the money she would certainly demand it.

The money order lay fresh and crisp in the fold of paper. It would certainly come in useful, for since the birth of her baby son Wee Lily had been sunk in lethargy and depression, and it fell to Big Lily or any kindly neighbour to tend to the child, who looked like being even more neglected than Kitty had been, if such a thing was possible.

With a pensive expression Tibbie folded up the note and wondered what was most needed in the bothy. It would soon be winter and the baby had no warm clothes. Wee Lily carried him wrapped in her shawl but often put him down under a hedge and forgot to go back for him. Unless someone looked after him he was in danger of dying of exposure.

She decided to lay out some money by employing a lassie from the village to act as nursemaid to carry the baby around and remind his mother when it was time to suckle him. He was a big, lusty child who made a terrible howling din when he was hungry, so he obviously had the will to live.

She went in search of Wee Lily, whom she found half-heartedly searching the hedgerow for eggs from stray laying hens. The baby was tied to her back with her shawl and he was crying, his face purple with rage. Wee Lily did not seem to hear him, though his screams were being vented right beside her ear.

'Lily, I've had a letter from Kitty,' whispered Tibbie, for she did not want Big Lily, who was nearby, to hear.

Wee Lily had seemed much more feeble-minded since the birth of her son and Tibbie wondered if she understood what was being told to her. 'I've had a letter from your Kitty,' she said again.

Wee Lily's face crumpled up with tears. 'My bairn, oh I miss my bairn. My mother never should have sent my bairn away. I miss my bairn, Tibbie,' she sobbed.

Tibbie clasped the workworn hands. 'Kitty's all right, she's in London and she's well. She sends you her love.'

'I miss my bairn,' sobbed the inconsolable Wee Lily and the noise of her weeping brought out her mother, who shouted, 'Hush that din. What're you greetin' at? Between you and that howling laddie, I'm deived to death. What did you say that's made her greet, Tibbie?'

Tibbie wasn't going to show Big Lily the letter so she shook her head. 'Nothing, Lily. She's just sad, that's all. She misses Kitty.'

'Daft besom,' snapped Big Lily. 'She's lucky to have a laddie instead of that wild lassie. Bad blood, that's what's wrong with her. Jake's no' up to much but he's better than that navvy ever was.'

Tibbie put a hand on the squalling child in an effort to calm it. It had a look of Jake – round head, short neck, low brow, tiny eyes. There was little of its mother in it. Wee Lily was a good-looking woman, or at least she had been, but since the birth she'd lost interest in everything and no longer made an effort to keep herself clean and tidy. She had not even given the child a name and it remained unchristened, a scandal to the villagers, who referred to it as 'Jake's bairn', and Tibbie suspected that it would go through life as nothing else.

'Let me take the baby, Lily,' she said, holding out her arms.

It was quickly surrendered and she carried it down the street to a house where she knew there was a club-footed but clever twelve-year-old girl called Peggie, who would find it difficult, if not impossible, to get work either on the land or in a household. She'd look after the child better than its mother.

Tibbie gave this girl two shillings and promised her the same amount of money every week if she took charge of Jake's bairn from the moment Wee Lily appeared with it in the morning till she went to sleep with it beside her at night.

Neither of the bondagers made any comment about this arrangement and sometimes Tibbie wondered if they even noticed that Peggie had taken over as Wee Jake's mother.

When she was sure that her stratagem for having the child looked after was going to succeed, Tibbie wrote to Kitty telling her that, because Wee Lily was busy, she'd hired a nursemaid for baby Jake.

'He's a year old now and taking after his father in looks,' she wrote carefully, knowing Kitty would realise what she meant. 'Big Jake's moved away to Rosewell and doesn't live at the bothy any more, so things are quieter there. Your mother and grandmother are well. I told Wee Lily you'd written to me and she was happy to hear you're prospering. You must try to come back and see her one day. She misses you.' Because she did not realise Kitty was in the dark about what had happened to Walter Thompson, she did not mention Falconwood.

She finished her letter by saying that Marie was very busy, preparing for a big exhibition in Edinburgh where her pictures were going to be on display.

'I don't see so much of her these days because she's got friends in Edinburgh with a big house where she often stays,' wrote Tibbie. 'But when she's home next time I'll tell her about your letter and I know she'll be pleased. David's doing very well. The mill's thriving under his management and Mr Henderson's given him a fine dogcart to drive about in. He takes Marie and me out in it sometimes.'

This was a gloss over the facts. David still visited on Sundays but relations between brother and sister were very bad. Most weekends finished with them quarrelling.

What was more worrying was that in recent weeks Marie's mood had been very dejected. Gloom overwhelmed her, she looked white-faced and thin and the smiles that used to animate her and made her delicately pretty had disappeared. Tibbie did not know what was troubling her because when tackled about it, she always denied that she was sad.

She did show some animation and interest on the night Tibbie passed her Kitty's letter with the words, 'This came from your friend.' It was read eagerly and then Marie said, 'She sounds well, doesn't she? And she must be doing well before she can send money for Wee Lily.'

'Kitty's the kind that survives. I always said that,' Tibbie told her and Marie's face clouded, for she was wondering if she too was a survivor.

The reason for her unhappiness was Murray, whom she had not seen for weeks. She doubted that she could survive the loss of him. After he failed his examinations, they met a few times but he was distant and distracted, till one summer day when they sat alone in a secluded part of the Murrayhill gardens and held hands while he talked about his plans.

'I've to go through the exams again. Father says I didn't try hard enough last time. I've to study all the time, Marie. It's sickening. I won't be able to see you.'

'I'm sure you'll pass this time,' she said soothingly. In her estimation he was the cleverest of all his family and she could not understand how he managed to fail.

'I'll have to pass,' he said despondently, 'or we'll never be able to marry.'

Then he kissed her and sighed, 'Will you wait for me? It may be years before I can ask you properly.'

His kiss sent her into transports. 'I'll wait for you for ever,' she told him.

But that was nearly six months ago and since then she had only seen him twice and it was impossible to talk because they were surrounded by members of the Roxburgh family. All they could do was look at each other and yearn. Her news of him came through Amy, who consistently said how hard he was working, how determined he was to pass the examinations this time, but also gave out little details about outings and holidays he'd taken, or balls he'd attended. It struck Marie that he was leading much the same energetic social life as he had done the year before.

It also struck her that weekend invitations to Murrayhill, which used to be frequent, were now rare. She'd not been asked to spend a Friday to Monday for a long time, though she was often there during the week when Amy still took her home on Tuesday afternoons and she stayed till Friday when they went to their last class of the week together.

There was always a reason for weekend invitations not appearing – the family were having a houseful of guests or they were going away. Marie told herself that she was being over-sensitive, for all the Roxburghs were as kind as ever to her, especially Mrs Roxburgh, who was extremely interested in her painting and spent hours talking to her, encouraging her, telling her of the brilliant future that lay before her.

Sometimes Amy seemed annoyed by her mother's interest in Marie and would slam around the room making a good deal of unnecessary noise while they pored over books of engravings of old pictures or discussed Marie's work. Those moods passed quickly, however, and

Marie would end up telling herself that she was being ultra-sensitive about Amy as well.

She kept all her doubts and fears, and her love of Murray, to herself – at least she thought she did, but she was more transparent than she imagined. Tibbie knew something was wrong with her.

At first she was afraid that Marie was going into a physical decline, for she remembered the frailty of the girl's mother. If Mariotta had not been murdered, she would almost certainly have succumbed to wasting illness, for she looked the sort that died young and her daughter had the same ethereal prettiness, like a flower that only blooms for a few days.

When Marie was at Camptounfoot, Tibbie always plied her with bottles of emulsion or specially nourishing food but, to her disquiet, nothing seemed to make much difference. Marie remained thin and white-faced and her smiles were rare.

David's explanation of his sister's malaise was different. It seethed inside his mind, building up to a massive resentment against the people who were ruining her life by leading her into unsuitable circles and giving her expectations that were beyond her grasp. If she would only give up all the Edinburgh painting nonsense and go to live with him, she would become the old Marie again, he thought.

He arrived in his dogcart one Sunday morning and as soon as he stepped into the cottage, he said with a certain satisfaction, 'I hear your Lady Godolphin's come back to Bella Vista and is far from well. Folk say she's in some sort of decline.'

Marie was shocked. 'That's terrible. I must go up and see her. She's been so kind to me.'

He snorted. 'She's only kind because it suits her. But go by all means. If she dies, you'll lose your patron, won't you? Then what'll you do?' His sister whirled on him. 'That's not why I go to see her. I like her. She's a very nice woman.'

He smiled. 'And who'd believe you go crawling up there because you like her? She'll know the real reason and so will everyone else. You'd show more pride if you stayed away.'

She ignored him and went across the room to look among her drawings for a pretty one to take to Bethya. She'd make a frame for it and take it up to Bella Vista tomorrow, she decided.

Her brother's voice followed her, jeering and sneering. 'And what'll you do when you don't have a patron? Your fancy Professor won't go on teaching you for nothing. Maybe your fine friends, the Roxburghs, will pay for you. Do you think they will?'

Her tolerance of him snapped. He knew exactly how to needle her. 'You're jealous of my friends. But you needn't think that I'll crawl back to you. I've told you before that I'll never come to Maddiston and live with you, David. I'd sooner take a job as a governess than do that.'

He began to plead. 'But I could make you a lady. You'd have servants. I've a fine house and that dogcart. Henderson's going to give me shares in the mill. I'll be rich soon.'

She looked at him scornfully. 'No matter how much money you've got you'll never be a gentleman,' she said.

He shouted, 'And I suppose you know some gentlemen in Edinburgh, do you? Is that why you won't come back to your own place?'

Nettled she shouted back, 'Yes, I do know some gentlemen. They know how to behave. They don't yell and shout the way you do. They don't think the way to get what they want is by bullying.'

His face changed and a sneering smile twisted his lips. 'I'll wager you've not seen much of your gentleman friend, not since I wrote my letter to the Roxburghs. Have you? Admit it. You've not been in their fine house so much recently. That's why you're in such a bad mood all the time, isn't it?'

She felt her chest tighten with fear and her breath came rasping up from her lungs in spasms so that she felt as if she were about to faint.

'You wrote them a letter?' she whispered.

He nodded in demonic glee. 'Yes, I did. And I should have done it long ago.'

'When did you write?'

'About six months ago. I thought about it for a long time but that friend of yours, the bondager's bastard, said it was an awful thing to do. I shouldn't have listened to her. What does she know? When I saw how you were behaving, never coming home, looking down on Tibbie and me, I made up my mind. So I wrote it.' He seemed pleased with himself, as if he'd done something extremely clever.

Marie stared at Tibbie from eyes swimming in tears. 'I don't look down on you, Tibbie. I've never looked down on you,' she said in anguish.

Tibbie nodded. 'I know you don't, lass.'

Marie's voice was quavering as she asked her brother, 'What did your letter say?'

'I told the Roxburghs about us. I told them about our parents and the navvy camp and our mother being murdered by Bullhead. I also said that I was your only means of support when Lady Godolphin stopped patronising you and that they mustn't give you ideas that couldn't be fulfilled. I told them that I'd prevent you going to Edinburgh if I could because I thought it was ruining you, giving you ideas above your station.'

Tibbie was watching him with the same aghast expression as his sister and it was she who said, 'But that was a terrible thing to do, David. These people are Marie's friends.'

'Why was it terrible? They ought to know the truth about her. They ought to know that we're probably navvy bastards like that friend of hers she's always defending. She thinks it's shameful when people look down their noses at bastards so I didn't imagine her friends would be prejudiced.' He sounded triumphant.

Marie recovered herself with an effort. 'I think you're mad, David Benjamin, mad and evil,' she said coldly. 'Even if I had to go and live in a hovel like that bothy over there, I'd never share a house with you.'

It took an effort not to burst into a storm of tears or set about him with furious fists but she managed to, control herself and that made her reaction even more telling. He had expected her to back down, to do as he told her, and he was astounded by the way she was behaving.

'Didn't they tell you I'd written?' he asked.

She turned away from him. Now she knew why the Roxburgh family had been so different recently. She wondered if Murray had been told about the letter and if it would change the way he felt about her. Of course it wouldn't, she told herself, Murray was too sensible and too faithful for that, but it might make things hard with his family.

Hatred for David burned within her but she did not want him to see how much he had hurt her. 'The Roxburghs have been as kind to me as ever. Your letter didn't make a bit of difference,' she lied.

For the rest of the day she would not address a word to him. The days were growing short and at about half-past four, when the sky was beginning to darken, David came through from the parlour and lifted his boots off the hearth.

'I'll be going then,' he said.

Only Tibbie spoke to him. 'Take care. There's a storm coming. I can smell it in the wind,' she told him.

'I should be back at Maddiston before it starts. I've got a good pony between the shafts of my dogcart,' he said, pulling on his coat and drawing a hat down over his head.

Marie watched him stonily and before he left he ventured to say to her, 'See you next weekend then.'

'No,' she said. 'No, don't come back to see me. I don't ever want to see you again.'

All her life she'd looked up to and respected her brother, admired him for his determination and dedication to hard work, but now he seemed different and her feelings were different too. He had become shifty and sly, a schemer and a plotter, not a man to be trusted, for he was totally self-centred and would stop at nothing to gain his own ends. She felt sorry for poor Coleman who, she was sure, had been duped by him and wondered if even Adalbert Henderson knew what he was taking on when he put David in a position of power.

With a grimace she turned away from him and went upstairs to her bedroom under the eaves knowing that he would not dare to follow her there and risk being told some home truths. She was right. He looked with dismay at Tibbie as his sister left the room and the old woman shrugged as if to say, 'Well, you asked for it.'

'I'm off then,' he said lamely, pulling on his gloves.

'Like I said, take care,' Tibbie told him and added, 'You can't blame her. That was a terrible thing to do.'

He didn't want to think about it, however, he didn't want to feel remorse because that would challenge his certainty that he was right. All he said was, 'I'll come back and see you soon.'

As he drove along with his head lowered against the cutting edge of the wind, he went over and over the events of the day, justifying himself as if to an accuser.

'I did it for her own good. She ought to thank me. I'm realistic and she's a giddy romantic. She doesn't know what the world is like. She doesn't realise that blood's the only bond that counts. Friendships come and friendships go but it's your family that really matters in the end. She'll learn that. She'll come crawling back to me,' he told himself.

On the following week Marie returned to the painting class full of trepidation, but as soon as she entered the studio Amy came rushing over to her as if there had never been a shadow on their friendship. When she looked into her friend's smiling face Marie began to doubt that David had told her the truth – perhaps he had only been bluffing, trying to scare her into doing what he wanted.

Amy's easel was set up next to Marie's and as they worked, she talked about what she'd been doing during the weekend.

'Poor Murray,' she said. 'He's been working so hard. Mama was most upset when he said that he didn't want to go away with us for Christmas. He said he'd rather stay at home and study! Mama won him round though. She insists on having all her children with her at Christmas-time.'

Marie's heart sank. 'Are you going away?' she asked. She had secretly hoped for an invitation to Murrayhill during the festive period because Amy had told her that the family always held a dance and several parties then.

Amy's eyes opened wide. 'But I must have told you that! I don't blame Murray for not wanting to go. It's awful. Cousin Julia has invited us to the Highlands. We're to stay there for two whole weeks. She has this dreadful castle miles north of Inverness with ghosts and draughts and howling gales in all the corridors, but of course we have to go. I expect we'll freeze to death,' she said flippantly.

Marie managed a laugh. 'You'll enjoy it, I'm sure,' she said but her heart sank at the prospect of weeks without seeing Murray again.

Amy looked at her sharply and asked, 'What will you do at Christmas, my dear? Murray is so disappointed that you can't be with us.'

In spite of this concern, there was no mention of Marie being invited to Murrayhill that night, however, and she hid her sinking heart with a bright smile as she said, 'I expect I'll do a lot of painting. I'm gathering work for the show.'

On the way home in the train that night she pondered sadly, Of course, I've no reason to expect an invitation at Christmas and certainly no reason to believe that Murray would turn down the invitation to the Highlands for my sake. Perhaps I was the reason he didn't want to go, though. Poor Murray.

Snow began to fall that night and cut off the Borderland from every other part of Scotland, making it impossible for Marie to get to Edinburgh for the last classes of the year. No trains were running; a few brave people sallied out on horseback but only for short distances. The normal cart traffic that passed up and down the main street of the village disappeared and the world seemed strangely silent and waiting, as if it were holding its breath.

Still the snow fell, drifting down in a slowly waving curtain from the Three Sisters hills. Frost gripped the land and every twig, every dry flower stalk in Tibbie's garden stood up stiff and white.

Marie sat looking out of the window, brooding about her love. He'd made no move to contact her and over and over again she recalled Amy's warning, 'He's a bit of a flirt, you know.'

Yet she managed to reassure herself by recalling some loving thing he had said to her, the way he'd held her hand or slipped a kiss onto her cheek when no one was looking. Of course he loved her as much as she loved him.

She would have liked to go to Bella Vista to see Bethya but the snow made it impossible, so, desperate to occupy her mind and stop herself worrying, she started to draw the winter world.

A kind of fine frenzy of work gripped her and she found an old piece of canvas which she took to Jo's workshop and asked him to stretch over a frame. Then, having primed it, she set herself to paint the scene from the cottage window.

It grew under her hand into a thing of such dramatic beauty that Tibbie stopped beside her every now and again to exclaim in delight, 'Oh, lass, aren't you clever! Oh, lass, that's magnificent. That's just what it looks like.'

Marie painted in a frantic hurry, knowing she must finish the picture before the snow disappeared and also knowing that it was probably the best thing she'd ever done. When she stood back and looked at it, she felt no doubt about her ability. She had become an artist and was glorying in her skill.

She was still painting in the dim grey light of Christmas morning, putting the final touches to the background of snow-covered hills, when David turned up, covered with snow after a long and arduous journey from Maddiston.

He paused in the doorway and took in the scene. Tibbie was cooking and the kitchen was full of mouthwatering smells; the cat and the parrot were in their usual places, both snoozing gently; and his sister stood at the window covering a canvas with paint.

She looked over her shoulder at him. Her face took on a hard look and she said, 'Go away. I don't want you here.'

He left without a word, leaving nothing behind but a puddle of melted snow on the floor where he'd stood.

The snow lay for a fortnight and when the first thaw came, Marie varnished her painting of the hills under snow and, two days later, boarded the train to Edinburgh with a tremendous sense of relief.

Warm in layers of woollen shawls, with her carefully wrapped painting on the floor beside her, she sat in the corner of a compartment, her face pressed up against the window and marvelled at the immensely high walls of frozen snow banked along the line.

Where it was possible to get a view, the hills looked like roll upon roll of wool, piled up white and pristine as they must have been in the beginning of time before Man set a foot on them. There was not a soul abroad and everything was immobile in the grip of the cold.

The end of her journey, Edinburgh, was uniformly grey, not a city to cheer the downcast soul. Marie ran along Princes Street, slithering in the slush of the gutters, till she reached the Professor's door which was opened by a red-nosed Millie, who exclaimed, 'It's grand to see you. We thought you'd be gone till the spring!'

What delight it was to step once more into the brightly lit studio with its blazing fire. Chatter, banter and the usual delicious smells overwhelmed her. The flower painting she had been working on before Christmas stood waiting on her easel and the other students crowded round while Amy impulsively hugged her friend and cried out, 'Here you are, our brave explorer from the frozen Borderland!'

'Did you have a good Christmas with Julia?' Marie asked and Amy said in a sarcastic tone, 'Delightful! Very cold and horribly ghostly. I swear that castle hasn't just got one ghost, it has twenty and I saw them all. The food was foul too, game birds and venison *ad nauseam*. I told Murray that if we stayed there much longer we'd all be growing antlers.'

'How is Murray?' Marie managed to stop herself blushing as she asked the question.

'The same as usual. He sends you his love,' said Amy lightly, waving a paint-smeared hand.

Professor Abernethy then came across and beamed on his star pupil. 'It's good to see you again. Have you been working during the holidays?'

'Yes, I have. I brought a picture for you to give an opinion on because it's different from anything else I've ever done.' As she spoke she was untying the string that held the wrappings over her canvas. Everyone watched while the snow scene was unveiled and when she turned it round to face them there was a universal sigh of admiration.

'How beautiful… Oh, doesn't it look cold…? My goodness, it's masterly…' came the comments.

It was what the Professor said that mattered to Marie, however. She stood staring at him while he looked at her picture.

He took a very long time, chin on his fist and eyes veiled. Then he stepped a few paces back and stood staring at it again. All the girls were watching him with bated breath.

At last he switched his gaze to the artist. 'My dear,' he said, 'I thought that you were a very adept copyist. You seemed to be able to paint in any style… but this isn't derivative at all. This isn't the work of someone who is only a facile brush wielder. This is entirely original, I'm happy to say. You've made the breakthrough. You've become a real artist. My word, I'm overcome with admiration.'

Marie was so moved that she couldn't speak, only shake her head and try to stop her tears from flowing. The kindly old man put a hand on her arm.

'You mustn't weep. You've got a heaven-sent gift. It's something to rejoice about.'

'I painted it for the exhibition,' she whispered.

He nodded with enthusiasm. 'Of course, the exhibition. It's scheduled for February. This will be the best thing in it. This will make your name. The only thing that makes me sad is that this picture tells me I've taught you everything I can. You need someone better now. You've outpassed me by a long way.'

Marie was the heroine of the hour. The entire class clustered round her, looking at the painting, asking how she achieved her effects. She didn't have any secrets to impart…'I just wanted to paint it as it was, to show how cold and bleak it looked… I was low in my spirits and I wanted to show that too…'

She didn't tell them that as she was painting the picture she had been painfully conscious of the fact that on the slope of the hill that faced her, her murdered mother had lain dead in similar cold and wintry weather. All the desolation of her loneliness, her split with David and her unrequited love was painted into it.

Amy slipped an arm round her waist and said sympathetically, 'I can see you were sad when you did that. You must come home with me tonight and see the family. They're all longing to entertain you again.'

It was as if the sun emerged from behind a black bank of clouds. Light flooded the world and the blood throbbed faster in Marie's veins. She beamed with pleasure as she said, 'I'd love to. I'd really love to.'

When they emerged onto the street after the class was finished, the city seemed to have taken on a new face. A wintry sun gleamed down and gilded the windows, casting bright highlights over the grim stones of the castle. Marie beamed so joyously that Amy's coachman was infected by her high spirits as he tucked the girls into their seats and told her, 'It's good to see you again, miss.'

I've been worrying about nothing. Everything's going to turn out well, she thought as they drove to Murrayhill, which looked like a fairy mansion on the face of its hill, with its unmarked white lawn stretching down from the terrace to the road.

Mrs Roxburgh was waiting in her warm parlour and rose with both hands outspread when Marie entered. 'You've kept yourself away from us for far too long,' she cried.

This sounded as if Marie had been deliberately staying away but she made no protest and said with a delighted smile, 'It's lovely to see you again.'

Behind her Amy said breathlessly, 'Marie's done the most wonderful picture for the exhibition. The Profs in ecstacies about it. He says she's got too good for him to teach any more.'

Mrs Roxburgh fixed her sharp eyes on Marie's face and said, 'I knew you'd outgrow Professor Abernethy. You need someone better. I think you ought to go to Paris.'

Both girls gasped and Marie made her usual self-deprecatory noises but Mrs Roxburgh quelled them with an upraised hand. 'Listen to me. Paris is the only place if you're really serious about painting. Are you?'

Marie did not have to think about the question. Vigorously she nodded her head. 'Yes, I'm serious.' Painting was almost as important as Murray.

Mrs Roxburgh seemed pleased at this reply. 'You're a remarkable girl. You have to be dedicated to succeed as an artist, you know.'

Marie nodded. 'I know that but…'

'But?' Mrs Roxburgh was looking at her with interrogating eyes.

'But I'm poor. I've no money. How can I go to Paris?'

'What about Lady Godolphin?' Amy asked.

'I've no claim on Lady Godolphin. She helped me out of kindness. I expect nothing more from her.'

This did not put Mrs Roxburgh off, however. 'She helped you because she recognised your talent and that has grown. If she knows how good you are now, she'll probably go on helping you. Besides you'll make money from the pictures you enter in the exhibition.'

'If anyone buys them,' said Marie.

Amy laughed. 'You're such a pessimist. Of course someone'll buy them. They're all splendid. You'll probably make enough to take you to Paris.'

Marie looked from one to the other. They were both privileged women who could see no obstacle to any hopes and ambitions they held.

'I'd like to go,' she admitted, 'but not for too long.' She was wondering how she'd manage to live in a foreign land, so far away from Murray.

'Paris is a beautiful and enchanting place,' said Mrs Roxburgh, walking back to her chair. 'When you get there, there's no predicting how you'll react.'

To put the final touch to the delight of that day, Murray was at home and when Marie entered the drawing-room he jumped up and walked towards her with a smile of welcome on his face.

'It's so good to see you,' he told her.

All her fears disappeared in the twinkling of an eye. I was foolish to doubt him, she thought, as he led her to a chair and sat beside her, leaning forward as if she were the only person in the room.

Not only Murray, it seemed, but every member of the family went out of their way to please her that night. When they had dined, music was suggested and she sat in the midst of them listening to her favourite songs in a haze of happiness. Outside the window a full moon was shining on the snow-covered garden and the sky was a blanket of velvet studded all over with stars.

Murray saw her gazing through the uncurtained glass and leaned across to ask softly, 'Would you care to take a turn with me before you go to bed?'

His mother looked up sharply. 'Yes, that would be nice but wrap up well. It's so cold.'

He shook his head. 'We won't be long, Mama. Just a short walk to clear our lungs, a breath of fresh air. It's stuffy in here.'

A look passed between them and Mrs Roxburgh nodded. 'All right, but keep warm. Don't go far.'

He fetched a warm shawl for Marie and they set out, heading across the lawn to a little wooden summer-house that was tucked in a corner of the boundary wall. He took her arm to guide her over the snow-packed path and she felt as if she were in heaven. What she wanted most in the world was to lean her head against his chest and feel his heart beating beneath her cheek. Her emotions were so intense that she could not speak.

Murray was telling her how hard he had been working during the past few months.

'I really want to do well. If I pass the exams this time, I've been offered a place in a legal office in Queen Street, but they'll only take me as a probationer and it'll be several years before I'm on my feet...' he said.

She looked at him with shining eyes. 'I'm sure you'll do well. You deserve to for all the work you've done. It doesn't matter to me how long we've to wait, Murray.'

'That's just it,' he said. 'I won't be in a position to ask anyone to wait for me for a long, long time. It isn't fair on the girl, Marie.'

She laughed. 'I don't care. I'll go to Paris and learn to paint really well and then perhaps I'll be able to earn enough money to ask you!'

He smiled. 'You are a silly girl! But you'll probably meet someone else in Paris. I don't want you to think that you must wait for me...'

'I'll never meet anyone I love more than you,' she whispered.

'Now, now,' he said, as if he were calming a boisterous dog. 'You know we can't be serious about each other yet, don't you? You've your career to think about and I've got mine.'

'That's true,' she agreed, 'and I take my career very seriously too.'

'Of course you do,' he said in a hearty tone. 'And so you should. Everyone says you've a brilliant future before you. Even for a woman...'

The words chilled her. 'I think it's so unfair the way people think women painters are inferior to men,' she burst out. 'I have to sign all my work with my initials and not my full name. That's awful.'

Murray had a pragmatic mind. 'It's sensible, my dear, if you want to sell your work.'

'But don't you see that I want to be recognised as myself, Marie Benjamin, not as some make-believe man, not just a saleable commodity?' she sighed.

Money mattered to him, however, and he brushed that aside. 'When you've made your name, you can start a movement. Meanwhile make money, that's my advice to you.'

They seemed to be moving away from the matter of romance, however, and she leaned her cheek on his sleeve, saying softly, 'I've missed you so much, Murray. You've been on my mind a lot.'

'That's good, I'm glad,' he said awkwardly, squeezing her arm. She wondered why he didn't kiss her and decided to take the initiative, moving closer and whispering, 'Have you missed me?'

He was so handsome in the semi-darkness with the silver-gilt colour of the moon playing on his face that her heart beat faster as she looked at him. His gaze sought hers and she saw his eyes softening.

'I've thought about you a lot too,' he said vehemently. 'A great deal. More than you can imagine.'

Emboldened by this, she kissed his cheek. He sat very still for a moment and then stood up abruptly. 'Come on, it's getting cold and Mama will be wondering where we are,' he said, extending his hand.

Her face was so stricken that his resolve melted, however, and he aimed a peck at her cheek. 'Don't look so woebegone,' he whispered. 'It's best if we just stay friends for the meantime. It's so complicated. There's such a long time to wait… We can't commit ourselves. My family are anxious that I don't until I'm really settled.'

'Just tell me one thing,' she whispered. 'Just tell me you still love me.'

He held her hands to his chest and his wonderfully soulful eyes were fixed on her face. 'I still love you. If it was left to me, if I was independent, I'd marry you tomorrow. You're the sweetest girl I've ever met in my life.'

She almost jumped with joy. 'Of course I understand. I'll wait. It doesn't matter if I have to wait ten years for you,' she told him in a heartfelt voice.

He stroked her cheek and said, 'It's not just waiting, it's not being tied…'

She shook her head. 'We're not tied.'

He sounded relieved. 'I knew you'd understand. You're such a sensitive and sensible girl. I didn't want to hurt you because I thought you expected something to happen quickly, but it can't, you know.'

'Of course it can't. I know that perfectly well. But I do love you,' she cried out and threw out her arms to him again. He bent down and kissed her once more. Then gently he took her arm and led her back to the house.

When they re-entered the drawing-room, the family all looked up expectantly.

Marie beamed and happily told them, 'It's so lovely tonight. All the stars are out.'

Mrs Roxburgh looked from her to Murray and said slowly, 'You seem to have enjoyed yourselves.'

It was only when she was in bed that night that an unbidden thought struck Marie. Though she'd vehemently avowed her love for Murray, he had been reluctant to do the same. She told herself she was being stupid. He'd kissed her, hadn't he?

# Chapter Fifteen

The exhibition was fixed for 15 February 1875.

It was to take place in a large gallery along the road from Professor Abernethy's studio and was one of the social events of the Edinburgh year, because all the art masters, of which there were many in the city, periodically displayed pupils' work. The teachers vied with each other for the patronage of rich families with daughters and the Prof expected that Marie's work would stand head and shoulders above everyone else's. It would be better than any advertisement for him but he was not a selfish man and sincerely hoped that Marie would sell her pictures well because he had a shrewd idea that her circumstances were very different to those of his other pupils.

She shared his hopes and through the days before the exhibition she painted obsessively, every brush stroke expressing ambition. As she worked the Professor stood behind her gurgling with appreciation. 'You've never painted so well. But slow up a little, you'll wear yourself out,' he told her over and over again.

She didn't feel tired. She could have painted all night if necessary so he allowed her to stay on after the rest of the class had gone home and catch the last train to Camptounfoot, where she fell into bed and slept like the dead.

She was charged to a high pitch with energy and excitement, counting the days till the show.

The only cloud on her horizon was that she was too busy to go back to Murrayhill with Amy and as a result never saw Murray. Then one day Amy told her that he had been sent off to the Highlands to stay with Julia again.

'Papa insists that he can work there without distractions. He's afraid of Murray failing, but Julia'll keep his nose to the grindstone,' she said.

'I hope he manages to come back to Edinburgh for the show,' she said and Amy nodded enthusiastically. 'Of course he will. The

Roxburghs will be out in force. We wouldn't miss it for the world.'
Amy herself was exhibiting a highly coloured flower picture but did
not seem to care much whether it was admired or not. When the
Professor asked her to put a price on it in case someone wanted to buy
it, she laughed. 'It's not for sale. I'm keeping it for my grandchildren,
to show them what granny did when she was a girl.'

The exhibition was scheduled to open on a Tuesday and on the
previous Sunday Marie walked to Bella Vista with a printed invitation
for Bethya, whom she found in her elegant drawing-room, looking
even more drawn and pale-faced. There were purple circles round her
eyes but she brightened when Marie was shown in.

'My dear, how good to see you!' she exclaimed.

'I brought you this. I hope you'll be able to come,' said Marie,
handing over the invitation.

Bethya was delighted. 'This means your time at Professor Abernethy's classes is over, doesn't it? He wrote and told me how well
you've done. You've been an exemplary pupil apparently.'

Marie flushed. 'I owe you so much, your ladyship. I hope you'll be
able to come to the exhibition.'

Bethya exclaimed, 'Of course I'll be there. I wouldn't miss it for
the world. I've already heard about it actually and plan to go because
I had a letter from your friend Mrs Roxburgh.'

Marie was surprised. 'Mrs Roxburgh wrote to you?'

'Yes, she did. She's very enthusiastic about your work. She suggests
that you go to study in Paris for three months and I think that's a good
plan.'

It was astonishing that all this had been going on without Marie
knowing anything about it. She shook her head. 'But I can't go to
Paris, Lady Godolphin. I can't afford it. And besides I don't know if
I'd learn very much in three months. I'd be better to stay here and try
to get commissions. The Professor says I might… if people think I'm
a man. That's why I've to sign my work as M. Benjamin.'

The wry note in her voice made Bethya cock an eye at her. 'Be
sensible. Women learn that lesson very early,' she advised in a strange
voice.

Then she assumed her normal tone and went on, 'I can afford to
send you to Paris. Mrs Roxburgh is thinking of sending her daughter,
Amy, there and she suggested that you might go as well. You're good
friends I believe. There's a highly recommended École des Peintures

that Mrs Roxburgh knows about. I think Paris is a good idea. After three months you'll know if you want to stay and by that time you might have started to sell your work. You should try it. You have to gamble in life. Sometimes it comes off...'

Marie sat forward in her chair. 'I don't think I can take so much from you, Lady Godolphin. I don't want to presume on your generosity. You've been too good to me already. When you come to the exhibition, I want you to tell me which picture you like best and I'll give it to you. I can't do anything else to show my appreciation and I'll be very hurt if you refuse it.'

Bethya could tell that this offer was genuine and that a refusal would hurt.

'Thank you,' she said. 'I'll tell you which one I like and I will accept it. It's very thoughtful of you. But think about Paris, please. I can well afford it. Besides, it has given me great pleasure to have sponsored you and seen you do so well.'

Concerned at how ill Bethya looked, Marie stood up and said, 'I must go now because I don't want to tire you. I only came to bring your ticket for the show. I look forward to seeing you on Tuesday. And I'll think about your offer.'

When Marie was emerging from Bella Vista's gates, she was almost bowled over by a fast-trotting horse pulling a smartly painted dogcart with a man at the reins. She hopped onto the grass bank and glared at the equipage, and her look was so fierce that the driver pulled up and apologised. 'I'm so sorry. I didn't see you. I hope you're not hurt or frightened.'

'I'm neither,' she said stiffly, 'but you really should go a little more slowly.'

He looked contrite. 'I'm sorry,' he said again and then added, 'Can I offer you a lift? Are you going to Camptounfoot?'

'Yes, I am,' she told him.

'You live with Tibbie, don't you? I've seen you once or twice when I've been in the village. I'm Robbie Rutherford from across the road,' he explained.

She recognised him. This was the famous Robbie whom everyone in the village talked about, the most famous son of the place, the lad who'd gone into the world and made good. He looked well set up and respectable, not too tall but broad in the shoulder and his brown hair flopped down over one eye giving him a perennially boyish look. Yet he had a shrewd gaze and a firm chin. Not a man to take lightly, that was obvious.

'Let me drive you to the village,' he said again and she smiled.

'All right. Thank you.'

He jumped down and she noticed that he limped as he came round toher up to her seat. He proved to be a cheerful, talkative companion, asking intelligent questions about her painting and enquiring about the coming exhibition. His evident interest made Marie blossom. He had a good effect on her, making everything, even a trip to Paris, seem possible.

The carriage was high and beautifully sprung, far superior, she realised, to anything the Roxburghs owned. It must have cost a great deal of money. She told him about her visit to Bethya Godolphin as they bowled along and he listened with keen interest.

'I'd like to come to your exhibition,' he told her suddenly and she beamed.

'I'd like you to come.' But she did not think he would.

She had been invited to spend the night before the show with the Roxburghs in Murrayhill but before she left Camptounfoot, she tried to persuade Tibbie to take the train to Edinburgh on Tuesday morning.

'Please come and see the exhibition,' she pleaded, but Tibbie shook her head.

'I'm feared of the train. And I'd get lost in a city. I'd like to see your pictures all hanging up and hear folk saying nice things about them but going to Edinbury's no' for folk like me. I'd not be easy in my mind there.'

Marie knew it was impossible to change her mind. Because she herself was going in early, and would not change that plan because she was longing to see Murray again for the first time since their encounter in the summer-house, and because there was no one else to escort Tibbie to Edinburgh, she accepted defeat.

She had not told David about the exhibition and had no intention of doing so, for she had not forgiven him over the mysterious matter of the letter to the Roxburghs. They had not seen each other since Christmas, for he no longer came to Camptounfoot on Sundays.

At Murrayhill, Mrs Roxburgh and Amy greeted her with enthusiasm.

'The Professor says that your pictures are absolutely marvellous,' cried Amy. 'He's hung ten of them and he said that the snow scene is as good as anything in the landscapes of the big collections! You're going to do very well and Mama thinks you'll earn enough to keep yourself in Paris for six months at least.'

They seemed to accept the expedition to Paris as a certainty and Amy was full of what she'd bought to wear for the trip but Marie shook her head.

'I've not decided if I can go yet. I've no money,' she said.

Her objections were briskly swept aside. 'Lady Godolphin has written to Mama and said she'll still sponsor you and I can't go on my own, can I? It's all arranged. We're going! Mama's written to the École. Isn't it wonderful?'

Amy pranced around with her hands clasped and eyes shining but though Marie pretended to be equally excited, her spirits were low, for there was no sign of Murray and none of the family mentioned his name.

Where is he? Surely he's coming to the exhibition? she wondered in anguish. At last she found out from Amy when they were parting on the upstairs landing in preparation for retiring to bed.

'Murray's still in the Highlands,' she said, dropping her voice so that none of the others downstairs could hear, 'but he's promised to be back by tomorrow so don't look so forlorn.'

What Marie did not know when she retired to her usual bedroom with a heavy heart was that Tibbie had gone for a trip that day too. She took the carrier's cart to Maddiston and called on David in his office at Henderson's Mill.

He was surprised to see her standing in the office doorway and jumped from his chair to hurry towards her. 'What's wrong? Is it Marie?' he asked.

Tibbie shook her head. 'Nothing's wrong. I've come to tell you that your sister's showing her pictures in a big exhibition in Edinburgh and it would be a great thing for her if you went to see it. It's tomorrow and I've got the address here in my bag.'

His face went stony and its unguardedness disappeared.

'But...' he protested and she silenced him with a wave of the hand. 'No buts, just listen to what I have to say. Your sister's on the verge of a big success. Lady Godolphin's talking of paying for her to go to Paris. They all think she's a very good painter. You should be proud of her. Go and show her that you are or you and she'll lose each other for ever and I wouldn't want to see that happen.'

His eyes were narrow and his mouth a tight line. 'Why didn't she come and tell me this herself? Why didn't she ask me to go to the exhibition? I'm a success too and I did it for her as much as for myself but she's not grateful, is she? She lets those *people* patronise her and cuts herself off from her brother, her only blood relation.'

'David,' pleaded Tibbie, 'listen to me. You're both stubborn, and you've hurt her badly. One of you must make it up or it will never heal. This is the perfect time.'

He was beyond reason, however. 'Anything I did was for her own good. I've tried to protect her from being used by people who like to feel that they're helping the poor and needy. We're not poor, we're not needy. I earn a lot of money now and soon I'll earn more. She doesn't need to go cap in hand to those people in Edinburgh and Lady Godolphin. We're as good as they are! If she goes to Paris, I'll not care if I ever see her again because it will prove to me that she's a fool with the soul of a beggar.'

Tibbie sighed and pulled on her gloves, for she saw her mission was hopeless. 'I'm sorry. I hoped you'd have more understanding. Don't bother to see me out, I can find my own way. Come in and see me whenever you're down in Camptounfoot…'

He was still going over and over his old arguments and self-justifications when she left. Shaking her grey head, she wondered if he was not a little mad and felt afraid for him.

Next morning she got up early and dressed herself in her best black bombazine. Then, trying to quieten her quivering nerves, she walked the path to Rosewell station.

If David wouldn't go to Edinburgh to back up Marie, Tibbie would have to go in his stead though the prospect terrified her.

She was climbing the station brae when she heard the clip-clop of a trotting horse coming up behind her.

'Mrs Mather, Mrs Mather, wait,' cried a voice and she turned to see Robbie Rutherford being driven in his dogcart by a solemn-faced servant.

He jumped down and took her arm. 'Where are you going?' he asked.

'For the train. I'm going to Edinbury,' she said staunchly.

'So am I. I went to your cottage to collect you but you'd gone. I thought you and I might go to Edinburgh together,' he told her.

Tears came to her eyes. 'Oh Robbie, you were aye a good laddie,' she said with a sob in her voice and he laughed.

'Folk in this place are always telling me that. I wish the opinion was more widespread.'

While Robbie and Tibbie were jaunting into Edinburgh in the train, the morning at Murrayhill dawned bright and fresh. From her bedroom window Marie looked out onto a sea of white, purple and golden crocuses carpeting the vast lawn and her heart lifted in delight.

She breakfasted alone, for the rest of the family were still in bed but before she finished Amy appeared in a flannel wrapper and told her, 'The gig's ordered for you at nine o'clock. Mama thought you'd want to get into the gallery as early as possible and see your work hanging before the crowds arrived. I'll come on later with the rest of the family.'

By this time Marie was in such a state of excitement that her throat felt as dry and rasping as sandpaper, so talking was difficult. It was a relief that prattling Amy was not riding into Edinburgh with her. There was a funny pulsing in her temples like the onset of a headache which never actually came to full flowering, but Amy's chatter would almost certainly cause it to erupt and she did not want anything to spoil this perfect day.

She went first to Professor Abernethy's studio but found it empty apart from Milly, who was there looking very stately in a high-waisted silken gown and a frilled lace cap, a costume which, like her father's clothes, was many years out of date.

Marie's footsteps sounded hollow as she walked the polished floor of the room where she had done so much work. The easels stood empty and no welcoming fire burned in the grate. Its desolation made her sad as she realised that her days of working there were over. Another chapter of her life was about to close.

'Everything's been taken along to the exhibition rooms. Papa's there and I'm just going too. Come with me,' Milly said. 'I hope you like the way Papa's hung your pictures. He's taken a great deal of trouble to display them well. We both want you to have a good sale,' she said encouragingly.

When she set foot in the marble halled gallery, however, Marie's nervousness miraculously disappeared.

It was a long, white-walled room illuminated by an overhead glass roof. In the middle of the empty wooden floor was a circle of red plush seats around a trio of potted palms and the walls were closely covered with canvases, some brilliantly coloured, some subfusc.

The wall facing the door was given over to the Benjamins, ten pictures, glowing and vibrant. Marie stared at them as if they were works that she had never seen before and then recognition dawned. I did those, I remember painting that flower, I remember putting that layer of paint on the canvas, she thought, rushing across the floor with her hands out as if greeting old friends.

Standing in front of her pictures, she closed her eyes, then opened them wide and really looked. All the people who had been so complimentary to her were right. The pictures were magnificent. She knew that without worrying about false modesty or overweening pride.

The Professor had taken the trouble to put her flower and fruit still lifes in ornate, gilded frames which he kept in a storeroom behind the studio and these set them off so well that they could hold their own with the famous Dutch canvases that she had used as models for her copies.

The two pictures that Marie liked best, however, were not the clever copies but the ones she had done in Camptounfoot during the previous Christmas: a cosy interior showing Tibbie's parlour with the cat asleep on the rocking chair before a blazing fire, and by far the best canvas in the show, her snow scene. When she looked at it she shivered because it brought back the desolation and sadness she felt as she painted it. Bleak and forbidding but undeniably magnificent, it overawed her.

What she was looking at was the result of two years' work, for she had brought all her hard-earned skill into play to create that picture. It also represented the story of her life, for looming up at the back of the scene was the slope of hill where her mother's body had been found.

Suddenly she wished her brother was with her. She wanted to grasp his hand and stand beside him, for they had travelled a long and dangerous road together and she was sharply aware that without the kindness of strangers, their story could have been very different.

At last she tore herself away from the snow scene and walked along the line of her work. There was the harvest scene she'd done after Kitty went away; there was a romantic flower study done at the time she first fell in love with Murray. She had kept a diary in pictures but only she knew what it said.

Before she realised that time had passed, people began to flow into the room and one of the first to rush up to her was dear Tibbie, escorted by a beaming Robbie Rutherford.

The old woman and the young one embraced as if they had not met for years and Marie sobbed, 'Oh Tibbie, I'm so pleased you've come. You said you wouldn't and I didn't expect you, but I'm so pleased…'

Tibbie, extremely proper-looking in the bombazine and a neat little bonnet with a striped ribbon round the brim, said, 'I couldn't have done it except for Robbie. He held my hand all over that big bridge Emma Jane and Tim built. I'd have died of fright if he wasn't there.'

Marie turned to him in gratitude. 'That was kind of you. I did want Tibbie to be here but she absolutely refused to consider the idea. I'd given her up.'

Robbie laughed. 'I know that, but she was coming anyway though she was scared stiff. I met her at the station. Just look at her now… Before we know it she'll be engaging all the grand folk in conversation.' And he pointed to Tibbie's little figure pushing her way with grim determination through the press of people in order to get nearer to Marie's pictures.

While she was speaking to Robbie, Marie saw Bethya arriving and, apologising to him, hurried over to greet her.

Bethya grasped her hands and said, 'Where are they? Don't tell me! I'll pick them out… Yes, there they are, on that wall. No one else but you could do such wonderful pictures!' Still holding Marie's hand, she walked through the crowd, which parted in front of her because she had such an air of distinction.

They stood together in front of the winter landscape and Bethya sighed, 'That's the Three Sisters. I hunted over them when I was young. How wonderful you've made them look. Enchanted, in fact.'

'I want you to have it,' said Marie.

Bethya looked at her and shook her head. 'Oh no, not that one. It's too sad. I want one of your flower pictures… I need a summer picture to make me happy, especially now. Let's see which one I like best.'

They walked down the line and after much deliberation she chose a study of lilac blossom in a glass jar which Marie remembered had caused her a great deal of trouble in the painting.

It was only later, when looking at the price list, that she saw the Professor had put a price tag of ten guineas on the lilac picture but the snow scene was sixty, the most expensive picture in the show. She was sure that Bethya had refused to take the big picture in the hope that it would be sold to some other enthusiast.

When the little red spot went up on the lilacs and people heard that it had gone to Lady Godolphin, there was a rush to buy Benjamins, for Bethya was well known as an influential art collector. By the time the Roxburgh family arrived, all the flower pieces had been snapped up, for they came late, just before midday, but Marie's heart leaped into her throat when she saw that Murray was with them.

He looked well, handsomely clear-skinned and smiling and she wished she could go over to him and take his hand, for she longed to show her link with him, to mark him out as hers.

Mrs Roxburgh, a leader of smart society in spite of her affectation of despising it, was soon surrounded by a group of chattering ladies. They told her that Lady Godolphin was in the crowd and, leaving them, she hurried over to where Bethya was resting on one of the red plush seats, for her strength was ebbing and her face was white.

Mrs Roxburgh sat beside her and said, 'I do hope you don't think its presumptuous of me to introduce myself to you like this but we've communicated by letter and I feel as if I know you already. Our mutual interest in Marie Benjamin has made a bond between us.'

Bethya smiled wanly. 'She is so gifted. I'm proud to be associated with her. It would have been a terrible thing for such talent to be neglected. Even as a child, her pictures were remarkable.'

'I agree,' said Mrs Roxburgh, nodding. 'My daughter Amy and she have become very close friends and she has spent a good deal of time at our home, Murrayhill. We've become very fond of her and I do think it's a good idea for her to go to Paris. Her horizon must be widened.'

Bethya looked at the noisy crowd around her. Everyone seemed to be studying Marie's pictures and there was not much interest in the others. 'I think she's well launched on her career already,' she said.

'Yes, she is, but Edinburgh's not big enough for her. She should get away. I hope she makes enough today to send her to Paris, for that's what she needs, but it's an expensive city. My husband and I intend to pay Marie's fare there if she will accept it. She will be a good companion for our Amy. We feel that we could not let our girl go to that city alone and Marie is so sensible...'

Bethya knew what was being asked. 'I'm happy to go on backing Marie financially but she's a very proud girl. She's never taken any money from me, all she has allowed me to do is pay Professor Abernethy's fees. It would be insulting to offer her money now.'

'The classes at the École des Peintures where Amy is going are not cheap. I doubt if Marie could afford them for more than a few weeks even if she sells all the pictures she has here today,' said Mrs Roxburgh.

Bethya turned her lovely dark eyes on the woman by her side. 'I'm prepared to pay her class fees,' she said sweetly. 'How can we arrange it without hurting her feelings? Perhaps we can tell her that the fees are much cheaper than they really are...'

Mrs Roxburgh was delighted. 'That's extremely kind of you. I'll arrange it all and Amy and I will persuade Marie to go. We want to make it possible for her to spend long enough to benefit from the teaching there. As you were saying, it would be dreadful if her talent was wasted.'

Marie, unaware of all this planning, was acutely conscious of Murray no matter where he went in the big room. When he stood in front of one of her pictures, her eye followed him, trying to discern from his expression what he was thinking. She could not approach him because she was besieged on all sides by admirers and every now and again Milly, who was keeping the purchase sheet, would rush up to whisper out of the side of her mouth, 'Another one away!'

At last she could stay away from Murray no longer and succeeded in pushing her way through the crowd to stand beside him. She tried to slip a hand into his but he had them in his pockets, though the smile he turned on her was fond enough to make her heart melt.

'Which picture do you like best?' she whispered.

He pointed to the scene with the sleeping cat in Tibbie's kitchen. 'That's the one. It's so peaceful, so homely.'

'It's my home,' she said softly, thinking how very different it was to Murrayhill.

'In that case,' said Murray, 'I'm going to buy it.'

'Oh no,' she protested. 'You can't do that. You mustn't waste money. I'll paint you another one and give it to you as a present.'

He shook his head. 'No, no, I want to buy it.' He consulted his catalogue sheet. 'It's only ten guineas. I can easily afford that – especially now.'

'Especially now?' she repeated in surprise.

He looked slightly taken aback. 'I mean especially now that I've finished studying and will soon go to work.'

Just then Milly came over again with a lady admirer who'd asked to be introduced to Marie so her tete-a-tete with Murray was broken up and he was swallowed up by the crowd.

By half-past twelve people had started to drift away and Robbie appeared at Marie's elbow.

'I'm taking Tibbie for a meal at the hotel at the far end of Princes Street. Will you join us?' he asked.

She looked around for the Roxburghs but they had disappeared, so she accepted his invitation and they lunched in great style with the waiters fussing around Robbie who seemed to be known to them.

He ordered wine and toasted Marie with it and she felt tears rise to her eyes as she looked at the two smiling faces beside her. Dear Tibbie, whose cheeks were bright pink with the unaccustomed wine, and Robbie, who was openly proud of his achievements but not so proud that he could not acknowledge Marie's as well.

She wished that she was not acting a part, pretending to be as happy as they were, and not secretly sorrowing over Murray, wishing it was he who was sitting with her, not Robbie.

Before they returned to the station to catch their train home, she said, 'I'd like to go back to the studio and find out how many pictures have been sold altogether.' Tibbie and Robbie went with her and she hid from them her hope that Murray had left her a message with Milly, but disappointment awaited her over that too.

The Professor exclaimed in delight at the sight of his star pupil and rushed across to take her hands. 'My dear, my dear, you've sold everything except the big snow scene. You've made ninety-eight guineas! It's a fortune, well done.'

'Is that enough for Paris?' she asked him.

'It would keep you there for about a year providing you're cautious,' he said. 'It's a pity the snow scene hasn't gone, though, because it's the best of the lot but I priced it high, perhaps I went over the top. I thought it so masterly, you see…'

'But all the people at the show would know it was by a woman, wouldn't they?' said Marie bitterly and the Professor nodded.

'Perhaps you're right. But don't despair. There's another four days of the show. It might go before the end.'

For the next two days she waited in Camptounfoot, wondering about Murray. On the third morning after the show Robbie arrived to say goodbye, for he was going back to London, having been unexpectedly recalled because of pressure of business.

Tibbie was more disappointed than Marie by his departure, for she had high hopes of a romance flourishing between them but they had not had long enough to get to know each other. Marie was too concerned with wondering whether Murray would contact her to give much thought to anything else.

On the fourth morning, a footman from Bella Vista turned up with a note from Bethya. She too, said the note, was preparing to go south but had been in contact with Mrs Roxburgh of Murrayhill about the trip to Paris. If Marie would go up to Murrayhill as soon as possible, the final plans could be made.

Marie was on the next train to Edinburgh and found Amy and her mother closeted in the parlour at Murrayhill with French dictionaries and railway timetables piled on the table beside them.

'How do you feel about crossing the Channel?' asked Mrs Roxburgh jocularly when Marie appeared.

She shook her head. 'My snow scene hasn't sold. I might not have enough money.'

Mrs Roxburgh laughed. 'Of course you do. Mr Roxburgh and I want to pay your train fare to Paris. Now, don't refuse out of hand. If you accept our offer, it will get you there and Lady Godolphin has negotiated specially reduced class rates for you because of your talent… They're pleased to get a girl who can paint so well already.'

This was a lie. Bethya had undertaken to pay the full fees but Marie was not to know that.

She looked starry-eyed as Amy's mother went on. 'That means the money you've earned from the exhibition will be sufficient to pay your accommodation and food. Will you do it? Will you go?'

Amy chipped in, 'Do say yes. They won't let me go alone. You must come.'

I wonder if they're grooming me for acceptance into the family? thought Marie, for she was still acutely self-conscious when faced by the barrage of Roxburghs and aware of her social shortcomings.

Mrs Roxburgh put the clinching touch to her argument when she said, 'You'll learn so much more than painting in Paris. You'll come back a woman of the world…'

'It's very kind of you. I would like to go,' she faltered. They had won.

'Good, good,' cried Amy, clapping her hands.

'Good, good,' echoed her mother. 'I'll arrange things from this end. You must write to Lady Godolphin immediately and say I've spoken to you and that you'll go to Paris with Amy. You'll love Paris. It's such a lovely place to be in when you're young.'

## Chapter Sixteen

Cora White's Excelsior Club was famous with London's sporting men and, in spite of being in an unfashionable area, it was very smart indeed.

Bothy-born Kitty never ceased to admire the elegance of its furniture and fittings, the gleam of the paint, the sumptuousness of the carpets which, she was sure, would not be surpassed for style in Windsor Castle itself.

The front of the house was a reception area with an elegant entrance hall and sitting-rooms where clients lolled around reading newspapers or gossiping while pretty girls hurried to and fro serving drinks.

Behind were a series of sweat rooms and plunge baths where the clients went to lie wrapped in towels, enduring heat that could almost melt the flesh from their bones. The heating system was worked by an ingenious network of piping that connected with a huge furnace in the back yard, where a dust-stained gang of men were continually employed shovelling coal into its maw.

Clients could turn up at any time, day or night, and while they sweated, they called up food or refreshments, though the more serious of them took neither and sometimes fainted from lack of nourishment and weakness, so extreme was their regimen.

After a session in the hot rooms, they lay on cots in white-curtained cubicles to be massaged by well-muscled men who looked like, and sometimes were, ex-pugilists. For many of the clients the club was a sort of home from home and they held dinner parties there for their male friends or conducted long card games at the baize-covered tables.

Apart from her own girls, Mrs White did not admit women, even as guests of the clients, and the Excelsior was a male paradise. The stokers, the masseurs, the never-seen kitchen staff and Laverty were men; the rest of the staff pretty young women who were not averse to sitting on a client's knee if so requested.

There were seven girls, including Kitty Scott, working in the house. Though some of them appeared to do nothing more than walk about with trays of iced water, they all were handpicked for their looks. In this line up of beauty was a creamy-skinned Nordic blonde; a beautiful mulatto girl from Madagascar with eyes of jet-black surrounded by astonishingly brilliant whites; an Irish colleen called Brigid with hair like a raven's wing; and three pert Cockney girls whose doll–like faces belied their sharpness of wit and steely characters. Kitty was the only one with red hair and she stood out because she was the tallest of them all.

When she made her first appearance in the lavender gown Laverty had picked out for her, she was met by a wall of suspicion and distrust from the other girls. They had formed alliances among themselves; there were rivalries and dislikes simmering beneath the surface. Each faction wondered where this stranger would fit in.

As she looked from face to face an old singing game that used to be played at Camptounfoot school came unbidden into her head. 'Bow to the East; Bow to the West…' the children sang as they skipped round in a ring. The one in the middle picked out her friend and that went on till only one was left unchosen. That one was usually Kitty.

Which of these women, she asked herself, was the ringleader, the equivalent of Bella? Being on the road with the boxing show had taught her a lot about life and she knew that it would not do to set herself up in defiance. She would pick the winning side and placate it.

She smiled and the Irish girl smiled back. The only one who did not smile was the shortest and sweetest-looking of the Cockney girls, whose name was Gladys.

That's the leader, thought Kitty and smiled directly at her.

Her reward was a grudging nod. 'Where you from then?' the girl asked. It was an acknowledgement of her existence. Kitty was in.

At first Mrs White attempted to recruit the new girl as a bearer of drinks but she rebelled against sweeping around with a tray in her hand, knowing that the eyes of men were following her every move. She hated having to be scrupulously polite to boors whose faces she would gladly have slapped. Her manner was so offhand that it was obvious within one day that another position would have to be found for her, but she was so eye-catching that Mrs White was reluctant to put her behind the scenes.

'You said you were good at counting, didn't you?' she asked after a minor incident when it looked as if Kitty was about to bounce a silver tray off the head of an amorous client.

'Yes, I am.' Kitty did not believe in false modesty.

'I need a bookkeeper. The old man who used to do it died last month and I've been doing it myself but it takes me away from other things. You'd have to tally up all the chits for drinks and services that the girls bring in and enter them in my big ledger. Some of the patrons run accounts with me, you see.'

'I could do that,' said Kitty confidently.

'The only thing is you'll have to do it at a desk in the front hall. I want the customers to see you. It's a pity to hide you away.'

Kitty glared. 'You're dressing the window, are you? I don't mind so long as I don't have to sit on their knees and put up with them pawing me.'

Cora sighed. 'I'll let them know you're off bounds. Just don't hit them, will you? This isn't a boxing show, this is a gentlemen's club. I'll try you at the bookkeeping and see how you get on. If you don't, I'll have to let you go. I can't afford passengers, even if my sisters send them to me.'

Kitty bridled. 'I'm no passenger, Mrs White, but I'm no baggage either.'

Cora laughed. 'I like a girl with a quick tongue. All right, come into my office and I'll show you how the books are kept. If you suit me, I'll pay you a pound a week and your keep.'

Clients signed for anything they bought or received. Each day piles of paper chits appeared on Kitty's desk that had been set up beside an immense potted palm in the entrance hall. These chits had to be added up before being entered in the ledgers under each client's name. Bills were sent out monthly and Kitty prepared them too. She accomplished this task with ease and far quicker than any bookkeeper Cora had employed before, so her reluctance to flirt with the customers was soon forgiven by the owner of the club but not so quickly by the other girls, who felt that Kitty's disdain for the customers reflected on them.

Hardbitten Gladys put a restraining hand on Kitty's arm one night as she was climbing the stairs to bed in the tiny attic beneath the eaves.

'You too good to chat up the customers? Some sort of a lady then? Do you think we're all tarts?' she asked. Her breath smelt of gin as she pressed her face near Kitty.

'Of course I don't. I just don't like men much.'

Gladys's eyes glinted but her tone softened. 'You should have said so, dearie. We don't mind. It takes all sorts. But you don't look like one of those.'

That night Kitty took the precaution of sleeping with her knife beneath the pillow. There were dangers to be faced apart from the customers, she guessed.

Once Kitty was accepted, none of the girls made any secret of the fact that they were prepared, and expected by Mrs White, to sleep with the clients of the club, providing they were paid enough.

'You're silly not to do it too. You'd get plenty of offers. And what's wrong with it? It's all over so quickly and none of us are virgins, so we've nothing to lose,' exclaimed Brigid.

Gladys laughed. 'And they're always so pleased with themselves afterwards, like little boys! That's when you get the big tips.'

Kitty remembered making love with Gerry on the grass above the waterfall and shook her head. 'I couldn't.' She didn't see any point in having stabbed Thompson in order to save her integrity only to give it away for a few pounds to anyone who had the money.

Because she was so valuable as a bookkeeper and because Cora was genuinely afraid of annoying her sisters, no pressure was put on her and when a client drew the proprietrix aside and enquired about the red-haired girl in the hall, she shook her head and said, 'You'll have to ask her yourself, dear.'

Unknown to Kitty some of the girls and a few of the customers were making bets among themselves about how long it would take before she fell from her haughty perch. By the time three months had passed, the ones who set their time limit too short had lost their money.

Summer came and Kitty had saved enough money to send another five-pound note to Tibbie for her mother. Again she cautioned Tibbie not to let anyone else know where she was but pleaded, 'Please tell me how my mother is and if there's any news of Marie. I miss them both.'

The hot weather in the city unsettled her. For day after day the sun shone down from a copper-coloured sky and it seemed as if heat were trapped between the buildings, radiating out like a blast from an oven.

The atmosphere in the club was oppressive. The stokers in the back worked naked and sweat coursed down their bodies, leaving runnels of white on the ingrained coal dust.

In the attics under the slates it was impossible to sleep and when they were not working, the girls sat in the back yard with their dresses open at the neck and their skirts lifted up over black-stockinged legs. They sent Laverty out to the Plume of Feathers for jugs of beer and regaled themselves through the long lazy hours with drink and gossip.

Kitty sat with them but did not drink much because if she did, she could not do her work properly. When she got tired of listening to the gossip, she went for a walk, but the tar in the city streets bubbled up and stuck to the soles of her shoes, her hair clung damply to her neck and temples and the sweat ran down her back in an uncomfortable trickle. She longed for open country, for a gentle summer breeze and fresh air, for the sight of a tree-covered hillside and a silver, unpolluted river.

Sometimes she walked to the Thames and stared at its sluggish, scum-topped water, thinking about Camptounfoot where the swifts would be dashing over the surface of the river and Jo would be casting his line in the hope of catching a trout for his supper. Homesickness caught at her heart but she drove it away.

She was restless and knew that though she was happy at the club, soon she must leave. There was another adventure waiting for her round the corner.

On the hottest day in August she came in from a walk and sat down to sort through piled-up chits on her table in the hall, thankful for a faint breeze that came through the frequently opened front door. The work was engrossing and she was deeply involved in it when she heard a voice coming from Cora's office that made her sit up in surprise.

It was a lilting Irish voice that she thought she recognised. It took her back to Camptounfoot and the day a tall, dark man with a curling beard had given her a half-sovereign. A terrible feeling of disappointment seized her.

'Surely Tim Maquire isn't *here*?' she thought. Hearing about the peccadilloes of the Duke of Allandale and Lord Godolphin had only been a mild surprise but to find Tim Maquire patronising the Excelsior Club would be a blow, her childhood idol would be smashed, her illusions gone.

Laying down her pen, she slipped off her stool and tiptoed quietly to the office door. The voice was louder there and she listened with her head cocked. It was so like Tim Maquire's with the same soft Irish lilt, the same note of amusement running beneath whatever what was being said. She groaned beneath her breath. Turning back to her desk, she grabbed the first sheet of paper that came to hand and hurried towards Cora's sanctum and the voices.

The little room seemed full of people. Cora was standing in the middle surrounded by four men and she was speaking directly to one of them, a thin young fellow with curly brown hair and a wide humorous mouth. They heard Kitty's approach and all looked at her with undisguised interest as she hurried up to Cora with the paper outheld and a frown on her face.

'I wondered if those figures could be right, Mrs White... They seem larger than usual,' she said.

As she spoke she was scrutinising the men. To her infinite relief Tim Maquire was not among them. She relaxed and gave a long, deep sigh that made the curly-haired man grin at her and say, 'That sounded nice. Like you've been running. You're in a terrible hurry to do your sums, eh?'

He spoke exactly like Tim Maquire, the same tone, the same pleasant Irish accent. His voice turned the letter 'r' into 'rh' which gave a softness and sibilance to anything he said and made his merest utterance sound caressing.

Kitty's relief that he was not Tim was so overwhelming that she smiled at him while Cora White took the paper from her hand and pored over the figures.

'What's wrong with them?' she asked crossly. 'They're much the same as usual.'

Kitty took the paper back and apologised but with a light-hearted air. 'It must be the heat getting at me,' she said. The men laughed and the Irishman said, 'Come and have a bath with me then. That'll cool you down.'

Kitty frowned and Mrs White said primly, 'This girl is my book-keeper, gentlemen. She doesn't go into the bathhouse.'

'Now isn't that a pity,' said the man with the enchanting voice. 'And her with such pretty hair too, like a fall of autumn leaves, so it is.'

His eyes were on her face and Kitty felt herself colour up beneath his scrutiny but did not look away. His very bright blue eyes held her in their beam.

'What's this beauty's name?' he asked, still looking at Kitty.

'Kitty Scott,' said she and Cora White in unison.

'I'm Freddy Farrell,' he said, holding out a hand to her. She looked at him blankly. Though she had heard the name, it did not immediately strike some recognition in her.

He did not seem to mind that she was puzzled and laughed. 'You must be the only person in Whitechapel who hasn't heard of Freddy Farrell. I'm the jockey.'

Cora White chipped in, 'And he won the Derby and the Two Thousand Guineas this year.'

'That was lucky,' said Kitty.

Freddy Farrell laughed again. 'And so it was, so it was! Come on, my beauty. Share a bottle of champagne with me.'

Kitty stepped back. 'No, thank you. I've work to do.'

But Mrs White was behind her giving her a shove in the back. 'That can wait. Have a little drink with Mr Farrell, Kitty my dear.' It was obvious she was speaking through gritted teeth but Kitty was not going to be coerced.

'I don't like champagne,' she said and turned sharply on her heel, back to the sanctuary of her table. Behind her she heard Freddy Farrell laughing. He was not in the least put out.

Later that afternoon, when her head was aching with the heat and she was leaning her elbows on the desk to support it, the office door opened. She did not even look round, taking it would be Cora White who was probably still angry about her refusal to drink with the Irish jockey.

'Do you really not like champagne? It's a lovely drink,' said the lilting voice that so beguiled her.

She looked up and saw him standing in the middle of the floor with both hands behind his back and feet slightly apart. He was not as tall as she was herself but wiry and tight-muscled as a steel spring and his clothes were those of a dandy. He was obviously a man who took a great deal of care of his appearance and Kitty, who also loved clothes, could appreciate that.

His face was flushed from his sessions in the baths – or from the champagne – and his eyes were sparkling.

'I've never tasted champagne,' she said.

'Didn't I just know that. There's a girl with too much taste not to appreciate champagne, I said to myself. When you try it, you'll love it.' As he spoke he produced from behind his back an open bottle of gently frothing wine. In one of his waistcoat pockets he had stuck a wineglass and he pulled it forth like a magician producing a rabbit from a hat.

She laughed, she couldn't help it. 'I didn't expect that,' she said and he grinned back.

'I'm famous for doing the unexpected. You'll find that out.'

Kitty accepted the glass of wine he was holding towards her and said, 'Will I? That's doubtful.'

'Freddy walked closer and perched himself on the edge of her table. I'm at my best with outsiders,' he told her. 'I'm always bringing them home when no one expects me to.'

'But I'm not a horse,' Kitty said to him, sipping the wine which was deliciously cool. Bubbles tickled her nose and made her want to sneeze. After only a few sips she felt unaccountably cheerful. It couldn't be the wine, it must be the influence of the irrepressible jockey who was pressing another glass on her, she thought. She shook her head and held her glass away from his outheld bottle.

'One's enough,' she told him.

He looked downcast. 'Don't say I'm wrong about you. Don't say you don't like champagne after all. Don't say you're one of those Bible-thumping teetotallers. Don't tell me you're an abstainer!' He rolled his eyes and sounded anguished.

She reassured him. 'I do like it but I've got work to do. If I drink any more I won't be able to add up.'

'What does it matter? It's a lovely day outside. You've only got one life. Have another drink and come for a drive with me… I'll take you to the Strand and show you off.'

She bridled. 'I'm not for showing off. Thank you for the drink. Go away now please so I can finish what I was doing.'

He went without protest but next morning, when she came down from the attic, the hall was packed solid with baskets of flowers. It was almost impossible to make a path through them. Roses and lilies, huge sprays of gladioli and brilliant white daisies with yellow hearts filled the space with a riot of colour and the scent from them was almost overpowering. The girls were crowded at Cora's office door admiring the floral tributes while more messengers kept arriving with other bouquets which had to be stacked.

Mrs White was vainly trying to remonstrate with the florists' messenger boys.

'Take them away. We don't want any more. Take them back to the shop,' she was crying, holding out her hands to bar the way of a man carrying a huge sheaf of heavily scented white lilies, but he would not listen. He'd been told to leave the flowers at the Excelsior Club and that was what he intended to do.

At eleven in the morning the last gift arrived, a spray of pale yellow and green orchids. They alone bore a card and it was addressed to Miss Kitty Scott... 'Give me and champagne another chance, Freddy Farrell' was all it said.

He arrived at noon, with his followers behind him. This time he stood at Kitty's flower-encircled table and bowed very low.

'Will Miss Scott agree to take a little turn with me in my dogcart? I promise not to bump and bore, not to drive too fast or cut anybody else out at the corners and Miss Scott can sit with her parasol up if she doesn't want to be shown off.'

He gazed at her, both eyebrows raised and mouth wide in a grin. His impertinence was so engaging that she laughed.

'I shouldn't but I will if it's going to stop you emptying the flower shops of London and sending their stock here,' she said. 'Mrs White's desperate about what to do with all those flowers. They're even in buckets in the kitchens.'

His face looked downcast. 'Now don't tell me that as well as not liking champagne, you don't like flowers!'

'I love flowers,' she protested. 'But I don't like to see them dying for nothing. Poor things, they were wilting away when I got down here this morning.'

He walked over to her and laid his hand on hers. She noticed he had long, tapering fingers and a broad palm. It looked a very competent hand. 'You come with me, Kitty, and I'll give you a garden,' he said softly.

She could not resist him. It wasn't so much the way he looked, for he was three inches shorter than she was and till now she had always preferred dark men and his hair was a much lighter brown than Gerry's. As a child he would have been blond.

It was his voice which did it, that lilting voice that seemed to turn her bones to water and took her back to the time when she cherished the hope her father would look and sound like Tim Maquire.

When she agreed to go driving with him, she was not in the least surprised to see that he had the same effect on horses as he had on her, for when he stroked the silken ears of the smart little bay mare harnessed between the shafts of his dogcart that stood outside the Excelsior Club and whispered to her, the mare perked up, stood tall and whickered through her nostrils back at him.

'Where would you like to go?' he asked Kitty when they were seated side by side on the soft, cushioned seats.

'I don't know,' she said. Apart from occasional tram journeys with Brigid 'up west' and her walks to the Thames on sunny afternoons, she knew nothing of any other part of London except Whitechapel.

'I've an errand to do. I'll show you Camden Town,' he said, and gave the reins a little shake to which the mare responded immediately as if she had been listening to him.

They bowled along at a smart trot and people recognised him on the street, waving and shouting greetings like, 'Well done, Freddy. Win next year too.'

He acknowledged their calls with a waggle of the whip that stuck up from a holder by his side but which, Kitty noticed, was not used on the briskly moving mare. He encouraged her by words, crooning 'Come along, lass, clever lass, that's good now, step it up a bit, slow down here, girl, that's a good girl...'

There seemed to be some special bond between the man and his horse, which made Kitty warm to him.

They bowled along road after road, through street after street all full of shops and people, until they came to a leafy district with long avenues of pretty but tumbledown-looking houses.

'This is pleasant,' said Kitty, breathing in the clear air.

'I live up here,' he told her.

The street where he stopped the dogcart was lined by red brick houses with leafy gardens in front and front doors approached by a flight of steps. The house where Freddy pulled up was the only untidy one in the row and this surprised Kitty, for he seemed so fastidious. Its garden was filled with rubbish and dirty-faced children were running around it, yelling and screaming like savages.

They crowded up to Freddy, grabbing his legs and fighting for his attention, but he cut a way through them, holding Kitty by the hand. In the house he introduced her to a blowsy woman called Peg, who, it appeared, was the mother of the children in the garden plus another five who were older and not at home.

Peg was large and slatternly and sat with her huge arms on the kitchen table and a jug of beer at her elbow. She was also the most blatant flatterer Kitty had ever heard in operation, crying out to Freddy over and over again, 'Oh, aren't you a grand fellow, Freddy? The finest fellow walking the streets of London today. There's not a man to touch you in the capital.'

To Kitty she launched into a eulogy about Freddy's personal qualities that made him sound like a cross between Angel Gabriel and Samson. He didn't pay much attention to her except for laying a half-sovereign on the table and saying, 'There you are, there's your money. You can send one of the children out for more beer to keep you going tonight.'

'God bless you, Freddy,' she cried, grasping his hand and kissing it. 'I praise the day that you stepped into this house, I surely do.'

Kitty was mystified as to why she had been brought to see this gargantuan woman. They left after about fifteen minutes, and she said curiously to him, 'Was that your mother?'

He was genuinely surprised. 'My mother? Of course not. What made you think she was my mother.'

'All that adoration of you. How can you stand it?'

He shrugged. 'I don't listen to her. She's my landlady and just afraid I'll move on and leave them now that I've hit the big time. Her old man drinks his wages every week and they live on what I give them. I owed her some money so that's why I went there today.'

'How long have you lived with her?' she asked, curious at how Freddy could turn himself out so well when he lived in such a mess of a house.

'About fifteen years but I've rooms in London too. I keep my place with Peg though because she needs the money and I don't want to hurt her feelings.'

'Fifteen years!' she was astonished because he didn't look much older than she was herself. That meant he must have been with Peg since he was a child.

'Come on, ask. You're wondering how old I am, aren't you?' He grinned. 'I'll tell you if you tell me.'

She laughed back. 'All right, I'm nearly twenty. I've been in London for almost a year.' It was almost true.

He nodded. 'I'm twenty-five but I tell people I'm twenty-nine. They like age and experience on their horses' backs. I've been in

London since I was ten. I came over to work in a hotel stable. Then I rode a winner at Ally Pally and it was the turf for me after that. I'm the highest-paid jockey on the turf. I scooped up six thousand on the Derby. Aren't you impressed?'

'Six thousand! I didn't know jockeys were paid as much as that,' she gasped.

'They're not but you've heard of betting haven't you?'

She nodded and her mind went back to what he had said about his youth when he left home. 'Weren't you scared coming to London on your own at ten?' she asked.

He raised his shoulders in a shrug. 'It was that or starving. I'm an orphan and I had an uncle working in the hotel who said he'd take me when my folk died. The priest in our village paid my fare. Father Corkery his name was. I say a prayer for him every time I go to chapel... but that's not very often, I'm afraid!' Again the grin changed his face as if he were reluctant to show that he had a serious side.

Kitty looked hard at him, her brown eyes brooding beneath the pale lemon brim of her straw hat.

'I ran away from home because I stabbed somebody,' she heard herself saying and for a moment his façade slipped and his eyes revealed startled surprise but again he hid it quickly.

'I knew you looked dangerous. That's what I first liked about you,' he told her, grinning.

She did not smile back and he knew that she was sad so he asked, 'Where's home? I come from a village near Waterford. What about you?'

'From Scotland. A village too. It's called Camptounfoot and it's in the Borderland but no one's ever heard of it. It's very quiet and very beautiful.'

'And you were the local bad girl,' he said jokingly.

She nodded in agreement. 'Yes, I was. They called me a bondager's bastard because my mother was made pregnant by an Irish navvy. She didn't even know his real name.'

'I knew you were an Irish girl. It's that hair, pure Irish!' cried Freddy.

'I used to hate it. The other girls called me Carroty Kate,' she told him. It was difficult to understand why she was revealing herself to him in this way but he seemed to be drawing her secrets out of her.

They were silent for a bit and as he drove the mare along, he glanced at her from time to time and she felt his regard moving over her face like a touching finger.

Then he said softly, 'It's lovely hair, not the colour of any carrot I ever saw. It's the colour of amber with the sun shining through it. You and I have things in the past that we want to forget, don't we? Let's live for today and not look back. Let's be friends.'

'All right. Friends,' she said. 'And I'll not look back.'

It was almost evening by the time he delivered her back at the Excelsior and Mrs White was adding up her own account books but amazingly she did not say a single word of protest or ask where Kitty had been. Freddy Farrell could, apparently, get away with anything he wanted.

The courtship of Kitty Scott and her Irish jockey was exciting and tumultuous. Every day when he was not racing, he came to the Excelsior Club and besieged her with gifts and lover-like words. Sometimes she was sweet to him and sometimes cutting. He never knew what to expect.

He pleaded with her to sleep with him. 'Haven't you heard what they say about jockeys being good lovers and since I'm a better jockey than the others, it would be a pity to miss what I can offer,' he said, leaning over the table in Mrs White's hall.

'I can manage to live without it, I think,' she said teasingly, for she enjoyed the cut and thrust between them, though she had already decided that she would give in to Freddy one day.

He laughed. 'You don't know what you're missing.'

'Then I'll not care, will I?' said Kitty. She was secretly glad that he refused to be rebuffed. He worked on the principle that water dropping steadily on stone gradually wears it away.

All through that late summer and autumn he plied her with compliments, took her out driving in the parks when her work was finished, and insisted on buying her many presents in spite of her protests.

One bright winter afternoon he arrived, bunch of flowers in hand, with a smart new dogcart pulled by a bobtailed chestnut cob and said, 'It's not a pleasure outing today. I need your help. I've decided to take a bigger set of rooms in London and want you to look at the ones I've found.'

She raised her eyebrows. 'But what about Camden Town?'

'I've not lived there for a long time. I got tired of Peg's cooking. I've a place in Newmarket because I have to go up to try out horses but I need a smarter base in London now that I'm making big money. I want a place with some style and who better to tell me what's stylish than you, my beauty.'

'I'm thinking of moving on myself,' she said sweetly.

'Where to? Let me move in with you or come with me,' was Freddy's reply.

She looked innocent. 'I was thinking of going back to Scotland actually.'

This time he was the one who laughed. 'No you weren't. You'd be like a fish out of water up there now and anyway, you can't leave me. I'm meat and drink to you. If you went away, you'd miss me something terrible. Who'd you be rude to every day? Who'd you treat like a lapdog if you didn't have me?'

'Some lapdog. More like a fighting mastiff,' was Kitty's reply. Then she asked, 'What exactly do you want? I've work to do even if you don't.'

'I told you. I want you to come and look at a suite of rooms off the Strand that I've been offered. I want you to run your woman's eye over them and put the fear of God into the landlady. You know me, I'm far too soft with women,' he wheedled.

'I've work to do,' repeated Kitty but she was intrigued by his suggestion because in spite of the game they were playing, she knew that she and Freddy would eventually become lovers. He was wearing her down, not that she had ever been really averse to the idea of sleeping with him, but she sensed that the more difficult she made it, the more Freddy would appreciate her once their affair began.

The point of decision was near because she was far too shrewd not to know that he wouldn't dance on the end of a string for ever. Besides, she had been abstinent for too long and was longing for love. Blood and passion ran strong in Kitty Scott's veins.

'Forget the work. I've spoken to Cora. She said I could borrow you for an hour,' he whispered in her ear.

The sun was out but there was a brisk, cold breeze so she wrapped herself in a beautiful iridescent shawl that he had given her and topped it with a big hat that she had to hold on with her hand as they bowled off down the street together, pursued as usual by the cries of Freddy's admirers.

He proudly held her hand – and she did not draw it away – when they walked into the imposing doorway of a large block of newly built flats in a narrow road leading down to the river from the south side of the Strand.

The landlady, Mrs Dawkins, was waiting to take them on a conducted tour through the rooms she had on offer; a luxuriously furnished bedroom with a vast half-tester bed, which Kitty deliberately did not allow her eyes to rest on, and a long parlour crammed with fussy bits of furniture, a bathroom, a kitchen and a little boxroom for a servant.

The nicest thing about the rooms was the outlook from the parlour, like a Canaletto painting of the Thames on which barges floated in slow and stately procession.

Mrs Dawkins knew who Freddy was and could not contain her delight at having such a famous person as a tenant, but she was not so sure about Kitty. Towards her she behaved with strained politeness, which much amused Freddy, who realised she had been mistaken for a tart. He played up to this and wasted no opportunity to caress her hand, kiss her cheek, and display her as if she were a trophy of war.

At last Mrs Dawkins could contain herself no longer and asked, 'When are you and Mrs Farrell thinking of moving in?'

'Oh,' said Freddy, 'there's no Mrs Farrell. This is my friend, Miss Kitty Scott.'

He turned to Kitty and asked, 'Do you like this place, my dear?'

She glared at him and snapped, 'What does it matter if I like it? I won't be living here.'

In fact, the apartment with its view of the river entranced her although the finicky little tables and low chairs got in her way wherever she turned.

Freddy looked at Mrs Dawkins and raised an eyebrow as much as to say, 'She doesn't want you to know the situation between us.'

Then they discussed the rent, which seemed extortionate to frugal Kitty, who longed to intervene and knock down the venal landlady's price, but she had precluded herself from the discussion and was furious at having done so.

After they'd been shown everything for a second time, including a luxuriously fitted bathroom with a deep white bath surrounded by intricate brass piping out of which jets of water spurted and made both of them widen their eyes in surprise, Freddy ushered the landlady out into the hall saying, 'Thank you, Mrs Dawkins. Could we have a look round by ourselves before we make up our minds?'

As soon as the door closed behind her, he advanced on Kitty with his arms widespread and whispered, 'Did you ever see a bath like that in your whole life? I can't wait to get into it. Come on, my beauty, let's christen this place properly.'

She laughed and threw her hat onto the bed like a quoit as Freddy bent down and pulled off his boots. Giggling they struggled out of their clothes – Freddy's white silk shirt and tight breeches; Kitty's skirt, boots and high-buttoned blouse.

Laughing and whispering, for they knew that Mrs Dawkins probably had her ear pressed to the door, they stripped each other naked. Hand in hand they ran to the bathroom and turned on all the brass taps. Water spurted out in all directions, hitting the ceiling and splashing over the tiled floor, as they clambered into the deep bath. It deluged over their heads, trickled down their backs and their legs, jets pelted off their flanks as they stood kissing and caressing under the flow.

Freddy had a brown, sinewy, tightly muscled body and his skin was very silken. Passion rose in Kitty as she pressed against him and ran her hands down his back to the neat, tight buttocks. She felt his penis, hard and long, against her groin. His hands were incredibly gentle, skimming over her, lighting here and there like little kisses.

When he entered her standing up, she threw her head back so that the long wet curls stuck to her back and moaned aloud in ecstasy. His mouth was against her shoulder and his teeth biting into her skin; his hands under her buttocks pulling her into him. She closed her eyes and gave herself up to making love.

They did not know how long it was before they ended up on the parlour floor, still wet, rolling in passion on the carpet with little tables crashing around them.

When he finally raised himself on his hands and looked down at her, Freddy groaned, 'Oh God, I hope Dawkins hasn't got her eye fixed to the keyhole. She'll have had an eyeful if she does.'

The sun streaming through the windows was gleaming golden on their skins by the time they were spent and lying side by side with their faces close together. Freddy's wonderful hands were stroking Kitty's long thighs and lifting the wet tresses of her hair as he whispered, 'You're every bit as exciting as I thought you would be. You're wonderful, Kitty Redhead. Come and live with me here and we can do this every day.'

'We'd kill ourselves with exhaustion,' Kitty told him, putting her hands on his tousled hair.

He kissed her. 'Not a bit of it. We'd get better with practice. Say you'll come Kitty and then I'll go out and tell Mrs What's-Her-Name that we'll take this place. It'll be hard to find another bath like that. I'll never feel the same about a tin tub in front of the fire again.'

Kitty laughed, pulling him down onto her. 'Come on, Freddy. I think we should try out the bed before we decide whether this place is suitable for us or not.'

They moved into their new home the next day. Kitty gave up her job with the Excelsior Club but agreed to Cora's suggestion that she go back once a week and bring the account books up to date. For that, she'd be paid the same wages as she'd received before.

Now that she was officially his mistress, Freddy took over her wardrobe. He liked her to look colourful and flashy, so he took her to the expensive shops of the West End where he picked out trailing cloaks of velvet or fur, gowns of vivid colours, and matched them with huge, outrageous hats loaded with ostrich feathers and artificial flowers many times larger than life.

'I can't wear that,' Kitty sometimes cried as Freddy made his selection, but when she was persuaded to put on the clothes and looked at her image in the long glass, she felt magnificent, for he was always right and the clothes he picked out made her look like the Queen of Sheba.

They stopped the traffic when she walked out with him and that was what he liked. The only flaw in their domestic life as far as Kitty was concerned was that Freddy was not happy unless he was accompanied by an army of flatterers, and every now and again the slatternly Peg and her bedraggled family would make a foray from Camden Town and settle themselves in at the flat on the Strand for the afternoon, eating, drinking and making a good deal of noise. They never seemed to annoy Freddy but they annoyed her very much indeed.

She was so taken up with her lover that she did not often think about Camptounfoot, but now and again she woke with a start in the middle of the night and found that she'd been dreaming she was back there. In her dream she was always in the orchard with the lichen-covered branches. Then she'd shiver and press herself against his back. She didn't know whether her dreams of home made her sad or happy.

## Chapter Seventeen

Everything happened very quickly for Marie after the painting exhibition.

It seemed that she had embarked on a runaway scheme that she was powerless to stop or control. All the decisions were taken by Mrs Roxburgh, who decreed that the girls should go to France as soon as possible in order to have three months' tuition before Paris went quiet at high summer. They would then return home and decisions would be made about whether they should go back again or not.

'I don't know if I'm doing the right thing,' Marie said to Tibbie when a letter arrived from Edinburgh giving details of travel arrangements. When she held this programme in her hand, it struck her that she was about to embark on a momentous adventure.

Surprisingly it was stay-at-home Tibbie, who had become much bolder after her trip to Edinburgh, who urged her on.

'Of course you should go. You'll enjoy it. It's a big opportunity for you and you might never get another chance,' she said encouragingly.

As her contribution to this momentous event, she took Marie to the best costumier and outfitter in Rosewell and bought her travelling clothes.

'You've been a good child to me and I don't want you going out into the world in old rags,' she said, though Marie had never worn rags in her life.

Marie, who was always ultra-cautious, was worried about money. 'I wish I could have sold the snow scene,' she said as she counted her takings from the exhibition and piled the money carefully on Tibbie's kitchen table. It was as if a good fairy were listening to her because next day a letter arrived from Professor Abernethy saying that the snow scene had found a buyer at last. He would give Marie the money when she came up to Edinburgh to join Amy for the start of their trip.

Saying farewell to Tibbie and her friends at Camptounfoot was hard. Bethya had gone back to London so Marie wrote a letter to

Berkeley Square promising to write again when she got to Paris. After that she went round the neighbours – the Rutherford family; Tibbie's brother the blacksmith and his family; and the bothy where Big Lily and Wee Lily stared at her with astonishment when she told them she was going to Paris. Wee Lily's baby boy was growing big and lusty, a greedy child who howled with frustration if denied anything he wanted. Tibbie shook her head when she talked to Marie about him.

'I doubt he's no' all there. There's something funny about him. He should be standing up and saying something by now but he's not,' she said.

As always the sight of the misery in which the bondagers lived depressed Marie and she did not stay with them long, but when she was halfway down the lane, she heard someone running behind her and Wee Lily came panting up.

'Oh Marie, Marie,' she gasped, 'if you see my lassie tell her I send my love and kisses. Tell her I miss her.' To Wee Lily, Paris was part of the big outside world into which Kitty had disappeared. She had no idea of distance. Paris might be as far away as Timbuktu or as close as Falconwood but she was sure that everyone there knew everyone else just as they did in Camptounfoot. She held her hands out in supplication to Marie who caught hold of them.

'If I see Kitty, I'll certainly tell her that,' she promised.

On her last night at Camptounfoot Tibbie asked, 'What are you going to do about David?'

'What do you want me to do?' asked Marie.

'I think you should go to see him and tell him you're going away.'

She shook her head. 'I don't want to. He'll try to stop me and I've made up my mind now. I don't want to have to argue about it or even think about it any more. I'll write him a letter and tell him what's happened. By the time he gets it I'll be on my way and he won't be able to stop me.'

Tibbie shook her head sadly. 'I always think it's best to do hard things face to face, lass.'

Marie protested, 'I can't. I'm afraid of him, afraid of what he'll do. I'd rather write.'

The letter she composed was short, saying that she was going to study painting for three months in Paris and would contact him as soon as she came back again. She sent her love and asked him to keep in touch with Tibbie.

Next morning when they rose in the grey mist of dawn Marie's resolution had weakened. She and Tibbie clung to each other and she wept. 'I wish I wasn't going. I wish I hadn't said I'd go to Paris.'

Wiping her eyes Tibbie said reprovingly, 'Now don't be daft. You're getting the chance of a lifetime, don't waste it. Everybody wishes you well and we're sure you'll be famous one day. Do it for us, lass.'

She had asked Jo to harness his pony and trap to carry Marie's bags to the station and in the grey dark they heard him draw up outside the front door, so they ran out to load the baggage onto the flat top of the cart and climbed up beside him. There they sat holding hands while Jo drove, making occasional gloomy comments about the weather.

At the station forecourt, he hefted the bags down and said to Tibbie, 'I'll wait for you, Tib, and tak' you hame again after the lassie's awa. See and do weel in Paris, and dinna forget Camptounfoot, Marie.'

Neither Marie nor Tibbie could speak as they waited on the platform and when the train arrived they clutched each other and sobbed but there was no backing out now. The die was cast.

In Edinburgh Marie left two bags in the left luggage office of the station and headed along Princes Street to Professor Abernethy's. He was delighted to see her, dancing about with his hands fluttering and exclaiming, 'My dear, I've a windfall for you. Last week I received a letter offering to buy the snow scene and a bag of money for the full price, sixty guineas! It was delivered by a bank messenger. Look... Here's the money.'

From a doeskin bag with a drawstring neck he poured out a pile of glittering coins that winked and sparkled on the dark wood of his table.

Marie clapped her hands in wonder. 'How amazing! Who bought it?'

The Prof shook his head. 'That's the strange thing. There was no name on the letter and the bank messenger didn't know who'd sent him. He was just told to come, give me the money and take a picture away with him. I was a bit suspicious as you can imagine but the coins are real enough.'

Perusal of the letter provided no clue either, for it was written in a clerkly hand on bank notepaper and seemed to have been dictated or copied.

'A mystery,' sighed the Professor.

'But a good one,' added Milly, scooping up the coins and putting them back in their little sac which she handed to Marie.

'This is wonderful,' she said. 'It means that I've more than enough money to keep me in Paris.'

At Murrayhill tempers were frayed as the last travelling plans were being laid. Amy sat sullen in the drawing-room and when Marie asked what was wrong, she snapped, 'We're being sent to London with Arthur and after that my horrible aunt's taking us on to Paris. They don't even trust us to travel on our own.'

She raised her voice so that her mother could hear and said again, 'We're being treated like children.'

Mrs Roxburgh was imperturbable. 'You'll travel to London with Arthur and your Aunt Agatha has kindly agreed to travel with you to Paris, for she knows that city well. She'll find you lodgings and register you at the class. Then she'll come home.' There was obviously no arguing against this, though Amy tried.

'We're perfectly capable of getting to London and finding lodgings in Paris for ourselves,' she whined.

'No, you're not,' said Mrs Roxburgh sternly. 'Neither of you know anything of the world and I want to be sure that you're in a respectable house. I owe that to Marie's brother at least.'

Marie looked up startled from the map of Paris she had been studying. 'To my brother? But he's not concerned in this. He doesn't even know anything about it.'

'Then you should have told him. It's only right that he knows because he's your closest relative, isn't he?'

It was then that Marie knew Mrs Roxburgh had not only received David's letter but that she believed, or at least sympathised with, whatever he said in it. A feeling of foreboding grew strong in her. Though members of the family were passing through the room there was no sign of Murray and she hoped that she would at least be able to say goodbye to him. Three months seemed a very long time to be away. Surely he would feel the same?

He did not appear at dinner and, unable to contain herself, Marie asked Amy about him. The reply was light. 'He's working like the very devil. His exams start next week but he'll come to see us off.'

Marie sighed. It seemed to her that Murray had done more work for his exams than anyone ever before. If he did not pass, it would certainly not be for lack of trying.

She slept little that night and when morning came she was dressed in her new travelling clothes before anyone else was up and sat for an hour at her bedroom window, staring down at the vast garden.

When she went down to breakfast, the sight and smell of food nauseated her. All she could take was a cup of tea. Then the servants started piling Amy's bags and trunks up in the hall, two carriages were waiting at the door and the family began to appear.

Oh joy! There was Murray. He looked so stern and handsome in a dark suit and long cape. Marie's heart leaped into her throat at the sight of him and she stood up from her place at the table to walk into the hall towards him. He greeted her with a smile.

'What an adventure for you,' he said cordially as if he were talking to a stranger.

'I wish you were coming too,' she whispered.

'So do I. Paris is lovely,' he said with a laugh. 'The time'll pass quickly,' he added.

His mother came sweeping into the hall, issuing orders. 'Murray, you ride with the baggage and make sure nothing's been left behind. Marie's bags are in the left luggage office at the station. You must take charge of them as well... Amy and Marie get in the first carriage with Arthur and myself. Now let's go!'

When Murray retrieved Marie's two bags from the left luggage office, he was obviously amazed.

'Is this all you're taking?' he asked, for Amy had three trunks and two bags, both of them bigger than Marie's.

'What else do I need?' she asked. 'When I want new clothes, I'll buy them, *if* I need new clothes. Things don't wear out in three months.'

'I hope some of your economy rubs off on my sister while you're away together,' he said with a grin and set off with a bag in each hand for the train, which was already steaming at the platform.

Everyone embraced. Marie found herself crushed to Mrs Roxburgh's bosom, pecked on the cheek by Mr Roxburgh and Amy's oldest brother and then, at last, in Murray's arms. He smelt of pomade as he bent his head to kiss her... on the cheek. Her lips stung with her longing to press them to his but she was very conscious of his mother's eyes on them.

'Goodbye, Murray. Don't forget me,' she whispered.

'I'll miss you. Have a lovely time,' he said in a formal voice. Then they were away.

The journey passed without incident except that with every mile they travelled Marie gained in confidence and Amy seemed to shrink into herself. While one girl enthused about the places they saw from the train window *en route*; while she relished the French coffee and sniffed the smell of French tobacco with delight, the other grew more and more disdainful, comparing all she saw to Edinburgh and never finding anything that equalled it.

The lodgings found for the girls by Amy's aunt, the snobbish Mrs Agatha Wyndham, were on the Boulevard Clichy in a large apartment owned by Madame Guillaume, widow of a pedagogue. For them she provided a stuffy sitting-room and large bedroom with two narrow beds.

The sitting-room had a long window overlooking the street, but they were denied a view because Madame preferred to keep it permanently shuttered. The whole apartment smelt musty and airless, made worse by the underlying aroma of aged dog which came from the curly-tailed white Pomeranian, the landlady's constant companion.

'As soon as Aunt Agatha goes home, we'll move,' Amy whispered to Marie when they first saw the room but they never did because French-speaking and apparently self-assured Amy was intimidated by Paris.

She walked the short journey from the apartment to the painting salon every day as quickly as possible and hurried home again at noon for the enormous meal which was always waiting for them in Madame Guillaume's gloomy dining-room where golden dust motes swam in filtered light coming from the lace-curtained windows. In the afternoons Marie drew while Amy slept and when evening came, they still stayed at home, sometimes playing cards with Madame.

Marie was frustrated because she felt life pulsating around her when she stood at the window, which she opened in spite of Madame's prohibitions, and stared down at the people passing by.

'Do come in,' said Amy when she saw her. 'Someone might see you standing there and Madame likes the window to be kept closed.'

'But look at those people sitting outside the café over there. Aren't they smart?' exulted Marie.

Amy would not look. 'They're horribly flashy. Don't let them see you. The French are awful about British people. They think every English girl is rich. They're quite unscrupulous.'

Marie hoped that Amy's caution would ease in time but she was wrong. In class she would only talk to other English-speaking students and if any French person, apart from a teacher, addressed a remark to her, she affected not to understand.

Marie, handicapped by her own lack of language, fretted when Amy would not interpret for her and remonstrated with her friend, 'Don't be so stiff with the French people. I think some of them are trying to be friendly.'

'We're safer with our own kind,' Amy told her stiffly.

On their third Sunday in the city the sun shone brilliantly and it was hot from early morning. By dint of much persuasion Marie managed to get Amy to agree to go sketching on the Île de France and they walked through a festively dressed crowd, across the bridge onto the island, and set up their stools and easels in the little garden behind Notre Dame, intending to draw the willow trees dipping into the river.

After they had been working quietly for about an hour, a group of young men came strolling over and stood behind the girls, making comments about their work. Marie saw Amy's cheeks colouring but since she could not understand what was being said, she did not mind. Then one of the men leaned over her shoulder and said, 'Very good, very good… *très bon.*'

She smiled up at him and he made a drinking gesture with his hand, inviting her to take a glass of wine with him. She brandished her pencil to indicate that she wanted to finish her sketch and with a grin he ran over to a café, returning a few moments later with a glass of white wine which he presented to her with a flourish. One of his friends followed with another glass for Amy.

Marie accepted her glass graciously and smiled her thanks. '*Merci,*' she said, for she had at least learned that word by now.

Amy, however, shook her head and said loudly in English, 'No, thank you. Take it away.' Then she turned reproachfully to Marie and hissed, 'You shouldn't drink it. They've been making very personal comments about us because they think we don't understand.'

Marie, sipping the wine, laughed and asked, 'What have they been saying?'

Amy's cheeks were red. 'They said I'm an amateur. Such impudence! They admire your work of course and they also like your hair.' It was obvious that Amy had not come out well in comparisons between the girls and she did not like it.

The young man who stood beside her holding out his offered glass suddenly said in accented English, 'But you too, Mademoiselle, are very pretty. Do not worry.'

'I'm not worried,' snapped Amy, rising to her feet. 'I don't have to worry what a party of Frenchmen think about me! I'm going home.' In her haste she scattered sheets of drawing paper over the grass and spilled her box of charcoal. The young men stood watching and, to her chagrin, none of them tried to help as she scrabbled about picking things up.

Marie sat still too. 'I'm staying here,' she said firmly.

'But you can't speak French. What'll you do? Take care you don't get into trouble. These men look very rough to me,' cautioned Amy, who was visibly angry and upset.

'I won't get into trouble. I know the way home. I'll stay here to finish my wine and my drawing. Then I'll come back to the apartment. Don't worry about me, Amy,' Marie said coolly.

When her friend stormed off, she started to draw again but the young men did not go away. Instead they settled down, sprawling back on the grass with their legs thrust out, and tried to speak to her. The one who spoke some English said his name was Pierre, and offered to be their interpreter. He invited Marie to have lunch with them in a café overlooking the river. 'You will be safe with us. We are also painters,' he told her.

That was the only encouragement she needed and soon she found herself in the middle of a group of rapidly talking, gesticulating young men, crumbling delicious crusty bread into oil and vinegar sauce while eating asparagus and sardines with her fingers. They filled her glass of wine again and she found her tongue, chattering in a sort of half-French, half-English, which amazingly they seemed to understand.

They laughed, they flirted, they asked questions and answered hers while the lunch-hour passed into afternoon and fashionably dressed women with little dogs on leads began to promenade along the side-walk in front of them.

'We're going to the studio of a friend now. Would you like to accompany us?' asked Pierre.

Marie turned to look at the café clock. 'Oh, goodness gracious! It's half-past four. Amy will be frantic with worry about me. I must go back to the apartment, I'm afraid.'

'We will walk with you,' offered Pierre but she shook her head. 'No, it's best if I go alone. I'm sorry I can't come with you, though. Perhaps some other time?'

She knew that sounded very bold but somehow, in Paris, it did not matter. She could be as bold as she liked.

'Where are you working?' asked one of the other men, whose name she had discovered was Luc.

'I'm not. I'm studying at the École des Peintures.'

A gabble of talk broke out over this and then Pierre told her, 'We think you are too good to be in that place. It is for fashionable dabblers. You are not a dabbler. We will meet you tomorrow at the same place and take you to see some real teachers if you like.'

For a moment she thought she ought not to accept this offer but her own misgivings about the salon surfaced, misgivings that she had been thrusting to the back of her mind ever since she arrived in Paris. It had not taken long to gauge the standard of work of the pupils who attended the same class as Amy and herself. They were all well-born young ladies who were even more unserious than the girls at Professor Abernethy's class and the teachers were more intent on gossiping and flirting with them than teaching them how to paint. The fees, Marie was beginning to fear, were a waste of money.

'All right. I'll meet you here tomorrow afternoon at three o'clock,' she said.

Pierre laughed. 'Not three. Meet us at seven. We are working, or sleeping, at three…'

She only hesitated for a moment. 'At seven then,' she agreed and hurried back to the gloom of Madame Guillaume's apartment.

It was best not to tell Amy about her afternoon, she decided, and Amy did not ask. They were scrupulously polite towards each other for the rest of the day and all of the next morning but as they were walking back at noon, Marie said, 'I don't think much of the standard of work in the class, do you?'

Amy screwed up her nose. 'It's all I want. Perhaps you're setting your sights too high.'

'I think it's a waste of time,' Marie protested.

'We're not all touched with genius,' was Amy's retort.

'Oh, Amy, I don't think I'm a genius. But I want to learn more. None of the teachers at that place seem capable of teaching me anything worthwhile,' she protested.

Amy sniffed. 'I don't think you've given them a chance. We've only been here for three weeks remember.'

Marie frowned, almost one month gone out of three. One month wasted when she could be learning something worthwhile.

And one month gone without hearing anything of Murray.

When they entered the apartment, however, there was a letter waiting on a tray in the hall. It was for Amy. She read it, folded it up and stuck in her pocket, saying casually, 'Murray sends you his love.'

'Is he well?' asked Marie eagerly.

'Very.' That was all that passed between them about him but Marie treasured the little bulletin from across the Channel and longed to ask Amy to let her see his writing, to let her read his message of love for herself but that would have been considered impossibly presumptuous. Amy's letters were private and she never left any of them lying about.

Their afternoon passed in boredom. 'Come and walk along the street to look at the shops. There's a lovely bookshop on the corner that I'd like to visit,' said Marie, but Amy shook her head.

'The books are all in French and you can't read French,' she said.

'I'm going to learn it,' Marie said with sudden resolve.

Amy laughed. 'You won't learn much in the time we've got left.'

'I might stay longer,' Marie said and Amy looked up with a light of interest in her eyes.

'Really?' she asked.

'Yes, I like it here and there's nothing much to go home for at the moment. Murray's so busy that I never see him...' Marie threw caution to the winds and spoke his name openly instead of carrying it around in her head all the time.

Amy flinched as if Marie had uttered an obscenity. 'I told you not to rely on Murray,' was all she said as she rose. 'I'm tired. I'm going to lie down.' Then she walked from the sitting-room into the bedroom next door.

She was still sleeping, or at least lying with her eyes closed, at half-past six when Marie dressed to go out.

'I'm going for a walk,' she whispered, leaning over the bed where her friend lay.

'Take care,' was the mumbled reply.

Pierre and Luc were waiting at the café near Notre Dame and when she arrived, they gave her a glass of wine and suggested that they go to Montparnasse where their friends lived. Marie agreed without hesitation because her initial liking for them was growing with further acquaintance.

Pierre, who had a streak of oil paint down his face but seemed oblivious of it, told her that he worked as a restorer, but Luc did less well because he scraped a living selling watercolours of local scenes to people strolling in the Boulevard St Germain.

He was very thin, his shoes were cracked and his clothes threadbare but he was ebullient and cheerful, always laughing and from the way his friend guffawed at his remarks, apparently very funny. Marie longed to know enough of the language to understand his jokes as well.

He'd been selling his work that afternoon from the rails outside the Church of St Germain and had seven francs in his pocket. He counted them out on the metal top of the café table and said he was going to buy the next round of drinks.

She demurred. 'Let me buy the drinks!' she said. It seemed awful to take Luc's last seven francs when she had a roll of francs in her purse. The men looked at each other and allowed her to pay.

'You are reech?' enquired Luc as he sipped his wine.

She laughed. 'Rich? Oh no, I'm actually very poor. Both my father and mother are dead and I was sent to painting classes by a lady who likes my work. I'm only here for three months and when the classes are over I'll have to go home again.'

Pierre understood what she was saying and translated for Luc who shook his head sadly. 'So you are poor like us! *Dommage*. A pity. We thought you and your friend were rich young ladies, Americans perhaps.'

Marie was shocked and remembered Amy's warning. 'Was that why you spoke to us?' she asked.

He laughed and admitted, 'Yes, at first, but then we saw your work and knew that you were serious. The other girl is rich perhaps? Her work is not serious.'

Marie shook her head. 'Amy's not rich either but she comes from a better-off family than I do. She'll go home and get married to someone but if I don't sell my pictures, I'll have to take a job as a governess or a schoolteacher if I'm lucky.'

Pierre reached over the table and grasped her hand, 'Then you really are like us. We are friends. Come, let's go to Montparnasse and you can meet other serious artists.'

Accustomed as she had become to the gloomy respectability of Madame Guillaume's block of apartments, the teeming building where Pierre's friends lived at the far end of the Boulevard Raspail in Montparnasse was a revelation. The ground floor was a laundry, the steamy, sudsy smell of which filled the whole place. The floors above were like a village because they contained warrens of rooms, full of people.

Built around an inner courtyard with all the windows looking into it, this community was entered through an arched doorway off the street and a twisting, precipitous stair led them up for floor after floor until Marie thought that her lungs were going to burst from the effort of climbing.

'How much farther is it?' she gasped.

'There are ten storeys but we are only going to level eight,' Pierre told her.

At last they reached their goal and she had to lean against the wall, fighting for breath while he knocked on a door of blistered wood. A woman in a long white gown and a brilliantly coloured turban answered. When she saw them she threw her arms around Pierre and kissed him on both cheeks, repeating the greeting with Luc. They introduced Marie and the woman kissed her too.

'This is Thérèse. She's a painter, and a very good one,' Pierre explained as they pushed their way into a room which seemed to be full of people. Canvases were stacked against the walls and a large half-finished work stood on an easel in the middle of the floor. It was of a glowing vase of flowers.

There were about ten people there already and all of them, women as well as men, were smoking little black cigarettes, filling the room with wreaths and coils of grey smoke. A large, portly man with very curly, grey-streaked hair half-sat and half-lay in a long chair by the window.

'*Entrez, entrez!*' he called out and looked at Marie with his eyebrows raised, obviously wondering who she was.

When Pierre introduced her the big man stood up, bowed, took her hand, raised it to his mouth and held it there for a long time. She felt herself colour beneath his scrutiny as Pierre told her, 'This is Adolfo Mancini, a famous painter, one of the best in Paris.'

Mancini pulled a face, 'Famous for flower pictures and I hate the smell of flowers. I have to paint with a peg on my nose or I spend all day sneezing! Isn't it bad luck that the thing people want to buy from me is the thing I least like painting.'

He spoke in French and Pierre translated for Marie, who murmured something she hoped sounded sympathetic. She could see from the picture on the easel that Mancini was an artist of great talent.

Thérèse called out something which Marie could not understand but actually was, 'Don't complain, Mancini. At least you're selling. Think of the rest of us.'

He turned to look at her and called back, 'You'd sell more if you spent less time with your lover and more at your easel.'

Everyone, including Thérèse, laughed, and she walked across the room to sit down in the lap of a beautiful young man with springing blue-black hair and the face of a fallen angel. He was at least twenty years younger than she and with a look of triumph on her face, she cupped his chin in her hands to kiss him on the lips before looking back at Mancini and saying, 'You're only jealous, Adolfo.'

Pierre sat down on a cushion on the floor and patted it indicating that Marie should sit there too. When she did so, he put a friendly arm around her shoulders and she did not draw away, for that would have looked too prim in such frank and uninhibited company. Someone put a glass into her hand and she sipped at the milky-looking liquid it contained. The taste was like the aniseed tea that Tibbie sometimes made from a herb growing in her garden.

'What is this?' she whispered.

'It's absinthe. Don't drink too much of it if you're not used to it. It's very strong,' he counselled. She took his advice and nursed the glass all evening.

Her heart was singing and it was midnight when she returned home. Amy was asleep. Next morning when Marie tried to tell her about the visit to the artists' colony at Montparnasse, Amy was dismissive.

'I think it's most unsuitable for you to be going about with people of that sort,' she said.

The idea grew in Marie's mind that the first thing she must do was to learn to speak and understand French. To help her in this endeavour she enlisted the assistance of Madame Guillaume's maid, Isabelle, who always smiled and nodded, whereas Marie had not yet seen one smile cross Madame's forbidding countenance.

Whenever she could, Marie followed Isabelle around, pointing at things and asking their names. Because she had a gift for mimicry, in a very short time she was speaking rudimentary French with a working-class Parisian accent which horrified Amy.

'It is really amazing,' she said scathingly one day after they'd had a disagreement about some trivial matter, 'how old sayings often prove to be true.'

'What do you mean?' asked Marie.

'I mean, sayings like "pride comes before a fall" and "you can't make a silk purse out of a sow's ear", that sort of thing, nearly always prove to be true in the end.' Amy's voice had taken on the silken quality that weeks of living with her had taught Marie meant she was trying to be nasty.

'I don't know. Perhaps you're right,' she said.

'Of course I'm right. People from poor backgrounds nearly always betray themselves in the end, no matter how hard they try.'

'Do they?'

'Yes, of course. I'm not meaning to be hurtful, but look at you. When you start speaking French you sound like a washerwoman... you really should try harder. Listen to the way Madame Guillaume speaks and try to imitate her instead of Isabelle.'

It was important to keep up a façade of friendship, so Marie bit her lip and said nothing but she was thinking of David's letter. That was what Amy was symbolically brandishing in her face.

While their friendship was seeping away like a receding tide, others were growing. She went to the restorer's workshop and watched Pierre giving a craquelure finish to what looked like an old painting but was actually a copy of one in the Louvre and he took her back to Mancini's where she met voluble artists who talked so quickly that her French could not keep up with them, but she enjoyed seeing their paintings. Mancini's work was her favourite and she would stand before his easel for a long time admiring his technique.

'You like my pictures?' he said to her one evening and she nodded vigorously.

'Very much, very much indeed.'

'You paint?' he asked. She told him that she did and that one of her favourite subjects was flowers.

'Ugh!' He screwed up his face. 'I am tired of flowers but there is always a market for them. Bring me a flower painting that you have done and I will tell you what I think of it.'

Next day, she abandoned the teaching of the salon and started to paint a flower still life, having bought a huge bundle of roses and delphiniums from the flower market on the Île de la Cité early in the morning. She kept them in a shadowy corner of the salon in a big vase of water that she changed every day. In spite of her care, however, they began to droop on the third day and she hurried to finish the picture before there was nothing left but stalks. It was still wet when she took it back to the apartment for varnishing and Isabelle threw up her hands in delight.

'I can smell them!' she cried.

'I hope Mancini can't,' said Marie but no one else understood her joke.

When she was varnishing the canvas, however, Madame Guillaume came into the bedroom and said stiffly, 'I do hope, Mademoiselle, that you do not intend setting up an atelier in my house. I do not like the smell of paint.'

That evening Marie went to Montparnasse and lugged the canvas up the flights of stairs. Mancini, as usual, was not alone. A thin woman wearing gold-rimmed spectacles on a face like a goat's was watching him paint. They looked up in surprise when Marie went in with her canvas and propped it against the wall.

'You said to bring you one of my flower pictures. Well, I did this one to show to you,' she announced.

Mancini sneezed, blew his nose on a vast red handkerchief and said, 'It is magnificent. You did this? You are my rival.'

The woman stepped across the floor and stood before the canvas. Her clothes, Marie noticed, were very elegant and expensive-looking and her long, narrow feet were clad in shoes of the finest, softest-looking leather.

'Hmmmm, remarkable,' she hummed beneath her breath.

'I'm not your rival,' said Marie to Mancini, 'because you can get colour and sheen into your pictures that I can't in mine. How do you do it?'

He laughed. 'You are asking my secrets! When I look at your picture I cannot believe that a woman painted it, it is too good.'

His female companion turned and said, 'Tell her Mancini. She'll work it out in the end. She's nearly there now.'

He shrugged expressively and said, 'All right. I do it with little dots of colour. I don't use strokes of the brush but I make tiny dots, thousands of them. It gives the glow, it gives the sheen. But it takes time to learn how to do it. I'll show you if you like but only if you work very hard.'

'I would like that very much but I'm afraid I won't be able to work in the flat where I live, the landlady doesn't like the smell of paint,' said Marie.

'Never mind her. Come here tomorrow,' said Mancini, but the woman gave a funny whinnying laugh and nudged Marie as she said, 'Beware. He's a goat of a man. He tries to seduce every woman he meets.'

Mancini fixed Marie with an earnest eye and told her, 'You come. I will not touch you because you are serious.'

The goat-faced woman laughed again and patted his bottom fondly. 'You are not all bad, old man,' she said.

Then she turned to Marie and announced, 'I too can help a young artist. My name is Félice St Laurent and I have a studio near here but I'm going south, tomorrow for two months. There are paints and an easel and canvases there. You can use them till I come back if you feed my cats. They do not mind the smell of paint.'

'That would be wonderful. Where is it?' asked Marie.

'Above the Café Flore at Montparnasse station. Come tomorrow morning. Ask at the café for Félice St Laurent.'

'You should not have accepted that offer,' joked Mancini. 'She asks everyone to look after her animals but what she does not tell them is that she has fifteen cats and they are all rabid.'

Next morning Marie did not go to class with Amy but hurried to Montparnasse where she found the Café Flore full of early drinkers. They all knew where Félice St Laurent's studio was situated and pointed above their heads. It was on the first floor with long windows to the front and the back, a little like Professor Abernethy's establishment except that this studio was full of a weird and wonderful collection of objects that seemed to fill up every corner.

Félice was inside, smoking a cigarette and stabbing at a canvas with a brush. She looked over her eyeglasses when Marie stepped through the open door and said, 'You're up early. I like people who are early risers.'

Marie's French was good enough to say, 'I was brought up in the country. Everyone rises early there.'

'I too am a country girl. I was born near Moustiers and go back there every summer. Now let me show you where everything is. I'll leave money for the cat food. Buy it from the fishmonger on the corner. Don't move anything in here. I know where everything is.'

Marie stared around at an incredible jumble of furniture draped with exotic pieces of material glittering with gold and silver thread; huge vases; spears; potted palms and rolled-up carpets.

'They're my props,' explained Félice. 'I paint portraits.'

As she spoke a stately black cat came strolling across the open section of the floor and rubbed itself against Marie's legs. 'Good, she likes you,' said Félice.

Marie stroked the cat. 'It won't be any trouble to look after her, she's so lovely,' she said.

'Oh there's more than her. I have eighteen of them but six are only kittens.' Félice was painting again and had an abstracted air.

Marie gasped, 'Eighteen cats! In here!'

It was then that Marie realised why Félice worked with the door open. There was a stench in the room that even turpentine and linseed oil could not drown.

Félice cocked an eye at her. 'You will still paint here?' she asked.

Marie looked around. In spite of the animals, the studio had the atmosphere of a place where serious work could be done. She'd clean it up and get rid of the smell.

'Yes, I'll work here. I'll look after them for you,' she promised.

Then the owner of all the animals handed her a key and a small sum of money, pulled a luxurious silk wrap over her shoulders, perched a beautiful hat on her head and sailed out of the door.

Marie sat down on the sofa and the black cat jumped onto her knee and lay purring happily. She surveyed her new haven with delight. Here, she knew, she would be able to paint in peace. Impatient to start, she put the cat on the floor and stood up.

There was a stack of primed canvases in a corner and she took one. Félice had left paints behind too and Marie lifted a brush. Inspiration was upon her and she started to paint the crowded and chaotic room.

She worked till evening and then went downstairs to buy the cat food. The money Félice left, she soon found, was not going to last for even one week because the fishmonger had parcels of fish awaiting her which cost more than Marie would have spent on herself for a week.

'Don't they eat scraps?' she asked.

He sniffed. 'Mademoiselle St Laurent only feeds her cats with the very best fish,' he said. Marie realised then that Félice was not so philanthropic as she seemed. If her rent was the animals' food, when she was in charge of them, they would eat scraps from different purveyors than the one their owner normally patronised.

It was dark when she reached home and Amy was reading in bed. She looked up and asked, 'Where on earth have you been? Madame is furious because you didn't come for luncheon or supper and the food was wasted.'

'I've found a studio. I'm going to paint there every day. I won't be needing lunch here any longer,' Marie said excitedly.

Amy exclaimed, 'You're not going back to the School?'

'No. I've given it up. I'm going to paint on my own.'

'I hope you've written to Lady Godolphin and told her not to pay any more fees in that case,' said Amy primly.

Marie said, 'I'll write to her tomorrow. I only found my studio today. I'd like you to come and see it with me. It's quite delightful – in spite of the animals.'

'What animals?'

'Some cats which belong to the owner. She's gone away for a few months and I'm looking after the place till she comes back.'

'What's her name?' asked Amy suspiciously.

'Félice St Laurent. The studio's in Montparnasse.'

Amy sat up in bed. 'Félice St Laurent! Are you sure? The girls at the salon were talking about her the other day. She's very well known. She paints portraits, good ones I believe. All the smart women sit for her. She makes a lot of money.'

They were friendlier and nicer to each other than they had been for ages as they undertook the journey to Montparnasse. Amy had received a letter from home that morning and read bits out to Marie.

'Murray thinks he's probably passed his exams this time. Things are working out well for him. Oh, yes, and he sends his love to you. He hopes you're not working too hard.'

'Is that letter from Murray?' asked Marie eagerly.

Amy folded it up and put it back in her pocket. 'Yes, it is. That's good news, isn't it?'

Marie's heart ached. Memories of him came flooding back. Why hadn't he written to her? Why would Amy not let her see his letter?

When they reached the studio her mood lifted again and she was eager to let Amy see her wonderful new discovery, so she ran up the stairs first and unlocked the door, throwing it back with a flourish. The smell that came out was nauseating and Amy reeled. 'Good God, it's like a zoo in there! You can't live in that.'

'It's all right when the air gets in. I'll open the windows and then you'll see.' Marie wanted Amy to like it as much as she did but the other girl hung back.

'Are you sure you won't catch something breathing this in?' she asked suspiciously.

Marie was opening windows and ushering out cats. 'Of course not. Do come in,' she said.

Amy stepped cautiously over the threshold and went straight to the jumble of furniture at the back of the room, exclaiming, 'But Marie, this furniture is exquisite. That's a boule cabinet! Look at that Louis Quatorze commode. And what a lovely sofa. Good heavens, there's a litter of kittens in it. What can that St Laurent woman be thinking of?'

'She doesn't care,' said Marie, who was standing back looking at the painting she'd done the previous day. It was good, as good as she'd thought when she left last night. Her spirits soared and she wished she could start to work again at once.

'Not care about a Louis Quatorze commode! She must be mad,' said Amy, who was pulling a length of shimmering material out of the jumble on the floor, 'And look at this. It's real silk gauze.'

Marie turned and said sternly, 'Amy, please leave everything alone. I promised I wouldn't touch Félice's things.'

Amy flounced towards the door. 'I can only imagine your upbringing makes it easy for you to live in a place that smells like a pigsty, but it makes me ill. I'm leaving,' she said and when Marie heard her footsteps disappearing down the stairs, she made no effort to stop her.

But the reproaches stung her so she rolled up her sleeves, lit the stove and filled a bucket of water from a tap in the hall, put the bucket on the stove to heat, went out to buy some soap and a scrubbing brush and set to work cleaning out the studio.

When she finished, everything smelled of soap. The cats hated it and sat on the window ledges watching reproachfully.

She painted at the studio every day and sometimes in the evening Pierre would come to call and she went with him to visit other artists.

She was becoming accepted in their circle and everyone called her Marie d'Écosse with a note of respect because they could see from the work she was doing in Félice's studio that her talent was impressive.

One Sunday afternoon they were climbing the stairs to Mancini's eyrie, when they heard a terrible noise coming from a flat on the sixth floor. A woman was shrieking and screaming, '*Putain, infidel...*' and there was the sound of smashing crockery and heavy thuds from behind the door.

Pierre looked at his friend and shrugged. 'It's Thérèse,' he said. 'She's fallen out with Tadi again.'

A particularly heavy thud made the floor rock when they were on the landing and a high-pitched scream stopped them in their tracks. '*Salope, vache,*' growled a man.

'No, no, take your hands off me,' screamed a woman's voice.

The door was unlocked and Pierre quickly pushed it open. 'Thérèse, are you all right?' he called.

'Come in. Save me from this brute,' she yelled and he ran into the room with Marie close behind him. Thérèse was lying on a bed with the black-haired man she had been kissing on the first night standing over her.

He was panting heavily and there was blood on his face from a long scratch that ran down one cheek.

'Save me, save me,' sobbed Thérèse, holding out bare arms to Pierre.

'What's going on?' he asked, turning to Tadi.

'The *vache* is mad. I'm not going to hurt her. She did this to me!' he growled, pointing to the bleeding mark on his face.

'He's a *putain*. He's been fucking another woman. Another two women in fact. I met him with one of them in the café and she told me he's been fucking her for a month!' yelled Thérèse, getting up on her knees and flinging a candlestick at her lover's head. It narrowly missed him.

'Get out you pig, get out and don't come back,' she sobbed, subsiding among the pillows again.

He ducked and said, 'I'm going. I don't want to stay with you. It's always you who comes crawling after me.'

'You're a liar!' she howled and appealed to Pierre, 'He's a liar, isn't he? I don't go crawling after him. Did you know about his other women?'

'Well yes, I did. Most people knew. He doesn't make any secret of it,' said Pierre. Tadi stood back with his arms crossed on his chest. 'I am irresistible to women,' he said proudly.

'You're a seducer,' sobbed Thérèse.

'Me a seducer! You'd been seduced hundreds of times before I met you,' he said ungallantly. Standing there, he looked handsome and disdainful as he glared at her with flared nostrils and rolling eyes like a mettlesome horse. His wonderful dark curls flopped over his brow and gave him the air of a romantic brigand.

Marie felt her stomach tighten as she stared at him. His hair was the same colour as Murray's, except that Murray always kept his neatly in place and would never have flaunted himself in such an arrogant way as Tadi now did.

Pierre turned to her and said, 'Come on, it's all right. It's just a lover's tiff.'

They headed for the door and Marie whispered, 'But are you sure she'll be all right?'

He laughed. 'Of course she will. He'll get into bed with her and they'll be as happy as larks in half an hour. They go on like that a lot,' said Pierre.

'So they don't mean it?'

Pierre shrugged. 'I suppose they do mean it at the time but it blows over. Tadi keeps three or four women on a string at one time and fights with them all. It's Thérèse's fault for being so silly about him. She's old enough to be his mother.'

'He's certainly very handsome,' said Marie, thinking of the furious demon lover Tadi towering over Thérèse.

'And a tiger in bed they say,' was Pierre's rejoinder. 'That explains it.' He was hankering after Marie, who was completely unconscious of his infatuation.

Later that evening Thérèse and Tadi came upstairs arm in arm as if nothing had happened. After a short time, however, he got up from her side and went over to sit next to Marie, lifting a stray lock of hair that was falling to her shoulders and saying, 'Your hair is like corn silk, such a lovely colour.'

She smiled and replied, 'I like the colour of your hair better.'

'You also have a lovely body. I would like to see your body,' he murmured, leaning closer to her. She flushed and leaned back.

He laughed. 'Do not worry. I am a sculptor, that is why I would like to see you. I would like to sculpt you. Will you sit for me?'

Marie saw Thérèse narrowly watching her from the other side of the room and shook her head. 'I've never modelled. I'm very shy,' she said.

Tadi sighed. 'You Englishwomen are so repressed. I am Hungarian and we are not repressed. We delight in our bodies! You should delight in your body It is a gift from God.'

'I don't think I'm repressed – and I'm not English,' protested Marie.

Tadi rolled his magnificent black eyes. 'Of course you are. You are afraid of men like all the women of your country. None of you enjoy yourselves in bed. No wonder all your men make love to other men.'

Marie wondered if she should stand up and walk away from him but he was holding her hand and pinning her down. 'I could teach you how to make love. I could teach you such skill that when you marry you will keep your man in love with you for ever. Are you in love with someone?' he whispered in a voice like honey.

She nodded her head. 'Yes, I am. I'm in love with a man at home in Scotland.'

He nodded. 'Ah yes, Scotland. They are even worse than the English in matters of love I believe. Does this man love you?'

'I think so. I hope so.'

'You *think* so. You don't know? He should be on his knees to you now because you are beautiful. I would be on my knees to you if you were mine. Why does he let you come here to Paris alone? He cannot love you enough.'

'He's different to the men here… He's very serious,' she said in defence of Murray.

Tadi snorted. 'You should forget him. It is bad to be serious in love. When you are in love you should be mad, careless, passionate, demanding. I am all those things when I'm in love,' he said but at that moment, Thérèse, with a purposeful look on her face, walked across the floor towards them, leaned over Marie and hissed, 'Take your hands off him. He's mine!'

Marie stood up, glad to be released from Tadi's grasp. 'I didn't have my hands on him,' she protested.

'Never do if you want to go on living,' was Thérèse's final threat.

The trees were in leaf along the boulevards and in the little squares of Paris; the street life of the cafés was in full swing; there was a wonderful lightness in the air that made it marvellous to be young and alive with work to do and friends to see.

Marie had never painted so well. As soon as she lifted her brush every morning, all her other cares and concerns disappeared. She even forgot Murray.

Pierre came to see her often and she was aware of his passion for her but did not encourage him. She wanted them to be friends but not lovers, though he courted her with tenderness that she greatly appreciated. He was also the greatest enthusiast for her pictures.

'You must show your work,' he said many times. 'Send one into the Salon des Beaux Arts. It won't be accepted because you've not made your name yet but on the strength of the refusal you'll be able to display at the Salon des Refusés. That's where all the best people show these days.'

Marie gave up the School completely. She wrote to Bethya explaining why she had quit the classes and received a sad little note saying that Bethya was sorry Marie had found the teaching at L'École so poor but hoped that her work had not suffered and that she was continuing to paint. There was a melancholy, a hopelessness, about the note that saddened Marie but she forgot about that too when she started to paint again.

She was drifting away from Amy and only appeared at Madame Guillaume's to sleep. Sometimes when she walked into the sitting-room she found Madame and Amy, who had struck up a sort of friendship, sitting whispering with their heads together. At the sight of her they jumped guiltily apart and she guessed they had been discussing her.

Without warning, one night in April, Amy said, 'Oh, by the way, I don't suppose this will worry you much but I'm leaving the day after tomorrow. I'm going home.'

Marie was astonished by this sudden decision and full of remorse that she had paid so little attention to her friend. 'But classes don't finish till the end of next month,' she protested.

'I know, but I'm going home to be a bridesmaid at a wedding,' Amy told her.

'Who's getting married?' Marie asked.

'It's Cousin Julia actually.'

Marie remembered the tall, disdainful girl dancing at the party in Murrayhill, the one who had the castle and the vast fortune.

'But I thought you said nobody would ever marry her because she's so frightening. Who's taken her on?' she asked in an amused tone.

Amy was standing at the window and turned slowly to say, 'It's Murray actually.'

Marie reeled. 'Murray! Your brother Murray?'

'My brother Murray. They've been bespoken for a long time, since the first Christmas we all spent in her castle as a matter of fact. I knew they were to marry this year but they've brought the date forward and they want me to be a bridesmaid. I've to go back now so that I can have fittings for my gown. Mama's arranging everything.'

Marie felt as if she had been hit in the stomach and it was difficult to breathe. She gasped, 'Arranged for a long time! Why didn't you tell me?'

'My dear, how could I? You've been mooning over him for ages, haven't you? I did try to warn you. We all knew he was going to propose to her when we went north and she accepted him, I'm glad to say.'

Amy's voice was light as if she were trying to imply that this was of little consequence to Marie.

The other girl's face was ashen and her voice was little more than a whisper. 'But he said he loved me… He said that we should wait till he found a position in a law firm and then he'd speak to your parents about us… He kissed me, in the summer-house when there was snow on the lawn… it was so lovely. He said he loved me…' Marie found it hard to understand what was happening to her.

Amy turned away, saying briskly, 'Don't be silly. He was only flirting. He can't help it. He does it all the time. Mama was very angry at him when she saw how you'd taken it. She thought it would be better if we came away to Paris and everything would be arranged by the time you got back. She hoped you'd meet some dashing Frenchman and be swept off your feet. She really likes you Marie… Oh, don't look like that. I warned you that he was fickle. You can't say that I didn't.'

'But I love him,' whispered Marie. Her world had crashed around her.

'You're being very silly,' said Amy. 'How can you deceive yourself about this? He's not given you any encouragement for months. You must have guessed it was nothing. If he was going to marry you, don't you think he'd have done something about it by now?'

'He said he would. I've been waiting.'

Amy looked interested. 'You're such an innocent, aren't you? You'll get over this. It was only an infatuation. You couldn't really have thought that you and Murray would marry. After all, there's such a difference between you.'

Marie stared at her one-time friend. 'What do you mean?' she asked.

'I mean you're from a very different background to us. Though Mama admires you as an artist and likes you as a person, she and Papa were really worried when Murray was mooning over you and they would have gone mad if he suggested marrying you...'

Even the insensitive Amy was beginning to falter a little when she saw that Marie's face was chalk-white and she was trembling all over like someone on the verge of a fit. However, she collected herself enough to ask, 'Your mother got a letter from my brother, didn't she? It was all right before that, wasn't it?'

Amy nodded. 'Yes, she did get a letter. She didn't like the idea much before but when she got that letter... when she heard about your mother being murdered by the navvy she lived with and all the rest of that scandal, she was genuinely shocked. She's a great believer in heredity is my mother...'

'That's not fair,' said Marie. It was all she could think.

'It wasn't only that, of course,' Amy told her. 'Julia's very rich. Murray's marrying money. He's the second son and he's ambitious.'

'But he's clever and he passed his exams. You told me he'd got a place in an office in Edinburgh,' Marie sounded stunned.

Amy shrugged. 'He failed the exams again in fact. He's working as a clerk till the wedding but he's not the type to knuckle down in an office all his life. This marriage is ideal for him. He'll be a gentleman of leisure.'

Marie felt as if her heart had been ripped from her body. She put a hand on her chest where the ache was and closed her eyes. Then, after a moment, she rose from her chair and walked slowly into the bedroom where she began pulling clothes out of her drawers and stuffing them into a bag.

Amy stood in the doorway watching and asked, 'Whatever are you doing?'

'I'm packing. I'm going to sleep in the studio tonight. I don't want to stay here.' Marie told her.

'You're being stupid. How will you be able to sleep with all those cats crawling over you?'

Marie turned and said fiercely, 'I'm not staying here!'

The last of the clothes were rammed into the bag, which would not shut, but she held it together with one hand as she turned towards the door. On the way out she paused and said to Amy, 'Will you do something for me?'

'If I can.'

'Will you tell Murray that he's broken my heart?'

She walked down the hall to Madame Guillaume's parlour where she rapped on the door. When the landlady answered it, she said, 'I'm going away, Madame. I won't be coming back.'

The sloe-black eyes were hard and unfeeling. 'Very good, Mademoiselle. But your rooms have been paid for till the end of the month and I cannot give you a rebate.'

'I don't want a rebate. I'm only telling you that I won't be requiring the rooms after Miss Roxburgh leaves.'

'Very good,' said Madame, closing the door.

Isabelle was in the hall when Marie left her key on the plate that lay on top of a large credenza.

'I'm going away, Isabelle,' she said. 'If any letters come for me, will you keep them please? I'll call now and again to collect them.'

Isabelle whispered, 'Yes, I'll keep them.'

Marie walked all the way to Montparnasse, through brightly lit streets, past busy cafés where people were sitting watching the passers-by. The bag she carried was heavy but she did not notice its weight. Her eyes were blank and her expression rigid as she trod the familiar pavements.

'I've been such a fool,' she thought over and over again. 'I shouldn't have believed him when he said he loved me. It was only a game for him.'

That was a painful idea but it hurt less than thinking that he had loved her and David's letter killed his love.

Amy's cruel words burned in her memory... navvies, murder, heredity... But it wouldn't matter to me if I was told that he was a bastard with bad parents. I would still love him for what he was, not for what had happened in the past to people he never knew, she thought.

Her rage against David mingled with her sorrow about losing Murray and confusion overtook her till she was barely able to remember who she was or where she was going. At last she could continue no longer and stopped at a café she had walked past many times before.

Throwing her bag on the ground she sat down in a metal chair by an empty table and stared blankly into space. Soon a waiter came and stood before her with his tray outheld and a questioning look on his.

'What would you like?' he asked.

She remembered the milky drink that tasted like aniseed. 'Absinthe,' she said. 'Bring me absinthe.'

He arched his eyebrows disapprovingly but brought the order, clear liquid in a thick glass tumbler and a carafe of water with which to mix it. Her hands were shaking as she lifted the carafe and when the drink was the colour of milk, she drank it down in one.

The waiter was standing with his back to a pillar watching her.

She nodded to him. 'Bring another.'

By the time she'd had four her head was swimming and all she wanted was to sleep. Standing up giddily she swayed as she bent to lift her bag and the waiter was beside her in a flash.

'Three francs fifty,' he said, indicating the little pile of saucers on the table that showed the number of drinks she'd consumed. She fumbled in her pocket and brought out five francs. When he handed her the change she shook her head. 'Keep it,' she said.

It was only a short distance from the café to her studio but she felt incapable of making it alone. Clutching at him she said in a slurred voice, 'Walk with me to the corner. I'm afraid I'll fall down if I go alone.'

He did not argue but tucked his apron up into his trouser waistband, winked to his friends and took her arm. 'Lean on me, Mademoiselle,' he said sympathetically.

At the street door of the studio he helped her put the key in the lock and tried to slip into the hall with her.

She pushed him away and told him, 'Go back to the café.'

He was angry and shouted insults at her through the door but she did not care. Safe behind the closed door, she laid her forehead against the wall and wept.

## Chapter Eighteen

After Marie went to Paris, Tibbie was depressed. Nothing could cheer her until the day Tim, Emma Jane and Christopher turned up in Camptounfoot to take her by surprise.

When the first flurry of excitement was over Emma Jane said, 'We heard that Falconwood House is for sale and Tim decided to come north before we started on the London project to see if he could make Mr Raeburn an offer for it.'

Raeburn, Falconwood's owner, had been one of the directors of the railway company that hired Emma Jane's father to build the bridge across the river Tweed. Since then he had frittered away his fortune and was known to be in need of money.

'We only want the house and its park,' said Tim. 'We don't want the farm but it should be easy enough to sell on. Laidlaw, Raeburn's steward, wants to buy it and he and I'll probably do a deal if I get it.' Tibbie gasped and clasped her hands. 'Imagine! You came here all those years ago as a navvy and now you're going to buy Falconwood!' Emma Jane and Christopher stayed with Tibbie while Tim drove off for a meeting with Raeburn. He was gone for two hours and when he came back, he was jubilant.

'I think we'll come to an agreement. He's asking too much but his wife's a sensible woman. She'll talk him into selling. They're going to let us know soon, so we'll sit it out till then.'

Next morning, news came that Raeburn had accepted Tim's offer. He was delighted and waving Raeburn's letter of acceptance he cried, 'We've got Falconwood. It'll be ours at the end of the summer. Raeburn says we can have a tour of the property tomorrow. You must come with us.' Though she'd lived almost in the shadow of the big house for her whole life, Tibbie had never even been in its garden, far less across its threshold.

The next day was brilliantly sunny and Falconwood looked its best as they drove through the gates and up the long, straight drive.

It was a Georgian house, built of weathered pale yellow sandstone, unenlarged and unchanged by Victorian fashion because Raeburn never had enough money for rebuilding.

The façade was two-storeyed and long, with a pillared door in the middle and two well-proportioned wings stretching out at each side in a u-shape. Because it was built on the side of a hill, the kitchen premises and staff rooms were below the façade level, at the back, looking out across the river valley.

Its park stretched in front of the house to the south, dotted with old trees, oaks and beeches, maples and chestnuts, that gave shelter to the sheep and cattle grazing in their shade. There was a walled garden on the west side with a little turret-like teahouse in one corner and it was full of fruit trees and old cottage-type flowers that had been established there for over a century.

Tactfully the Raeburn family were not in evidence when the new owners were shown around by the housekeeper, who turned out to be an old schoolfriend of Tibbie's. Because of their acquaintance she was a good deal more informative than she would have been to strangers and did not hesitate to tell Emma Jane which chimneys smoked or which rooms were bitterly cold in winter.

The house was beautifully proportioned and not large. It opened off to the east and west from a large central hall with pale-grey-and-white marble pillars and a black-and-white-tiled floor. On one side ran the drawing-room that opened into a smaller salon and a dining-room; on the other was a library, a parlour and a room that Raeburn used as an office, dominated by a huge rent table with drawers around its circumference. The bedrooms were all at the back looking down over the sweep of the river.

Emma Jane wandered around with her eyes dancing, not afraid to enthuse over the magnificent plaster ceilings and finely carved marble fireplaces which, the housekeeper informed her, were the work of the famous architect William Adam, who had also had a hand in designing the house.

Everything had been allowed to fall into disrepair, however, for there were greenish damp marks on the walls, soot marks above the chimney pieces and in the shut-up drawing-room a lovely old Chinese wallpaper was hanging in loose and forlorn strips.

Emma Jane was glad that she and Tim had husbanded their money carefully and would be able to give this jewel-box of a house the care it required. She had no ambition to modernise it, or to cover the pale pastel colours of Adam with the heavy wood stains and embossed wallpaper that were currently in vogue. She'd rehang the Chinese paper, repaint in the original shades and try to re-create the sort of life that had been lived there long ago.

Tim broke into her reverie by saying, 'Come and look out of this window, my dear.' Taking her hand he guided her to an eastern-facing window at the end of the dining-room and when they stood together in its embrasure, he pointed out.

There, in magnificent outline and bowered in trees, the bridge they had built together stretched over the tranquil river. It was a view of their creation that they had never seen before and they gazed at it entranced.

'Doesn't it look wonderful?' they said together.

–

A few days later Kitty received a letter from Tibbie which fascinated her, especially the bit about Falconwood.

She could think of nothing more suitable than that her hero Tim Maquire should own that lovely house which she knew well from her wanderings as a child.

She wondered if he would take over the farm as well, and what would happen to all the people she knew there: Laidlaw, MacPhee, the horrible Liddle? She still did not know if Walter Thompson was alive or dead.

Thoughtfully she folded up her letter and stuck it behind a china ornament on the mantelshelf. She was going out with Freddy and had to get dressed up in her best.

They were very happy together. They stayed in bed most of the day, then sallied out grandly to go shopping or to visit fashionable restaurants where Freddy picked at lettuce leaves and smoked cigars while Kitty sampled the menu. No matter where they went people knew him and he was greeted by claps on the shoulder and shaking of hands.

Marriage was not discussed between them. Kitty did not care because she did not want children. Freddy never asked about her precautions and she never told him. It was something she preferred to keep to herself, like lots of other things, including details of the bank account into which she paid the money she earned from the Excelsior Club and anything Freddy gave her when he came home flush with cash after a successful outing to the races. Sometimes he would come back with a leather satchel stuffed full of money and throw it on the bed with a whoop, crying out, 'I won today.'

His success grew till it seemed that any horse with Freddy on its back was a guaranteed winner and owners vied with each other to get him to accept their horses as his mounts. The public loved him and would have backed him if he turned out to race on a rocking-horse.

When he walked out with Kitty, the acclaim of the people on the street, who recognised him from drawings and sketches in the popular press, for he had an easily caricaturable long face, roguish eyes and a wide, wry mouth, sometimes made getting about difficult.

He loved his fans and distributed generous tips to any street sweeper, flower seller or poor beggar who greeted him on his way. Because of his generosity, his reputation with the common people grew even more.

Kitty was slightly piqued that he never asked her to accompany him when he went off to ride but that was something else they did not talk about. They kept parts of their lives separate. It suited them that way.

As the start of another racing season approached, he had to go to Newmarket to try out horses and they were separated for several days at a time. In his absence, Kitty took the omnibus to Whitechapel and sat at her old desk catching up on Mrs White's paperwork. It was often dark by the time she returned to the Strand.

One night she went back to find Freddy sitting in the dark parlour with a glass in his hand. He had been drinking and was in a foul mood, glaring when she entered the room and snapping angrily, 'Where the hell have you been to this hour?'

She took off her hat and stared at him in surprise. 'I've been at the club,' she said. She had never seen him so aggressive before and guessed it was the drink that had done it.

He stood up. 'Doing what? Entertaining the clients were you?'

She turned away from him. 'Of course not. I went to tally up Mrs White's accounts. You know perfectly well I do that.'

He put a hand like iron on her shoulder and whirled her round to face him. 'I don't want you going there. I want you here when I get back at night.'

She shrugged her shoulder in a vain attempt to dislodge hjs grip and told him. 'You don't own me. If I want to go to Whitechapel, I'll go. I was late because there was more work than I expected. Get your hands off me!'

He kept hold of her and shook her hard as he said through gritted teeth, 'How much does she pay you?'

'One pound a week.'

Freddy laughed. 'That's nothing! I give that to the man who blacks my boots. You don't need money. I give you anything you want.'

This time Kitty made a determined effort and wrenched herself out of his grasp. Her shoulder hurt where he'd been holding it. 'I want my independence. I like having my own money. It makes me feel free,' she told him.

He lunged towards her, eyes blazing. 'I don't want you free. I want you to be mine.' He raised his hand and slapped her across the face, a stinging slap that sent her head back. She reacted immediately, for her old practice in the boxing booth still stood her in good stead and Grandma's training had not been forgotten. With a swift jab to the chin she put him on his back. He lay at her feet, hand on his chin, looking up at her in astonishment.

'You knocked me down,' he gasped.

'And I'll do it again if you ever slap my face like you did just now. Nobody hits me.' Kitty was blazing with a rage that sobered him.

He clambered to his feet and put his arms round her. 'Aw, Kitty, my lovely Kitty, I was mad with jealousy. I thought you'd run off with another man. I've had a bad day. I never rode a single winner and I was sitting here burning up with anger when you came in. I didn't mean to hurt you, I really didn't. Forgive me, say you forgive me, please, please,' he pleaded.

He kissed her face, he kissed her hands, he crooned in her ear and of course she forgave him. They made up their disagreement in bed but in spite of Freddy's blandishments, Kitty would not promise that she'd stop going to the club. She was more determined than ever to keep her independence.

The thing about their life that really annoyed her was that Peg and her family still turned up regularly and it was obvious from their talk that they went to race meetings and watched Freddy in action. Kitty always stalked into the bedroom when those conversations began, for she could take no part in them.

May was warm but the beginning of June was hotter. Freddy rose early one morning to say to Kitty, 'Let's go up West to buy you a hat for the Derby.'

She gaped at him from the bed. 'For the Derby?'

He was knotting his stock. In defiance of the trend for ties that had come in with fashionable men, Freddy still preferred stocks. They were more horsemanlike.

'Yes, I'm riding in the Derby of course and it's next week. Don't you want to see me?' he asked.

She sat up excitedly. 'Of course I want to see you. What's your mount called?'

He laughed. 'Five Per Cent.'

'Will you win?' she asked.

He shot her a sharp look. 'I could. It's a good horse. It all depends.'

'On the other horses, I suppose,' said Kitty.

'On more than that,' Freddy told her.

He crossed to the bed and tickled her. 'Come on, get up. I want to buy you a hat that'll stop the old Prince of Wales in his tracks. I want him to say, "Who's that lovely woman?" and his equerry'll reply, "That's Freddy Farrell's lady, Your Highness!"'

She laughed. 'You're silly. All right I'll get up, but I've fifteen hats already. I don't need any more.'

Freddy's face was unusually solemn. 'But this is to be a very special hat. This is to be a lucky hat. I want it to be the best and biggest hat in the crowd.'

They went out arm in arm and had a wonderful morning shopping for hats in Bond Street and Piccadilly with Kitty pirouetting in front of mirrors and Freddy admiring her while all the shop-girls admired him. Eventually he bought an immense hat of beechleaf-green straw with big cabbage roses around its brim and pale green ribbons fluttering from the back. It would not have been Kitty's own choice but Freddy had his heart set on it.

It was so heavy that Kitty had trouble perching it on her head and the effort of keeping it in place meant that she had to sail along with her back very straight, as erect as a dowager.

The effect delighted him. 'No one'll miss you on Derby Day. You'll be the best-looking woman on the course,' he cried.

To go with the hat, they also purchased a cream-coloured silk gown with fine voile ruffles round the neck, the wrists and on the skirt. The narrow waist was encircled by a sash of green the same colour as the hat. This ensemble was completed by a pair of ivory-coloured shoes and a silver-handled cream parasol with a ruched frill. When Kitty was arrayed in this outfit, she had to admit that she did feel like a queen.

On Derby Day Freddy was up at five, more nervous than she had ever seen him. He ate no breakfast, for he had to keep his weight down for Five Per Cent's light weight and he bustled about from first light, getting his things together, packing and repacking his leather satchel.

When she eventually emerged from their bedroom in all her finery, he stopped, stared and exclaimed, 'Aw, Kitty my love. That's wonderful. I want you to show yourself off today. I'm really proud of you.'

It was overcast but dry and Freddy, wrapped up in a thick overcoat so that he could sweat off another few unwanted ounces, drove them to Epsom in a high dogcart with a Hackney gelding between the shafts.

Though it was still early, not yet nine o'clock, in Piccadilly and along by the Elephant and Castle, traffic was flooding like a river into the streets… carts, vans, shandrydans, dashing drags and donkey carts, omnibuses and phaetons. It seemed like all of London was heading for Epsom.

The carts and carriages jostling for position in the streets were full of shouting people, some wearing false noses, paper hats or feather boas and waving paper streamers. Men, women and children were out to enjoy themselves and when they caught sight of Freddy they cheered him.

As they dashed along the Surrey Road, they saw many crashes and collisions. In front of them a four-horse phaeton turned upside down and deposited its cargo of two men and two women in the dust but none of them was seriously hurt, though their picnic hamper burst open and bottles of wine, a huge ham and lots of fruit went rolling along the road, to be gathered up by urchins who were cheering as they bore off their unexpected booty.

Kitty sat forward in her seat, loving the thrill and excitement. She greatly admired the way Freddy handled his horse, for he could make their equipage nip in and out of the traffic, overtaking everything in their way.

She clung to his arm and laughed. He looked at her and grinned back. 'This is our big day, my darling,' he told her.

When they arrived at the course, there were already hundreds of people on the ground. Some of them had camped overnight and Kitty saw sideshows and clusters of showmen's tents in the middle of the Downs. The strains of an oom-pah-pahing band drifted across to her ears and she gasped, 'I'm sure the boxing show's here. I must go to see if I can find Grandma and Sophia.'

But Freddy scowled and said, 'No, no, I don't want you wandering off. I want you near me all day. Don't wander off onto the Downs or you'll get lost. I want to see you all the time.'

She was perfectly well aware that she wouldn't get lost but she did not argue with him because she could see he was very keyed-up.

'Where are you going?' she asked.

'To Stamford's stables. That's where the "crack" is, but I'll come back to see you. I've a job that I want you to do later,' he told her.

She humoured him, patted his arm and said, 'I'll do whatever you say.' Proudly he took her hand and strode with her into the Grand Stand where he installed her in a reserved seat overlooking the course and the Royal Enclosure.

'I'll come back as soon as I can. Stay here,' he told her.

There was plenty to see, for the sun had come out from behind the clouds and was shining brightly. Under its beams throngs of people were arriving on the other side of the course and she could see buses and charabancs by the hundreds; coaches and gigs; flat-topped carts and donkey carriages all disgorging their human cargoes of men, women and children, bent on enjoyment.

The distant band began calling to her again… She wanted to see Grandma and Sophia very much.

There was no sign of Freddy. If she hurried, he wouldn't even know she'd gone. Gathering up her lovely skirts, she left the elegant stand and ran across the course to the part where the touts and tipsters, the loose ladies and their gentlemen friends, the families with children, the costers and the Cockneys were all gathering.

She strolled among them like an ocean liner among fishing smacks. Heads turned to watch her, fingers pointed behind her but she ignored the stares and whispers. Led on by the music she found the boxing booth in the middle of a large cleared area, surrounded by gypsy caravans and a canvas-walled square in which an immensely fat man in a bowler hat was roaring out his claims to know the winner of the big race.

Bill the busker was rolling up some ropes on top of the platform when Kitty paused at his feet to stare up at him with a smile on her face. He looked down in surprise. Such elegantly dressed women were not normally seen around boxing shows, so he raised his eyebrows and asked, 'Anything I can do for you, mum?'

'Don't you know me?' she asked, holding out a gloved hand.

'Bless me, it's Carroty Kate! Blow me, Kate, who's paid for all this?' he cried, leaping down from his platform and hugging her in delight.

She held onto her hat and laughed. 'Freddy Farrell actually.'

Bill threw back his head and guffawed. 'Trust you. I knew you'd do well. Freddy Farrell, the best jockey in the world. Nothing but the best for you, Kate, eh? Come on up and we'll surprise Grandma.'

He hauled her up and they hugged each other again, laughing and not caring that Kitty's grand hat was pushed to the back of her head.

Grandma was in the tent at the back, as wrinkled and intimidating as ever. She too glared at the fashionable apparition that came sailing through the tent door but then took a second glance and shouted out, 'Well bless my buttons, it's Kitty. Hey, Sophy, Kitty's here dressed like a duchess.'

Sophia appeared from the gloom at the back of the tent and stood with her hands on her hips and a grin on her face. Kitty ran towards them and hugged them both, while words poured out.

'What are you doing here?'

'I couldn't sit over there in the stand and not come to see you… How's business?'

'How's your business? You've done well by the look of you.'

When all the excitement died down, Kitty reached into her bag and said, 'I've brought you back the money you gave me when I ran away from Newcastle. How's Poole, by the way?'

Grandma grimaced. 'Bolted. It doesn't matter because we've got a new young punk who can punch his way through a brick wall. We've no girl though. Your place is still here if you want to come back… Not that it looks as if you'll need to.' And she laughed as she fingered Kitty's gown.

'I miss it sometimes. I miss the travelling,' Kitty told her, but Sophia piped up, 'You stay in one place, lass. That's the only way to gather moss.'

'Talking about moss, here's your money. I want you to take it because I've plenty now,' Kitty said, delving into the cream silk purse that she carried on one wrist.

As she snapped its tortoiseshell clasp she paused in astonishment because as well as the small roll of money that she had put there in the hope of seeing Grandma, a fat wad of notes lay at the bottom of the purse. It looked like hundreds of pounds because she could see at a glance that the bundle was made up of five-pound notes. Freddy must have slipped it into her purse before they left home.

She felt as if she had been carrying a primed gun through the crowd of hucksters and pickpockets of the Downs crowd. No wonder he hadn't wanted her to leave the safety of the stand. What if she'd lost it!

She hid her consternation and passed a ten-pound note to Grandma, who raised her eyebrows but accepted the money. 'Can't say I expected to get that back,' she said with a crooked grin.

The presence of the money in her bag worried Kitty and she knew she had to find Freddy.

'I can't stay. I've got something to do. Have a bet with my money on the Derby. Freddy's going to win. He's on Five Per Cent,' she told them and with more embraces all round, she left.

Back at the stand, the seats were almost all occupied and smartly dressed men and women strolled to and fro, showing themselves offand chatting with acquaintances. The Royal Enclosure had filled up.

She opened her parasol and held it over her head because the sun was out but she did not have long to enjoy the shade because Freddy, dressed in the Prince of Wales's racing colours of red and purple silk with gold epaulettes and hogging over his chest, came rushing up and hissed, 'Put down your parasol. It hides your hat. Put it down.'

Slightly bewildered, she did as she was told and put a hand on his arm while she whispered, 'Why did you put all that money in my bag? How much is there?'

He grinned. 'Five hundred, but it's for later. I'll tell you about it soon. Let's go for a walk now.'

There were thirty thousand people on the course, said Freddy, and all of them, it seemed, knew him, for he was continually accosted by fans asking, 'Will you win, Freddy?' or 'Are you trying?'

This question amused her and she looked at him with her eyebrows raised and repeated, '*Are* you trying, Freddy?'

'Of course I'm trying,' he said defensively. His well-wishers kept offering him champagne, brandy, any drink he cared to take but he always refused. 'I'll make up for it later,' he promised them.

He introduced Kitty to dozens of people, saying, 'This is my lady friend. Meet Miss Kitty Scott,' and her hand was shaken so many times that the palm of her pale glove was soon black and stained.

The Derby Stakes was the third race.

Freddy won the first for the Prince of Wales and the second for another owner. Kitty beamed with pride when she saw him streaking past the winning post and heard how the crowd yelled his name.

He's mine. That wonderful man is mine, she thought.

Each time he won he raised one arm above his head in a victory punch and Kitty ran down to be by the winner's enclosure when he rode in. After he'd been weighed, he came out to embrace her in full view of the people who were crowding around him. He even introduced her to the Prince of Wales, who, her keen nose noted, used the same pomade as Freddy.

It was when they were making a victory stroll after his second success that a voice rang out at Kitty's elbow and she saw blowsy Peg from Camden Town, with red-faced husband and assorted children in tow, pushing her way through to hug Freddy and exclaim, 'Isn't he a lovely man! Isn't he a hero!'

Kitty received them coldly, but to her wrath Freddy seemed genuinely pleased t;o see this motley crew, hugged Peg and then said to Kitty, 'Peg'll tell you what I want you to do for me before the big race starts.'

Kitty glared at him. '*Peg*'ll tell me what to do, will she?'

'Yes, I haven't time now. I've got to go. Listen to Peg and do what she says,' he said as he kissed her cheek and strode off towards the weighing room, leaving her with Peg, who was smelling strongly of gin.

'Come on, dearie, listen to me. You've got a wad in your bag, haven't you? What you've got to do for Freddy is go round the bookmakers and lay twenty pounds on him with as many as you can. He's not meant to bet you see… it's against the rules.'

Kitty frowned. 'Why can't I put the whole roll on with one bookmaker?'

Peg shook her head. 'Freddy don't want it done that way. You've to walk along the line and lay your money like I said. It's easy. Do you want me to come with you?'

'No,' said Kitty, 'I don't.'

And she strode off, seething with anger against Freddy who'd landed her with this commission and with Peg.

The bookmakers were all gesticulating arms as they yelled out the odds. They were dressed up to catch the eye in colourful suits, white bowler hats, and with huge flowers in their buttonholes.

'I'll give you three to one on Five Per Cent; I'll give you seven to one on Agra; I'll give you ten to one on Patrimony,' was the cry.

When Kitty started laying her money, Freddy's Five Per Cent stood at three to one. By the time she'd got to the third bookmaker, it was down to even money. Her mathematical mind told her that Freddy wasn't going to make a fortune laying five hundred pounds at evens but she went on doing what she was told. It was his money.

In her progress along the bookmakers she was followed by a crowd of people who recognised her as Freddy Farrell's woman and bet on him too in the belief that, if she was backing him, he was certainly out to win.

The odds fell to six to four on and then three to one on but by that time all Freddy's money was gone.

What's he up to? she asked herself as she went back to her seat to watch the runners for the big race parading on the emerald-green sward before the stand.

Brilliant silken colours, gleaming-skinned horses, bright sunshine and viridian grass made a magnificent spectacle as thirty hopeful entrants cantered past the cheering crowd. The favourites received the greatest ovation and hats were thrown in the air when Freddy Farell appeared on Five Per Cent, because by this time it was the runaway favourite.

Five Per Cent was a tall chestnut colt and Freddy set him off well in the owner's colours of green and gold.

The horse which received the worst reception, catcalls and yowls, was a leggy grey called Cockney Boy, ridden by a young apprentice in pale blue colours. Cockney Boy had no fanciers because he was famous for being what racing people called 'not genuine', always there at the finish, always looking as if he were going to win but if challenged, he always gave up.

The start was delayed because of the difficulty of getting thirty horses to stand in a line and jump off at once. At last they were off and the crowd fell silent, all eyes straining to catch the first glimpse of the runners coming round the far bend.

When they appeared, sitting tall in their saddles, whips in hand, the yelling started again. They charged round Tattenham Corner with the speed of a runaway train. Then one horse slipped and fell among the feet of the front runners. The crowd yelled, standing up in their seats and Kitty put her hands to her throat, worrying about Freddy. But her panic subsided when she saw his gold-and-green silks in the first group of galloping horses.

'Freddy, Freddy, come on, Freddy,' she called. Three horses were out in front now: Freddy on Five Per Cent; a jockey in red on Agra and the slim young lad in blue on Cockney Boy.

People in the stands were screaming, thumping their fists into the palms of their hands, throwing their arms in the air as the three challengers raced neck and neck in a line towards the winning post.

Agra was the first to weaken. With his nostrils distended and scarlet, he dropped his head and fell back half a length. Five Per Cent and Cockney Boy stayed on, straining to the finish. Kitty could see Freddy standing up in his saddle, but – was it her imagination? – he did not seem to be urging his mount on in the same way as he had done when he won the previous races.

His arm with the whip was flailing the air and his features were distorted into the image of a man under pressure but he lost the race by a head. Cockney Boy, a rank outsider which had started at a price of two hundred to one, was the winner.

It had only taken three minutes to run the greatest race of the year. After the horses flashed past the stand, there was a moment of silent and stunned disbelief as the crowd took in what had happened. Then a chorus of booing broke out.

Kitty shrank as she realised that they were booing Freddy. He was being booed because he had carried the money of most of the people at the races on his back and they thought he'd thrown it away. Some people were turning and staring at her as if she were responsible too.

People were flocking to the winner's enclosure, but she sat still, wondering how she could comfort Freddy in this terrible defeat. She was alone when he came walking towards her. He had changed back into his ordinary clothes and though people were shouting at him, he did not seem to hear. His eyes were on her face.

'I'm very sorry. It was such a close thing,' she said.

He took her arm and squeezed it tight. 'Thanks,' he said, but she saw to her surprise that his eyes were sparkling, not with tears but with triumph.

A gasp escaped her and he squeezed her arm again. 'Let's go home,' he said. 'I've no other rides today. Let's go back to London as soon as possible. I want to get out of here.'

Without a word she allowed herself to be led away. When they reached the place behind Stamford's stables where their dogcart was parked, she saw Peg waiting beside it.

'Aren't you the hero then?' she said, patting Freddy's back.

'Did you get it all?' he asked her.

'I did indeed,' she said, and indicated a battered leather satchel that lay on the dogcart floor.

'You took yours?' asked Freddy.

'I did and God bless you. My children pray to God for you every night, Freddy lad,' she said.

Bewildered, Kitty allowed herself to be helped into the dogcart and Freddy jumped up beside her as Peg's husband expertly backed the Hackney between the shafts and buckled up the harness. He was grinning and adding his praise to Peg's, which seemed very excessive for a man who'd lost the big race by a short head.

Kitty sat grim-faced and silent while Freddy negotiated the dogcart out of the field where carriages were standing. More insults, more shouts followed him but he did not turn a hair. When they were on the open road and bowling smartly along, she turned to him and said, 'You are a bastard, Freddy.'

He looked at her and now he was openly laughing. 'What do you mean?' he asked.

'You made use of me. You drew people's attention to me and gave me money to bet on you so people would think you were sure of winning and then you pulled the horse.'

'I didn't pull it. I just didn't help it,' he said. 'And I don't know why you're angry. We've made a clear profit of twenty thousand pounds today.'

'Why didn't you tell me what you were doing? Why did Peg know and not me?' she asked.

'Peg's bet for me in the past. She's great at it. And it was better that you didn't know. You'd be more natural then.'

'Did you fix it up with that jockey on Cockney Boy?'

Freddy nodded. 'Yes, I got a whisper that it was running well in gallops and they thought it would win if it wasn't challenged so I contacted the lad who rode it. I gave him a thousand and he's well content. He's won the Derby after all, so he'll keep his trap shut.'

She shook her head under the heavy hat. It was beginning to irk her, especially now that she knew it had been bought for the purpose of making her conspicuous. 'But doesn't it matter that people have lost their money on you?' she asked.

He raised his shoulders in a shrug. 'That's gambling. I won for them last year. I could win next year. This was a chance to make some real money and I didn't want to turn it down. I won't be able to go on race-riding for the rest of my life you know. I don't want to be a stable strapper when I'm old like other ex-jockeys. I'm going to be rich, Kitty, see if I'm not,' he told her fiercely.

'Doesn't it matter to you that what you did was crooked?' she asked.

Freddy looked at her. 'I don't know the meaning of that word but I know what having twenty thousand pounds feels like,' he said. 'Come on, Kitty, cheer up. Who've I cheated? Just a fat gent who owns a horse and thought he'd win the Derby with it. Why are you so mad?' He was genuinely surprised at her reaction.

'I'll tell you why I'm mad. I'm mad at you for not trusting me,' she said angrily. 'That's what makes me angry. You used me as if I was a silly child. You set me up. I went and told Grandma and Sophia to bet on you and all the time you had no intention of winning. You've made me into a fool. You dressed me up in this fancy gear to catch the eye when I went around putting money on you, that's all.'

Her temper was up and her face flaming. At that moment they were crossing the Thames and Kitty ripped the big hat from her head and skimmed it out over the bridge parapet. It soared into the air and then floated gently down onto the water where it bobbed along like an offering to a Hindu god.

Freddy looked askance at the flower-bedecked hat in the water and then he laughed. He laughed and laughed till the tears ran down his face. It was impossible for Kitty to sustain her rage against his merriment and though she did not laugh as well, she thawed a little.

That night they stayed at home and people came to them carrying parcels of money. They were the others whom Freddy had sent out over the course to lay bets on Cockney Boy for him. Kitty watched amazed as he sat at the table in the window counting the takings. Money lay in piles in front of him.

Each of his runners was paid off with a hundred pounds and when the last of them left around midnight, Kitty said, 'What I can't understand is why they bring you the money. Why don't they just keep it?'

Freddy laughed. 'They're afraid of me. If they didn't bring me the money, I'd send somebody round to break their legs. It's as simple as that.'

—

The owner of Five Per Cent was Mr Stanley Melford, a rich Yorkshire mill owner with a short temper and a long memory. He was furious at Freddy and although he could not prove his horse had been cheated out of the Derby, he had a shrewd suspicion that was the case.

The next time Freddy went to Newmarket to ride out he was met by Melford's trainer who shook his head and said, 'I've been told to keep you out of the yard. Mr Melford says you'll never ride for him or any of his friends again.'

Freddy affected outraged innocence but, in fact, he was not surprised. He still had his circle of aristocratic owners, however, including the Prince of Wales, who treated him with friendly condescension and for the next month he made superhuman efforts, pushing home horses that had never won for any other jockey.

He notched up seven winners at Ascot which almost re-established his reputation but he felt it was best to give the scandal time to die down.

'I think we should go away for a bit,' he said to Kitty when he arrived home after achieving his seventh winner. 'I've made enough money this year to take a break. Let's travel, Kitty.'

'Where will we go?' she asked, for the idea of going away always appealed to her.

'The toffs go to France, don't they? You and I should go to France, and swan about like they do.'

Kitty thought of Marie and said, 'My friend went to Paris. Maybe we could go there.'

Freddy shook his head. 'I don't want to go to Paris. I want to go to one of those smart resorts where old Eddie and his crowd spend their time. Let's go to Biarritz.'

They arrived in Biarritz in the middle of a rainstorm. Only a few old people in cane Bath chairs were in residence and they sat in the salon of a vast hotel staring bleakly out at lashing waves on the rocky seashore.

To Freddy's disappointment, none of the other guests knew who he was and looked askance at him and his flashily dressed consort.

By the second day he was ready to leave and told Kitty, 'I've been asking around. We'll go to Menton, that's where the smart people are.'

Three days later they were installed in the small but luxurious Hotel Prince de Galles on the seafront of Menton.

When he found out what the hotel's name meant, Freddy was delighted. 'What's good enough for Eddy is good enough for me,' he said as he threw himself back on the bed in their suite and opened his arms to her.

They still made love with the same fervour but Kitty was more guarded now. His Derby coup had never ceased to rankle with her and she was constantly on her guard against him trying to exploit her again.

In Menton, to her chagrin, all he wanted to do was gamble and she went with him to the casino behind the hotel but, while games of chance enthralled him, they did not appeal to her. She hated to lose and grew irritable if she saw him laying tall piles of counters on a single card, for he preferred card gambling to the roulette wheel, which he was convinced could be fixed.

His pleasure in the casino increased when some of the patrons found out who he was and, after that, everyone fêted him the moment he set foot in the establishment.

'I'm tired of the casino. I'd like to see the town. I want to go and sit in a café on the seafront,' complained Kitty after five days had elapsed and they'd spent every one of them sitting by tables covered with green baize.

Absentmindedly Freddy reached into his pocket and drew out a roll of notes. 'Go and buy yourself something,' he told her as he bent over the cards again.

Angrily she slipped the money into her reticule. She had no intention of spending it all and would keep it to swell her secret bank fund. She was preparing herself to leave Freddy, though she had not consciously made the decision yet.

He did not even look up as she walked out and that angered her too.

Outside the sun was brilliant. Neatly polled palm trees cast black shadows onto white paving slabs. It was four o'clock and the late afternoon fashion parade had not yet begun. She went into a café facing an azure sea and sat at a table in the cool shade of a green awning. The air was full of the smell of brine mingled with jasmine.

She stretched out her long legs and sighed while she sipped a glass of cold white wine. The corsets that Freddy liked her to wear, very tight-laced because they nipped in her waist and swelled out her breasts, chafed her, and she wished she could take them off. At least she could remove her hat, another flower-bedecked creation chosen by Freddy.

The long skewer-like pins were drawn out and she put it on another chair where it lay like a discarded bouquet. Then she shook her head and loosened her hair a little, closed her eyes and leaned back listening to the susurration of the sea and the rustling of palm fronds above her head. A deep feeling of peace overwhelmed her and she dozed.

She was wakened by the sound of someone coughing beside her. Her eyes flew open and she saw a smiling man standing by her table.

'Please forgive me, but I'm sure I know you,' he said.

He was standing against the light and her eyes were still shrouded by sleep so she glared at him, thinking this was only another male gambit.

'Go away,' she snapped.

'No, no, it's not what you think. Your name is Kitty Scott, isn't it? No one else has hair like that.' His voice was pleasantly accented and she recognised a Scottish lilt in it.

She sat up straight and tried to see him properly. He was a broad-shouldered upright man with a pleasant and honest-looking face, a broad brow and merry blue eyes. His nose looked as if it had been broken at some time and his smiling mouth had well-marked lips, full and humorous. His hair was brown and a bit stuck up at the back, like an exclamation mark. She was sure he spent hours trying to brush it down but never really succeeded.

'Don't tell me! You're from Camptounfoot, aren't you? You're Robbie Rutherford,' she gasped.

'I am. I'm glad you recognised me. I knew you at once though it's a long time since we met. I couldn't believe it. Kitty Scott sleeping on a café chair in Menton! I had to speak to you,' said Robbie.

She indicated the chair beside her and said, 'Sit down, it's wonderful to meet you. Have you been back in the village recently. How is

346

everyone there?' Now at last, she thought, I might find out about Walter Thompson.

He accepted her offer and sat down fastidiously, pulling up his smartly tailored trousers at the knees as he did so. Robbie was obviously a bit of a dandy in spite of the errant cow's lick of hair. 'I was back three months ago. I saw your mother and your grandmother. They're – they're all right,' he told her.

She looked sharply at him. 'All right? What does that mean?'

'Just the same I suppose. But the baby's not right… I mean it's a simpleton. Tibbie's been very good, paying for a lassie to look after it and everything or else it would be dead by now I suspect. Your mother doesn't bother about it much.'

Robbie saw he had upset her but hurried on. 'Big Lily's getting very lame. She worries about what'll happen when she can't work any more. She thinks she and Wee Lily'll have to go into the Poors' House. And the laddie too, of course. He'll never be able to work.'

Kitty's expression hardened. 'My granny was bitter cruel to me when I was wee,' she told him.

He nodded. 'I know. She's not at the Poors' House stage yet and Craigie's sisters still need her. She's worrying about nothing I think.'

'I don't care,' said Kitty sharply, but she did. She cared about Wee Lily. For a moment she wished she had not asked Robbie to sit down. She should have pretended she didn't know him and kept her peace of mind.

Robbie began telling her village gossip. Jo was dead, found lying by the riverbank with his fishing-rod in his hand; Bella and Mr Arnott had produced four children and she had taken over the shop from her parents. Kitty's expression changed with every piece of news she was given… sorrow about Jo, amusement about Bella.

'Tim and Emma Jane Maquire are thriving. They've bought Falconwood,' he said and Kitty nodded, remembering Tibbie's last letter to her.

'And they're spending a lot of money on it,' said Robbie slightly enviously, but added, 'I've bought a house too. In fact, I've bought a place here in Menton. It's called the Villa Favorita and I'm laying out a garden there. That's why I'm here'at the moment. Would you like to see it?'

She hesitated, thinking of Freddy and his reaction if he found out she'd gone off visiting with another man. Then she made up her mind. Freddy was quite happy gambling.

'I'd love to see your house, Robbie,' she told him.

He lifted her hat off the chair seat and stared at it. 'That's lovely, all flowers. Do you love flowers too, Kitty?'

She looked round at him and smiled so that her eyes danced. 'Yes, Robbie, I love flowers.'

He took her arm after she'd skewered the hat in place again and told her, 'Everyone at home'll be so pleased to hear that I've met you. They often speak of you.'

She stopped dead and her arm went stiff. 'You can't tell them. You mustn't say where you saw me.'

'Why not?' he asked in surprise.

'Because of Walter Thompson. Because I stabbed him.'

Robbie was genuinely amazed. 'Stabbed Walter Thompson? Who's Walter Thompson?'

'He worked on Falconwood. He tried to rape me and I stabbed him. That's why I ran away.'

Robbie said softly. 'And you thought you'd killed him, didn't you? Well, you didn't. There's not been a murder in Camptounfoot or anywhere near it since Craigie shot…'

'Since Craigie shot my father,' Kitty finished the sentence for him. Then she asked again, 'You're sure about Thompson? You're sure they're not looking for me?'

'I can assure you that if they were looking for you, I'd know about it. My mother tells me everything that happens in the village in detail. Nobody can sneeze but she reports it to me. Her letters are never less than five pages long and she writes every week,' said Robbie with amusement.

Kitty couldn't believe it. All those years she'd been sure Walter Thompson was dead. Even now she felt that there was a danger Robbie might be wrong but he kept telling her, 'No policemen ever came asking after you. You didn't kill him, Kitty.'

He was holding her arm and limping slightly as he guided her down the broad promenade. 'We'll take a fiacre. It's about a mile and a half,' he said. 'Isn't it odd that two people from Camptounfoot should meet in France?'

Robbie's property took her breath away. Villa Favorita was built on an outcrop of tumbled red sandstone rocks sticking into the sea. The low, rambling house had a roof of pale pink tiles and cream-painted walls. Green wooden shutters covered the windows. There was a jetty

348

at the tip of the point and a grove of umbrella pines on the east side. The garden rose up behind the house in a series of tiers, one above the other, each planted out with many different trees and flowering creepers.

The effect was magical.

Kitty stood on the flagged terrace and stared out to the expanse of sun-dappled sea with her eyes wide. 'This place is beautiful,' she sighed.

Robbie was pleased at her reaction. 'I think so too. When I'm away from it, I dream about it. I'm trying to make a garden here that'll be the best in the whole district. I'm growing things that no one else has. I have plants sent from India and China.'

Kitty smiled at him. 'It's the sort of place that you could go on working at for the whole of your life.'

He took her arm and guided her to the doorway which stood wide open in welcome. There was no one around, though somewhere in the distance she could hear a low murmur of voices and the clatter of pots.

The hall was cool, painted a pale yellow colour that seemed to reflect the sunshine outside. Its floor was laid with interlinking red tiles worn down by the passage of many feet. A long table stood in the middle of the floor with a shallow Chinese bowl on top of it. Facing them from the shadowy back of the room was a large painting. As Kitty walked towards it, she felt a strange pain grip her heart.

'Oh, it's the Three Sisters. That's just what they look like on a winter's day,' she said with a break in her voice.

Robbie said softly, 'Yes, Marie Benjamin did it. I think it's her masterpiece.'

Kitty walked closer to the picture and looked for a long time at the cloud of snow drifting down the flank of the nearest hill. Marie had painted the little gate that she so often walked through when she went on her wanderings. The hedge where she had her secret hiding-place ran along the foreground. The silver orchard was in the left-hand corner. She put up a hand and gently touched it.

Then she wiped some tears away. 'I miss it,' she said brokenly.

'You mean Camptounfoot?' he asked.

She shook her head. 'No, the land. I miss the land. It's part of me. I was rooted in it.'

'You could go back,' he suggested, but she said, 'No, not while my grandmother's alive.'

'I told you, she's failing. She's losing her powers,' he said, but she shook her head again.

'I hate her. I feel strong when I'm away from her but if I saw her again, I'd remember what it's like to be afraid. But this picture breaks my heart.'

He walked up to join her in front of it and said, 'It takes a masterly artist to make you feel like that. I like to look at it and remember where I came from. Mind you, I nearly didn't buy it. I walked away from the exhibition without it but it preyed on my mind and in the end I knew I had to have it. It's pitiless somehow. There are no illusions in it.'

Kitty understood. 'Poor Marie,' she said.

They walked out to the garden again and admired Robbie's plants before ending up sitting on the terrace, talking about the past and the people they knew. She told him she was in Menton with Freddy Farrell and he exclaimed, 'He's a magnificent horseman. Are you married to him?'

She looked him straight in the eye and said, 'No, I'm not. I'm his mistress. I don't think I'll marry him.'

Robbie did not turn a hair. 'It would take a very special man to tie you down,' he said.

When it grew dark a woman servant with white hair and a creased face brought out wine but talk of Freddy had brought Kitty back to the present and she got up hurriedly.

'He'll be finished in the casino now. If I'm not in the hotel, he'll be very worried.'

'I'll take you back,' said Robbie, ringing a bell to order a carriage and they bowled along the coast road in sweet-smelling, velvet darkness. Overhead, stars like diamonds spangled the sky and, in the sea on their left, little lights from tiny fishing boats sparkled on the water.

When they turned in at the hotel gate Kitty's heart sank, for Freddy was walking up and down the strip of lawn like a caged lion. Even from the distance she could tell that he'd been drinking and she knew what effect that had on him.

When he spotted Robbie handing Kitty down from the carriage, he came running over and grabbed the stranger by the lapels.

'What are you doing with my woman? I'll kill you, you bastard,' he fumed, lowering his head and preparing to attack.

Kitty stepped between them saying urgently, 'Calm down, Freddy. He's an old friend. We're from the same village.'

Freddy shook her off and charged at Robbie shouting, 'I'll kill you.' His fists were up and his face contorted with fury. Robbie put out an arm and held him back. 'Keep your temper, keep your temper,' he said soothingly, but Freddy was beyond reason.

He grappled with Robbie in an attempt to throw him to the ground and nearly succeeded, but between them Kitty and Robbie took hold of him, twisted him round and flung him away, while Robbie jumped into the carriage and disappeared, waving a hand in farewell.

She said furiously, 'You're mad. He comes from Camptounfoot. I met him in Menton this afternoon.'

There was no question of Freddy admitting to a mistake, however. He grabbed her arm and hissed, 'That's it. I've had enough of this. We're going home. We'll go tonight.'

And they did. That was the end of their holiday.

Neither of them were speaking to the other when they boarded the train for Paris at midnight.

Next day they were still sullen and though Kitty would have liked to spend a few days in Paris to look for Marie, she did not suggest it. They sat in brooding silence in the first-class waiting-room of the Gare du Nord till it was time to catch their train for the Channel packet and home. She saw nothing of Paris and burned with resentment. Not till they reached the Strand did he apologise and they made up the quarrel in bed, but afterwards she lay awake with one arm behind her head, wondering how much longer she would stay with him. The love affair was growing cold.

# Chapter Nineteen

If it had not been for the hungry yowling of the cats, Marie could have stayed huddled up on Félice's studio sofa until she died of starvation, but her sense of responsibility for the animals drove her out every day to fetch them food.

She slipped downstairs and hurriedly bought a few fish-heads from a stall in the next street before running back upstairs like a wraith. When she boiled the fish on the stove it stank out the room but she no longer noticed things like that.

The thought of eating anything herself was nauseating. She lay on the sofa with her face turned towards the wall and was dozing there when someone came rapping at the door. Her whole body went rigid and she hardly dared breathe in case the unwanted caller heard her. But there is some strange way in which people can tell when a listener lurks behind an unanswered door and the caller would not go away. The rapping continued, urgent and concerned. It was Pierre but she did not want to speak to him.

'Marie, Marie,' he called, but she sank her face into the pillow and put her hands over her ears. He went away at last.

Day after day, foetus-like she huddled, knees up to her chin, and thought and thought and thought until her brain ached.

She was thinking about Murray, reliving every meeting she had ever had with him, every word that had been exchanged between them. She turned her hand on the pillow and stared at the palm. He had held that hand. She put the hand to her cheek. He had kissed that cheek.

She clenched her fists and cried aloud, 'How could he? How could he? Why did he make me think he loved me when all the time he was hoping to marry Julia?' She could not bring herself to admit that she had made herself a willing victim.

It was money that had taken hint away from her, of course, she told herself. Julia was born to money, so she got Murray too. She, Marie, was born to poverty and got nothing. She sobbed her grief to the cats, who sat staring hard-eyed at her, waiting for their next meal.

Her mood became even more melancholy when she started to think about her brother's letter to the Roxburghs. She hated David with a hatred of such intensity that it made her whole body tense. Because she would not go to live with him, he had cut her off from the man she loved, from the family who had taken her up and shown her a life which she never imagined. In her confused mind, David, the past and Camptounfoot all became mixed up together.

'I'll never go back there,' she swore.

On the sixth day of her self-enforced isolation she made a sorry sight. The stall owners stared in astonishment at her when she went out to fetch the cat food. She had always been a clean and tidy young woman but now dirty clothes hung on her, her fine hair was tangled and in need of brushing, her manner *distrait* and strange. She did not notice their curiosity.

When she made her purchases and was hurrying back to the studio she heard a voice calling her name. Pierre came running along the street towards her with his arm raised in greeting. 'Marie, Marie, wait, wait. I want to speak with you,' he shouted.

Panic-stricken she ran like a greyhound up the stairs to the studio, slamming the door in his face, but this time he would not go away and knocked, frantically, calling her name. 'Marie, Marie. What's happened to you? It's Pierre. Let me in. Are you sick? Let me in and I'll help you.'

She stood in the middle of the room holding the parcel of foul-smelling fish to her breast and listening to his entreaties, but he was determined because he had been trying to make her answer the door for a long time and was shocked when he caught sight of her in the street.

When she would not reply to his pleading, he said loudly, 'If you don't open, I'll fetch a gendarme to break this door down. I really mean it, Marie. You need help.'

Still she did not reply so he said it again. 'Please open or I'll have to go to the police.'

When she heard his footsteps descending the stairs, she ran to the door and threw it open. 'Don't do that. I don't want any police here. Come in.'

The normally fastidious girl was unkempt and dirty; the room she had cleaned with such care was stinking and filthy. Cats were everywhere, sitting on window ledges, perched on the furniture, all yelling hungrily because of the smell of fish.

He thought she must have gone mad and tried to treat her gently. 'Come and sit down,' he said, leading her to a chair.

To his relief she was quite amenable though her eyes were swollen and her cheeks sunken. It was obvious she had not been eating.

'What's happened? What's wrong? Tell me and I'll try to help,' he said, taking the fish and putting it in the pot on the stove. The cats crowded round him yelling and rubbing themselves against his legs.

Marie started to weep, shoulders heaving. 'The man I love is marrying someone else. His sister told me. But he said he loved me. He said I was to wait for him...'

Pierre said sympathetically, 'He doesn't sound like much of a man. You're well rid of him.' He came across the room and knelt beside her, holding her hand.

She protested through her tears, 'No, he is a good man. I love him. He's marrying his cousin because she's rich. And his family wouldn't want him to marry me because my father was a navvy and my mother was murdered.'

Pierre said, 'Tell me about it.' And she did. The whole story poured out: Nanny Rush and Tibbie; David and his terrible letter; the Roxburgh family and Amy... and Murray, always Murray; how she loved him, how she didn't really blame him but tried to lay blame on other people.

Pierre listened, nodding and never contradicting, from time to time brushing her disordered hair from her face with his paint-stained hands. His love for her shone from his eyes but she did not notice it.

When her story was told, he asked, 'Have you eaten anything today?'

She shook her head surprised. 'No. I don't want to eat.'

'Did you eat yesterday?' he persisted. She shook her head again.

He frowned. 'This won't do. I'll take you out for a meal. You can't eat in here because it stinks.' The smell of cat and boiled fish was making him nauseous.

He combed her hair, brushed down her skirt which was covered with cat hair, found a clean blouse in her unpacked bag and persuaded her to put it on.

Then he helped her downstairs to the Café Flore where they found a table in a shadowy corner.

'What would you like to eat?' he asked, studying the menu. 'How about an omelette?'

She nodded dully. 'Yes, an omelette and could I have some absinthe please?'

Pierre frowned. 'An omelette and absinthe! That's not a very good mixture.'

She looked at him with enormous eyes. 'Oh please. I need a drink and absinthe will make me feel happier.'

She was visibly shaking so he decided to humour her.

'All right, absinthe,' he said.

When she finished eating, he asked her, 'What are you going to do? You can't stay shut up in that flat for day after day with those cats. Will you go home?'

She shook her head violently. 'No, no, I want to break away from everything in the past.'

'You should stay in Paris. No one here cares who your mother or your father was. All they know is that you're going to be a great painter. Stay here and keep on painting,' said Pierre.

She looked at him from tragic eyes. 'But what if I'm doomed? What if Amy's right about heredity. What if nothing will ever turn out right for me? I'm so scared.'

He briskly set about dismissing these notions. 'Forget all that. Start thinking optimistically and things will turn out better.'

She drank a second glass of absinthe. Perhaps he's right, she thought. If I concentrate on happier thoughts, things can only get better. I've still got money. I can afford to stay here for a while.

It was easy to feel happy when she had absinthe fumes in her head so she drank a third glass and when Pierre helped her up the stairs to the studio she was drunk. He made her lie down on the sofa and covered her with one of Félice's glorious wrappers, chased out the cats and banked up the stove before he went away.

When she woke it was the following morning and her head was splitting. Pierre returned with bread and milk, chivvied her to eat and when she did, he said, 'Now the next thing you must do is finish your picture.'

The food did make her feel better and after she'd tended the cats, she could lift a brush and make a few daubs.

Pierre had to hurry away to his own work. 'I'll come back tonight,' he promised.

But the moment the door closed after him, she put the paintbrush down again. Her head was throbbing, she could not concentrate. She knew what would cure her – absinthe.

In the café, she liked the feel of the glass in her hand and appreciated the numbing effect the alcohol had on her mind. She remembered someone had told her – was it Bella? – that her mother drank. It was easy to understand why.

A week later, made brave by drink, she walked to Madame Guillaume's and collected her letters from Isabelle, who exclaimed in shock at the sight of her.

'Oh Mademoiselle Marie, you are so thin! You look ill. Come in, come in. Madame is out and I'll give you something to eat.' The maid was horrified to see that the girl was not only looking ill but that she was drunk, for she staggered, slurred her words and reeked of absinthe.

Marie allowed herself to be plied with bread and strong black coffee which sobered her slightly and sharpened her perceptions.

As she walked back to the studio she realised for the first time that summer was over and autumn had begun. The trees in the Luxembourg Gardens were assuming their autumn colours of brown, gold and copper. Soon it would be winter. Slowly she walked along with her head lowered, kicking at fallen leaves as she used to do with Kitty long ago, now and again bending to pick up a gleaming chestnut and slipping it into her pocket like a treasure.

It struck her that though Félice had originally intended to stay away for only two months, her absence had stretched over the whole summer. Time had passed without Marie noticing it. Félice would return soon and then where would she go?

The next day she received a *petit bleu* from Moustiers. The telegraphed message said, 'Returning 15 October. Please vacate. Félice.'

She laid the message on the table beside the unopened letters she'd collected from Isabelle and did nothing about it, but fortunately it was spotted by Pierre on his daily visit. He lifted it up and read it with a worried expression on his face.

'Where are you going to go?' he asked.

Marie shook her head. 'I don't know.'

'But you've only two days left. She'll be furious if she comes back and finds you still here.'

356

'I'll get a place,' said Marie despondently.

'How? You won't unless you start looking. Have you any money left?'

She frowned. 'Yes, I have money. I haven't spent much.'

'Where is it?' he persisted.

She turned out her purse and her pockets – a search that produced ten gold pieces and about thirty francs.

'But I've still got about eighty English pounds in the bank,' she added when they'd counted up all the coins.

That was a fortune to him and he looked at her in amazement. 'You've been living here like this and you've all that money!' he gasped.

'I forgot about it,' said Marie weakly. Money had ceased to be important to her, as had almost everything else. All she needed was enough to buy a bottle of absinthe and a pile of fish pieces every day.

'Where is your bank?' asked Pierre, who was a practical man.

'In the Champs-Elysées.'

'Come on,' he said, pulling her to her feet. 'We'll go and take out enough to rent you a place to live.'

'But I don't want to be among strangers. I don't want to have to speak to people,' she groaned as he hurried her along.

He paused and looked at her. 'Would you like to live at Mancini's? It's friendly and people know you there. They won't bother you. And you might start working again.'

'Yes, I'd feel safe at Mancini's,' she said. The reason she'd done nothing about Félice's message was that she was afraid of ending up again in dark and gloomy rooms like Madame Guillaume's. Though Mancini's building was ramshackle and none too clean, it was not disapproving.

'Let's go,' said Pierre, hauling her downstairs and onto a passing omnibus.

They took out some of her money and then went to Mancini's where she was lucky. An old woman who sold flowers in the street had died recently and her room was empty. When she opened the door, Marie said, 'Oh yes, I could live here.' It was the first sign of real animation she had shown for weeks.

The room contained only a sagging bed, a wooden chair and a little table with a pottery jug on it. A pot-bellied stove with ashes spilling from it stood in one corner and a big window looked north, the best aspect for painting. It was a homely place and there was an atmosphere

357

in it that reminded Marie of the security she'd felt when she lived with Tibbie.

'I'd like to live here,' she told Pierre again.

The owner of the building was Mancini and he did not need any persuading to take Marie on as a tenant. She paid fifty francs as an advance and was told that another fifty would be required on the first day of every month. If no relatives of the old flower seller turned up to claim her bits of furniture, she could have them too.

When all was arranged she seemed transformed, laughed gaily and flung her arms around Pierre saying, 'Thank you very much. I don't know what I'd have done without you.' For the first time since Amy told her about Murray's impending marriage, she felt that there was some point in living.

Pierre and Thérèse, however, were worried about her. The quick way she had gone from almost catatonic misery to high enthusiasm seemed unbalanced to them and Thérèse resolved to keep an eye on her.

'I'll watch her for you,' she whispered to Pierre when he turned to go.

Though spartan, the little room was clean and it was a relief that it did not smell of cats. Marie fussed around, going out to buy food and setting up her easel in the best possible light. Then, even before she unpacked her clothes, she began to paint again and there was no longer any hesitancy in her style. She did not stop until it was too dark to see what she was doing.

Next morning, Mancini looked in on her and found her putting the finishing touches to a picture of roses. He stood in the doorway with his arms crossed and said, 'I shouldn't have told you about the dots.'

She looked round and smiled. 'I'm glad you did.'

'That is a magnificent picture. You'd easily be able to sell it to one of the dealers on the Quai Voltaire for a thousand francs,' he said heavily.

She carefully signed it in the right-hand corner with tiny letters – 'M. Benjamin', as Professor Abernethy's friend had advised.

'Do you really think someone will buy it,' she asked.

'I wish I could say "no" but that would be a lie,' he said, walking away.

The news that Marie had painted a picture that was so good it put Mancini off his midday meal went round the colony in no time.

Thérèse was amused that their landlord felt upstaged by one of his tenants and told the story to Tadi, who returned that night from a visit to his family in Hungary.

His eyes lit up because he liked to hear such tales and he resolved to pay a call on Marie to see the picture for himself. He did not tell Thérèse what he meant to do, however.

Her door was ajar and he gently pushed it open wider so that he could lounge against the upright, watching.

Her sheet of pale hair was flowing down her back like a veil of yellow silk. It was poker-straight and so long that it reached her waist. She was very thin and her skin so pale it was almost translucent. She seemed to glow in the shadowy little room like a will-o'-the-wisp.

'You have made a difference here,' he said and came strolling in, idly fingering the drapes of bright colours which she had bought from the local flea market and placed over the chairs in imitation of Félice.

There was a pot of coffee on the top of the stove and without being invited he poured himself a cup, sipping it while he looked at the girl. His stare made her blush, for his eyes were very dark and soulful with long, girlish lashes and he could use them to devastating effect.

She was wearing a thin blouse deeply open at the neck showing the cleavage between her small breasts and her feet were bare. She looked as if she had only just risen from bed. His gaze made her very conscious of her state of undress and she reached out to lift a shawl off the back of a chair and drape it over her shoulders.

'Aaah, do not cover yourself up. You have a beautiful body. I think I told you that before,' he said softly. Slowly he walked across the floor towards her and ran his hand down her bare forearm. 'It's like marble and so cold,' he said. His face was close to hers. She could feel the warmth of his breath on her skin. He smelt of the black tobacco all the artists in the building, except Marie herself, smoked.

She stood transfixed, watching his hand as it moved up to her elbow and gently turned her arm over so that the palm was upwards. Then he bent his head and planted a kiss in it.

'Hold that,' he told her and without thinking she curled up her fingers.

She closed her eyes and gave a little sigh. One hand cupped her head to turn it towards him. He kissed her on the lips.

'Do not be sad my pretty one,' he said. Then, as abruptly as he had appeared, he left and she stood like a statue in front of her easel with a stunned look on her face.

He did not come back the next day, or the day after that, but on a very rainy morning when the window glass was gleaming with a sheet of running water, he turned up again.

Her door was unlocked and she was arranging a still life on the table. Pierre had persuaded her to paint a few 'pretty' pictures which he offered to take to a dealer he knew.

While she was positioning some oranges and apples beside her pottery jug, Tadi materialised at her shoulder, reaching his brown hand over to adjust the setting she had made.

'No, let me show you how to do it. You must contrast the colour, like this… It's like eating food or making love, variety is necessary…'

She looked up at him, and tried to step away so that there was no body contact between them but he would not let her go. His arm went round her shoulders and he held her to him.

'Why are you afraid of me?' he asked, putting his other hand on her shoulder and gently squeezing the taut muscle there.

She shook her head. 'I'm not afraid.'

'But you are! Your muscles are so tight it shows you are terrified. You must let them go soft, loose, easy.' His hand ran down her arm, touched her waist and went on down her flank. She felt the muscles loosen out under his touch. It was magical.

He felt the relaxation too because he smiled. 'You see?'

His teeth were beautiful, unmarked and very white, contrasting with his sallow skin.

'I've come to ask you to model for me,' he told her but she shook her head.

'I couldn't pose. I'm too shy. I'm sorry.'

'I am not asking you to take your clothes off. I wish to sculpt your feet. When I was here the other day I saw that you have beautiful feet. I wish to make a model of them.'

'Just my feet?' She sounded disbelieving.

He nodded and laughed. 'Your feet only. Are you disappointed?'

The colour rushed to her face again. How she wished she did not blush so easily. It was disconcerting. 'Of course not. When do you want me to sit for you?'

He shrugged. 'I do not know. Soon. Perhaps tomorrow or the day after. I will come when I can. You can paint while I work. You will not even know I am here.'

Before he left he looked gravely at her canvas and said, 'You are very talented. But you are too virginal. You should paint with more passion. Perhaps you do not know what passion is?'

He did not come the next day or the next, but one evening there was a knock on her door and he stuck his head round to say, 'I have not forgotten about your feet. I will come tomorrow morning.'

He banged the door shut and she heard his footsteps running up the stairs and his voice calling out for Thérèse. She felt like a fish, being lured by an irresistible bait.

When he came he brought a beautiful pineapple, with bright green leaves sticking out of its top. 'You might want to paint it, or you might want to eat it,' he said, laying the fruit on the table beside the still life arrangement.

She thanked him and he sat on the floor in front of her. 'Take off your shoes,' he ordered. 'I will draw your feet.'

'But I thought you were going to carve them?'

'Not here. I only carve in my own place. Here I will draw them.'

They both worked silently for about an hour and then he rose, stretching his long arms and legs like a black panther. 'I need coffee,' he said and disappeared.

He did not come back that day, or the next. When he did reappear she was genuinely pleased to see him and pointed her paintbrush at the coffee pot on the stove and said, 'There's coffee here if you want it.'

He poured two cups, bringing one to her and holding it out in such a way that her hand had to go over his as she took it. The contact made every nerve in her body jump and Tadi smiled.

'May I draw your legs, up to the knee?' he asked.

'Yes,' she whispered and very gently he lifted up the hem of her skirt to reveal first her calves and then her knees.

'As I thought, exquisite, so pale, so fine, so elegant. You have the legs of a fine horse…' he said, letting his hand linger, cupping one of her knees and holding it softly. He drew for about an hour and then slipped away without saying goodbye.

That evening, when she was preparing her supper, he turned up again. His hair was tousled and his shirt open at the neck. She thought he looked handsome and wild, as Murray would have if he could have shed his restricting ambitions and polite Edinburgh manners.

Tadi came prowling over the floor towards her. She could neither speak nor move.

'Lie down,' he whispered and she walked to the bed where he helped her onto the mattress and arranged the coloured cushions around her.

'Show me your legs,' he told her.

She lifted her skirt and draped it over her knees. He stepped backwards and gazed at her.

Her racing heart was beginning to calm a little and she asked him, 'Are you going to draw me now? It's very late…'

He shook his head. 'No, I am going to make love to you.'

She made no protest while he climbed on the bed beside her and kissed her on the lips. His practised fingers loosened her clothes and slipped them off her till she was completely naked. Crooning gently as if to a child, he soothed her, relaxed her, made her yield herself to him and became her first lover.

The violence of the feelings he awoke in her surprised her. It was as if he had opened a capped well inside her heart, and all the love she had felt for Murray, all the frustrated passions of her life, came flooding out and overwhelmed her.

She was completely without shame or artifice. Because he told her how much he enjoyed her body, how he loved lying with her, she thought that by making herself available to him at any time she would keep him, she would win him away from his other women, for he made no secret that there were other women, many of them.

The thought of where he went when he left her made her want to scream and she clung to his arm pleading, 'Don't leave me, stay with me.'

Sometimes he cursed her and told her she was too easily seduced but he never stayed away from her for long and when he came back she received him with delight. When he found out about the money she kept in the room, he asked for some and she gave it gladly, not as a loan but as a gift. She thought that if she gave him money, he would always return to her. She would have done anything he asked.

If days passed without him coming to her, she was inconsolable, pacing her room like a caged animal, weeping and heartbroken. When he did turn up, she threw herself at him, tearing at his clothes, pulling him into her bed. He could not believe that such an ice-cold, virginal-looking woman, who had been so reluctant to yield in the first place, could turn into such a demanding, abandoned mistress.

He tried to caution her when she cried aloud in passion, 'Keep quiet. No one must know about this or Thérèse will stab you. Keep quiet for God's sake.'

He was not coming to her so often now and his cooling terrified her. She began following him when he left the building, running along behind him, begging him to take her with him. Her insatiable passion and uncontrollable behaviour began to repel him. It was as if he'd let a genie out of a bottle and could no longer control it.

He said cruel things to her, comparing her unfavourably with other women, turning away from her when she reached out for him, deriding her, taking money and then telling her he'd used it to entertain one of her rivals.

Nothing worked. The more he abused her, the more eager she was for him. He began to wish he had left her alone and wondered about her sanity.

Pierre knew what was happening. She did not tell him but it was impossible to keep a secret in Mancini's building and Marie had no guile in her.

Thérèse waylaid him on the stairs when he was going up to see Marie and said, 'Tell me one good reason why I should not stab that girl.'

He stared at her. 'Because she's no danger to you. She's a very sad person.'

Thérèse sighed. 'You're right. That's why I haven't done anything to her. It's Tadi I should stab and you should stab him too.'

Pierre shook his head. 'What good would that do? It would only make her love him more. She has got to come to her senses alone.'

Thérèse nodded. 'I've told him to leave her but he says she won't let him. I really do think she's mad, Pierre. All of those brilliant artists are a little mad.'

When Pierre went into Marie's room she jumped up and came running to the door but stopped with a disappointed look on her face when she saw who stood there.

'You were expecting someone else?' he asked sadly.

'Yes, I was. I thought you were Tadi.'

Pierre groaned. 'He's broken many hearts, that man. He's without feeling. The only woman who's able to control him is Thérèse.'

'Oh Pierre, I love him,' she said brokenly. 'I don't care about his other women. I just want him. I can't face losing him the same way as

I lost Murray. If I'd gone to bed with Murray, I might have kept him. I'm desperate.'

'He might not come back,' said Pierre, thinking of Thérèse's warning to her lover.

Marie shook her head. 'He must come back. I love him.'

'But I love you,' groaned Pierre. He'd never said it before but now it didn't matter. She wasn't listening.

'You're my friend,' she told him. 'It's different with us. I couldn't sleep with you. I couldn't do the things with you that I do with Tadi. He's my lover...'

He grabbed her arm. 'Listen, he'll destroy you. He doesn't love you. He doesn't love anybody except perhaps Thérèse and if you don't stop this, she might do something awful to you.'

His pleas fell on deaf ears. Terrified that things might get out of hand and that Thérèse's patience might snap, Pierre went to see Mancini and explained the situation.

The big Italian groaned. 'Oh those virgins! They are so much trouble! The girl's out of her mind. I'm worried about her,' he said.

'She's lonely. She's got no one to love her,' said Pierre.

When Tadi had stayed away from her for two weeks, Marie started drinking absinthe again and fell down the stairs because she was too drunk to walk.

Alarmed by the unpredictability of her behaviour, Mancini told Tadi, 'Go to Budapest, go to Prague, go to Vienna, go anywhere but get out of Paris till she gets over this. If you're not here, she'll have a chance to forget you.'

'Women do not forget me easily,' said Tadi.

Mancini spat at him and pushed him out of the door.

One of the other women in the building told Marie that Tadi had gone away.

'How long for?' she whispered.

'Who knows? His family have a castle in the country outside Budapest. But he'll come back. He always comes back to Thérèse eventually.'

When the mornings were dark and wet she did not bother to get up, but huddled in bed listening to the rain on the window. Her excursions into the outside world were to get money from the bank so that she could buy absinthe.

One day she made the disturbing discovery that she was down to her last ten pounds. That night she completed a still life with a pineapple and when Pierre arrived she asked him to sell it.

He returned in an hour with five hundred francs and said, 'Do another. The dealer likes your work. He'll buy everything you paint.'

She didn't paint another, however, because five hundred francs would keep her in absinthe for a long time.

Rather than face Isabelle's disappointed face, she asked Pierre to collect her letters. The little maid was delighted to see that Marie had a respectable-looking male friend and handed over a couple of envelopes. They were both from Tibbie.

Marie put them on the table but never opened them. She did not want to be reminded of home, she did not want to be reminded of anything.

Pierre worried about her. 'You are ill. You're so thin. You are not eating.'

'Yes I am eating,' she lied, but he did not believe her and hurried to the café, where he bought bread and coffee. With disquiet he saw a line of empty absinthe bottles behind the stove where she was attempting to hide them.

One morning Thérèse heard her retching. She paused with her ear to the door. The retching went on and on. The door was unlocked, for Marie always hoped Tadi would come unexpectedly and surprise her.

The girl was bending over a basin beside the bed with her hair falling down like a curtain.

'You're pregnant. You're having his child. You foolish girl,' cried Thérèse angrily, for she had seen this sort of thing often enough to know what it meant.

Marie pushed her hair back with a thin hand and stared up. 'Am I?'

'Of course you are. You didn't know any better, did you? You didn't take any precautions and *he* wouldn't.'

Marie shook her head. The possibility of a baby had never occurred to her. Thérèse was speaking urgently. 'He's been away for over a month and he wasn't with you for a long while before that. You must do something soon or it will be too late.'

'I can't think,' sobbed Marie.

'Then start thinking. You haven't got much time,' said Thérèse. Next day she appeared again in Marie's room and said abruptly, 'Get up. We've an appointment with a friend of mine.'

For a moment Marie thought she meant Tadi and sat upright in bed but Thérèse continued, 'She lives in the next street. It's not far.'

'It's cold. I don't want to go out,' Marie protested. But Thérèse would brook no refusals. She hauled off the bedcovers and said, 'Get up and get dressed. I won't leave here till you do. God knows why I'm bothering about you but you remind me of my sister who died a few years ago. Get up.'

Marie did as she was told.

They walked without speaking along two streets till they came to a narrow lane. At a green door Thérèse paused and rapped sharply. It was opened by a gypsyish-looking woman with curly black hair and large golden earrings, who gestured with her hand for them to come inside.

The front room was immaculately clean and warm with a glowing stove and stiffly starched white curtains at the windows. There was a gleaming tablecloth and white antimacassars on all the chairs.

'This is my friend who needs your help,' said Thérèse, gesturing at Marie. The woman ran her eye up and down the girl, frowned and asked her, 'You don't look well. Are you sick? Do you cough?'

'A little,' said Marie.

'Do you cough up blood?' was the next question.

'Sometimes.'

The interrogator turned to Thérèse and said, 'She is fragile. She could be consumptive.'

Thérèse's face showed consternation, for though she had known Marie was physically low, she had not imagined things were as bad as that. 'All the more reason for her to get rid of it,' she said.

Then the woman turned back to Marie again and asked, 'How far gone are you?'

Marie had not realised they were going to an abortionist. She'd only allowed herself to be swept along by Thérèse because it was too much of an effort to refuse. Now she panicked. 'I haven't made up my mind what I want to do about the baby...' she gasped.

The woman shrugged. 'From the look of you I'd say you're at least four months gone. You'd better make your mind up quickly.'

Confusion overwhelmed Marie. She had not considered what it meant for her to have a child. She looked at Thérèse and asked, 'What should I do?'

The answer was unequivocal. 'You should let Madame Robert do what she can for you. She is very skilled.'

They told her to lie down on a white-covered bed in the corner and Madame prodded her stomach. 'She's so small it's hard to tell, but it's four months as I guessed. It has to be done now.'

Thérèse helped the girl to sit up and said gently, 'Do you have any money?'

'Yes, I have some. How much does an abortion cost?'

'Three hundred francs.'

'I have three hundred francs.' It was all she had left out of the money Pierre brought her for the painting.

Madame asked, 'Do you want it done now?'

Marie shook her head. 'Not today. I'll come back with the money tomorrow. I want to think about it, to be sure that's what I want to do.'

When Thérèse took her home, she said, 'I'll come back for you tomorrow morning. Tadi will never help you and it's hard to bring up a child on your own. I know because that's how my mother brought me and my sister up. It was bad for all of us.'

The night was long and troubled in spite of the bottle of absinthe that she bought to make her sleep. When she went out to buy it, the man in the little shop eyed her speculatively as he handed it over.

'You're young to be drinking so much of this stuff. It's bad for you, you know,' he told her.

'It doesn't really matter,' she said.

When morning came she was snoring and was wakened by Thérèse crying out, 'Get up, fetch your money.' Marie did as she was told and soon they were out in the wet, grey street heading back to Madame Robert's.

As they reached the door, Thérèse said, 'Madame Robert knows what she's doing. I'll come back later to take you home.'

'I thought you'd be angry with me,' Marie whispered.

Thérèse shrugged her magnificent shoulders. 'I'm sorry for you. You're not like the rest of his women, that's why I'm helping you. If we don't help each other, nobody will.'

Madame Robert was very business-like, taking Marie's money first and then making her lie on the bed which was draped with a sheet of oilcloth. A large kettle was boiling on the stove.

Marie was shuddering so badly when she lay on the bed that Madame had to put a hand on her ankles to try to calm her. 'Let me give you something to soothe you,' she said and brought a tiny ball of black paste out of a saucer on the cupboard.

'Chew that,' she said.

'What is it?' asked Marie.

'Opium. It'll calm you down.'

The effect was miraculous. Not only was Marie calmed but her mind seemed to clear and she began to see everything in a different light. She even felt optimistic again.

When Madame saw that her patient's nervousness was abating, she said, 'Raise your legs and let me feel your baby.'

Before she could do what she was told, however, the child within Marie moved for the first time. It heaved round and kicked her side. She gasped and put her hands on the place where the movement had occurred.

'I felt it, I felt it!' she cried. Madame grimaced. She did not like aborting a child that was moving within its mother.

'Hurry up, raise your legs,' she urged, turning to fetch her instruments which were sterilising in the boiling kettle.

'I felt it, I felt my baby,' said Marie sitting up. All of a sudden the child became a living person to her. It was within her, depending on her. She could not have it ripped out and thrown away.

'Lie down,' said Madame roughly, but her patient was on the floor, barefooted and staring-eyed.

'I don't want it taken away. I want to keep it!' she cried, backing towards the door. She wrenched open the door and ran into the street leaving her cloak, her shoes and her three hundred francs behind.

## Chapter Twenty

There was a little furrow of worry between Tibbie's brows and Emma Jane, sad at seeing her old friend fretting, asked her, 'What's the matter? Are you ill?'

'Oh no, nothing like that. It's just that I've not heard anything from Marie and I'm sure she's in some kind of trouble. Of course I know I've no claim on her. I'm no blood relation or anything like that, but she used to write so regularly...'

'When did you last hear?' asked Emma Jane.

'More than four months ago.' Tibbie's face was deeply concerned. 'She's not a good letter writer but she's not left it so long before.'

'Does she keep in touch with her brother?' was Emma Jane's next question but Tibbie shook her head. She did not know the answer to that because she saw David rarely. The last time was a few months after Marie went away when he came to tell her that he was buying Henderson's Mill in Maddiston from old Adalbert. He'd seen to it that takings dropped for two years before he made his offer and Henderson had been relieved to get rid of it. Since then output had tripled.

Emma Jane said in a decided tone, 'Our carriage can take you to Maddiston. Go and find out if he knows anything about the girl.'

David was in the mill counting-house when Tibbie arrived and his expression hardened at the sight of her. Nonetheless, he seemed cordial enough as he ushered her into his private office and showed her to a comfortable chair.

She stared around, much impressed by his working place for it was like a gentleman's library with solid mahogany furniture, well-polished brass firedogs and fender, and gilt-tooled, leather-bound books on the shelves behind his desk. He too looked impressive in a dark suit and very white linen. He seemed much older than his actual years but that had always been his way.

'It's good to see you, Tibbie,' he said, wondering why she'd come. 'It's about Marie,' she told him.

'What's wrong with her?' he asked.

'I've not had a letter for months and that's not like her. I wake up at night worrying about her. I wondered if she'd written to you...' Tibbie was twisting her fingers together nervously as she talked.

He leaned back in his chair. 'No, she hasn't. It looks as if she's cut us both out of her life.'

Tibbie shook her head. 'She wouldn't do that. I wondered if you'd make some enquiries. You're her brother...'

'What sort of enquiries?'

'With those friends of hers in Edinburgh. You could write to them and ask if they've heard from their daughter. She went to Paris with Marie. They were only meant to be there for three months and that's more than a year ago.'

David frowned and pressed his fingers down onto the wooden top of his desk. 'Of course she should never have gone to Paris in the first place. Maybe she realises that herself. Perhaps she's run out of money and can't come home,' he said grimly.

Tibbie was prepared to grasp at straws. 'If that's all it is, I could send her money. Will you write to the Roxburghs and find out please, David?'

He nodded. 'All right but I think you're worrying unnecessarily. She s gone off and we'll have to accept it. She'll be moving around with swanky people who are better than us. That's what she liked.'

'You're not being fair to her,' said Tibbie, rising to go. He was annoying her. He saw her reaction and changed his attitude. 'I'll write today,' he told her placatingly.

A few days later he arrived at Tibbie's cottage and said solemnly, 'I'm afraid it looks as if you've been right to worry about my sister. I had a letter from her friend Miss Roxburgh today and it was quite upsetting. Apparently Miss Roxburgh came home a year ago and left Marie in Paris. She'd stopped attending her classes by that time and was going around with a very rackety crowd of people, artists who sold drawings off railings in the street, that sort of thing. Miss Roxburgh would have nothing to do with them.'

Tibbie was horrified. 'In that case she shouldn't have left Marie with these people. She should have written to you or to me.'

David raised his eyebrows. 'I don't think we can blame her. You know how stubborn Marie can be. Miss Roxburgh wanted her to return home too but she wouldn't. She quit their lodgings and went to live in some room that was full of cats. The Roxburghs didn't know Marie wasn't in touch with us.'

Amy's letter had scrupulously avoided mentioning Marie's anguish over Murray and the tone of her missive was tolerant and long suffering, as if Marie had given her a good deal of trouble that she was loyally glossing over.

'Cats?' asked Tibbie in a bemused voice.

David consulted his letter. 'Eighteen cats apparently.'

Tibbie leaned back in her chair with a gasp. 'We've got to find her, David. Something's very wrong.'

'I'll write her a letter,' he said solemnly. 'You have her last address in Paris, haven't you? You write too. Surely she'll answer one of us. This nonsense has got to stop. Eighteen cats indeed!'

That night, when Tibbie was trying to compose a light and non-accusatory letter to Marie, Emma Jane and Tim appeared at the cottage to tell her that Bethya Godolphin had died in Bella Vista, very suddenly of a heart attack. Both of them were weeping and Tim said with a groan, 'We've sent for Sydney. He wasn't with her when it happened. I know he'll be devastated…'

'And those poor children left without their mother,' sobbed Emma Jane. 'It's so terrible.'

–

Two weeks after Bethya died, Pierre made one of his periodic visits to Madame Guillaume's and collected Marie's mail, two letters which Isabelle handed over with good wishes for Miss Benjamin. Rain was pouring down and all the cheerful cafés were battened down against the cold; the trees in the Jardins de Luxembourg were leafless; no vendors stood on street corners and Paris seemed to be hiding from itself.

Back at Mancini's he found Marie huddled in bed. Her face was as white as a winding-sheet and the bones stood out prominently under strangely shiny skin; her blue eyes seemed enormous and perpetually anxious.

'Oh Marie,' he groaned, 'I'm going to fetch you something to eat. The café downstairs has cassoulet today. It smells very good.'

She grimaced. 'The very idea makes me feel sick.'

He sat beside her and held her hand. 'Then what would you like?'

'Chocolate,' she said. 'Black chocolate and a bright red apple.'

'I'll get them,' he said, jumping to his feet. 'While I'm away read your letters. There are two of them today.'

When he came back he was horrified to find her lying face down on the bed sobbing bitterly. On the floor beside her were pieces of paper as if she'd torn the letters up.

'What's wrong. Is it bad news?' he exlaimed.

She lifted her head. 'Very bad, very bad. The woman who sent me to Paris has died. I can't believe it. She thought I'd be a great artist and I've let her down badly.'

For a long time she had done no work. Canvases, some only half-finished and with the unvarnished paint cracking, were stacked against the walls. If a picture looked saleable, Pierre took it to the dealer who gave him cash for it. He knew that Marie's paintings were subsequently changing hands for ten times as much as he was paid for them but there was nothing he could do about it. She desperately needed money and he was not in a position to bargain too hard on her behalf.

She looked up at him and said, 'And my other letter was from my brother. He wants me to go home.'

Pierre looked down at the bits of paper and she explained, 'That's his letter. He'd like nothing better than to see me crawling home, poor and sick and pregnant... Oh yes, he'd look after me for the rest of my life but he'd never let me forget what I owed him.'

'You don't have to go back to him. You could marry me. I'll be a father for your child. VVe could go and live in the country together and forget all that's happened to you here. My copies are selling well now,' said Pierre desperately.

She stared at him. 'You're offering to marry me?'

'I love you. I'm doing fakes for an American. He takes them to New York and sells them as Caravaggios. By next year I'll have saved enough to leave Paris, to go to the south, to Arles perhaps. It's lovely there. The sun shines all the time. It would be good for your cough.'

'Dear Pierre,' she said softly, 'I can't burden you with another man's child. And I can't marry you because I don't love you enough.'

The baby inside her was restless, heaving about and kicking. 'In spite of that I'd be proud to take you and your baby,' he said simply.

But she shook her head. She still cherished the hope that Tadi would come back to her.

Pierre knew what she was thinking. 'He won't come,' he said and left, closing the door quietly behind him.

Tears flowing down her cheeks, she rocked herself to and fro for a long time but then she got up and went out for a bottle of absinthe. After she'd drunk half of it, she started to write to Tibbie.

The words in the letter were disjointed and scrawled across the page. Sentences began but never finished; huge tear blobs made the ink run. She would never have posted it if she hadn't been very drunk indeed. Tibbie received the envelope from the postman with delight. 'It's from Marie. Oh thank God! She's all right!' she cried out to him but reading what was inside changed her feelings, for the letter was almost incomprehensible, like the ravings of a lunatic. Sentences petered out; phrases were repeated over and over again... 'Poor Lady Godolphin, I owe her so much... I'm well and happy. Paris is beautiful. I'll stay here for a bit... Poor Lady Godolphin, she was so kind to me... I'm staying here for a little longer. I have cried and cried about poor Lady Godolphin. I can't believe she's dead...'

Then, at the foot of the page was written, 'I miss you so much, Tibbie. I dream about you and the cottage at night. I hope we'll meet again one day...' Shocked, Tibbie read it over and over again. Then she took it to Falconwood to show to Emma Jane, who tried to conceal her misgivings for Tibbie's sake but could not help saying, 'If someone was speaking to me like that I'd think she was drunk.'

'*Drunk!*' Tibbie was shocked. 'Marie never had a drop of liquor pass her lips in her life.'

'Then maybe she was just shocked and homesick. Bethya's death must have been a terrible blow to her,' suggested Emma Jane. She succeeded in soothing Tibbie's fears a little but not completely because she decided not to show David the letter. However, since he did not visit her, she was not put to the test.

It was a long winter, uniformly grey and wet. Towards the end of her pregnancy, Marie drifted into a state of suspended animation which made her more tranquil. Her frail prettiness returned, she stopped drinking and even managed to eat some of the food brought by the faithful Pierre, who still looked after her in spite of her rejection of him.

Thérèse had been furious at Marie when she ran away from the abortionist but as time passed, she forgave her, especially when she saw how pathetically helpless and ill the girl was. She or one of the other women in the building looked in on the girl every day to see that she was all right. All Marie's energy was concentrated on the baby who heaved around inside her. She spent hours sitting with her hands on her belly, feeling it swimming around like a vigorous little fish.

She could not stir herself to paint any more. The colours on her palette caked hard, the stacked canvases gathered dust. She was waiting, waiting, and hoping that Tadi would come.

She marked a chart of her pregnancy on the wall of her room and ticked off each day. Other ticks she made also represented the number of days since she had seen Tadi... two hundred and ten, two hundred and twenty...

Every morning she thought he would appear, every day she did not go out till it was dark in case she missed him. The nights were hideously long, made terrible by the yowls of cats and the hurrying feet of solitary pedestrians on the cobbled street beneath her window. If she was careful the money Pierre had got for her pictures would last till the baby came. She did not think any farther than that.

One dreadful, lonely night she remembered the relief she'd been granted by the opium that Madame Robert gave to her. Next day she slipped downstairs to the laundry and bought a bit from an old Chinese woman who worked there. After that she bought it often and spent her days in a daze. Pierre and the other women did not realise what gave her such serenity. They were only glad that she was not drinking so much.

She neither knew nor cared how her appearance had changed, for she never looked in a mirror. Her belly was sticking out as if she were carrying a ball under her dress but her arms and legs were stick-thin. Her beautiful hair was lank and her peaked face looked like that of a starving child.

The disease that Madame Robert had spotted in her had taken a firm hold during the winter and the cough was worse. She did not know that the pinkness which flooded her cheeks was not a healthy sign but a hectic flush. Nor did she particularly worry when she woke in the morning and found bloodstains on her pillow. When her cough got too bad, Pierre went to a pharmacy and bought her linctus but he knew that she would almost certainly forget to take it.

'Please marry me, Marie,' he asked again but she dreamily shook her head she said, 'I can't, Pierre. I'm waiting for Tadi, you see. When the baby's born he'll love me again.'

He rose angrily. 'I heard last week that he's gone to Berlin with some rich woman. He's even left Thérèse. Can't you accept that he's a bad lot?'

But it did not matter to Marie.

On a bright spring morning, Thérèse paused at her door and heard her groaning.

As always the door was unlocked so she rushed in calling out, 'Have you started?'

Marie had been sweating and writhing in bed all night and the tumbled covers were half over the floor.

'Help me, please,' she said through gritted teeth.

'How long have you been like this?'

'I don't know. It was still dark when I woke up. I can't move… it's so painful…'

Thérèse threw up her hands in horror. 'Have your waters broken?' she asked.

'The mattress is wet,' admitted Marie through clenched teeth. The pains were agonising. She felt as if her body were being torn in half.

'Then it's coming. We'll have to do something. I'll get a midwife.' Thérèse went rushing out and soon came back with a mild-faced little woman who was rolling up her sleeves as she walked into the room.

She took one look at the convulsing Marie and said, 'Oh dear, this is bad. I can't do anything with her. I think the baby's upside down. We'll need to take her to the nuns. They'll know what to do.'

There was a convent hospital for mothers and babies a short distance away so Mancini carried Marie there in his arms. She weighed next to nothing.

Gentle nuns received her. Through the spasms of agony that racked her, she knew she was being cared for, given medicines, put into a high bed, covered with a pure white sheet, her brow stroked, a sponge passed over her face.

She caught hold of someone's hand and squeezed it hard every time a convulsion racked her. She screamed and wished she could die so that she would be delivered from such torture.

After a prolonged and agonising labour, the child was eventually dragged out of her by forceps. She was so weak and ill that she did not know she'd had a daughter until the following morning, because she collapsed into merciful sleep and did not waken till twenty-four hours had passed.

When she opened her eyes she stared about in amazement. She was in bed, in a high-ceilinged room with windows down one side and a parquet floor that gleamed in the sunlight. A sweet-faced little nun bent over her and whispered, 'Do you want to see your daughter?'

Marie nodded. 'Yes, please.' It seemed a miracle that the bulge that had been in her belly and impeded her movements for so long should now have become a child, another human being. For a moment panic seized her because she had no idea how she was going to look after it.

The baby was beautiful, with an elegantly shaped head covered in Tadi's black curls. Its face was tranquil and it was sleeping peacefully because it was being suckled by a strong woman who had given birth on the same day as Marie and was producing enough milk for two.

The nun put the baby in Marie's arms and asked, 'What are you going to call her?'

Just as she had never speculated about her feelings when the child was born, she had not thought of a name either. She smiled feebly and said, 'I don't know. My mother was called Mariotta…'

'That's a pretty name,' said the nun.

Marie shook her head. 'But I can't call her that because my mother had a very sad life. No, I can't call her Mariotta.'

She felt as if that name carried some sort of curse with it. It would not be fair to pass it on to an innocent child.

'Call her after yourself then. Marie is a lovely name. Call her after Our Lord's mother,' suggested the nun.

'No, I don't think so. I've not been very happy either. I'll find another name for her. I know, I'll call her after Kitty. Then she'll be strong and brave.'

Though the child was feeding well, the nuns christened her that night. It was not the baby they were worried about, it was the mother. They wanted Marie to know that her daughter had been accepted into the care of the Church because they were afraid that she was going to die very soon.

When the doctor in charge of the hospital examined her, he shook his head and whispered to the nun by his side. 'Her lungs are riddled with tubercular lesions.' Then he patted Marie's shoulders and said more loudly, 'Lie down and sleep, my dear. You're going to be in the hospital for a little while longer.'

## Chapter Twenty-one

Freddy was beginning to irk Kitty though at first she denied this, even to herself. She found that more and more she wanted to be alone, to wander off and please herself where she went or what she bought. The constant company of Freddy and his noisy entourage was beginning to annoy her and she resented the role he had forced her into, the role of Freddy Farrell's concubine.

Peg and her family still turned up unannounced and uninvited at the Strand about once a week. They were prodigiously hungry and thirsty, maudlin in drink and unashamed in their flagrant flattery of Freddy.

She disliked Peg most of all because she was always conscious of the woman's pig-like eyes following her around, assessing her clothes, guessing at how much she cost Freddy.

'I hate the way she flatters you,' she said to him after one interminable visit, but he only laughed.

'Don't mind old Peg. She's kissed the Blarney Stone.'

'What relation is she to you anyway? Why does she have to come here with her starving – and thirsty – family practically every week?' demanded Kitty.

'She's my auntie,' said Freddy lightly.

'Exactly how?' persisted Kitty, 'Is she your mother's sister or your father's sister?'

Freddy frowned. 'Neither really. She's a sort of distant relation, a kind of cousin three times removed.'

'Then I wish she'd remove herself out of here for good and stop leeching on you because that's what she's doing. You can't owe her all that much surely!'

'Kitty,' he said irritably, 'don't make a fuss. Irish families are like that.'

He had always been a considerate lover and now he began to treat her even more ardently, from time to time even asking her to marry him.

The first time he did that she was genuinely surprised.

'I don't think that's a good idea. I'm not the marrying kind,' she told. He didn't argue and it seemed to her that he'd made the offer as a sop to her and that he was relieved when she did not take him up on it.

One spring day he came bounding into their apartment in high good humour. 'Melford's forgiven me!' he cried. 'He's asked me to go to Ireland with him next week. He's going to buy horses and wants me to go along and ride them for him.'

'That's good,' said Kitty, glancing up from a book she was reading.

'I'll be away for a month,' said Freddy tentatively and she had to fight not to show her delight at the thought of being on her own for such a long time. If he knew how the idea pleased her, he probably wouldn't go.

'Oh, must you?' she sighed.

'I'm sorry,' he said. 'It's an all-male expedition. I can't take you along.'

She pretended to be upset which meant that he went off feeling guilty and without lecturing her about what she should do and who she should see in his absence. He didn't dare.

While he was away, she spent her afternoons in the Excelsior Club and passed happy hours gossiping with the girls there. In the mornings, she luxuriated in the silence and emptiness of the rooms off the Strand or strolled round the shops of the West End.

One day she wandered into the imposing premises of a picture dealer in St James's and found herself transfixed by the paintings on show. She walked slowly in front of them, studying each with interest and though there were several she liked, there was not one that was anything like as impressive as Marie's view of the Three Sisters, in Robbie Rutherford's house.

She became interested in art and started to tour the dealers and galleries. When I make my fortune, she decided, I'll buy paintings. In the meantime she'd get her eye in by looking at what was good.

When she walked home from those outings she thought about Marie. Once or twice she asked dealers if they'd ever heard of Marie Benjamin but none of them had. I wonder what's happened to her?

said Kitty to herself. She knew she was a very different person to the girl she'd been at Camptounfoot and guessed that Marie would have changed as well. Would they still like each other if they met?

It was not till the third week of Freddy's absence that she had a visit from Peg and family. When she opened the ground-floor door she heard the sound of their voices coming from the stairs and her heart sank. She wondered if they had been told to keep an eye on her.

They usually came on a Sunday and it was only Thursday but there they were, sitting on the stairs, drinking beer from bottles and scattering scraps of food on the floor. Their attitude was that they were visiting Freddy's house. He paid the rent, they were his friends. Kitty would have to like it or lump it.

She lumped it with ill grace.

'I didn't expect you,' she said haughtily to Peg, who was unabashed.

'We just thought we'd pay you a call and see how you were doing without Freddy,' she said, rising from her perch on the top stair. Her husband was sitting beside her as was one of their daughters, a girl of about fourteen, and a villainous-looking four-year-old boy, who could have been anybody's. Peg called him 'Our Pat', but whether he was hers or one of her daughter's, Kitty had never found out.

Our Pat was scraping Mrs Dawkins' paintwork with a knife, for which he received a clip on the ear from Peg that made him howl like a banshee, and they all trooped after Kitty into the apartment.

She stood in the middle of the parlour floor with her arms crossed, determined not to offer them any refreshment.

'Well, you've seen me. Now you can go home again.' she said.

'Isn't this a lovely place? Hasn't Freddy done it up well?' said Peg to her daughter, who, Kitty realised, had not been there before. Other daughters had, but since they all looked very similar, she never could tell them apart.

'Oh yes, as well as being a great jockey, Freddy's a champion house decorator,' she said sarcastically.

'And so he is, so he is,' agreed Peg, who was smiling happily and settling herself into the most comfortable chair. Obviously she intended to stay.

'The brass is shining something lovely,' she said to Kitty.

'Freddy doesn't do it,' she said. 'We've got a maid for that.'

Peg rolled her eyes upwards. 'A maid, and Freddy from a little turf cottage! He's come a long way.'

There was nothing that could not be laid to Freddy's credit. Kitty felt her temper rise and said, 'I'm going out again soon. I think you'd better go home. Freddy's away at the moment so you won't be seeing him.'

'We know he's away,' said Peg, making no effort to restrain the grubby child from looking for sweetmeats in the little china boxes on the side tables. 'It's making my heart sore not to see poor Freddy. We've come to see you though.'

'Freddy's gone to Ireland,' snapped Kitty, ignoring the allusion to herself.

Peg threw up her hands. 'Of course, he's gone home! He's crossed the sea to Ireland. God bless him! Did he say if he's going to see his mother?'

Kitty had never heard a word about Freddy's mother but was not going to admit that to Peg.

'He didn't mention it. He's gone to look at some horses actually,' she said.

'And to see Eileen. He's gone to see Eileen and the little ones,' said Peg slyly.

'He didn't mention any Eileen,' said Kitty sourly.

But Peg persisted, 'Oh yes, he's gone to see our Eileen and the wee ones. He's so proud of them.'

'Who exactly is Eileen?' asked Kitty, though she knew she was playing straight into Peg's hands by asking the question.

Peg lifted an eyebrow and her ruddy face beamed in triumph, 'Sure don't you know that Eileen's my own daughter, our eldest girl and her father sitting over there is bursting with pride for her... She's Freddy's wife of course. She met him in my house but she didn't like England and went back to Ireland after they were married for a bit. He goes over to see her once a year or so and he's very good to her. Sends money every week and she's bought a grand little farm. She and the children live in luxury I can tell you. He's a good husband and father is Freddy. We all understand how it is with you and him. He's only human after all and Eileen won't travel.'

'The children? How many children?' asked Kitty in shock.

Peg looked round at her husband who was standing behind her with his hands in his pockets.

'How many is it now, Thomas?' she asked.

'Eight, the last I heard,' was his reply.

'And it'll probably be nine by this time next year if his past record's anything to go by,' laughed Peg merrily.

Kitty smashed her hand down on the top of the most fragile of Mrs Dawkins' tables and sent the china flying.

'Get the hell out of here,' she shouted and drove them before her like a herd of sheep, pushing them down the stairs with no regard for their safety. To her satisfaction she could see that she had even succeeded in frightening the terrible Our Pat, who was crying.

When their outraged voices died away, she slammed the door and leaned against it. Her mind was in turmoil... Eileen and eight children... a farm in Ireland... living in luxury... Freddy, you swine! she thought.

While he was courting her in the Excelsior Club, plying her with flowers and sweet words, he must have visited his wife. He might even have visited her after he and Kitty moved into the Strand. She did not know whether to laugh or cry. A few months ago she would have been devastated but now – what did she feel now?

She felt relieved. She leaned her back against the door and laughed.

Long ago she'd given up any idea of marrying Freddy, though she always believed that he would be the one who would feel rejected if the matter was ever seriously discussed. She'd been afraid of what he'd do should she ever try to leave but now Peg had handed her the excuse on a plate.

Outrage, that would be her reason. How could he live with her, propose marriage to her even, while he was married to another? If she'd accepted him, he'd have been a bigamist.

What made her really angry was the depth of Freddy's duplicity. Once again he had taken her in, used her, just as he did when he sent her to lay his bets at the Derby.

Her pride was hurt especially when she remembered Peg's snide comment about the family understanding the relationship between Kitty and Freddy. She was regarded as a home comfort, like an eiderdown or a pair of comfortable slippers, for the lord and master.

'Damn him, damn you, Freddy!' she shouted aloud, making the listening maid in the next room jump with alarm.

Then she stormed into the apartment calling, 'Get out the valises, get out every bag you can find. I'm leaving.'

She took with her every present he'd ever given her as well as the things for their rooms that they had bought together. She crammed every piece of her colourful clothing into bags and hatboxes, then sent the maid out to summon a cab.

For Freddy she left a note propped, on the mantelshelf. It said, 'I hope you had an enjoyable time with your wife and children in Ireland. Peg came round specially to tell me about Eileen. You should have told me yourself but you're a liar to the core. I'm going away. Don't try to follow me because if you do, I'll cut your balls off. Kitty.'

She was angry enough to do it too and the knife still rested in her skirt pocket.

It took two cabs to carry away all her possessions and she sent the contents of one of them to a furniture storage emporium that the cabbie knew. She and half of her extensive wardrobe went back to Cora White's, where she spent one night before finding a room a few yards along the road.

'If Freddy comes looking for me, don't tell him where I live,' she warned Cora.

In fact, it was a relief to get away from Freddy and make it look as if it were his fault. That let him off the hook and he would not pursue her too hard.

Of course he did turn up at Cora's the day after his return from Ireland. Kitty was there, working in the office, totting up columns of figures, when he appeared. She looked up and saw him standing in the office doorway and her heart did not even miss a beat. He was like a semi-stranger, someone she used to know, and he had no effect on her heart at all.

'I'm sorry, Kitty,' he said but she held up a hand magnanimously.

'Don't go on, Freddy. It's over. It was wrong of you not to tell me. You should have let me make up my own mind whether I wanted to take up with a married man or not.'

'I couldn't help myself. It's like this…' started Freddy in his most silken voice but she got up and pushed him backwards out of the door.

'Go away. It's over. It was good while it lasted. I'm not asking you for anything. Let's leave it at that,' she said. He did not push back.

When he left she was jubilant. It was as if a burden had been lifted from her and a whole new horizon revealed. She could do anything she liked, go anywhere she liked, answerable to no one but herself… Kitty Scott was free!

To celebrate she took the rest of the day off, hailed a cab and went to the West End. She'd go and look at some more pictures. She might even buy one because while she was living with Freddy she'd managed to amass a fair amount of money.

The fashionable crowd always thrilled her because it seemed so wonderful that she, the bondager's bastard, should be moving among them, accepted as one of them, with money in her purse and fine clothes on her back. She was sauntering along, pausing to look at the pictures in dealers' windows, when the cries of a newspaper vendor caught her attention...

'Tunnel collapse at Hyde Park... Fifty men entombed... Engineering peer feared among them...'

Why did a cold hand clutch at her heart when she heard those cries? She hurried across the road to the newspaper man and bought one of the sheets he was holding out.

'Tragedy in London Tunnel', screamed the headline across the front page.

The story beneath it said that rescue teams were working frantically to try to reach a party of men trapped below ground by the fall in a new tunnel being built beneath London. The man in charge of the project, Sir Timothy Maquire, had gone down with the first party of rescuers but there had been a subsequent fall and he was trapped as well.

Kitty's eye ranged down the close print, looking for the location of the accident...

'Hyde Park, near Apsley House, the home of the great Duke of Wellington', it said. She dropped the newspaper on the ground and started to run. Apsley House was not far away.

As she ran she became ragged Carroty Kate again. Tim Maquire's gold half-sovereign bounced up and down in her pocket. She always carried it with her. In her mind she had a vivid memory of him, the most handsome man she ever saw in her life. The epitome of glamour.

The end of Piccadilly was packed with people and horse-drawn ambulances. Frantic policemen were trying to disperse the crowd of onlookers, who stood with shocked faces watching injured men being helped out of a gaping hole in the ground.

Beside it was a building site with tarpaulin-covered shelters and huge steam-powered diggers, now silent. Solemn-looking men were standing about in groups. The crowd gave a groan whenever a group of dirt-covered men came out of the mouth of the cavern carrying a stretcher on which lay a body with a piece of sacking thrown over its face.

There was an ambulance waiting and one by one, five dead men were laid inside it. When it was driven away another ambulance took its place and the terrible procession of stretcher-bearing parties went on. As each body was brought up, a shaken-looking man wearing a bowler hat looked at their faces and shook his head as he called out a name.

She pushed her way unceremoniously through the crowd, glad that she was tall and could see over most people's heads. She found a viewing-place beside a grim-faced policeman.

'You shouldn't be here, madam,' he said disapprovingly, thinking she was a sensation seeker.

When she turned to look at him, however, he saw that her face was streaked with tears. 'I know Tim Maquire. I've known him since I was a child. I want to make sure he's all right,' she said.

The policeman's heart was touched.

'I'm sorry,' he told her, 'but they brought his body out ten minutes ago. Sir Timothy Maquire is one of the victims. I think you should go home. This is not a place for you.'

She walked all the way to Whitechapel in a state of shock, weeping as she went, oblivious to the curious eyes of people she passed on her way. She was mourning the dreams of her youth, mourning the loss of her beau ideal.

–

The work on Falconwood was almost finished. The beautiful old house was slowly being restored to its former glory and on a fine summer evening its new owner, Lady Emma Jane Maquire, sat with her son Christopher and his grandmother-by-adoption Tibbie Mather, on the lawn and admired the transformation that had been brought about. While the women chatted, the child played on the grass with his dog, a sprightly little fox-terrier that ran barking after twigs he threw for it.

The women watched him indulgently and Emma Jane said, 'It'll be lovely when we're all here together. Tim's going to be so pleased when he comes up next week and sees the improvements in the house. The workmen have done a fine job.'

The words were barely out of her mouth when a horse came cantering up the drive, scattering gravel as it went. She anxiously called Christopher to her as a man jumped from the saddle and came running towards them.

'It's all right,' said Tibbie. 'It's only Dr Robertson from Maddiston, but what in the name's the matter with him!'

Alex Robertson looked distraught, eyes stricken and hair flying, when he stood before them. To Tibbie he said, 'Take the child away please, Mrs Mather.'

Emma Jane stood up with consternation in her face and gasped, 'What's wrong? What's wrong? Is it Tim?'

Tibbie hurriedly did as she was bid but before she was out of earshot, she heard Robertson saying, 'I'm sorry, Emma Jane, I'm afraid it is…'

She seemed to crumple when the terrible news was broken to her. Never a big woman, she looked as if she contracted and shrank when she heard what he had to tell her.

'Oh no, oh no, not Tim, not Tim,' was all she said over and over again. Robertson wished with all his heart that he had not been the one Sydney chose to be the bearer of such awful tidings.

He held the sobbing Emma Jane in his arms and tried to comfort her. 'I'm sorry, I'm so sorry. He was too brave. He didn't need to go down…' he told her.

'Why, what happened?' she asked, looking up at him through a sheet of tears.

'Sydney sent a telegraph message to say that ten men were trapped in a fallen part of the tunnel. Tim went down with a party to try to dig them out but more of the tunnel fell in. All of the rescue party was killed… that's what Sydney said.'

Emma Jane's eyes were wide and staring in horror. 'In the tunnel. It must have been dark. Oh my dearest Tim. There must be a mistake. I'd have known if he was dead. I would have felt it… I love him so much, you see… He couldn't go without me knowing,' she whispered, grasping at straws.

Robertson shook his head. 'No, my dear, Sydney sent me a telegraph message. He would know all the facts before he did such a thing,' he told her.

'I can't believe it, I can't believe it. I can't live without him. He's everything to me,' she sobbed and laid her head on his shoulder for comfort.

Robertson was in anguish. Having to comfort her was agonising for him and he wanted to weep as well but he knew why Sydney had sent him the message. Such terrible news had to be told by someone who cared for Emma Jane. It could not be broken by a stranger.

'Ssh, ssh,' he said to her, 'come and sit down. I'll give you something to calm your nerves.'

She shook her head. 'That won't help. It wouldn't change anything. Oh God, what am I going to do without him? He was everything to me.'

Robertson looked across the grass and saw Tibbie standing beneath a copper beech tree holding the boy by the hand. He was a sturdy little fellow with his father's curly black hair and well-built body but it was obvious he was upset and puzzled by his mother's grief, for though Tibbie was trying to divert him by talking and pointing in the other direction, he kept turning his head to look back over his shoulder.

'Will I tell Tibbie to take the boy away?' asked Robertson, but Emma Jane shook her head.

'No, I'm going to tell him. He has to know. He's lost a father and I've lost my husband. God, how cruel! How could this happen!'

'I think you should wait before you tell him. It's bad for him to see you in such a state,' advised Robertson, but she sat up straighter, a visible effort to pull herself together, and said, 'No, I must tell him now. He knows something's wrong and I don't want to fob him off with lies. And there's poor Tibbie as well. She loved Tim like a son.'

She rose and walked across the grass with such dignity that Robertson felt a surge of love and admiration for her. Hurriedly wiping his eyes on the huge handkerchief he wore flopping from his top pocket, he walked behind her and heard her say, 'Christopher, Tibbie, my dears, darling Tim's dead. He's been killed in a collapse of the tunnel he was building... He died trying to save other people.'

She gave a strangled sob and held out her arms to receive her son and her old friend, who both ran towards her, Christopher clinging to her legs and sobbing brokenly. The women bent down to him and held him close though they too were convulsed with tears.

'Oh bairn, don't cry, don't cry,' wept Tibbie. 'Your daddie's in Heaven. He'll be watching out for you.'

'But I want him here, I want him here,' sobbed poor Christopher. I want him here too, thought Emma Jane, only Tim can help me through this.

Next morning Alex Robertson escorted her by train to London. In spite of her protests he advised that she leave Christopher behind because he thought that attending his father's funeral would be too gruelling for such a young child.

Tibbie broke her lifelong rule about never sleeping outside her cottage and moved into Falconwood to watch over the little boy, whom his mother did not want to leave in the care of servants at such a terrible time.

Sir Timothy Maquire's funeral service, and the service for the other men killed in the tunnel collapse, was held in St Peter's, Hanover Place, the church Emma Jane attended when they were in London, for they had taken a town house nearby while the tunnel construction was going on.

Tim, though nominally a Roman Catholic, had long ago abandoned his religion. Somehow it was suitable that he be buried with his workmates, the other navvies, his friends.

The huge church was packed to the door and the mourners came from every section of society. There were weather-beaten old navvies who had worked with him long ago and peers of the realm sitting side by side in the pews.

Kitty Scott, elegant in black, was one of the last to arrive and slipped into the back of the church as a line of immense silver-decorated black coffins was being borne down the aisle. She did not know which one was Tim's but guessed it was the last in the line because alone on it rested a single red rose, a token of love from Emma Jane, who sat with her head bowed in the front pew.

Kitty knelt and prayed for Tim, not to a conventional God but to the gods of the woods and the fields, the gods who still seemed to rule and frolic around the fields of Camptounfoot. Somehow Tim Maquire seemed to belong to them more than to the solemn God of the established Christian Church.

The funeral service was long and impressive, dominated by a sonorous sermon and a eulogy, extolling Tim's bravery in giving up his life trying to save his men, but at last the congregation began filing out, following Emma Jane, who was walking with her sister-in-law Amelia. They were both shielded from view by long black veils that completely hid their faces.

Walking behind like two sentinels were Sydney Godolphin and Dr Robertson from Maddiston, both of them grim-faced.

The mourners gathered in the church's pillared portico and watched as the coffins were carried out into the churchyard. Kitty stood at the back of the crowd and was about to walk away when she felt a hand on her arm.

'I saw you in the church but I didn't have a chance to speak to you,' said a voice she recognised and she looked up into the solemn face of Robbie Rutherford.

'Oh, Robbie,' she said brokenly, 'isn't this awful! He was such a good man. I'm so sorry.'

He nodded. 'So am I. Tim was one of the finest men I ever met.'

He took Kitty's arm and said, 'I need something to drink and so do you, I expect. There's a cold wind blowing. I've written and told Emma Jane how I feel so I'm not going to any funeral reception. I can't stand those ghoulish affairs. Why don't you and I go somewhere and talk about Tim Maquire in comfort.'

They went to a hotel off Piccadilly. A string quartet was playing and Robbie ordered brandy without asking Kitty what she wanted. When it came he raised his glass to her.

'To Tim Maquire, to Camptounfoot,' he said solemnly.

The fiery liquid made her eyes water but she was crying anyway so it did not matter.

Robbie put his hand on hers and said, 'Don't cry. He was the sort of man who had to go out with a flourish. He wouldn't have wanted to get old and crippled or senile and querulous. He died a hero.'

'I know he did. It's not that, it's everything – people dying, people changing, time passing, not knowing what's coming next… it's everything, Robbie. Since I heard about Tim's death I've been thinking so much about the people at home. My mother, Tibbie Mather and Marie Benjamin. I've made up my mind to go back to see my mother. I've been putting it off for too long.'

'She's all right,' Robbie told her. 'I saw her three months ago. I told her I'd seen you and she was delighted. Tibbie buys her things with the money you send and she's very careful about it. Big Lily doesn't know.'

Kitty sighed. 'I've only just realised that I need to see her, though. I must go back to sort things out before I can go forward again. I'd like to see Marie too. We weren't good friends when we parted. I'd like to make it up with her.'

'Are you still with your wild jockey?' asked Robbie in a careful voice. Kitty shook her head. 'No, I'm not. We parted. It was over.'

'I guessed that was about to happen when we met in Menton,' said Robbie. 'Who are you with now?'

She bridled. 'Nobody. I'm with myself. I don't need a protector. I'm not a tart.'

'I wasn't suggesting that you are. I was only asking if you were free to do something,' he said in apology.

She looked sharply at him and asked, 'What?'

'I've heard from my mother that Tibbie's very worried about Marie. She didn't hear from her for a long time and then she got a letter that was distracted, as if it were written by someone out of their mind. Her brother's no help. He's a hard case. All he'll say about his sister is that she cut herself off from him and she should stay cut off. He wrote to her and told her to come home but she never replied and he's furious.'

'That's awful,' exclaimed Kitty, looking at him in dismay. 'Somebody must know what's happened to her? Didn't she go to Paris with her friend from Edinburgh?'

'Yes, but that girl came home months ago, over a year ago in fact. She wrote to Marie's brother and dropped dark hints about her keeping bad company. That horrified him,' said Robbie solemnly.

Kitty sighed. 'Poor Tibbie. She'll be grief-stricken about Tim Maquire and now she has Marie to worry about as well.'

'I want you to go to Paris to find her,' said Robbie, leaning forward eagerly in his chair.

'Why me?' asked Kitty.

'Because you're her friend and you've got your head screwed on. I can't imagine anybody who'd be better. I can't go myself because I've to travel to America on business and besides, she wouldn't come home with me. There's not many people she would trust but I'm sure you're one of them. I'd like to ease Tibbie's mind, especially now she's grieving over Tim. It would be a great happiness to her to see Marie again.'

His eyes held Kitty's as he talked and she said, 'You're interested in her too, aren't you?'

'Yes. I think she's a great painter and it would be a pity if she wasted her talent. I got her last Paris address from Tibbie, the one the letters were sent to. I'll pay all your expenses if you'll go.'

She frowned. 'I'd like to go but I can't speak French.'

He laughed. 'I'll wager you can make yourself understood in any language. Just go to this address. You'll probably find she's there or they'll know where she is. Find out why she hasn't written to Tibbie and bring her home if she'll come.'

Kitty nodded. 'Marie always needed somebody to look after her, didn't she?'

Robbie agreed. 'She's a gentle soul and gentle souls need nurturing.'

'Not like us,' said Kitty but he shrugged.

'I don't know. We both need nurturing too at times, I suspect.'

She'd known from the moment he made his proposition that she was going to Paris but the sum of money he brought out of his pocket and pushed across the table towards her was an embarrassment.

'I don't need your money. I've plenty of money of my own. I don't need bribing to go,' she said drawing back.

'Please take it,' he pleaded with her. 'You don't know what'll be needed when you get there. Stay at a good hotel and bring her home with you if you can. I wish I could accompany you, but I can't.'

'I'll keep an account for you,' said Kitty primly, putting the roll of notes into her purse.

Travel always energised her but this was her biggest adventure so far because this time she would be crossing the Channel alone. When she went to France with Freddy she had only seen the interior of two Parisian stations but now she was to walk the city's streets, see its sights, become one of the throng that filled Paris with life. So after she left Robbie, she hurried back to her room, packed a bag and caught the midnight train. She was wasting no time.

Next day she found a hotel off the rue de Rivoli and was soon in a fiacre rolling over cobbled streets on her way to Madame Guillaume's at the Boulevard Clichy.

She asked for Madame when she rang the polished brass bell. Her reception was icy.

'Marie Benjamin?' said Madame with a rising note of disapproval in her voice when Kitty announced the reason for her visit.

Kitty nodded. 'Yes, yes. I've come to see Marie Benjamin.'

'Not here,' said Madame shaking her head.

'Where?' asked Kitty, spreading her hands in an imploring gesture.

'For a long time not here,' said Madame.

'How long?'

Madame puzzled, searching her mind for the English words. 'A year, more…'

'Where did she go?'

'*Au diable,*' said Madame.

Kitty had a phrase book with her and she flipped through the pages… '*Diable, diable,*' she muttered as she turned the pages but Madame stopped her by holding up a hand.

'To the bad,' she said.

That was all that could be elicited about Marie from her and Kitty turned to go but the maid who held the door for her had obviously been listening and raised her eyebrows with an air of complicity.

Kitty lingered on the landing outside the door and was rewarded a few moments later by the door opening a crack and the maid peering out.

'Marie Benjamin?' asked Kitty.

The maid lifted a plate off the top of a cupboard and showed her a letter lying in it. Kitty looked at it and saw that it was addressed to Marie.

'You mean she hasn't come to collect her mail?'

The maid nodded, came out, took Kitty's arm and pulled her in the direction of the kitchen door where she motioned to her to sit down. Then making another gesture that told her to stay where she was, hurried out of the room again.

Within a few moments she was back with a white-haired old man who bent over Kitty's hand and said, 'I am a neighbour of Madame Guillaume. I speak a little English and Isabelle, the maid, tells me that you are enquiring after a girl who used to live here.'

'Thank heavens!' gasped Kitty. 'Yes, I'm trying to find Marie Benjamin. Her friends in Scotland are worried about her.'

'Marie Benjamin,' said the old man to Isabelle, who nodded vigorously. She knew that already.

Then she started to speak rapidly and he listened with his head cocked to one side, making encouraging noises when she paused for breath.

At last he turned to the curious Kitty and said, 'Marie Benjamin left here more than eighteen months ago but till Christmas of last year she used to come for her letters.'

'Latterly she was very thin and pale. Her friend, an artist, came for them then. He told Isabelle she was ill. He has not been for some time and Isabelle is worried too. She was fond of the girl.'

'Has she any idea where she was living after she left here?' asked Kitty and he addressed this question to the maid, who went off on another tirade.

Then he told her, 'She was a painter. She went to live with other painters. Isabelle does not know their names. She never said where she was staying but Isabelle once saw her going into a house near Montparnasse station. That's the district where many painters live.'

Kitty got to her feet. 'Thank you very much. Montparnasse station. I'll go there now.'

'Would you like me to go with you?' offered the old man in a kindly way. He was frail but his eyes sparkled and he was obviously interested in her quest.

'That would be very kind of you. I would appreciate your help because I can't speak the language at all,' she said in acceptance.

'Wait till I fetch my overcoat,' he said and bustled off while Isabelle wrung her hands with excited little moans and sighs.

Kitty and her guide found their way to Montparnasse station without any trouble.

'The best way to find anything out in Paris is to ask at the local café,' he told her and went into the nearest one where he engaged in colloquy with the customers and soon came out again, his face shining with triumph.

'A woman painter lives upstairs! They think she might know something about your friend,' he exclaimed.

Félice was working when they knocked on her door. She opened it to find two strangers there. One, a woman with brilliant red hair, stared at her and then said, 'No, that's not her.'

Félice, who had been pedantically educated as a girl, could understand English and asked, 'Who is it that you are seeking?'

'Marie Benjamin,' said Kitty.

'Her! She left my studio a long time ago.'

'You know her! She's been here! That's wonderful!' cried Kitty.

'Yes, I know her,' Félice sounded guarded.

'Where is she?' asked Kitty. 'I'm her friend from Scotland and I've come to find her.'

Félice glared over her spectacles and said, 'You should have come a long time ago. The last I heard she was living above the laundry at Mancini's place.'

Kitty's guide interjected, 'Where does Mancini live?'

Félice gave him directions and once more they were off on the trail.

Mancini received them cordially and could not stop himself from casting admiring eyes at Kitty, who was exactly the sort of woman he admired.

'Poor little Marie,' he said, rolling his liquidly expressive eyes to heaven. 'Poor child, she's with the nuns.'

Kitty gasped, 'She's a nun?'

'No, she's a mother,' said Mancini.

Kitty looked at her guide for elucidation and he found out that Marie had given birth to a child and was lying ill in the nuns' hospital, which was marked by a large green glass light outside the front door, a few streets away.

'Alas, she will be there till she dies,' said Mancini dolefully.

Kitty could see from the expression of her kind guide that something unfortunate had been said and she grabbed his arm. 'What did he say?' she asked.

'He said she will be in hospital till she dies,' he explained and she gasped in horror, 'Dies!'

The old man hastened to reassure her. 'He is Italian. Perhaps his French is bad. He may only mean that her life could be in danger.'

By now Kitty was in a fever to find the hospital and her friend. 'Let's go, let's go,' she urged him, pulling at his sleeve.

It was evening and the lamps were lit when they left Mancini's so it was easy to see the large lamp in a green globe at the doorway of the hospital where Marie was lying. Kitty could not stop herself from running when it was pointed out to her from the other side of the street.

She grabbed hold of her guide's hand to hurry him along but he gasped, 'Wait, wait, I am an old man.'

She barely slacked her pace, however, and in the hospital entrance hall urged him, 'Please ask for Marie Benjamin, ask where she is.'

He stopped a black-clad sister and whispered to her. A long white hand appeared from beneath the drooping sleeve and she pointed along a corridor.

Kitty was halfway up it before the nun had time to speak. There was a door with a glass panel in its upper half at the end of the passage and she looked through it into a narrow room containing four beds. Her eyes went from occupant to occupant till they reached the bed by the window. The woman lying there had her face turned away but there was a skein of pale yellow hair on the pillow.

'Marie, Marie,' Kitty was crying as she burst in.

The patient in the bed turned slowly. Her face was very thin, almost ethereal, but it looked as it had done when she was a girl. Time had turned back for Marie Benjamin.

She stared at the gloriously dressed stranger running towards her and frowned, but for only a moment. Then she whispered, 'Is it Kitty? Oh, Kitty, I've been thinking about you.'

Kitty bent over the high metal bed and took the thin hand that lay on the cover. 'I've been thinking about you too. That's why I came to find you. I'm going to take you home,' she said.

At that moment a hand descended on her shoulder and a red-faced nun hissed, 'You shouldn't be exciting this patient. She's very ill. You must not upset her.'

Kitty shrugged the hand off. 'I won't upset her. I've come to take her home.'

From the bed came Marie's voice. 'She's my sister. She's come for the baby, she's come for little Kate.'

Kitty looked down at her with wondering eyes. 'For Kate?'

'Yes, for my baby,' said Marie. 'You've come to take her home with you.'

'You've called her Kate,' whispered Kitty. 'Yes, I've come to take her home.'

The kind old man was standing in the open doorway beside another nun. Kitty went over to him and said, 'She's here. We've found her. I'll have to stay with her now. Thank you, I'd never have found her without you.'

He shook her hand. 'I enjoyed it. I'm glad you found your friend.' Then he turned and walked away.

There were two nuns in the room now: the angry one and the serene one who had directed them to the room where Marie lay. Surprisingly the first one was English.

'You must not upset her. She has consumption and is in the final stage. She is very weak. In fact, she is dying,' she told Kitty angrily when she tried to walk back to Marie's bed.

Kitty shook her head. 'I won't upset her. We're sisters. I've come a long way to find her.'

'You don't look like sisters,' said the nun.

'We had different fathers,' said Kitty, remembering Grandma and Sophia… 'It's the women who count,' she said in tribute to them.

'You will take her baby?' was the next question.

'Yes, she wants me to have it. Can I see the baby please?'

Kitty, who had never had any desire for a child, longed to hold Marie's baby in her arms.

'We would keep the child. We told her that,' said the nun but Kitty shook her head.

'No, I'll take the baby back to her village, back to Scotland. Is she really dying, Sister? She's so young…'

The angry nun softened. 'Yes, she is, I'm afraid. She knows it now. She is peaceful so do not upset her, please.'

Kitty swallowed the lump in her throat. It was essential to maintain her composure. 'I won't upset her. Can I see her baby?'

'It's in the nursery. We keep it there for fear of infection but she likes to be shown it every day. We bring it to the door and hold it up for her. I'll fetch it now,' whispered the nun and hurried off.

Kitty went back to the bed and took Marie's hand again. 'You're going to get well,' she said with determination.

'Am I? Did they say that?' Marie's voice showed how much she hoped this was true but she was very weak and did not have the strength to sit up.

'Yes, they did, and I'm going to stay with you till you're well and then I'll take you back to Camptounfoot,' said Kitty, defying facts.

From the doorway she heard a little cough and turned to see the English nun standing there with a white-wrapped bundle in her arms. Holding the baby out she tenderly pulled the cover back from its head and Kitty cried out quite spontaneously, 'She's lovely! What a beautiful child!'

Without thinking she rose from her seat and went over to the nun with her arms held out. The baby was placed in them and she clutched it to her heart, staring down at a perfect little face. Marie's child had a cap of silky black hair that curled on her neck. Her face was like that of a cherub and she had very finely drawn, arched black eyebrows and long silky lashes. The lashes flickered as she slept. Kitty lifted one of the curled little fists and slowly opened the fingers. They were long and tapering.

'Aristocratic hands,' said the nun softly.

It was impossible for Kitty to put the baby down. She held it to herself, breathing in its sweet smell, and felt something deep inside her open and blossom like a flower. This, she knew, was love.

Marie's huge eyes were watching intently. Kitty smiled across at her and held the baby tighter.

The nun intervened. 'The child must not stay here for too long – all the patients in this room have consumption and there are germs, you see... She's still being breast-fed and we'll keep her till she's weaned. You will be staying in Paris with your sister...?' Her voice trailed off and they looked at each other searchingly.

Kitty nodded. 'I'll stay as long as it takes,' she said and handed the baby back with reluctance.

The nun had sharp blue eyes which she fixed on Kitty's face as if trying to tell her something. 'Before you leave, come and speak with me,' she said.

Marie tired quickly. She fell asleep in a short while and Kitty walked back along the corridor in search of the English nun, whom she found in a tiled pantry.

They looked at each other and the nun spoke first. 'Your sister will never leave here, you know. If you wanted to save her you should have come at least a year ago,' she said sternly.

'No one knew where she was. No one knew she was ill. How long has she got?' asked Kftty bleakly.

'She is very weak. When she came to us a month ago she had been drinking and there were signs she'd also taken opium but that wouldn't have killed her. She has advanced disease of the lungs and we do not think she will last more than another week. I'm sorry.'

This was received in silence and Kitty stood twisting her gloves with her head down. Then she looked up and said, 'I'm living in a hotel on the other side of the river. I'll move so as to be nearer to her.'

'I know she has a room in the artists' building over the laundry. It was women from there who brought her to us. We know many of them. You might be able to live there,' suggested the nun.

Kitty said, 'I know the place.' All she wanted was to go somewhere private so that she could think, make plans and shed tears for Marie.

She had always possessed a good sense of direction and found her way back to Mancini's building without trouble. His room was full of people and when he introduced Kitty to them, a young man jumped up and came across to her.

'My name is Pierre. I'm a friend of Marie,' he said in English, extending a hand.

She looked at his dark hair and asked, 'Are you the father of her child?'

He shook his head. 'No, I'm not. I wanted to marry her but she wouldn't. The father's a Hungarian sculptor called Tadi. He's gone to Berlin.'

Mancini growled from the back of the room, 'It's a good thing for him he's gone away. He'd better not show his face here again.'

Pierre undertook to show Kitty to Marie's room and when they opened the door, she was appalled by the grime and squalor of the place. A few canvases were propped against the wall and her guide waved a hand at them saying, 'Those she did not really start. I sold the others one at a time for her. They fetched good prices. She could have been famous.'

'What have you done with the money?' asked sharp-minded Kitty.

'I gave it to her. She drank it. Poor Marie. She was very sad.'

Suddenly Kitty was overcome with a feeling of intense weariness and sank down on the tumbled bed.

Pierre went towards the door saying, 'You're tired. I'll leave you now but I'll come back tomorrow and we can discuss things more deeply.'

Though the bedding was filthy and there were mice scrabbling around on the floor, Kitty fell asleep and did not wake till morning. Then, galvanised with energy, she dragged the covers off the bed and took them to the laundry downstairs; borrowed a pail and washed the floor and threw out all the accumulated rubbish and empty bottles Marie had left behind. She lit the stove, went out to shop for food and was eating it when Pierre returned.

He looked around with approval but made no comment as he sat on a rickety chair and asked, 'What are you going to do about Marie's child?'

'She's given the baby to me,' said Kitty. She was utterly determined that no one else was to have the child. It was her legacy from her friend.

'The nuns said they would like to keep her,' said Pierre, but Kitty shrugged.

'They can't. They think I'm Marie's sister. They can't stop me taking the baby back home with me.'

'You are a married woman?' he asked, looking curiously at the statuesque redhead with the imperious face.

'No, but the nuns don't know that. They call me Madame and I haven't corrected them. Don't worry, I can afford to keep a child. It won't suffer if it comes to me.'

'I'm sure it won't,' said Pierre with respect.

Every day the people in the building watched Kitty stride with her countrywoman's walk to the hospital. She held her head high and, wearing one of Freddy's big hats, made an imposing sight as she swept over the Parisian pavements.

Every day she found Marie weaker. It seemed that she was melting away. By the time a week had passed, her flesh looked transparent but her cheeks were often hectically red and her eyes blazing. When fever seized her she liked Kitty to sit by the bed and talk about their childhood. Her scarred thumb lay upwards in Kitty's hand and she stroked it gently while she talked about Camptounfoot.

Though sometimes Marie seemed to have accepted the fact that she was going to die, at other times she allowed herself to hope and whispered of how she longed to see the village and Tibbie again. Kitty did not tell her anything sad. She did not talk of Tim's death or of David's hard intransigence until she saw that the end of her friend's life was drawing near.

Then she whispered, 'Would you like me to telegraph to your brother and ask him to come to see you?'

Marie shrank back in bed. 'No, no, no,' she said emphatically. 'I never want to see him again. He wrote awful things about me to Amy's family and that was why Murray wouldn't marry me.'

She whispered the details of her love for Murray and how devastated she had been when he married Julia.

'I'd never have allowed Tadi to make love to me. I'd never have needed him the way I did if it hadn't been because of losing Murray,' she said brokenly.

Kitty soothed her. 'Don't cry. It doesn't matter any more. Everything's going to be all right now.'

Marie smiled through her tears. 'I know it is. You're here.'

At the beginning of the second week, she was only intermittently conscious and Kitty sat by her bed for hours till one of the nuns forced her to go home to sleep.

Next morning the sun rose in glory and she woke feeling unaccountably light and free. When she looked out of the window she saw that the streets were gleaming slickly with water and the people all looked fresh and cheerful as they went about their business.

She did not wait to eat breakfast but hurried to the hospital, hitching up her skirts and running through the streets. She was met at the door by the English nun whose name, she had learned by this time, was Sister Dominique.

'I'm afraid Marie has gone,' she said softly, taking Kitty's arm and leading her to a small room with a crucifix on the wall.

It was not really a surprise. She felt she had known from the moment she woke but still a rush of tears burst from Kitty.

'You should have sent for me. You shouldn't have let me go home last night,' she sobbed.

The nun patted her arm consolingly. 'She wouldn't have known you. She died in her sleep. Do you want me to help you with the interment arrangements?'

'Yes, yes, please,' sobbed Kitty wiping her eyes.

Marie was buried in the nuns' tree-shaded graveyard behind the convent. The mourners were the nuns, Kitty, Isabelle, Mancini, Thérèse, Félice, Pierre and Luc. No one informed Tadi or David and they would not have taken the trouble to attend even if they had known.

The careful nuns had been supervising the weaning of little Kate and on the day a week later, when Kitty set out to take the train back home, she carried a baby in a basket.

## Chapter Twenty-two

The first thing Kitty did when she got back to London was deliver a message to Robbie's London office saying that Marie was dead and telling him how well she'd been cared for by the nuns. With the note she enclosed the money left over from the sum he had given her. She did not mention the baby.

Then she went to the Excelsior Club to say goodbye. The girls enthused over little Kate, who Kitty carried around on her hip in the same way as she had seen women carrying their children at Camptounfoot.

'You never looked as if you were pregnant. Where did you get her? She's not Freddy's, is she?' asked May-Belle.

'She's my sister's,' said Kitty. 'I'm taking her home to Scotland.'

At last she was going home and she was in a fever to start.

First, however, she spent a fair amount of her hoarded savings on clothes for the baby. She wanted them both to arrive in Camptounfoot in style. She travelled first class on the train and hired a carriage at Rosewell station to drive her to the village.

The cab-driver had known her as a child but did not immediately recognise her in her new transformation as a fashionable lady, for her giveaway hair was tucked under her hat.

As they drove along, he kept glancing over his shoulder and at last could contain himself no longer.

'I ken you, don't I?' he asked.

Kitty stared haughtily back at him. 'You might.'

'Whereabouts in Camptounfoot are you going?' he asked.

'Tibbie Mather's.'

'She's no' in. She's ower at Falconwood with Lady Maquire, looking after the poor soul. Her husband was killed in London last month.' Cab-drivers were great sources of information in the country.

'In that case take me to Falconwood and wait for me there,' said Kitty grandly. She was not going to satisfy his curiosity but, knowing the locals, she guessed it wouldn't take long before he found out who she was.

Tibbie was alone in the drawing-room when the maid announced a caller. 'A Miss Scott has come to see you, madam,' she said.

'Miss Scott?' Tibbie frowned. The only Miss Scotts she could think of in her acquaintance were Craigie's sisters. Joan had recently died but the surviving sister, Helen, would never visit Tibbie at Falconwood or anywhere else.

She did not have long to wonder, for a tall, elegant woman appeared at he maid's back. She was carrying a baby basket.

When Kitty saw that she was not immediately recognised, she slowly took off her hat, shaking her head, and then Tibbie gasped, 'Kitty! Kitty! It's you, Kitty! What are you doing here? Is that your bairn?'

Kitty told a lie. 'It is,' she said. 'But I didn't come about the baby. I've something sad to tell you, Tibbie.'

'Oh, lassie, I don't think I can take much more sadness. You'll have heard about Tim, have you?' said Tibbie brokenly.

'Yes, I heard. I went to his funeral as a matter of fact. This is about Marie. Sit down and listen to what I've got to say.'

Taking Tibbie's hand she led her to a chair and kept hold of her as she said, 'I've just come from Paris. I went because Robbie Rutherford sent me to find Marie. She was very ill when I got there. She had consumption and there was no saving her. I'm sorry to have to tell you that she died, but it was very peaceful. She was in a little hospital looked after by nuns and they were wonderfully kind to her.'

Tibbie looked up at Kitty's face with tear-filled eyes and nodded. 'Poor lassie, poor, poor lassie. I knew something bad had happened to her. This is heartbreaking. Her brother David'll go daft when he hears. I'll ask Dr Robertson to tell him. He comes down here every day to see Emma Jane…'

'No, don't ask the doctor to do it. I'll go to Maddiston and tell him about Marie,' said Kitty firmly.

She wanted to see David in order to decide whether she should tell him about Marie's baby, though already she was so fond of the child that she doubted she would ever give her up.

'Will you?' asked Tibbie. 'The trouble between him and Marie wasn't all his fault. He's never got over losing his mother and he tried to stop his sister going away too. All he lives for is work. He's rich but he doesn't enjoy it. Poor David and poor Marie. What a sad story... first their parents and now them. They never had a chance somehow. It breaks my heart.'

Kitty put an arm round the old woman and hugged her tight. When Tibbie dried her eyes, she looked down at the baby in the basket at Kitty's feet and said, 'That's a lovely bairn you've got. Your mother'll be pleased to see you with a bonny baby. Wee Jake's not all there, I'm sorry to say...'

Kitty lifted up the sleeping child and handed her to Tibbie.

'She's never going to be a bondager. She'll never work for Craigie, I'll make sure of that,' she said fiercely.

Every time she looked at Kate, she was overcome with the wonder of her and had quite forgotten her old dislike and fear of children.

Tibbie hadn't forgotten, however, and looked curiously from the woman to the child. Kitty had certainly changed, she thought. There was sleek dark hair on the baby's head and she asked, 'Is your man black-headed?'

Kitty laughed. She was not going to tell the secret of the child's parentage till she'd seen David. 'I haven't got a man but, yes, the baby's father had black hair.'

'What's her name?' asked Tibbie, holding out a finger which the baby grasped tightly.

'She's called Kate.'

'After you?' asked Tibbie looking up.

'After me,' agreed Kitty proudly.

She put the baby back in the basket and said, 'I'll have to go to the village now. I want to see my mam. How is she?'

Tibbie's face went solemn. 'They're in trouble, lass. One o' Craigie's sisters died in the winter and the one that's left is the daftest of the two. She's absolutely away with the fairies now. Sits huddled in the house all day and won't even speak when she's spoken to but she's told Big Lily to get off the farm. They're going at term time.'

'That's in a week,' gasped Kitty.

'Aye, that's right. They're going to the Poors' House because Big Lily's past working. She's fair crippled with the rheumatics. She canna walk properly any more. Your mother can't do the farm work on her own and Wee Jake's no help to her. He just wanders the village all day long.'

Kitty stood up. 'I'll have to go to see them first. Will you let me leave my baby here while I go to Camptounfoot? I've a hired carriage outside so I won't be long.'

'Of course the bairn can stay here. You must stay with us as well. I won't have you going anywhere else. Emma Jane's told me this is my home as well as hers and I can entertain anybody I like. We've plenty of empty bedrooms. I'll find a nice sunny one for you and your baby. Off you go to see your mother. Take it easy how you go about surprising her. Seeing you is going to be a shock.'

The carriage dropped Kitty at the end of the village and she walked along the main street, looking at everything she passed. First of all she pressed her eye to the splits in the door leading to the orchard and saw the silver wilderness inside. Little pink and violet flowers were growing among the moss that patterned the stones of the wall.

In the lane that led up to the bondagers' bothy, she could hear the chink, chink, chink of hammer on iron as she passed the smith where Tibbie's brother and his son were shoeing horses, but there was no rattle of a loom from the Rutherfords' window and that surprised her till she remembered that they had not done any weaving since Robbie made his fortune.

She walked on slowly and saw Jo's forbidding-looking house looming at the end of the lane. Jo was dead... Poor Jo. He was the only person in the village apart from Tibbie and Tim Maquire who had shown any sympathy for her when she was young.

She turned into the narrow vennel at the top and saw the tumbledown cottage where she was born. Its thatch was even more ragged and grass-covered than she remembered; the windows still stuffed with rags and bits of paper. A trickle of smoke rose from a hole at the end of the roof. There was not a sound to be heard except the chirping of birds in the orchard trees.

When Kitty pushed open the door she was blinded for a moment after going into semi-darkness from bright sunlight. The smell of smoke from the fire made her nose itch.

Somebody was sitting hunched by the hearth. 'Whae's that? Come closer. I cannae see you,' croaked her grandmother's voice.

In spite of her new confidence Kitty felt the cold hand of fear grip her gut but she stood up taller and said, 'It's Kitty.'

There was silence for a moment and then Big Lily asked, 'Kitty Scott? My lassie's lassie?'

Kitty walked slowly up the uneven floor. 'Yes, your lassie's lassie. The navvy's bastard,' she said when she was close to the seated woman.

'Why've you come back? To laugh at me? Are you pleased we're going to the Poors' House? Is that why you've come back? To see me taen awa on the back of a carrier's cart?'

Kitty said nothing. She stood like a figure of doom against the light and stared at Big Lily with disbelief. The once tall, vigorous woman was bent almost double and the hands that were folded on the top of a stick that supported her were red and swollen-jointed.

'I've not come back to laugh,' she said at last.

'Then you should,' said Big Lily, turning her head and staring into the fire. Kitty could see a white membrane over the pupils of both her eyes. She was almost blind as well as crippled.

'I hope you dinna expect anything from us because we've naething to gie you,' was Big Lily's next remark.

'I don't need anything from you,' said Kitty coldly. 'I've come to see what I can do to help my mother.'

'You've left it a bit late. If you'd come sooner we wouldn't have been sent off because you'd have been able to do the work,' Big Lily sounded hopeless and bleak.

'Tell me what's happened,' said Kitty.

'You see what's happened. I'm old and I cannae work so Craigie's sister's sending us away. She says she's going to sell the farm. She's a daftie and doesnae ken what she's daein'.'

'Does Craigie know she's selling the farm? Does Craigie know she's sent you off?' asked Kitty.

'I dinna ken. She doesnae tell me anything and I canna go to Edinbury any more.'

'I'll speak to her,' said Kitty, but Big Lily only snorted, 'That'll no' do any guid. She's been waiting to send me off for sixty years. She'll no' change her mind noo.'

'But surely you've got rights. Surely my mother's got rights too. She's Craigie's child…' Kitty was angry and her rage made her forget her fear and hatred of the woman by the fire.

'Bastards. That's what we are, bastards. You too. Bastards haven't any rights,' said Big Lily.

'This bastard does, this bastard certainly does,' shouted Kitty and ran out of the bothy.

Her mother was in the dairy, washing out the milk-pans. She did not hear Kitty coming into the shed and the girl was able to stand for a moment watching her at work. Her head, in the cotton sunbonnet, was bent over the pail she was scouring and her sleeves were rolled up showing brown muscular arms. When she turned round, however, her face was older, weather-beaten and worn. Her eyes were blank.

'There's nae milk till evening time,' she said.

At first Kitty couldn't speak for the strength of her emotion. All she could do was walk forward and hug her mother. 'Oh dinna you ken me, dinna you ken your own bairn?' she sobbed.

'It's Kitty. It's my Kitty. Oh my word, it's my wee Kitty!' sobbed Lily, kissing the young woman's face and running her hands up and down her arms. 'Aren't you braw! Aren't you bonny! I'm that glad to see you. I was awfy feared you were dead.'

They clung together and Kitty ran her hands gently over her mother's face as she said, 'I've come back to take care of you, Mam.'

Wee Lily looked into her daughter's eyes and asked, 'And my mither. You'll take care of your granny and Wee Jake too, won't you?'

Outside the sky was darkening. It would soon be evening. There was a rustling in the shed that meant the animals were preparing for their rest. Birds twittered softly in the eaves and the whole steading seemed to sigh as if the ancient stones from which it was built were settling down. Those sounds were among the most evocative of Kitty's life.

She was holding her mother's hand as they walked back to the bothy when a young boy emerged from the shadows and clung to Wee Lily's skirt. When she saw him, Kitty mentally thanked Tibbie for the way she'd managed the money she'd sent because he was properly dressed and had thick boots on his feet.

'Jake, this is your sister Kitty,' Wee Lily said and he grinned broadly at the stranger. His head was almost completely spherical, like a cannonball, and his eyes small and red-rimmed.

Kitty bent down and put a hand on his shoulder. 'Hello Jake,' she said.

He grinned even wider and touched the skirt of her dress, fingering the fine material. 'Pretty,' he said.

In the bothy Big Lily was still brooding by the fire and did not look up while Wee Lily prepared the supper, laying out plates of soup and bread. While they ate, Kitty told them about her time with the boxing show, and of living in London and Paris.

When she said that Marie was dead, Wee Lily expressed surprise but little grief. Big Lily was trying to make it seem she was not listening so she said nothing, but Kitty could tell that she was.

Kitty said nothing of Marie's baby though that bit of news burned on the end of her tongue.

When the meal was finished she gathered up the plates and took them out to the water barrel at the back door for rinsing as she had always done. Then she announced, 'I'm going over to the farmhouse to speak to Craigie's sister. Which one is it that's left?'

'Helen. Joan died,' said Big Lily who'd been silent till now.

The lamp that Jo used to tend on the gable wall of his building was still guttering when Kitty came out to pick her way over the farmyard and across the street to the old farmhouse.

Tiny pipistrelle bats swooped above her head, making funny little twittering noises, and she looked up towards the dark outline of the three guardian hills that loomed on the southern horizon. Nothing had changed. Time stood still in Camptounfoot. Lives came and went like water flowing along the river... Marie, Jo, Tim Maquire and Lady Godolphin, Joan Scott, in time Kitty herself, and still the village would nestle in the evening beneath its sheltering hills as it had always done.

There was no one, real or spectral, about when she reached the tall gable of Townhead farmhouse. The door was at the back, facing the ghostly orchard that Kitty loved so much. The lichen had overtaken even more trees and it seemed as if she were in a snow-covered world when she walked among them.

No one answered her knock. Then she hammered more loudly on the chipped door. No one came. Undeterred she went to a window and cupped her hands round her eyes in an effort to see through the dirt and grime that clouded the glass. The faint flicker of a lamp shone in the darkness within. She knocked again and was rewarded by a voice calling out, 'Go away!'

Instead of obeying she dropped the latch of the door and stepped inside. The cold was deadly. Even though the day had been warm the chill cut through to her bones.

She had never been in the house before and looked around curiously. The floor was laid with huge, flat stone slabs and the walls covered with tongue-and-groove panelling that had once been painted green but was now in the same flaking condition as the front door. A carved oak cupboard, more than seven feet tall, stood against one wall, and facing it was an elaborately carved chair with lions' heads on the ends of the arms and a tattered cloth seat.

A wall-eyed sheepdog lay under this chair with its lips lifted in a snarl, showing ferocious fangs. Seeing a shepherd's crook lying by the door, Kitty grabbed it in case the dog should take it into its head to attack her. As soon as it saw she was armed it slunk away.

'Where are you, Helen Scott?' she called. The uncanny silence told her Craigie's sister was nearby, holding her breath.

'Where are you, Helen?' she called again and walked towards a closed door on her right. It opened into a little parlour, also furnished with fine Georgian pieces including a huge pedestal table, but everything was dirty, dusty and uncared for.

Craigie's sister, looking like a scarecrow in ragged clothes, sat in a wooden chair by the unlit hearth. She had a broadsword in her hand and was using it as a walking stick. It was unsheathed.

'I told you to go away,' she said.

'I'm Kitty Scott. We're related,' said Kitty boldly.

Amazingly Helen knew who she was and shouted angrily, 'We are not, we are not, you're mother's a bastard. Nobody kens who her father was. They tried to blame it on Craigie, but it wasnae his fault.'

Kitty shouted back, 'My mother's your brother's child, so she's your niece and my grandmother's your half-sister. You can't put them off this farm. They've probably got legal rights anyway.'

Helen stood up, trying to raise the big rusty sword above her head but it was too heavy for her.

'Get oot. You've no right in here. I didn't ask you in. It's too good for the likes of you,' she shouted.

'Put that thing down before you hurt yourself,' said Kitty scornfully. 'I've come to tell you that it's wrong to send my mother and grandmother to the Poors' House after all the work they've done for you. You can well afford to hire another labourer and let them stay in the bothy till they die. That's how other farmers repay people who've worked hard for them.'

'Craigie's the boss here. He's the one who gives the orders, not you,' shouted Helen.

'And I'll be bound he doesn't know what you're doing with my mother and her mother,' snapped Kitty.

'He does, he does, he wrote me a letter telling me to get rid of them,' stuttered the old woman rummaging around among a pile of papers on the table as if in search of the order.

She was lying. It was not there.

Kitty looked scornfully at the pile of envelopes and said, 'If that's the case I'll have to go to Edinburgh and speak to him myself.'

She turned on her heel and left the house. When she closed the door, the sheepdog flung itself against it on the inside, snarling viciously.

Next day she left Kate in Tibbie's care again and took the train to Edinburgh. The prison, high on its hill at the end of Princes Street, loomed over the station and she kept it in her eye as she walked towards it.

Would Craigie be sufficiently sensible to discuss the problem of his bondagers? she wondered. She'd never seen him and only had local gossip to give her a picture of him. What she'd heard was not very good. 'Craigie was aye funny, even before he went off his head and shot the navvy,' Jo used to say when she asked about her grandfather.

The guard at the prison gate was bribed with a florin and she was admitted to the governor's office. Her assurance and the expensive clothes she wore gained her an audience when she said that she wanted to speak with her grandfather, Mr Craigie Scott.

The governor was cordial. 'You've come to see Craigie? And you're his granddaughter! Well, well, I didn't know he had any children. He said he wasn't married, the old rogue.'

Calmly Kitty said, 'He's not married. My mother is his illegitimate child. My name is Kitty Scott.'

The governor coughed and said, 'Quite, quite, I understand...'

'How is he?' asked Kitty, who hoped Craigie was not senile.

'He's been here a long time,' said the governor carefully.

Kitty nodded. 'I know, twenty-one and a half years...' Craigie had shot Bullhead for raping her mother on the day she was conceived.

'Exactly,' said the governor. 'He's not been very well recently but it's only because of his age. When you speak to him, don't excite him or tire him too much please.'

It struck Kitty as touching that the governor of such a big prison would have the time and the sympathy to worry about one of his longterm inmates, but she could see that the man had a kindly face and he seemed to have established some sort of friendship with Craigie.

He nodded to the clerk and said, 'Take Miss Scott to the hospital ward. Craigie's there now, isn't he?'

Once more he shook her hand and told her, 'I'm pleased to have made your acquaintance. Your grandfather is an interesting man. Very knowledgeable.'

That last remark ran in her head as she followed the clerk down a long, dank corridor to a gloomy room in which there were two lines of metal beds, half of them occupied by men who looked as if they were breathing their last… I hope I'm not too late, I hope I'm not too late, thought Kitty as she walked past them.

They stopped at the last bed. The man in it was sitting up against a coverless pillow. He stared at the clerk without speaking. Then his eyes moved to Kitty and she saw something spark in them, some kind of recognition woke there. It seemed to amuse him.

'What's this, what's this?' he asked. His accent was old Camptounfoot, like Jo's had been.

'This young woman says you're her grandfather and she's asked to come and see you,' explained the clerk.

'Has she indeed?' said Craigie. His eyes were fixed on Kitty's face and, yes, he was amused.

The clerk indicated to an attendant that a chair be brought for Kitty and then said, 'I'll leave you now. One of the guards will show you out.' There was silence for a few moments after he left. Her eyes met Craigie's and they both looked as if they were sizing up the opposition. It reminded Kitty of going into the boxing ring and she mentally raised her fists. It was Craigie who broke the ice, however.

'And how's your grandmither?' he asked.

'Not well. She's got bad rheumatics and can hardly walk.'

'She'll no' be able to do much work then, will she? How's your mither?' was his next remark.

'My mother's well enough but you know how it is with her, she can't take decisions, she needs guiding.'

He nodded and Kitty went on, 'Your sister Helen has told them they've got to leave Townhead at the term, that's in four days' time.'

'And has Helen got someone else to do their work?' Craigie was completely unsurprised by anything she said and she wondered if he had been writing to his sister with his instructions.

'No. She told Big Lily she's going to sell the farm.'

That made him sit up. His coolness disappeared and he snapped, 'The daft bitch, she can't sell Townhead. She doesn't own it. I do and I'll never sell. Never, never. There has to be a Scott in Townhead. We've been there for four hundred years...'

'She may be able to sell because you're a certified lunatic and she's your nearest kin,' Kitty told him.

He bristled and his prominent grey and ginger eyebrows seemed to stick out even farther. 'I'm no more a lunatic than you are,' he snapped.

'The law says you are,' she told him.

'The law! I've no time for the law. It's made to be broken. It's only cowards and women who bother about the law,' he growled.

'Well you didn't get away with it the last time you broke it, did you? If you had, you wouldn't be here,' said Kitty, giving as good as she got.

'You're a lippy besom, aren't you?' he said but not without respect.

'I must have taken it off somebody,' was her reply and she was astonished when Craigie actually laughed.

Then he asked her, 'What do you want coming here? Was it just to tell me about Helen? Was it just to get me worried?'

'No, I came to ask you to stop my mother and grandmother being put into the Poors' House. They don't want to leave Townhead. They were both born there and they've lived there all their days, though I must say I'd be happier if they were living in more comfortable conditions.'

'It's a good enough bothy,' said Craigie.

'It could be a damn sight better and you know it. The cows are better housed,' was Kitty's reply.

He made a mollifying move by saying, 'We shouldnae be fighting about the bothy. You want me to keep them on the farm? But why should I do that if they cannae work? And you don't look as if you'll be working with them, not with all that finery you've got on you.'

'I was reared to work with them but I got away and I'm glad I did. I'm not going back on the land either. But I love my mother and I don't want her to be shut up like a prisoner – you should know what that's like – for the rest of her life.'

'Take her away wi' you then,' suggested Craigie.

'I would but she'll not leave Big Lily.'

He stared at her and said, 'And you don't like Big Lily. You'll no' take her.'

Kitty nodded her head without speaking.

'Was she hard on you?' asked Craigie.

'Very hard,' Kitty told him.

'It doesnae seem to have done you much harm,' he said, looking pointedly at her golden jewellery and expensive clothes.

She ignored that and went straight to the point. 'I've a proposition for you. Instead of Helen selling the farm to some stranger, why doesn't she sell it to me? That way, Scotts would still be there, people of your own blood.' She accurately guessed that this would strike a chord with Craigie.

His eyes narrowed. 'And what sort of price would you be offering? It's worth a lot of money.'

She was cool. 'We could have it valued. I'd offer a fair price.'

She had not enough capital to buy a farm but was confident that she'd find it. She'd borrow if necessary. Robbie Rutherford or even Freddy might lend her the money. She'd pay it back with interest. That problem would come later, however. At the moment she had to persuade Craigie to see her point of view.

'I don't need money,' he said bleakly. 'What do I need money for in here? And I'm not going to sell my land. It's been in the family too long.'

'It would still be in the family if you sold it to me,' said Kitty. Pride in her family's long association with Camptounfoot made her eyes shine.

With his talent for guessing what was in people's minds. Craigie knew what she was thinking and said caustically, 'I dinna ken how long your Irish father could trace his ancestry, though. Not very far I'll be bound.'

She glared at him. 'Ancestry's all very well providing you look after the people you're related to. You're not doing much about Big Lily and Wee Lily, are you? If you really cared about your family, you'd let them stay in the bothy till they die, even if they couldn't work. They've both been good servants to you and they've never received much for it, either in money or in thanks. That farm would have gone back to thistles after you were sent up here if it hadn't been for my grandmother. She ran it as well as any man could have done and now she's being put out because she's too ill to work! You wouldn't do that to a horse, would you?'

411

Craigie's eyes glimmered while he listened to this outpouring but then he grinned wickedly and said, 'No, I'd shoot a horse that was too old to work.'

She groaned and stood up. 'I can see I'm wasting my time. But I'm warning you that Helen may get permission to sell the farm, and then there'll be no Scotts there any more. You'd do better to sell it to me.'

'And what would you do with it?' he asked sardonically.

'I'd hire men to work it and I'd let my mother and grandmother stay there to oversee what was being done. Big Lily's body might be worn out but there's nothing wrong with her mind.'

'And what about Helen?' asked Craigie.

For a moment Kitty was nonplussed. She hadn't given much thought to Helen. 'I'd find her a house in the village. She's living in misery in the farmhouse. I'd find out what she wanted to do…'

Craigie waved a hand, dismissing Helen. 'She's daft. Always has been. She'd do what she was told. But nobody's said I'm going to sell, have they? I'd have to see the colour of your money first.'

Kitty was preparing to leave. 'A minute ago you said you didn't care about money. You're only playing with me, aren't you?'

Craigie leaned forward in his bed and she could see how painfully thin he was. 'I don't have to care about money. I've got treasure in the farmhouse, treasure beyond what you ever dream about. Even Helen doesn't know what I've got there. That's why I'm not selling anything…'

Kitty snorted. 'And what good will it do you? What good has it ever done you? It'll lie where you've hidden it till some stranger digs it up.' Craigie groaned as if in pain and a guard came hurriedly up to say to her, 'You'll have to go now, miss. He's an ill man.'

She lifted her gloves off the bed and stood up. 'Goodbye Grandfather,' she said coldly.

He lifted his head, which had fallen forward when he groaned and looked up at her. His eyes were pale yellow like the dog that guarded his sister's house.

'What's your name?' he asked.

'I told you. Scott,' she said surprised.

'I know it's Scott. What's your first name? What did they call you?'

'Kitty.'

'Just Kitty. Not Katherine.'

'Just Kitty.'

Craigie grinned. 'I don't suppose they'd be able to spell Kath-erine...'

'You know damned well that neither of them can even write,' was her last riposte.

She was furious when she walked back to the station. I shouldn't have come. He was just playing with me. He's a horrible old rogue and not mad at all. He's totally sane. He was very lucky not to be hanged for shooting Bullhead, she was thinking.

On her return to Camptounfoot, she went to the bothy and told the bondagers. 'I'm going to find you a house in the village. I'll pay the rent for you. You won't have to go to the Poors' House.'

Big Lily glared bleakly at her. 'And what will we use for money? We'll have nae wages coming in.'

'I'll give you money,' said Kitty.

'I dinna want your money. I'd rather go to the Poors' House,' said Big Lily.

Wee Lily was sobbing quietly behind her mother. 'I dinna want to leave Townhead. I'm feart to go away.'

Her mother turned on her, saying sharply, 'I dinna want to leave here either but there's naething else to do. You should have taken Jake back when I told you to and had another bairn and this would never have happened.'

Kitty tried to make the peace. 'I'm going to find you a place to live,' she said firmly to Big Lily, 'and I won't give you any of my money. I'll give it to her...' She pointed at Wee Lily as she spoke.

'Pshaw,' spat her grandmother, 'how long'll that last? It'll be the Poors' House for us in the end.'

Though she asked everywhere, there wasn't a house for rent in Camptounfoot. She could have got a cottage in Rosewell for five shillings a week but she knew the bondagers would regard going to live in Rosewell with the same dread as they would have felt about emigrating to America. She hated the idea of failure but it looked like she had failed.

# Chapter Twenty-three

On the morning of the bondagers' last day in the bothy, Kitty woke up in her room at Falconwood with a splitting headache and a terrible sense of having lost a battle.

Wee Kate was in her cot in the same room and Kitty lovingly cared for the child before she dressed herself. She'd have to go into Christopher's nursery later because Kitty had to go to Townhead and force her grandmother to do what she wanted. The thought of the tussle ahead made her head ache even more.

She was hurrying to leave the house when Tibbie came along the hall crying out, 'There's a letter come for you, Kitty. It looks very official. It's got a big seal on it with a stamp and a lawyer's name.'

With an expression of dread on her face, Kitty split the seal with her fingernail and drew out a sheaf of closely written sheets of paper. The first page was headed with the name of an Edinburgh lawyer.

Tibbie watched with undisguised curiosity as the covering letter was perused. She saw Kitty shake her head and furrow her brow as she read it again without giving any clue as to its contents. After she'd gone through it a second time, she gazed at Tibbie for a few seconds and then said very slowly, 'I can't believe this. There must be some mistake.' Tibbie anxiously clasped her hands because she was afraid that the girl had received bad news. 'Oh what's the matter?' she asked.

'Matter? Tibbie, dear Tibbie, nothing's the matter! It's amazing.' Then Kitty grinned, the old impish look taking over her face. She threw the papers in the air and whooped, 'I can't believe this! I simply can't believe this! I thought he didn't like me...'

'Who didn't like you?' asked the confused Tibbie.

Emma Jane Maquire, hearing the noise, came out of the breakfast-room and looked curiously up the stairs to the landing where Kitty was throwing her arms around Tibbie and clasping her so tight that she gasped, 'Don't, you're hurting me. What's happened?'

'He's left me the farm… I mean he's given me the farm. Craigie's given me Townhead,' she cried.

'Oh never,' gasped Tibbie in disbelief. 'Craigie never gave anything away in his life and certainly not Townhead.'

Kitty was kneeling down collecting the papers she'd so carelessly thrown around. Reaching up she thrust the covering letter from the lawyer into Tibbie's hand. 'Read it for yourself. Read what it says there…'

Tibbie read, and like Kitty, she had to read it twice before she cried down to Emma Jane in tones of wonder, 'The lawyer says that Craigie was so impressed by Kitty that he's made a deed of gift and passed his ownership of the farm and all its contents on to his granddaughter, Kitty Scott. Isn't that amazing?'

Then she added in a softer tone to Kitty, 'It says he's done it because you look like his mother. You reminded him of his mother, that's why he's done this.'

Kitty shook her head disbelievingly. 'He never said anything at the time. He was quite hostile really.'

'I remember his mother,' said Tibbie, 'though she died when I was just a bairn. Craigie must have been twelve then. She died in an accident, something about a cart overturning. She was a big, upstanding woman with red hair. I haven't thought about her for years. Isn't this the strangest thing! Who'd ever have expected it!'

Kitty was rereading the legal papers enclosed with the letter. 'It's all very official, all in lawyer's language… I can't understand half of it. I'll have to go to a lawyer in Rosewell and have it explained before I do anything. I'd better go there now.'

She was away for an hour and the lawyer she consulted could hardly believe what he was reading either, for he knew Craigie Scott's reputation for meanness.

He folded the papers up eventually and said, 'It's perfectly legal. You own Townhead farm, Miss Scott. He's given it to you. His sister Helen's still living there, you say. There might be trouble with her.'

'Yes, I thought that too. Perhaps you'll come with me when I go to see her,' said Kitty, mindful of Helen's broadsword.

'I'd be delighted,' said the lawyer, sensing that he'd just acquired a good client. 'When will be suitable?'

'Now, straightaway, immediately,' Kitty told him.

Helen was not surprised to see them. When she answered the door she was carrying a letter similar to the one Kitty had received. 'Craigie says I've to do what you tell me. He's sent me money and told me that's my share. I dinna understand any of this,' she said distractedly.

The lawyer took the letter from her hand and read it. 'He's sent you five thousand pounds, Miss Scott. That's a lot of money. It's your inheritance. You're a rich woman.'

'Am I?' asked Helen. All the financial transactions in their family had been handled by Craigie and it could have been five pounds or five hundred for all that it meant to her.

'What will you do now that young Miss Scott here has been given the farm?' asked the lawyer gently. Kitty stood back and left this delicate matter to him, for she guessed he'd be better at it than she would.

'I don't know,' said Helen, looking round the cobwebbed hall.

'Would you like a nice little house in Rosewell and a maid to look after you?' suggested the lawyer, who'd seen the decrepitude of the place.

Amazingly Helen nodded. 'Aye, that'd be nice. I'm sick o' this place and if Craigie's no' coming back, I don't think I'll stay.'

It seemed too easy to be true but Helen meant what she said. In her mind she'd been holding the fort for Craigie and now her responsibilities were at an end. She turned and wandered off into the gloomy depths of the farmhouse while Kitty and the lawyer stared at each other.

'Do you want me to handle her moving?' he asked and Kitty nodded.

'Oh, please do.'

Now that Helen was taken care of, Kitty was at last able to go to the bothy where she found her mother pottering frantically about among bundles and bags. There was not a lot because they had few possessions. Her grandmother sat staring into the black hearth. It was the first time Kitty had ever seen the fire out.

'You're late. I thought you said you were coming early. This isn't early,' snapped Big Lily.

'Has the cart come yet?' Wee Lily asked.

'It's not coming, Mam,' said Kitty, ignoring her grandmother but Big Lily refused to be cut out.

'Why not?' she growled.

Kitty turned to her. 'Because you're only moving down the road to the farmhouse. You're going to live there from now on.'

'I am not,' snapped Big Lily. 'That's a cold, cheerless place. I never liked it.'

'It's better than the Poors' House,' protested Kitty, wishing that they'd ask how this turn of fortune had come about because she wanted to astonish them.

She turned to her mother. 'Don't you want to live in the farmhouse, Mam?'

Wee Lily was cuddling little Jake and they both looked confused. She said, 'No' really. I'd rather stay here.'

Exasperated, Kitty had to break the news without them asking. 'Well, listen to this. I got a letter this morning telling me that Craigie's given me the farm. Helen's moving to Rosewell and you can live in the farmhouse.'

Slow-thinking Wee Lily didn't take it in properly but Big Lily reacted immediately. 'You're daft. Craigie wouldnae gie his farm away – especially to you.'

'He did and I've a lawyer's letter to prove it. He said I looked like his mother so he gave me the farm.'

Big Lily sighed. 'The police must have been right when they shut him up for being daft. Like his mother, you say. I cannae remember much about her but folk used to say that she had a sharp tongue on her – like you, I suppose.'

If Kitty was downcast at the reaction to her great news, she was even more disappointed when both her mother and her grandmother refused to leave the bothy.

A compromise was reached in the end. They would allow the bothy thatch to be repaired, new glass to be put in the windows and a proper fireplace built. They would even allow her to divide the barn-like structure into rooms and make a new front door but they wouldn't leave it.

'How are you going to manage when all the building's going on?' she asked.

'That's no trouble, we'll just live in a corner,' they said. Anything rather than move out.

When she announced that she was going to hire a ploughman and a labourer they were shocked. 'What a waste of money!' cried Big Lily.

'It's not,' said Kitty. 'This farm hasn't been looked after properly since Craigie went away. You tried but there was too much work for you and I don't want either of you working any longer. You can retire now.'

But they didn't want to retire either.

'What would we do wi' oursel's?' asked Wee Lily piteously.

'All right, go on working if that's what you want but not so hard, please,' pleaded Kitty. At least, she thought, she'd be able to give them money, even if it was in the form of a wage because that was all they would accept.

While she was waiting for Helen to be moved out of the farmhouse and to take possession of her property, Kitty determined to do something about David Benjamin.

The thought of giving up Kate saddened her but she knew that she had to go to see Marie's brother eventually. She had to decide whether it would be better for the child to go to him or stay with her.

Legally, she had no claim on the baby. If anyone did, it was David because Kate's document of birth registration gave only the name of her mother, Marie Benjamin. It was necessary to go to see him. What she did after that depended on whether she judged him capable of giving Kate the love and attention she needed if she was going to grow up well and happy.

Kitty's pride in the child was so strong that she could not hide her away from her family at Camptounfoot much longer. Already, she guessed, the Falconwood servants would be spreading the news that Kitty Scott had arrived back with a baby in a basket and no father for it.

That afternoon she left the baby with Tibbie and hired a cab from Rosewell station to take her to the Maddiston mill.

David Benjamin had matured so much that he looked like a man of forty and was excessively respectable. His blond hair was oiled and slicked down and any resemblance he'd ever had to Marie was long gone.

He shook hands with Kitty gravely and stood watching her while she perched on a chair before his desk.

'I've come about Marie,' she said.

He held up a hand. 'I heard she's dead. Robbie Rutherford sent me a note. I got it last week. He said he'd asked you to go to Paris to find her and that you were with her when she died.'

Kitty nodded. 'I was…' Her voice trailed off sadly as she wondered if she should describe Marie's death to him. Even thinking about it brought tears to her eyes and she feared she would break down.

He apparently did not want to hear, however, for he turned to the window and said in a remote voice, 'It was inevitable that she'd destroy herself, I suppose.'

'She had consumption!' protested Kitty.

'Her way of life made it worse. Her friend, Miss Roxburgh, told me she drank alcohol.' He sounded totally uncompromising.

'Lots of people drink alcohol. They don't all die of consumption,' snapped Kitty.

He turned, eyes blazing. 'I do not approve of drinking. I discharge any man or woman in my mill who drinks. It's a sign of moral weakness.'

Greatly daring, Kitty said, 'I remember once finding you the worse for drink yourself.'

He was infuriated. 'That was my one lapse, the only time I ever yielded. What exactly have you come about Miss Scott? I'm a busy man.'

She stood up. 'I came to tell you about your sister but you don't seem to want to hear. I'm sorry I'm taking up your time.'

'My sister is dead. In fact she's been dead as far as I'm concerned for a very long time. She was the one who broke off the connection between us. I have no wish to be reminded of her.'

'That's all I need to know,' said Kitty and she left.

It's perfectly possible to bring up a baby on my own, her heart was telling her. No matter where I go, Kate will go with me. We'll have a wonderful time. The thing she had to do now was bring Kate out and act as if she were hers.

She turned up that evening at the farm with the baby on her hip. Big Lily greeted the appearance of a baby with a loud sniff but held her tongue because Kitty fixed her with a fierce eye, daring her to say anything.

Wee Lily and Jake were delighted with the child, cooing over her, waggling their fingers above her face, expressing their admiration for the pretty clothes that Kitty had dressed her in.

Soon the neighbours dropped in, apparently casually, to catch a sight of Kitty's child, for though she had not said Kate was hers, she hadn't said otherwise. It was assumed that she'd followed the way of her mother and grandmother and given birth to another bastard. Not that she cared.

The gossip reached the village shop where Bella, very fat and matronly-looking, served behind the counter. When Kitty failed to appear in the shop herself, Bella's curiosity was too strong for her to resist walking up to the farm dairy with a milk-can in the hope of catching sight of the returned prodigal.

Kitty, with Kate on her hip, was directing the workmen who had started repairs on the bothy, when Bella appeared.

'It's good to see you again, Kitty, after such a long time... and in such happy circumstances,' she gushed.

Kitty glowered. She'd never liked Bella and was not going to start pretending now.

In an effect to be friendly, however, Bella looked at Kate and exclaimed, 'What a pretty baby. Such black hair.'

Kitty, hoisting the child higher up on her hip, said, 'She looks like her father. He was a Hungarian.'

Bella gasped, 'A Hungarian!'

Let's give her enough gossip material for the next year, thought Kitty, so she smiled and said, 'He was living in Paris... He was a sculptor.'

Bella's jaw dropped. A Hungarian sculptor in Paris!

'You've travelled a bit since you left Camptounfoot then,' she said.

Kitty furrowed her brow. 'Yes, I went off with the boxing booth first and then I lived with Freddy Farrell, the jockey. Have you heard of him? He won the Derby the year before last. Then I went to Paris...'

It was all true. She'd only missed out bits like the baby being Marie's and not hers.

Bella was thunderstruck... Freddy Farrell, boxing booths, Paris... she was thinking as she hurried as fast as her bulk would allow her back to the shop to spread the news.

When she told her mother what Kitty said, the old woman shook her head. 'If she's been running about wi' Hungarians in Paris, she'll no' stay long in Camptounfoot, mark my words.'

In fact, that was exactly what Kitty was thinking herself. Having seen the world, she was still too young and eager for adventure to settle back into Camptounfoot, where gossip and speculation were the main recreation. It was inevitable that she would provide most of it. She must travel again soon.

At last the lawyer fixed up a house for Helen and arrived to collect her. She and the sheepdog were to be installed in a cottage in Rosewell where her respectable neighbours would be outraged to see her ragged, unwashed state. In spite of hints from the lawyer, Helen had done nothing to spruce herself up and intended to lead the same hermitical existence in Rosewell as she had at Camptounfoot.

She was taking some of the best pieces of furniture from the farmhouse with her but Kitty did not care because she reckoned she was lucky to be rid of her with so little trouble.

As soon as the wagon carrying Helen's furniture rolled away, Kitty, carrying Kate, and accompanied by her mother and Jake, took possession of the old farmhouse. It was even dirtier and more broken-down than she'd imagined but Wee Lily gaped all around as if she were in a palace.

'My mother says Craigie has treasure hidden in this house. You'll have to find it,' she said.

They started looking for it at once. Kitty expected that it would be buried beneath the floor but in fact it was far more accessible than that because it had been Craigie's greatest pleasure to take it out and turn it over, estimating its value night after night. So he kept it in a big wooden trunk in the cellar. Since he'd gone to prison, however, the chest had rarely been opened and finally Helen lost the key.

Kitty called in Tibbie's brother William, the village blacksmith, to break its hasp and the sight that met their eyes when the heavy lid was heaved up made even the phlegmatic blacksmith gasp. Silver ewers with handles covered with clusters of grapes, huge silver platters, a gladiator's golden face-mask and embossed breastplate, golden horse armour, glittering weapons (for Craigie had burnished everything he found), small statues of Roman gods in bronze or gold, bracelets, toga pins, bead necklaces, a big bag of coins from the reigns of the Emperor Sevcrus and Governor Agricola… it was a treasure trove indeed.

Also standing around the walls of the cellar were huge earthenware amphorae and smaller black pottery jugs with hunting scenes embossed round their necks. Craigie had used them for storage of home-made beer and grains or pulses, so Kitty kept them there, happy with the idea that they could still be put to the use intended by the long-dead potters who made them.

The great value of Craigie's treasure was an embarrassment to Kitty who consulted the lawyer about it and he decided she should bequeath the most valuable items to an Edinburgh museum under the name of the Craigie Scott Bequest. It turned out to be the most valuable gift the museum had received in its whole history.

When the treasure was crated up for its journey to Edinburgh, Kitty made a return visit to the prison to tell Craigie what had happened to his possessions. She found him very ill and feeble, worse than before, and apparently not capable of taking in all she said.

'Just sit by the bed and talk to him, miss. He doesn't look as if he's listening but he is,' said the guard who was caring for him. Kitty did as she was told and reeled off the recent events...

'Helen's in Rosewell with the dog. She seems quite happy, or as happy as she's ever been, let's say.

'The hay's in and it was a good crop. We've stacked it and I've bought ten more calves to fatten up. We're going to plough the river meadow and the back field and put one of them into turnips for the sheep and the big one into corn again. The house is being repaired and so is the bothy. I'm living in the house... my grandmother and my mother are still in the bothy.'

Craigie's closed eyes fluttered at that and she knew he was hearing her.

'I found all your treasure,' she whispered leaning forward. 'It's safe. I sent it in your name to a museum. It's made you famous. There have been articles in the newspapers about it.'

He smiled for the first time since she sat down beside him.

Before she left she said, 'The farm's in good heart and I'll take care of it. Thank you for giving it to me.'

He made no sign that he'd heard her and it would have seemed false to try to kiss him, so she only patted his hand and went away.

Ten days later, she was informed by the prison authorities that Prisoner number 7942, Craigie Scott, aged eighty, had died and been interred in the prison burying-ground. At his own request the burial had been conducted without any of his family being informed in advance.

Craigie's death made Kitty unsettled. His going had freed her and she did not want freedom yet because that meant that she would have to start contemplating what lay ahead.

She was living in the farmhouse and when she rose in the morning, she drew back the curtains of the room in which she and Kate slept and gazed out towards the Three Sisters brooding on the horizon.

The orchard swirled around her like surf. Only a few trees were still productive and she knew she ought to cut down the lichen-covered ones but could not bring herself to call in the fellers. Some of the trees were hundreds of years old and she loved their spectral appearance.

The place awed her; it seemed to cast some strange spell on her, a sort of enchantment that was frightening because she knew if she yielded to it, she would be in thrall for ever and would never get away. One morning she would gaze out and find that she had become an old woman. Time would have passed in a kind of dream.

She still carried Big Lily's knife in her skirt pocket and was afraid to let her grandmother know that she had it, not because she feared violence any longer, but because she would be branded as a liar. Big Lily's bad opinion of her granddaughter would be justified.

She kept Tim Maquire's half-sovereign as well. This she stitched into the corner of the coverlet that was spread over Kate at night as she sprawled in her wooden cot. Kitty hoped that its protective magic would be passed on to her adopted daughter.

Though she loved the farm, Kitty felt very alone, as isolated as she had been when she was ostracised because of her bastardy and the circumstances of her conception, for now she stood outside local society because of the elevation in her status. The Scotts of the farm had always possessed power in the little, close-knit village. The bond-ager's bastard who now owned Townhead assumed the mantle of local ruler and people drew back from her, fearful that she might think them to be currying favour. Only Bella gushed over her and Kitty was too wary of Bella ever to consider her a friend.

One afternoon she walked over to Falconwood farm in search of familiar faces. MacPhee, she was told, was dead; Laidlaw, the steward, had bought the land and lived in lordly state with his young wife, a farmer's daughter twenty years his junior. Liddle, too, had died but Walter Thompson was still skulking around the cattlesheds. He pretended not to know her and she returned the compliment.

When she asked about Effie, one of the married women bondagers who had not been on the farm when she worked there, said that the once happy, flirtatious girl was living on a farm in Berwickshire with her ploughman husband who beat her and had given her six children already. Kitty decided against going to see Effie, for she knew that the gulf between them would have grown too great.

She walked home from Falconwood farm over her own land and wondered why she could not be content with the miraculous turn in

423

her fortunes, but she still longed for travel and adventure and, most of all, she longed for love.

She was lonely but she knew that her imposing appearance and self-possession intimidated local men, including the ones who might have been tempted to pay court to her because of her inheritance, and those she would not want.

Even the sorrowing widow, Emma Jane Maquire, had more male companionship than Kitty, for the besotted Dr Robertson was her constant visitor and people were already beginning to whisper that when her period of mourning was up, she would marry him. The company she and Tim had started and run so well was still in existence with Lord Sydney Godolphin at its head. He had taken over the management of it after Tim's untimely death.

What am I going to do? Kitty wondered. The farm would soon be settling down into its winter hibernation and did not need her. She built a pair of workers' cottages and hired two good hands. Everything would go perfectly well even if she was far away. But still she did not go. She was waiting for something though she did not know what it was.

–

Robbie Rutherford got off the train at Rosewell deadly tired and his injured leg ached as it always did when he was overworked or overwrought. He whistled for a cab and climbed in stiffly. On this trip he had not sent up his own carriage because it seemed to him that his attempts to impress the people at home had been infantile. He'd grown out of needing to be admired so much.

The cabbie knew him of course. 'Weel, Robbie, you're lookin' awfy braw. That's a grand coat you've got on,' was his first remark. The night was chilly, for the first frost of autumn was silvering the hedges, and Robbie was wearing a long coat with a thick fur collar which he had purchased in New York. He liked it because he thought it gave him a dashing appearance.

He bit back a remark about buying the coat in America. A year ago he would have said it and boasted about his success there but tonight he only laughed and murmured, 'It keeps me warm.'

The cabbie kept talking as he drove along. 'You'll have heard about what happened wi' Craigie Scott's farm. Thon Kitty Scott, the navvy's lassie, got it. Craigie gave it to her because her mother was his daughter by Big Lily… and Big Lily was his half-sister of course. Some family the Scotts, eh?' he said sarcastically.

Robbie leaned forward with interest. 'Yes, I heard. My mother wrote to me about it. It certainly seems to have given folk up here something to talk about.'

The cabbie laughed again. 'Talk? You've never heard the like. They'll still be talking about it this time next year.'

'How's she getting on?' was Robbie's next question.

'Grand, grand. She's got her heid screwed on that yin. She's a real Scott. She's hired men to work for her and the farm's looking better than it's done for twenty year. Folk are scared o' her though. She's a tough one.'

'My mother said that Craigie left her the farm because she reminded him of his mother and she was a capable woman apparently,' agreed Robbie.

'I heard that too. There's still old folk around that mind Craigie's mother. She was a besom, they say, wi' a tongue that could cut through leather and she had hair that colour, reed as fire,' the cabbie told him.

Robbie leaned back in his seat and closed his eyes. He had only recently returned from America after months of negotiating, arranging, estimating and winning contracts. His company, which he now owned entirely, was about to expand into America, for he had secured so much work for it there.

He was tired and he wanted to spend more time at the Villa Favorita where his garden called him. He longed to be able to relax.

The cab took him to the arched gate in his parents' garden wall and when the driver saw how badly Robbie was limping, he got down and offered to carry in his bag for him.

'Look after yourself, Robbie,' he said, clapping him on the shoulder. 'Nane o' us are gettin' any younger.'

Robbie responded with a laugh but he was not really amused. The advice worried him. Life was moving on too fast. Though he looked younger, he would soon be forty years old. The years were flying by and he felt that, in spite of his huge worldly success, he had missed something.

As usual he was greeted like a conquering hero. People stopped him on the street when he strolled out next morning and they all had the same thing to say, 'Isn't it amazing about Craigie giving his farm to Wee Lily's bairn?'

He went up to Townhead in search of her and found her in the yard with a baby on her hip. This was a surprise. He had not expected her to have a child. No one had mentioned it.

She saw him staring at her from the farm gateway and a brilliant smile lit up her face, making her eyes dance. 'Robbie, it's wonderful to see you,' she exclaimed.

The word 'wonderful' made him feel strong again. His leg didn't hurt so much any more. He straightened up and walked smartly towards her.

'Well, well, this is some turn up, isn't it? I didn't expect you to be mistress of Townhead when we next met.'

A laugh gurgled from her. 'I didn't either.' Then she sobered. 'Did you get my letter about Marie? I sent it and what was left of your money to your London office.'

'Yes, I got it. Thank you. It must have been a comfort for her to have you there when she died. I hope it wasn't too painful.'

She shivered at the memory. 'It was very sad.'

Instinctively when she remembered Marie, she always thought of little Kate and patted the curly dark head peeping out of the bend of her arm. The child's brown eyes were fixed on Robbie as if she were wondering who he was.

Seeing the solemnity on his face, Kitty said, 'I'm sorry that I had to give you such awful news about her. You must have been very upset.'

'It was tragic, but somehow she was always marked for tragedy, I think,' said Robbie.

Kitty was surprised that he did not seem more affected and decided that he must be hiding his feelings.

'That's a handsome child,' he said, admiring the picture they made standing in the yard.

She smiled proudly. 'Yes, isn't she? And she's very good, an angel. I always used to think that I didn't like children but I adore her. Come over to the farmhouse Robbie and see what I've done to it. I've got crocks of whisky in the cellar that must have been there for years and years. I'll give you a tot so that you can toast the future.'

He grinned. 'That would be very appropriate. I don't usually drink whisky in the morning but this time I'll make an exception.'

He'd only ever been in the gloomy front hall of Townhead farm but even that surprised him because she'd knocked a new window through the wall and painted the wood panelling a pale colour that reflected light from outside. There was a huge vase of autumn flowers, Michaelmas daisies and mop-headed chrysanthemums, on the polished pedestal table that dominated the middle of the floor.

Robbie laid a hand on its gleaming surface. 'That's a fine bit of old furniture,' he said.

Kitty agreed. 'It used to be in the parlour and I was glad Helen didn't take it with her. She took a lot of the other good pieces but the place was so crammed full that there's more than enough for us both.'

She chucked the baby under the chin and said, 'It's time for your dinner, isn't it, Kate? We'll get the maid to take you into the kitchen.'

'You call your baby Kate?' asked Robbie in surprise.

She looked around, checking that no one could hear her and whispered, 'She's not my baby. She's Marie's. When she was dying she gave her to me and I'm keeping her. I don't tell people she's not mine though because I'm afraid that David will want her if he knows she's his sister's child. He's horrible, Robbie. He'd not be good to her. That's why I didn't put anything about Kate in my letter to you. It's a secret.'

Robbie could not help himself from exclaiming, 'I'm glad she's not yours.'

'What do you mean?'

'I'm glad she's not yours because when I saw her I thought you'd found another man.'

'Another man?' For once Kitty's composure faltered. She looked girlish.

He threw caution to the winds. 'I love you. I think I've loved you since that day we met in the farmyard when you were looking for your mother, do you remember? I didn't realise it till we met at Menton and I showed you my garden but you were with that jockey then… When you went to Paris for me, I thought about you all the time. I had to go to America but I thought about you there as well.'

Kitty was clutching Kate tight as she said, 'But I thought you were in love with Marie. You bought her big picture from the Edinburgh show, the one in your villa. You said you had to have it… I thought it was because you loved her. That was why you sent me to find her in Paris too – that's what I thought.'

He was standing close to her now with his earnest blue eyes searching hers. 'I admired her as an artist but I didn't love her in any other way. Love never crossed my mind with Marie. I was sorry for her. She seemed so doomed… from the beginning she seemed doomed. It was an evil inheritance that she had.'

Kitty sighed. 'An evil inheritance. I suppose she did. I've a strange inheritance too. You could call that evil as well.'

Robbie shook his head. 'No, not yours. Your inheritance was vital and maybe even brutal but it wasn't self-destructive like Marie's. You're a survivor. That's one of the reasons I'm in love with you.'

She was listening to him intently with her lips half-parted. 'I remember watching you in your garden at Menton. I remember admiring you there. I compared you with Freddy and you had all the things Freddy lacked, all the good things.'

'But you were in love with him,' said Robbie.

'It wore off. When it did, there was nothing left. I needed more than Freddy could offer me… Over the last few months I've been realising how much I need them,' she told him.

Robbie's doleful expression had lightened. 'I'm not a saint. I'm not going to pretend that I am. I've had a few adventures in my time.'

'I'm glad of that,' she cried. 'I wouldn't want to live with a saint. That would be too much for me!'

They both laughed and Robbie held out his arms. She and the baby walked into them.